GW00503580

IT WAS A MEDICAL MIRACLE
AND A CRIMINAL'S DREAM

CRY
IN
YOUR
SLEEP

BRUCE HEWETT

HEWETTWRITES.COM

Copyright © 2021 by Bruce Hewett.

The right of Bruce Hewett to be identified as the author of this work has been asserted.

All rights reserved.

No part of this book may be reproduced, stored in a retrieval system, or transmitted, in any form, or by any means (electronic, mechanical, photocopying, recording or otherwise) without the prior written permission of the author, except in cases of brief quotations embodied in reviews or articles. It may not be edited, amended, lent, resold, hired out, distributed or otherwise circulated, without the publisher's written permission.

Permission can be obtained from www.hewettwrites.com

This book is a work of fiction. Except in the case of historical fact, names, characters, places, and incidents either are products of the author's imagination or are used fictitiously. Any resemblance to actual persons, living or dead, events, or locales is entirely coincidental.

Published by rodericgrigson.com

ISBN: 978-0-6484190-1-3

Cover design, illustration and interior formatting:
Mark Thomas / Coverness.com

Original photograph: *Tagimoucia Flower Medinilla waterhousei* by John Game on Flickr.com
Licensed under Creative Commons: Attribution 2.0 Generic (CC BY 2.0)
Original photograph short link: https://flic.kr/p/QM7JYp

To my wife Beverley, for her encouragement and support during the highs and lows of the writing process.

For all those out there that think they cannot write a book, give it a go!

PROLOGUE

Long, long ago, a beautiful princess lived in a village on the Fijian island, Taveuni. The princess's Tamana (Father) was a powerful village chief and, unbeknown to her, had arranged a marriage for her to the son of a leader in another village. She had, however, fallen in love with someone close to where she lived, contrary to her Tamana's wishes, and she did not want to marry his choice of a husband.

The princess's Tamana was truly angry. He refused her permission to marry the man of her choice, which made her distraught and inconsolable. Not wanting to have any part of an arranged marriage, she decided to run away from her village.

In her desperation, the princess left the village and made her escape by fleeing to the heights of the nearby mountain. She climbed higher and higher up the steep trail leading her away from her home to escape the forced marriage. Finding herself exhausted, she collapsed under a tree growing beside Lake Tagimoucia, located at the crown of the island.

The tree took pity on the princess and provided her with shelter and protection. Feeling safe and secure under the tree, the princess fell into a deep sleep and began to cry while she slept. Tears rolled down the princess's cheeks. The tears turned into the magnificent red flowers we know today as the red flowers of the Tagimoucia plant, the national floral emblem of Fiji.

Tagimoucia means literally, to 'cry in your sleep'.

CHAPTER 1

It was Monday morning, the day after the return from his disastrous trip to Fiji. Just before nine am Adrian Nicholls stepped into Giuseppe's Café, located a short distance from Sydney's busy ferry terminal at Circular Quay. He wore a black NY New York Yankees baseball cap and dark, large-lensed sunglasses, masking much of his face. A black Nike jacket, zipped up, with the collar turned up, sat on top of a white polo shirt and his beltless dark grey chinos. There were no socks inside his well-worn navy-blue boat shoes.

After graduation from University, he had worked in Sydney's CBD in the marketing division of a large department store chain. Giuseppe's had been his regular café before departing Sydney, like many young Australians, to seek fame and fortune in London. It was one of his first stops on his return to Sydney, to take up the position of President of Anux Pharmaceuticals for Asia Pacific. The café was located at street level, at the entrance to his office block, the towering Credit-Suisse building, which over-looked Sydney Harbour. The Anux offices were housed on the 42nd floor and enjoyed panoramic views of the City and Harbour.

With his previous regular patronage of Giuseppe's, Adrian had struck up a friendly relationship with Sue Powell, the waitress. Sue was in her late twenties, an athletic, attractive blonde standing 5 feet 6 inches tall in her sockless black trainers. She wore jeans with the compulsory rips around the knees and thighs, over which was tied a small black, pocketed apron, housing her order pad and pen. Her muscular, tanned arms protruded out from her tight-fitting, black, zip-up vest. Topping her off was a black brandless peaked cap, with a ponytail hanging out the rear like a horse's tail.

"Hi Adrian," Sue greeted Adrian, initially unsure it was Adrian behind the cap and sunglasses. "Was that really you on television last night?"

"Unfortunately, yes," Adrian sounded crestfallen and did not meet her eyes. "Can you find me a quiet corner and just a long black coffee with two sugars, thanks? I don't want to be spotted by any of the staff."

"Take the rear booth near the door to the kitchen," Sue pointed to the rear of the café. "Don't worry about the reserved sign. I'll have your coffee shortly."

Sue watched Adrian head towards the booth. Adrian always made her heart flutter. He was a little over six feet tall, with a washboard like stomach and broad shoulders tapering down to a narrow waist. He obviously looked after himself.

She knew from over-hearing staff from his business, that he was returning to Australia. Surely there could not be two Adrian Nicholls. The gossip she heard was that he had been remarkably successful in London and projected to be on a rapid career path. Sue had certainly looked forward to seeing him again, hoping he remained unattached.

It was obvious to Giuseppe the proprietor of the café that Sue had the hots for Adrian. However, he always seemed oblivious to her smiles and the extra attention she paid to him, or the extra cookie that found its way onto his plate with his coffee order.

"I can't believe what they wrote about him in the paper. He is such a nice guy."

Adrian had nearly an hour before his meeting with Linda Campbell the Human Resources Manager for Anux. He sat in his quiet corner of the café and while sipping on his coffee, reflected on all that had transpired over the last 24 hours, since arriving back in Sydney from Fiji. The more he thought about how he had been treated by the company and his boss, the angrier he got.

"I will not rest until I get my revenge on them all."

"Here's your coffee Adrian," Sue caused Adrian to lift his eyes from staring at the tabletop. "I got some good news on Friday."

"Take a seat I could do with hearing some good news," replied Adrian.

"Well, I have been accepted for the advanced course in Pilates at the North Sydney Technical College. The guy who runs the gym where I go, reckons he would look at adding Pilates classes on to the program," beamed Sue. "It would be a great opportunity to get out of waitressing. I have been wiping down tables for far too long."

"A good friend of the family, Johnnie Miller runs a gym out at Mt Willsmore. He may also be interested in adding Pilates to the gym's offering. He also mentioned a PT course being offered at the local technical college. I reckon I will enrol," said Adrian, almost thinking out loud.

"Wow, that would be great. We could work together. Let me know." Sue stood and headed off to greet a new customer arriving at the entrance to the café.

"*There's some food for thought,*" smiled Adrian. "*Mmm…after this morning with Linda Campbell I will certainly be looking for a new career.*"

Adrian left a good tip for Sue on the table and gave her a smile and a wave as he headed for the exit. No doubt this meeting would signal the end of his career in the pharmaceutical industry, given the media's worldwide coverage of the incident in Fiji.

*

A lot had happened since his first morning back in Sydney from London, when he was on his way to the office, to start his first day in the Anux Sydney Office. Adrian could clearly remember when he had entered Giuseppe's café near the entrance to his office building, catching Sue's eye. As he entered the café, she rushed over and gave him a big hug. She looked him up and down, noting the transformation from the university graduate, starting his first job, into the well-groomed businessman in his navy-blue suit, crisp white shirt, and red power tie.

"Well, if it isn't Adrian Nicholls," she grinned with her hands on his shoulders. "Table for one?" she smiled.

"That would be excellent, thanks," Adrian followed her to his table. "I never thought I would see you again," stated Sue, as she pulled out his chair.

"I start work in this building today and will no doubt be a regular again, if the coffee has improved," Adrian joked.

Sue led him to a table by the window, which looked out into the street. "Would you like to see today's paper while you wait for your usual double espresso and almond croissant?" she asked, handing him a copy of the Sydney Daily Express.

"Perfect, thanks." Adrian took his seat and placed the newspaper on the table. He was carefully unfolding it, conscious of not wanting to get any ink on his fingers or his crisp, white shirt. His eyes were immediately riveted to the headline on the front-page, *Aussie Scientist Decries the Approval of the New Powerful Analgesic AnuxuDine in Australia*. Creases in trousers and getting ink on his fingers were suddenly forgotten, as Adrian became agitated and focussed on the headline article.

"What the bloody hell is this about?" he muttered to himself, with eyes starting to rapidly scan the article, as his stomach churned.

The article quoted a Dr Jacob Bryant from the Pharmacy Department of Sydney University, stating that "*the unusual fast track approval by the regulatory authorities in Australia of the powerful, new opioid analgesic AnuxuDine was irresponsible. Opioids have the potential to do more harm than good due to the potential for the development of addiction. More testing is required.*"

When Adrian was the London based Marketing Manager for Europe, he had spearheaded the launch of AnuxuDine, throughout Europe. It was the latest product to be launched by Anux Pharmaceuticals, the giant US based, global pharmaceutical company. The successful launch in Europe had earned him and his sales and marketing team large bonuses. This resulted in him having a dedicated team, motivated to work hard for him, driven to exceed their sales targets. Many in the company regarded him as somewhat of a golden-haired boy and rising star. So, it was no surprise when his promotion to the position of President Asia Pacific, based in Sydney Australia, was announced.

Meeting corporate expectations in Australia was imperative for the company's continued global product rollout. Achieving company targets in Australia and ultimately into Asia, would ensure his meteoric rise through the company echelons would continue. Who knows, a Vice-President's position in the New York Head Office and all that entailed – share options, a big US Dollar paycheck and all the trimmings that attracted; all within his grasp.

On the flight out from London to Sydney, he chuckled to himself, as he reflected on his rapid rise through the ranks of Anux Pharmaceuticals. After a brief period working in marketing in a Sydney department store, he took the chance as a recent graduate in Commerce and Marketing from Sydney's prestigious Macquarie Business School to head off to see the world. Joining Anux in London, he started out as a sales representative and quickly worked his way through the ranks into senior marketing roles. Rumours abounded that he was happy to step on his fellow employees in his drive to succeed. As a rising star he knew he had created some enemies within the company.

It was also rumoured that he had been involved in activities related to inappropriate product promotion, in contravention of international product promotional codes. Allegedly he had arranged for educational seminars to be held at Disney World in Florida. Leading medical professionals were provided with business class airfares and accommodation to attend the seminars. There were whispers that these airfares were somehow converted into economy tickets, enabling families to accompany the conference attendees. Mysteriously, paperwork relating to the seminars had disappeared. The company appeared to be happy to ignore allegations surrounding Adrian's activities, given the huge sales of AnuxuDine in Europe since launch. It appeared that as long as no hard evidence surfaced of his actions, the company was happy to leave him to continue as he pleased.

Along the corridors of power, it was whispered that the company had even forced the early retirement of the popular former President of the Asia Pacific business, to make way for an aggressive and successful Adrian. This made him the youngest person ever appointed to the position of President in the Anux Empire.

He was a long way from the boy, who escaped from a state housing commission estate in Sydney's western suburbs. He was raised by his devoted Mum as a solo parent, who struggled to raise him while living on social welfare.

He never knew his alcoholic Dad who disappeared soon after his birth.

Adrian had spoken to his Australian senior management team via videoconference the previous week, from the Anux London office, in preparation for this his first day in the office. He wanted to get up and running as quickly as possible and had arranged for a meeting first up on Monday morning at nine am to start the week. He had arrived on the Saturday morning into Sydney, so as to provide some time to recover from the punishing 24-hour journey from London. He wanted to make a big impression on the team from day one.

Despite his relative youth as a senior Anux manager and his Australian origins, he wanted to convey an image of the consummate business professional coming from the office in London. He expected a high standard of performance, with a "no prisoners" attitude and wanted to replicate the success in Europe in the Asia Pacific region.

The newspaper article had destroyed Adrian's good mood in a matter of seconds. Addressing the newspaper article was going to be a major priority on day one and would certainly be a baptism of fire for him, in taking charge of the business. There would be little time for pleasantries with the staff. It would be straight down to business.

Adrian continued to mutter to himself. '*Who did he think he was, this Australian nobody of an academic? Doesn't he know Anux has invested over $600 million US Dollars to get this new analgesic to market!*' Even though the Australian market was relatively small by international standards, approval in Australia was well-regarded by the regulatory authorities. An Australian approval would assist in securing marketing approvals in the major markets of Asia, such as China and Korea.

He needed to get to the office and immediately fire up the marketing and regulatory teams. They needed to minimise the damage that may come from the publication of the newspaper article, on the eve of the launch of the product in Australia. Leaning down, Adrian grabbed his computer satchel, into which he shoved the copy of the newspaper and was standing just as Sue arrived with his order.

"Sorry Sue, got to get going", he said with urgency placing a $20 note on the tray as he headed towards the door, "keep the change".

"*What's got into him*", Sue pondered as Adrian strode towards the exit.

With his mind ticking into gear, Adrian stormed purposefully out of the café. Some colonial hick of an academic from Australia was not going to impede his career, or the company's success, by trying to impact the launch of their new blockbuster drug.

His mind continued to churn as he stood on the footpath gathering his thoughts amongst all the morning office commuters, their eyes transfixed on their smart phone screens. It was if they were like ostriches, with their heads down and eyes and ears riveted to their smart phones, somehow avoiding collisions. People appeared to be able to navigate along the footpath and cross busy city streets as if they possessed an onboard radar system, detecting any hint of danger that may fling them or their expensive mobiles to the pavement.

Adrian paused at the entrance to the building and looked at his reflection in the huge glass window adjacent to the automatic doors. He straightened his tie and checked for any specks on his jacket. He was conscious of one of his Mum's old sayings, that first impressions were lasting impressions and there was no second chance to make a first impression.

Before finally entering the building, he took a final look around, gathering his thoughts. The morning sun reflected like a beacon off the building's windows, as though it was lighting the way for those working in the building. At the bottom of the street, there was a busy stream of ferries arriving at the ferry terminal with people being rapidly disgorged like ants onto the wharves. The glint of sunshine, like laser beams, bounced off the myriad of car windscreens as they streamed across the Harbour Bridge and finally, the morning sun glistened off the cream-coloured sails of the Opera House. Someone brushing past him quickly brought him back to reality and it was onward, to this his first day in the office. There were more important matters at hand, which would need his immediate attention in light of the damned newspaper article.

Entering the building's lobby, he quickly identified the location of the elevators to take him to the Anux office level and strode with purpose towards the signs identifying L 31 to 48. He pressed 42 on the panel and the light above elevator door G immediately started to pulse. He stepped inside as the door opened with a ping. The door silently glided closed behind him and the elevator rose rapidly, causing some discomfort in Adrian's ears, which he cleared with some vigorous swallowing. A quick glimpse of his Rolex revealed it was 8.15, well before the scheduled nine am introductory meeting with the Australian management team.

The newspaper article had certainly changed things and a gentle easing into the running of the business was not going to be possible. He was going to have to hit the ground running. It would be necessary to get everyone together to plan how to tackle the matter, as a priority. Nothing was going to halt his drive to reach the top.

Adrian stepped out of the elevator as the door silently glided open on Level 42. Feeling the cooling air-conditioned breeze, he paused to get his bearings. He noticed immediately to the left of the elevator foyer, was the reception desk for Anux Australia, with Anux displayed in big bold black letters on front of the white desk facade. Set behind the desk, via floor to ceiling windows, was a postcard view of the Sydney Harbour Bridge. "*Could anyone ever get tired of this view*?" He set off to approach the receptionist. To the right of the reception desk, he noticed there was a frosty, glass door marked PRIVATE, with a scanner mounted at chest height to the right of the doorway, for electronic access.

Behind the reception desk sat a well-groomed, middle-aged woman, with coiffured, blonde hair, who Adrian reckoned, would have been very stunning in her day. She looked very professional in a dark-grey suit, which sat on top of her white ruffled blouse. The name tag on her jacket lapel read Sheila McKenzie, which brought a smile to his face.

"Good morning Sheila," Adrian cheerfully greeted, "I am Adrian Nicholls the new boss."

"We are expecting you Mr Nicholls," Sheila stood and extended her right hand. "Welcome aboard."

"Thanks Sheila and please call me Adrian. How long have you been with the company?" asked Adrian.

"18 years' service Adrian," Sheila proudly replied.

"Let me compliment you on your very professional presentation," noted Adrian. He knew from experience that the receptionist was a key source of knowledge of what happened within the company and as the new boss, wanted to keep her onside.

"Thank you, so much Adrian. It is so nice to be acknowledged," beamed Sheila.

"Obviously, I do not have an entry pass as yet, so hopefully you can let me into the office area, while one gets sorted for me," queried Adrian.

"Certainly, Mister, I mean Adrian," smiled Sheila, as she led him to the door with her pass in hand.

"I have arrived a little earlier than expected as an important matter has come up in today's newspaper. I will need to dispense with the niceties on my first day and would ask you to assemble the Management team in the boardroom straightaway. We need to get on with addressing the front page in this morning's newspaper." he directed, adopting a business-like tone.

Sheila opened the door with her pass and led him into the boardroom which was set directly behind the reception desk on the harbour side of the offices. Again, Adrian was mesmerised by the view of Sydney Harbour. "*There was nothing in the London Office that could match this, I think I will enjoy my time back home in Sydney for sure.*"

CHAPTER 2

The modern boardroom featured three sides of pinkish-grey wood panelling along with floor to ceilings windows, framing Sydney Harbour like a postcard. Covering the length of the wall to the left of double entry doors was a credenza, which had been set up with bottles of chilled still and sparkling water. Also, there was an urn, steaming away with hot water, ready to brew a wide range of regular and herbal teas. There was also a coffee pod machine, with recyclable pods of various coffee intensities – Paris 10, Melbourne 11, and Florence 12. The wall to the right of the entrance was covered with a large smart screen television, fed by a projector mounted on the top of the boardroom table, along with a telephone console for conference calls.

The boardroom table had 12 seats, one on each end and five down each side of the boardroom table which matched the colouring of the wall panelling. Placed at each seat at the table was a metal coaster, upon which sat an over-turned glass.

"Nicely setup Sheila," praised Adrian. "Now please get everyone in here as soon as possible."

"On to it, Adrian," Sheila was increasingly warming to him, after further words of praise. She strode quickly out of the boardroom to round up the management team.

While he waited for the management team to assemble, Adrian strolled over to the boardroom window to take a glimpse of the magnificent Sydney Harbour and the famous Bridge once more. He then headed over to the coffee machine and made himself a double espresso before taking his seat at the head of the table, at the left-hand end, facing towards the projector screen. He sat preparing to meet the management team in person for the first time.

Cautiously, Adrian took a sip of his coffee and was surprised that the coffee machine had produced an exceptionally good espresso, nearly as good as Giuseppe's Café. After a short wait, he could hear the chatter coming from behind the boardroom door. The door appeared to tentatively open and in marched the team, comprised of the Australian company's five senior managers.

"Hi, everyone. I'm Adrian Nicholls," standing as he introduced himself in his most cheerful voice. "Sorry to drag you in like this, earlier than our scheduled nine am meeting I know, but I expect you have all heard about or read the front-page article in this morning's newspaper." There was a general consensus that all in the management team were aware of the situation. "We need to address the situation as a matter of urgency, given we are only days away from the official launch of AnuxuDine in Australia."

"Please take a seat," Adrian pointed to the vacant boardroom chairs. "It is good to see you all in person, following on from our videoconference session last week. To refresh my memory, I would ask you all to introduce yourselves. Tell me a little about yourselves and what your role is in the company."

Grant Davis was the Chief Financial Officer. Adrian guessed he was mid-forties. He had a good head of unkempt, collar length, salt, and pepper hair, needing a bit of a trim. He had been with Anux for around eight years. He wore a light-grey suit, with a white shirt and no tie. The black, lace-up shoes looked as though they needed a bit of a polish. His voice was confident, and he described a wealth of finance experience of the past 20 years, the last five years in the pharmaceutical industry. *"He will be my right-hand man."*

Linda Campbell was the Human Resources Manager, Adrian thinking, *"late-thirties and well-presented like the receptionist, Sheila."* She wore a dark-grey pants suit with buttoned up jacket, along with black, patent leather high heels. She was a graduate in Psychology and had been with Anux for three years. *"She looks very professional; no doubt she knows her stuff."*

Bob Williams the Sales Director was close to 50. Tall, balding with grey hair.

Typically, of sales personnel, he was a little more casually presented, with dark-grey trousers and a navy sports jacket, and scruffy brown suede shoes. He had been in sales all his working-life and had done the rounds with a number of pharmaceutical companies during his career, so was pretty well connected. He had been with Anux for five years, a lengthy stay by his standards. "*Getting too comfortable*," Adrian pondered.

Jenny Tang the Marketing Director spoke with an Aussie accent, which surprised Adrian, expecting a more typical Asian accent. She had been born in Australia and was very professionally presented in a black pants suit and white blouse. She was short, a bit over five feet tall and had entered Anux straight after graduating in Marketing. She reminded Adrian of himself and noted how she had worked her way quickly up through the sales and marketing ranks. In her late twenties, Adrian thought, "*great potential, maybe internationally with Anux eventually*."

Lastly was a confident Dr Premila Singh, Head of Regulatory Affairs. A pharmacist, she was probably in her late thirties and dressed in an eye-catching dark-blue sari and dark-brown, ornate leather sandals. Her plaited, jet black hair hung down her back, nearly to her waist. Anux brought her in from the business in India, to assist with the planned rollout of product launches into Asian markets. She spoke with a distinctive Indian accent. Adrian had heard she was very well-regarded within the Anux business. "*With her experience she will be a vital cog in the team for our launches into Asia*."

"I look forward to getting to know you all personally over the coming days," smiled Adrian, making individual eye contact with his team, "but as a priority for the business, we need to address the matter from today's newspaper. We need to minimise any negative impact from the article." He noted all their affirmative nods.

Reaching into his computer satchel, Adrian extracted his copy of the newspaper and placed it on the boardroom table. "If this rhetoric gathers momentum, it has the potential to severely impact the launch, not only here in Australia but in other markets around the world," Adrian's voice rose in volume with his increasing emotion. "This article could initiate very negative and damaging publicity on the eve of the Australian launch." Adrian was aware that the official launch for the Australian market was planned for the forthcoming College of General Practitioners of Australia, Annual Conference to be held in Sydney in two weeks' time.

"Does anyone know this academic Dr Jacob Bryant?" Adrian queried, looking around the table. "Maybe he could be persuaded to go away and maintain his silence, in return for some sort of research grant?"

"I have met with Jacob a number of times in regular continuing educational meetings held by the Pharmaceutical Society of Australia," replied Premila. "Jacob is one of those scientists dedicated to his work. His specialty is the medicinal use of plants, a field of pharmacy known as pharmacognosy. He is the type of person unlikely to be swayed in his beliefs by a research grant."

All eyes were on Premila. "We have further cause for concern," she added. "I came across him at a function last week, to thank the major sponsors of the forthcoming College of General Practitioners Conference. I overheard him speaking to the Head of the Sydney University, Department of Pharmacy, Professor Tim Baldwin. They were talking about an exciting project in Fiji and Jacob wanting to take some leave of absence from the University, to go to Fiji to work on a project."

"From what I gathered with the Fiji project, there is the potential for issues for Anux and our new analgesic. Not immediately, but in time," Premila added with a look of concern.

"Please share it with us Premila," asked Adrian moving forward in his seat, eyes fixated on her.

"I heard Jacob detailing an article recently published in the scientific journal, *Pharmacognosy*. It appears he has contacted a Dr Joeli Koroi and a Dr Mere Koroi from the Fiji School of Medicine." Premila paused then continued. "The Doctors Koroi published a study highlighting the analgesic properties of an extract from a plant unique to the Fiji Islands. I am not sure how to pronounce it, but it is spelt T-A-G-I-M-O-U-C-I-A. The flower of the plant is crushed and formed into an oral draft and was fed to rats. The study successfully demonstrated there was no pain response in the small sample of rats, who were placed on hot plates."

"We need to monitor this closely, given its possible future impact," Jacob instructed.

"From what I understand, Jacob is arranging to go to Fiji during the summer vacation period at the University, to work with the Doctors Koroi in their laboratory in Fiji," continued Premila. "He will help them design and conduct a second formal study using human volunteers, to confirm the positive response achieved in the first study. In addition, they would be able to access the resources of Sydney University, to assist in the project."

There was silence from the team as Premila continued, "Jacob indicated to Professor Baldwin, that with a second successful study in human volunteers completed, there was the potential to commence commercial discussions, with ethical pharmaceutical companies. As we know a partnership with a company would provide the capital to undertake the expensive development process, necessary to get a product to market."

"There was a particular point of concern to us they discussed," stressed Premila, with a worried look on her face. "Unlike our AnuxuDine I understand the Fijian plant is non-opioid, therefore, such a product if successfully developed, is unlikely to have the addictive potential of our opioid based product. A new powerful, non-opioid, non-addictive analgesic has the potential to replace our product in the market."

"OMG," stammered Adrian. "Such a competitor could destroy the huge investment the company has made in AnuxuDine. I have only just arrived back in Australia and the company has a possible competitor on the horizon, when we have not even launched in this market." He unexpectedly pounded the table with his clenched fist, causing the managers to sharply inhale and fully focus on the new boss. "We need to stop this in its tracks."

"I have already started working on something for our Public Relations agency," fired out Jenny. "This is a draft of a press release I worked on as soon as I got into the office. I have concentrated on highlighting the results that have already been achieved in Europe. I have included pictures and footage of what we have on file with images of smiling and happy families. Images of happy treated patients, are lapped up by the media."

"Great work Jenny for getting on to this so quickly," praised Adrian and nodded to acknowledge Jenny. "Make sure there is no mention of any patient reporting any side-effects, only positive information and how patients will benefit from our new wonder drug. Get this out forthwith. I want to stop any negative campaign gathering momentum, especially amongst healthcare professionals or the regulatory authorities, when we are so close to launch."

"That is for sure," added Bob Williams. "We have wholesalers loaded with stock ready for the first prescriptions to start hitting the pharmacies straight after the launch. The sales budgets are overly aggressive and there is a big incentive on for the sales and marketing teams, with a conference in Thailand on the cards if the budget is achieved. The promise of an overseas trip has the sales team hot to trot," assured Bob.

"OK everyone let's get on with it," emphasised Adrian, pounding his clenched right fist into the palm of his left hand. "Premila, would you mind staying for a moment. I want you to give me more detailed information on the Fiji plant situation. I am planning to speak with Newton Sinclair, the International VP of Marketing at the Anux headquarters in New York. I want to provide him with details of the immediate action we are taking and discuss with him a way forward in regard to developments in Fiji you have identified. I would like to stop anything getting underway in Fiji if possible."

After the update from Premila, Adrian sat by himself in the boardroom and reflected on what a baptism of fire it had been on day one as a president of a Anux business. He certainly had the adrenaline flowing and thought to himself *"there are no problems, only solutions."* This was one of his favourite business sayings, which had served him well on the rapid rise up the corporate ladder.

Adrian started thinking about his call with Newton. He knew from his reputation that Newton was equally as ambitious as he was and no doubt in time, a potential rival for higher office. From corporate gossip, he heard Newton was not necessarily to be fully trusted. However, he needed to share the day's revelations with him to avoid any political fallout. He needed to keep those at corporate headquarters in New York informed of the situation in Australia and assure them that action was being taken.

"*I will let him know we have taken immediate steps to rebut the article in the newspaper and I will raise the Fiji matter with him.*"

It was Sunday evening in New York, so Adrian would send an email to Newton, to arrange to speak with him Monday evening New York time. "*My first direct engagement with Newton should prove interesting,*" mused Adrian.

CHAPTER 3

As part of his daily ritual, Jacob sat astride his surfboard, bobbing up and down, a couple of hundred metres off Sydney's Mona Vale Beach. His eyes squinted into the sun rising over the Pacific Ocean, scanning the water for that one perfect wave to take him back into the beach. *"Whoa, you beauty,"* he roared, *"this is the one."*

He got into a kneeling position on his board and with powerful strokes from his muscular arms and shoulders, brought his board up to speed with the wave as it accelerated towards the beach. In a flash he was standing upright, knees braced and surging towards the beach, with the adrenaline rushing through his body. The wave broke about 25 metres off the beach and he dived into the water, re-surfacing with a huge grin on his face. *"There is no better way to start the day."*

Picking up his board he raced up the beach to the showers located adjacent to the carpark which overlooked the beach. He rinsed off the saltwater and looked at his watch. *"Yes, time for a coffee and some scrambled eggs on sourdough toast. Then the cursed commute, through the heavy Sydney traffic into the office at Sydney University."* The beachfront was a busy place most mornings, so he weaved his way through the joggers, dog walkers and tai-chi exponents, on his way to his favourite spot, the Beachside Café.

Jacob placed his board at the entrance and confidently strode inside. He shook the water from his straggly, sun-bleached hair, before peeling back the top of his wetsuit, revealing his well-tanned, muscular body. "Morning Zoe," he said, waving to the extremely cute blonde proprietor. "The usual thanks," his eyes admiring her long, slim legs, protruding from the very brief denim shorts. Combined with the small pink tank top, exposing a bare, trim midriff, complete with a gold navel ring, there was not much left unexposed of Zoe's sun-tanned body.

"Coming right up, Jacob." She smiled in reply, with a look of longing in her eyes. Her eyes appeared to move all the way from top to bottom of his six-foot plus frame, capturing every ripple of every muscle.

Jacob was about to sit down on one of the wooden benches when he heard the words Anux Pharmaceuticals coming from the radio behind the serving counter. "Zoe, would you please turn up the radio for a moment. There is something coming through on the news." A quizzical look crossed his face.

Jacob leaned forward on the counter trying to catch every word from the news reader," *A spokesperson for Anux, Ms Jenny Tang, said the company was disappointed in the comments expressed by Dr Jacob Bryant in yesterday's newspaper. The company had spent millions of dollars in developing AnuxuDine. Outstanding results have been achieved with its usage throughout Europe and Southern Africa, saving patients from experiencing severe pain. The company looks forward to shortly making their new blockbuster medicine available to the benefit of all the people of Australia."*

"Those self-serving bastards," cried out Jacob, turning heads in the cafe. "They have missed the whole point of what I was trying to say. Sorry Zoe, I need to cancel my order and get straight into the office," he said, turning to head out the door.

"Before you rush off, have you got a quick second," fired-out Zoe. "I need to ask you something."

"Sure, but I need to get away pretty quickly," he replied, looking rather edgy.

"Coming up in March, I have a wedding to go to and need a partner," she stated with an expectant look on her face. "I wanted to give you plenty of notice to see whether you would be my partner on the day. Be great if you could."

"Normally I would say yes, but I am heading off to Fiji in the next few days for a very important project." He started to move towards the door. "I will be in Fiji all through the summer break and not back till the end of February. Let me think about it. Gotta go, catch you later."

A crestfallen Zoe watched Jacob exit the café and stride-off determinedly with his board under his left arm, towards his nearby apartment which overlooked Mona Vale Beach. She received a sympathetic look from the other regulars in the café who knew how much she adored Jacob. Somehow, he never seemed to notice her. He seemed to be married to his work and his surfing.

After a quick shower, Jacob slipped on a pair of tight-fitting jeans and a white polo shirt which appeared a size too small due to his bulging biceps and broad surfers' shoulders. He ran his fingers through his scraggly hair to straighten it a bit, then slipped on his well-worn, navy-blue boat shoes. On the way out the door he grabbed a ripe banana, the remnants of his fruit bowl and thought," I *must get around to doing some shopping, or I could just drop in see Mum and Dad on the way home tonight*," he laughed to himself, "*Mum always has something for me to eat.*"

He fired up the engine of his aged, dusty dark-grey Volkswagen Golf. It was only ever washed when it rained and the backseat was piled with surfing gear and aged scientific magazines, that never seemed to move, just accumulate. The bumper-to-bumper slow crawl into the city, gave him a lot of thinking time, his brain racing. He wanted to get to Fiji and get the second study underway to stick it to those greedy bastards at Anux Pharmaceuticals, as quickly as scientifically possible.

Upon arrival at the office, he planned to meet with Professor Tim Baldwin. He wanted to firm up the arrangements for his sabbatical in Fiji to work with the Doctors Koroi at the Fiji School of Medicine. With that done, he would contact Dr Joeli Koroi in Suva to confirm everything was OK at the Fiji end, including his visa, before booking his flight. Hopefully, he could fly out this coming weekend.

While in the traffic Jacob went through everything in his mind that he had shared with the newspaper. He was sure nothing he said was incorrect and was speaking out in the best interest of patients. "*AnuxuDine was certainly a good analgesic, however, being an opioid there was the potential for addiction if abused.*

The company had obviously got the PR machine underway to minimise any impact from the newspaper article and the pending launch of the product in Australia."

Having reviewed his comments to the newspaper in his mind, Jacob confidently walked into the Pharmacy Department at Sydney University. He knew what he had to do and that was to get to Fiji and get the second study with the Tagimoucia flower extract underway. The sooner there was proof that the draft would work in humans, then the sooner it could be put in the hands of an ethical pharmaceutical company. Jacob was keen to help develop a powerful analgesic that was non-addictive.

"Morning Carol," Jacob greeted Professor Baldwin's PA. "Is Prof available?"

"Sure, he is expecting you," she replied with a flutter of long black false eyelashes, "go right in, he will make you a coffee on his new machine, his latest toy," she laughed.

Jacob entered and closed the door. Professor Baldwin being Head of Department, was more conservatively dressed than Jacob's casual style. He was dressed in pressed, dark grey trousers, along with a white shirt and dark blue tie. He had his back to Jacob tinkering with his new toy, a coffee pod machine. He was of average height, with a grey hairline starting to recede. The slight paunch overhanging his trousers was testament to his love and passion for Australian red wine.

"You must do something about Carol," noted Professor Baldwin, looking over the top of his thick, black-rimmed glasses. "She is like a sick puppy every time she sees you. Coffee?"

"Oh, Prof. She is not my type with those hip hugging skirts and tottering four-inch heels. I cannot see her anywhere near the beach and enjoying a surf," laughed Jacob. "Make mine a double espresso thanks," he said taking his seat, on the opposite side of Prof's cluttered desk. He moved a few piles of bulging files, to make room for his coffee.

"Prof I won't beat around the bush" started up Jacob. "I seem to have poked an angry bear in Anux Pharmaceuticals. They have come out strongly in response to the article in yesterday's newspaper and it was all over the news this morning."

"Unfortunately, the reality for the company, is that they will not get a quick return on the hundreds of millions of dollars of investment costs, by requiring them to do more clinical testing," sagely added Tim. "They will want to protect their substantial investment, by generating a sizeable return on investment for their many shareholders."

"I guess you are right, I should have anticipated a vigorous response to the newspaper article," reflected Jacob. "Anyway, the main reason for catching up with you this morning, was to firm up my sabbatical in Fiji, to work with the Doctors Koroi on a second study relating to their Tagimoucia plant project."

"I don't see any problems," noted Prof, "The final exams have been completed and as long as you have completed your marking of the examinations, I am happy to approve your sabbatical in Fiji. It is, of course, on the proviso you are back in time to resume lectures in late February next year. That will give you three months to get the second phase of the project completed."

"Thanks Prof," an excited Jacob responded. "In the conversations I have had with Dr Joeli Koroi and his daughter Dr Mere Koroi they sound pretty eager to get me over to Fiji."

"I know you are keen to get things moving and to confirm arrangements with the Korois but fill me in with a bit more background detail on what you will be up to in Fiji," queried Prof.

"As you know I came across an article in the *Pharmacognosy Journal* published by the Korois," began an enthusiastic Jacob. "I contacted them to see if I could assist them in their ongoing research and they were grateful for the offer of help. I understand from speaking with Dr Joeli, that his wife died tragically in severe pain. She had an accident, during a visit she made to family and friends on one of the outer islands in Fiji. Since then, he has devoted his life to identifying an analgesic based on derivates sourced from indigenous Fijian plants.

It is from this focus, that he identified the Tagimoucia plant as a possible source. Dr Joeli had received reports from the usage of the plant's flowers, on the island where the plant grows. His daughter Dr Mere, graduated in Medicine in Auckland, New Zealand and has joined her Dad, totally committed to their research."

"They sounded like a very dedicated team," mused Prof. "I can understand their motivation, given the tragedy in the family. When you speak with them today, please assure them that we are here to help in any way we can and can provide them with access to our facilities at the University."

"Thanks again for your support Prof. Your assistance with our laboratories, in helping to identify the active ingredient from the plant's flowers will be an extremely useful step in the project," Jacob finished his coffee and stood, "I will call them now to firm up the Fijian arrangements.

*

Jacob dialled Dr Joeli's mobile phone.

"Doctor Joeli speaking."

"Doctor Joeli, Jacob Bryant here."

"Hey, bula Jacob," Joeli using the world-famous Fijian greeting. "What's the news? Please call me Joeli."

"Dr Koroi, I mean Joeli," Jacob corrected himself, "Professor Baldwin has approved my sabbatical and I have three months available to work with you on the second study of the Tagimoucia project. Hopefully, that will give us enough time to complete the necessary work in a small group of volunteers."

"That is great news. Mere will be pleased to have the additional support," Joeli enthused before adding, "I can confirm that all is set with the Fijian immigration formalities. You just need to do take your passport into the Fijian High Commission in Sydney, for them to stamp your passport with your working visa."

"Fantastic news," Jacob stood and picked up his car keys. "I will head into the High Commission straight away to get the visa stamp, then I will book my flight. I have had a preliminary look and there are seats available for the Saturday flight, getting into Nadi International Airport on Saturday afternoon."

"Mere and I will drive around from Suva to pick you up and you can stay with us. We have a self-contained cottage at home which you can use while you are in Fiji," offered Joeli. "We will welcome the company."

"That would be fantastic Joeli. I am really looking forward to meeting you and Mere and getting the project underway." Jacob paused a moment before deciding to add, "I think you should know I have received a bit of flak in the local media from Anux Pharmaceuticals. I expressed opposition to the likely widespread usage of their new analgesic AnuxuDine, given its limited trialling. I am keen to assist you in the development of a new non-addictive analgesic that can be responsibly used throughout the world."

"You have my total support in that regard Jacob," Joeli sincerely added . "I look forward to your flight confirmation and seeing you on Saturday at the airport. Mere and I want to get things happening."

CHAPTER 4

Newton Sinclair, VP of International Marketing for Anux Pharmaceuticals was sitting at his antique oaken desk overlooking New York's Hudson River. It was early evening and the lights from the skyscrapers of the city that never sleeps, were starting to light up the night sky. Newton was waiting for the call from Adrian Nicholls in Sydney. Adrian's rapid ascendance through the corporate ranks was making him nervous. It was only a matter of time before he became a threat. Newton was quietly pleased that Adrian had needed to call him in regard to a problem and he was keen to learn what was the issue.

While waiting for Adrian's call, the October sales results had just come through on his computer. "*Another outstanding month,*" his mood lifting, "*we have already achieved the result for the year with two months still to go.*" The huge annual bonus was already in the bag and Newton was thinking, "*that might even keep pace with Lisabeth's spending habits and maybe I have earned a little celebration myself.*"

Newton stood and headed over to his office door and quietly locked it, before returning to his desk and kneeling on the floor, unlocking the bottom right drawer. He stretched to the very back of the drawer to retrieve a small, metal lockable container, which rattled as he placed it on his desk. Inside was a mirror, a pocket-knife and a re-sealable plastic bag containing a quantity of white powder. His dealer Pablo had said this was rather good stuff and was known as *Colombian Heaven*. "*It better be good at the price,*" he thought," *but I am worth it. I deserve a treat with this year's bonus in the bag.*"

As he setup to snort a couple of lines before the call from Adrian, he thought life was going pretty well, since his graduation in Commerce from the prestigious Rutgers University. A high paid job with big bonuses and a beautiful wife, life was good. However, he was approaching 40 and knew there were rising stars like Adrian Nicholls in the business who would no doubt want his job.

The corporate life was tough on his body with all those dinners and days travelling away overseas and Newton knew he carried a bit of extra weight. His burgeoning waistline was starting to put pressure on his navy-blue suit pants. *"Maybe I should get these taken out a bit, at least until I can get back to the gym,"* he agreed with himself, *"at least it may stop Lisabeth nagging me about the bulge starting to overhang my belt. Definitely a New Year's resolution to get back to the gym."*

Lisabeth his wife, was ten years his junior. She had been a finalist in the Miss New York beauty pageant and was his personal PA for a few months before they got a bit tipsy together at a company Christmas function. The partied into the small hours, waking up in each other's arms and after a whirlwind romance were soon married. With Newton's sizeable income, Lisabeth quickly retired from work, enjoying an extravagant lifestyle with her friends, in the stores, gyms and cafes, in the avenues of New York.

Newton looked longingly at Lisabeth's photo on his desk, *"Ah, her long blond hair and that body. I love her in that tight-fitting gym gear and oh, that butt of hers."* He was getting excited just thinking about it, but things had been much quieter on the home front in recent days. Lisabeth was happy to spend his money and live in their awfully expensive 5th Avenue apartment, but she had not been very forthcoming in the bedroom department, in recent days. *"Always complaining about my boozy breath and sweaty body. Maybe she could be seeing someone else? I don't know what I would do if she left me. I must get back to the gym and off the booze and coke."*

Thoughts of a change in lifestyle were quickly forgotten as Newton eyed the two lines of coke setup on the small mirror he had placed on his desk. With a finger over one nostril, he was lowering his head to take a snort. Just then his mobile phone rang, and he sat upright with his heart racing. "*Perfect timing Adrian*," noting the overseas number on his phone screen. "*You can hang on just for a moment*," and he proceeded to do the lines of coke. His head snapped back, and he leaned back into his black leather, high-backed office chair, letting out a mighty, "*wow, that Colombian Heaven. Thank you, Pablo.*"

Finally, he answered the phone with it persistently buzzing away like an annoying wasp on his desktop, "Newton Sinclair."

"Newton, Adrian Nicholls from Sydney, I was getting worried you were not going to answer the call."

"Sorry Adrian I just had someone on my other line. Great to hear from you. I hope all is going well in the land Down Under."

"Sydney is a great place Newton; I am sure you can arrange an excuse to come and visit us in Anux Australia at some stage."

"Anyway, enough of the small talk Adrian, what is this important matter you want to discuss, what can I do to help?" Newton asked getting down to business. "I need to get away shortly. I promised Lisabeth I'd be home early tonight," he added with a smirk on his face.

"Sorry for the late hour at your end, but the time difference makes it difficult." Adrian adopted an apologetic tone. "There was an issue in the local press with some crackpot Australian academic. He complained that the Australian authorities were too hasty in their approval of AnuxuDine. He is calling for more testing to determine if there is any danger with the likelihood of the occurrence of addiction in the use of our product."

"I don't like the sound of that," added a concerned sounding Newton. "If that initiative catches hold around the place, it could have severe ramifications for the ongoing global rollout. You know what that means, a big cutback in our future bonuses, especially, if there is any holdup in the registration here in the USA, the world's biggest market."

"Don't worry too much Newton, we stomped on it immediately", Adrian said assuringly. "We got the PR machine fired-up and had articles in all the media the following day. There was plenty of footage showing how we had successfully treated patients since the launch in Europe and in some trials in

Southern Africa. There was lots of coverage showing happy families with their smiling faces in hospital wards."

"I am glad you got right on to it," Newton sounding relieved. He did not want anything to go wrong that may impact the Anux share price and the value of his share options. He was planning to trade his options early in the new trading year, after the announcement of the full year trading result. The projected good result was likely to bump up the share price and enable a big payment on the apartment's large mortgage. That would ease the pressure on Lisabeth's spending habits in the stores which made him nervous each month while awaiting the monthly credit card statement.

"It has all calmed down," added Adrian sounding pleased with himself. "We have the launch in Australia in a couple of weeks, here in Sydney. The Minister for Health will be the guest of honour at the launch. He indicated he would be making an appropriate speech, reflecting the significant investment made by Anux in looking after the health of all Australians. A donation to the Government's political party coffers did not go unnoticed by the Minister."

"Sounds like you are on top of the matter raised in the media, but what about this potential future problem?" asked Newton with a hint of concern in his voice.

"It's related to some research having been published by some research scientists in Fiji," stated Adrian. "The study was published in an obscure journal called *Pharmacognosy*."

Newton jumped straight in, "Fiji, who's ever heard of research scientists based in Fiji!"

"The work was undertaken by a father and daughter research team who discovered the analgesic properties of a local plant," Adrian paused to think before he continued. "From our Head of Regulatory Affairs, Dr Premila Singh, we learned that they have enlisted the services of our Sydney crackpot academic to go to Fiji. He is a specialist in the area of pharmacognosy and is going to help them with a second, confirmatory study, on the therapeutic properties of the plant extract. I do not see an immediate impact on Anux, as it is likely to take several years before a competitive product could be developed, even if the second study proves positive. However, the major concern is that it is a non-opioid medicine and therefore not likely to have the addictive potential of our AnuxuDine."

"Positive results from the second study with a non-opioid analgesic would most certainly be detrimental to the Anux share price," Newton noted, his mind racing. Adrian's call had killed the effect of the cocaine hit. He was starting to get nervous. *"If there was any impact on AnuxuDine on his watch as the Vice-President for International Marketing then there goes a promotion to the Anux Board of Directors and any chance of additional share allocations."*

"I have come up with a couple of options for your consideration, Newton," Adrian commenced, "We need to nip the Fiji situation in the bud, preferably before any work gets underway. It would be great for us to agree on a way forward, rather than have to go through the multiple corporate layers for approval, which will take months. They will continue to ask for more and more information and no one will make a decision. The damage by then will have been done, with the results of a second study published."

"Before we discuss that, you know we had problems in Southern Africa?" Newton interrupted Adrian's flow. "We initiated some early supplies of AnuxuDine on a compassionate usage basis, in some emergency situations, however, reports quickly emerged of addiction developing in patients. Fortunately, the usage in Africa was not part of any official trial. I quickly arranged to bury any mention of the development of addiction during the treatment. A couple of payments to some willing doctors for "research" helped the problem go away. I will email you the information now." Hitting send on the email labelled CONFIDENTIAL to Adrian, Newton too late thought, *"maybe I should not have sent it."*

"That could be particularly useful, especially the bit about payments being made. Gives me some flexibility in what I can do in Fiji," acknowledged Adrian, hearing his Inbox ping from Newton's email.

"There is no one else with me in the office at this hour, so please feel free to let me know what actions you are recommending," encouraged Newton.

"However, we need to be careful and keep it between us. You do have a bit of a reputation, given some of the strategies you allegedly implemented with the launch in Europe. I understand a lot of files just suddenly disappeared."

"I can assure you I will be very discreet, and it will be just between us," reassured Adrian.

Newton quietly hit the record button on his recorder. He was thinking that it might be a good insurance policy to note Adrian's plans. He was not likely to remain content with being President of the business in Sydney, for a prolonged period of time. Adrian was one to keep an eye on and to be gotten rid of if necessary.

Adrian then started his discourse on his two main ideas he had for stopping matters getting underway in Fiji. Firstly, he proposed making an offer to the Fiji Government, via a meeting with their Minister for Commerce, one Mr Filipe Sitiveni Matai.

"We definitely need to secure the rights for the medical usage of any product that could be developed from the Tagimoucia plant," Adrian started out emphatically. His research had shown that Mr Matai had been responsible for negotiating various commercial deals on behalf of the Fiji Government, for enterprises such as fishing and mining rights.

"I see this as the best starting point," Adrian sagely noted. "I could make promises on behalf of Anux to develop a product for the benefit of all humanity. This would provide great kudos to the people of Fiji. Anux, of course, with their hands on the commercial rights, would then bury the project and it would never see the light of day. The Fijian Government would, of course, still have received a large upfront payment in US Dollars placed into their Treasury. We could also make a sizeable donation to the Minister's re-election account," Adrian concluded with a bit of a chuckle.

"OK, that sounds a reasonable approach," agreed Newton. "What is the Plan B you mentioned, if the Fiji Government doesn't play ball?"

"The problem I foresee is that any commercial negotiations with any Government will take time," Adrian continued. "Time, we do not have. We cannot allow the second study to be completed and published, bringing other potential competitors to the table and Anux unable to secure the commercial rights to the plant."

"Well, what do you have in mind," Newton laying back in his chair, awaiting the words of wisdom from Adrian.

"I have given the matter a lot of thought and want to destroy the plant at its source," was the business-like reply from Adrian. "No plant, then no study. Simple but effective. I, of course, would only put the plan into action if we cannot negotiate with the Government in a reasonable time-frame."

"What," Newton spluttered, sitting bolt upright. "You must be joking. How do you see yourself going about this in a foreign country? Not to mention without any corporate approval. I do not like the sound of this. I know there are rumours about some of your maverick promotional activities with the launch of AnuxuDine in Europe, but this takes the cake."

"I know it sounds extreme, but I would undertake this personally, so no one else would be involved from the company. Only you and I would know about the plan. There is the potential for a huge win for us and the company." Adrian added conspiratorially. "I have done some research and found out the plant is the national floral emblem of Fiji. It only grows in small quantities in an isolated area of Fiji, called Taveuni Island. It only flowers for a limited period during the year, being October to February and there is no current commercial cultivation of the plant. With no plant material, there would be no ability to undertake the second study. It would be our secret and protect the business, the share price and our bonuses going forward."

With a smile Newton was starting to relax, as he pushed the stop button on the recorder. *Either Adrian Nicholls gets rid of a potential problem and we can both take the credit, or if things go wrong, I will burn Adrian and remove a serious potential competitor to my own senior management ambitions within the Anux corporation.*

"Adrian, despite your plan sounding somewhat crazy, even unbelievable, you know you have my full support. You must make sure that we are the only ones in the company that are aware of this plan and please keep me informed," confirmed Newton. "We need no paperwork on this one."

"Thanks Newton, I knew I could count on you. Catch you later," Adrian quickly wrapped up the call.

Once Adrian had disconnected the call, Newton re-activated the record button on his recorder and clearly enunciated, "*Adrian, neither I nor Anux, can condone such unethical behaviour in seeking to destroy something as important as the national flower of a country. The company's reputation can in no way be compromised. The company does not condone and will never endorse you undertaking such activity. I therefore, suggest you focus your energies on the current priority of launching AnuxuDine in Australia and then seeing to its successful rollout into Asia, good night.*"

"*I am definitely planning to have a good night,*" Newton chuckled to himself, while patting his recorder. "*Either way I win with that potentially dangerous Adrian Nicholls.*"

He eyed the plastic bag sitting on his desk," *I think I have earned myself another couple of lines tonight and then straight home to Lisabeth. She is going to get it tonight, even if she says she has another one of those headaches.*" After snorting his *Colombian Heaven*, he carefully packed away his drug paraphernalia and locked the desk drawer, pocketing the key. He was humming cheerfully to himself as exited his office, heading for the elevator and home.

CHAPTER 5

"Mere will you hurry up." Concern was evident in Joeli's voice. "I checked with Fiji Airways and Jacob's flight is on time. I don't want us to be late to meet him."

"Nearly ready Tamana," Mere attempting to appease her Father. "*What to wear?*" holding a procession of outfits over her torso while standing in front of her bedroom mirror. There were a number of discounted outfits strewn across her bed. She could not make up her mind. Finally, after continued pleas from her Dad, coming from the loungeroom, where he was pacing up and down, she made her decision.

It was to be a tight fitting, full-length, cream chamba-sulu or dress, patterned with large red hibiscus flowers. The chamba-sulu enhanced her tall, slim body but maintained her modesty by covering her legs. There was a final quick look in her bedroom mirror, a pout of the lips, a dab of red lipstick. A final comb of her thick, wiry, black Fijian hair with her long-toothed, wooden Fijian comb and she was ready to go.

Joeli's face lit up as his beautiful daughter entered the room. "You look so much like your Tinana," he proudly declared. "*She has done so well, despite the tragedy of losing her Tinana (Mother) as a teenager.*"

"Come on Tamana, hurry up, or we will be late," Mere teased as she headed towards to the door.

"I will give you hurry up, Mere Koroi," Joeli proudly followed her out the door.

*

Jacob shuffled nervously in his seat as his ears started to feel as though they would explode. Flying was not his favourite past-time, it was a means to an end. The captain requested passengers to return to their seats and fasten their seatbelts. Turbulence was starting to rock the aircraft as it commenced a rapid descent to land at Fiji's Nadi International Airport. Adding to Jacob's concern, he could see the afternoon tropical thunderstorm starting to show its presence outside the plane's windows. There were flashes of lightning and rain started to run like rivers down the aircraft windows. He felt the butterflies fluttering in his stomach, as the aircraft began to swing more vigorously to and fro like a cornering rollercoaster, while making its final approach for the landing. *"Please hurry up and get this thing down."* Jacob's fingers dug into the armrests.

To take his mind off the pitching of the plane, he tried to focus on the week ahead. Mere and Joeli had arranged a busy introductory week. First up on Monday morning they would be meeting with the Minister of Commerce, Mr Filipe Sitiveni Matai. Joeli had arranged the meeting at the Minister's request. For some reason, the Minister was very keen to understand the process of developing a new medicine. In addition, there would be discussions around developing the protocol for the new study at the Fiji School of Medicine, before heading off to Taveuni Island on the Friday. Jacob was to accompany Mere on the trek to where the Tagimoucia plant grew and to collect quantities of its flowers to be used in the study.

Jacob was shaken back to reality as the pilot powered the aircraft into the runway to "stick" the landing. His upper body lurched forward, and the seatbelt grabbed tightly around his waist as the tyres screeched on the runway and the pilot engaged the reverse thrust. He began to continually swallow hard to try and clear his ears which had become blocked during the rapid descent. In the end, he resorted to pinching his nose and blowing hard, feeling the relief as his ears popped. *"Oh, so good to be on the ground."*

It was a relatively short taxi for the aircraft from the end of the runway to the terminal building. With the aircraft brought to halt, the seat belt sign was turned off with a ping. "Welcome to Fiji" announced the senior cabin attendant over the intercom, a signal to start a mad rush by the excited passengers to prepare to exit the aircraft. The passengers were largely families of holiday makers, keen to clear their hand-luggage and duty-free alcohol from the overhead lockers and to start their holidays. There was lots of chatter about swimming and cocktails by the pool, along with cruises to the offshore islands.

Jacob casually leant forward to retrieve his laptop satchel from under the seat in front of him. Being careful not to bump his head, he awkwardly raised his large frame from his cramped economy seat. He stood up in his aisle seat, to extract his carry-on bag stored in the overhead locker. In his hand luggage, he had some recent scientific magazines for Joeli and Mere, along with his Kindle and a few bits and pieces, such as a toothbrush, complete with a toothpaste tube less than 100ml carry-on limit. He also had a souvenir koala he had picked up on impulse, at the souvenir shop at Sydney Airport for Mere and was annoyed to find it was made in China. He would pick-up a couple of bottles of whisky for Dr Koroi at the Nadi duty-free store prior to clearing Fiji Customs. A friend indicated there was one located in the baggage collection area. He had been given a tip that Joeli liked a glass or two of whisky in the evening before heading to bed.

Standing in the aisle, Jacob was jostled by his fellow passengers, seemingly oblivious to anyone around them. They were set, poised with their hand-luggage, ready to make the dash to the passport control counters, collect their luggage, and get their holidays underway. As the aircraft door opened, Jacob sucked in his breath as his body was hit with a massive wave of heat and humidity. Within seconds of stepping out of the aircraft and heading towards passport control, Jacob could feel the perspiration starting to form on his brow and beads of sweat starting to trickle down his back. *"I thought the humidity in Sydney was bad, but compared to being in the tropics, it is nothing."*

After a welcoming utterance of bula and welcome to Fiji by the Immigration Officer and the scrutiny of his visa at passport control, Jacob headed downstairs to the ground floor to await his suitcase. While waiting for his luggage he noticed the duty-free store and its array of cigarettes, perfumes, and spirits. Jacob was not much of a drinker so what to get? *"I know Chivas Regal is a famous name," and* settled on two, one-litre bottles, the maximum duty-free allowance.

With suitcase in hand and passing through the quarantine x-ray inspection formalities, he stepped out into the arrival's hall. Jacob paused for a moment, his head turning to scan the waiting crowd. He saw a tall, well-built, well-dressed man, whip up a small cardboard sign which spelt out *Jacob Bryant* in black felt-tipped letters. Relieved and with a big smile on his face, he strode rapidly towards a beaming, welcoming Joeli.

*

Mere stood happily next to her Dad, behind the barrier in the visitors' arrival hall at Nadi International Airport. Jacob Bryant had texted her Dad to say he had cleared immigration and was waiting for his luggage. He should be out shortly. Mere wondered. "*What he will be like to work with? Will he be some introverted, quirky scientist?*"

Her towering Dad looked down at her with a proud smile, giving her a re-assuring pat on her arm. He was a bear of a man with a large barrel chest, accompanying large powerful arms and legs. He no doubt would have proven to be an extremely useful rugby player in his youth, while attending medical school in Auckland, New Zealand. Joeli still proudly wore a full head of short cropped, tightly coiled, dark Fijian hair, slightly greying at the temples. He was wearing the Fijian national dress for men, being a kilt-like garment known as a sulu. It was cream coloured, enhancing the darkness of his skin and covered him from the waist, down to shin length and came with trouser like pockets on each hip. It was complete with a bicep length, suit-like safari jacket. On his large feet he wore thick-soled, black leather sandals.

"I wish he would hurry up, it is hot out here," Mere starting to fidget nervously, awaiting the arrival of their guest and now fellow research scientist.

"He will be out shortly," Joeli said noticing her agitation. "I think that is him now," Joeli held up the piece of cardboard he had improvised as a welcome sign. He had scribed the name *Jacob Bryant* in large black felt pen lettering. "It's him," Joeli giving him a wave and big grin.

Mere watched him as he approached her Dad. He was pulling a suitcase in his right hand, had a computer satchel draped over his left shoulder and in the crook of his left arm, had what looked to be duty-free shopping bags. He looked handsome to her in a rugged sort of way. Tall but not as tall as her Dad. He had well-tanned skin and sun-bleached scraggly hair, no doubt from life on Sydney's beaches. He looked in good physical shape. "*Obviously looks after himself, no tummy like Dad,*" she chuckled to herself. He wore tight fitting blue jeans, over which he wore a loose-fitting, Hawaiian floral type, short-sleeved shirt opened to expose his dark hairy chest.

Losing her Tinana, unexpectedly in her teenage years had hit Mere hard. She had dedicated her life to her studies and the desire to study Medicine. She had studied at Auckland University in New Zealand, her Tamana's alumni. There was never much time for men in her life, with the dedication to her studies and now medical research at the Fiji School of Medicine. The oath she had made to her Tinana at her funeral, had always caused her to avoid getting involved in serious relationships, which would complicate her life.

"Bula, Joeli great to meet you," beamed Jacob, releasing the grip on his suitcase and extending his right hand. "Oh, here are a couple of bottles of whisky for you, hope Chivas Regal is OK?"

"You remembered to say bula," laughed Joeli. "Here let me take your bag and you can come to visit me anytime if you bring Chivas Regal."

Joeli felt a nudge in his back, "Sorry Jacob this my daughter Mere," Joeli was embarrassed at forgetting to introduce Mere.

Mere watched as Jacob seemed lost for words. He seemed to stare at her with his mouth dropped open, unable to say anything. Mere started to shift uneasily on her feet and blushed. "*What is he staring at?*"

They were all brought back to reality with a flash of lightning, followed almost instantaneously by an almighty clap of thunder. Mere wobbled on her feet and instinctively Jacob reached out to take her arm and stop her from falling over.

"You OK Mere?" a concerned Jacob asked.

"I'm fine, just got a bit of fright from that thunder and lightning," she replied, her heart rate starting to come back to normal.

"I nearly forgot Mere," Jacob passed Mere the remaining duty-free bag. "It's a koala. I would have got you some perfume, but it is such a personal thing selecting a fragrance. Hope you like it."

"He is very cute," smiled Mere snuggling the koala to her face. "It will sit nicely on my bed."

"I will quickly go and get the car from the carpark before the rain starts to come down," Joeli moved quickly for a big man. "Mere will guide you outside to the pickup area."

"Tamana, would like to get back home to Suva before it gets dark," Mere noted. "The main road back to Suva has large stretches that are unlit, and it can be quite dangerous with animals and people wandering over the road, not to mention the potholes."

"Tamana, is that Father in Fijian?" asked Jacob.

"Very clever, Jacob," smiled Mere. "I'll have to teach you some more words."

Joeli pulled up in the pickup area outside the terminal, in his white Mitsubishi Triton twin cab. Spits of rain started to descend from the ominous-looking dark grey, rumbling thunderheads that hovered over the airport. Another flash of lightning and rumble of thunder had Joeli quickly rolling out of the driver's seat. He dropped the tailgate and peeled back the protective, black cover on the vehicle's tray. With the intensity of the large raindrops increasing, Jacob quickly placed his suitcase in the tray and with Joeli's assistance moved to fasten the cover and close the tailgate.

With Jacob's suitcase safely stowed, Joeli moved rapidly to open the front passenger's door for Jacob. "Quickly Jacob, jump in, the rain is coming. It will not last long, but it will be pretty heavy until it passes over. Sit up front with me and Mere can sit in the back. She can look after that precious cargo of Chivas Regal for me," Joeli turned to smile at Mere, who tight-lipped, did not return his smile.

As Joeli headed back around to the driver's side, Jacob safely placed his computer satchel inside the vehicle. He then instinctively reached to open the rear door of the twin cab for Mere, just touching her hand, as she grasped the door handle. Jacob felt as though a shot of electricity surged through his body when his eyes met Mere's.

"Sorry," Jacob mumbled as he quickly removed his hand, while shuffling his feet, gathering himself and then opening the door for Mere.

"Thank you, Jacob," Mere smiled and looked into Jacob's eyes. "At least there is one gentleman in the car," she added loudly enough for her Dad to hear. Joeli smiled to himself while Mere climbed into the cab with Jacob quickly closed the door behind her.

The combination of rain, humidity, sweat, and heat caused an immediate fogging up of the windows, which brought a curse in Fijian from Joeli. "Tamana, please none of that profanity in front of Jacob," Mere gently chastising her Tamana. "We don't want his first Fijian words to be curse words."

"He will learn them from you fast enough," Joeli chortled, as he busily began using a hand towel to wipe the inside of the windscreen, while firing up the vehicle's air-con and demister. With the windscreen gradually clearing, Joeli had the windscreen wipers going at full speed. However, they seemed to make little impact on the heavy driving tropical downpour. With another flash of lightning and massive clap of thunder they were cautiously on their way to Suva.

"It will take me a while to get used to this heat and humidity," Jacob relieved as he felt the rush of cool air on his face, when the air-con kicked in. "I felt the humidity as soon as the aircraft door opened after we pulled up at the gate. The perspiration was starting to pour from me as soon as I started to walk from the plane to the immigration counters."

"You'll get used to it," Joeli smiled, as he gave Jacob a gentle punch in the arm.

With the thunderstorm quickly passing and disappearing into the hills surrounding Nadi Town, Jacob was able to start to relax and take in the sights. "This is my first trip to Fiji," he announced. "I look forward to working with you both on the study. Maybe on the way to Suva you can tell me about the Legend of the Tagimoucia?"

CHAPTER 6

Adrian sat at his desk looking out towards the Sydney Harbour Bridge. Enjoying the feel of the warmth of the sun on his face, he took the luxury to stop thinking about business for a moment and think about his journey through life. Life had treated him well and taken him a long way from that housing commission estate in Sydney, to a hectic commercial life in the busy streets of London. However, he still had the matter of his Mother at the back of his mind. One day, hopefully in the not-too-distant future, he would have enough money to get her a nice place, well away from the estate, where she could maybe get a dog. A knock at the door brought him to reality, it was Bob Williams.

"Hi Bob. Do you have an update for me?" asked Adrian. "Take a seat."

Bob launched into the update, "The public relations campaign has successfully shut down the media's interest in the matters raised by Dr Bryant and our plans for the launch are now well advanced. Based on preliminary orders from wholesalers, I am confident we will exceed our budgeted launch target."

"Great news Bob," thanked Adrian. "Keep me informed of progress. Please excuse me now. I need to make an important call. Close the door behind you, thanks."

Adrian's personal assistant had managed to arrange for a call with Fiji's Minister of Commerce, Mr Matai, stressing the importance of the call. Adrian was hoping to confirm a meeting with him in Fiji in the following week. He wanted to keep the momentum going with his plans to shut down work on the Tagimoucia project, as discussed and agreed with Newton Sinclair. Sitting down with Minister Matai, one on one, to discuss the acquisition of the commercial rights for the Tagimoucia plant, was the next vital step. "*I reckon it will be a win-win for Anux Pharmaceuticals and the Fiji Government*."

He picked up the handset and dialled. With a peep-peep-peep, followed by a short delay, the Minister's direct line rang in Suva, "Filipe Sitiveni Matai speaking."

"*He speaks better English than I expected. Sounds well educated.*"

"How do you do Mr Matai? Adrian Nicholls, President of Anux Pharmaceuticals in Sydney," speaking slowly and clearly enunciating. "Thank you for agreeing to speak with me at such short notice. I know you must be a busy man and I appreciate your valuable time."

"No problem. Please call me Filipe. I am quite interested to learn the interest your very large global pharmaceutical company has here in Fiji?"

"Filipe let me start by giving you a bit of background on Anux Pharmaceuticals," proffered Adrian.

"Excellent Adrian, that would be very useful," Filipe came across as sincere and interested in what Adrian had to say.

"Well Filipe," began Adrian. "Anux is headquartered in New York City and is a publicly listed, with a dual listing on the London and New York Stock Exchanges. Founded in 1965 by Mr Solomon Anux in New York, the company has grown rapidly from its humble beginnings. The company is now a global organisation, with an annual turnover in excess of five billion US dollars. Continued corporate growth and a subsequent rise in the share price, is expected with the recent launch of the company's new analgesic AnuxuDine in Europe and soon in Australia."

"Should I buy some stock in the company," laughed Filipe.

"Could be a good buy at the moment," Adrian relaxed with Filipe's casual style.

"Getting down to business," Filipe now sounded more business-like. "What can I do for you? My PA described your call as particularly important."

"The company is aware of some exciting Fiji based scientific research. The work having been published in a reputable scientific journal, *Pharmacognosy.*" Adrian continued, "The researchers, Doctors Joeli and Mere Koroi, identified the analgesic properties of a Fijian plant the *taggi-moo-chia*. Please forgive the pronunciation."

"Close enough," laughed Filipe. "There are some tricks in speaking the Fijian language. Maybe I can share them with you when we meet. Please continue."

"Anux is always looking to develop new sources of medicines," Adrian reverted to business mode. "The company needs to maintain an active product pipeline to maintain the growth of the business. To that end, Anux has done deals in other countries to acquire the commercial rights of various assets within those countries."

"Do you have an example of what you mean?" quizzed Filipe.

"Certainly, Filipe. There was a recent case in Brazil, where the company acquired the rights to commercialise medicines developed from a particular tree found in the tropical rainforests. An extract from the bark of the tree was found to relieve the sting of the fire ant. The company's laboratories are now working on a number of potential medical usages from various parts of the tree. There is the added likelihood of the company cultivating plantations of the trees, creating a large number of jobs."

"Fascinating. I like the sound of a large number of jobs." Filipe came across as being interested in acquiring more detailed information. "What do you have in mind for Fiji and the Tagimoucia, which by the way is our national floral emblem?"

"National floral emblem, that is potentially a significant fact. Imagine Fiji being credited with having the source of a new analgesic medicine," Adrian sensing Filipe's eagerness carried on. "With the growing commercial success of our new blockbuster analgesic around the world, Anux is looking for the next big opportunity to add to our product pipeline. With the initial study results of the Tagimoucia looking promising, I would like to meet with you face to face, at the earliest opportunity. The aim would be to discuss with you, the acquisition of the commercial rights to develop any medicine that may be developed from your national emblem."

"Please, go on. Explain to me what would be in it for the people of Fiji," Filipe prompted, now assuming a very business-like manner.

"For these types of arrangements, the company would typically be prepared to negotiate the paying of a very sizeable access fee upfront to the Fijian Government. In addition, there would be the likelihood of the payment of ongoing royalties, generated by the future sales of any products derived from the plant. The royalties would provide a revenue stream well into the future. There is a win-win for both the Fiji Government and Anux, in such an arrangement," Adrian declared attempting to sound his convincing best. "In addition, there would be major kudos for Fiji in being the home of a major new medical discovery."

"That sounds very interesting," mused Filipe. "It would definitely be worthwhile for us getting together for a chat, to explore the matter in more detail. How about we go with Thursday morning of next week, here in my office in Suva? Let me know if you have any difficulties in booking a flight and we can try and re-schedule for later in the month."

"Thank you very much Filipe for your valuable time. It would be good for us to get together at the earliest opportunity. So, I look forward to meeting you on Thursday of next week in your Suva office," Adrian giving a big air-pump with his right clenched fist.

"Great, I will put you back to my PA to firm up the time. Bye for now," Filipe paused to reflect on the call with Adrian. "*That was a very worthwhile chat. I must give my good friend Joeli Koroi a call.*"

*

Adrian immediately got on to his PA and asked her to arrange the flights from Sydney to Fiji, enabling him to arrive in Suva, by the Wednesday evening of the coming week. That would give him plenty of time to prepare for the Thursday morning meeting with the Minister. He decided on the Saturday for the return to Sydney. Staying the Friday would provide time for any follow up action that may be required in Fiji, after the meeting with Filipe.

Next on the agenda, Adrian called the management team together in his office. He gave them an update on what had transpired since they last got together on Monday morning. "It has been a busy few day's team and thanks to you all for your support," he started out. "I have had a call with Newton Sinclair in New York, and it has been agreed for me travel to Fiji, to meet with the Fijian Minister of Commerce, Mr Matai. The aim is for me to discuss the acquisition of the commercial rights to the Tagimoucia plant with him. If we can pull that off, that will enable us to block any further development from the Fijian source in the short term. With the rights secured we may decide to do something with it in the future, once AnuxuDine is established in the market.

There was a general rumbling amongst the team with the news. Consensus from the team was that this was a good way forward. "Do you want me to put any financials together for you for your meeting," asked Grant Davis the Chief Financial Officer.

"Good idea Grant. It would be good to have some information on what the company has spent on any similar acquisitions. It will give me something tangible to dangle in front of the Minister."

"Will do Adrian. I'll have it ready before you fly out next week," enthused Grant, busily making notes on his pad.

"I cannot emphasise enough, the confidentiality of what we are doing," Adrian going around the table, ensuring he made eye contact with each of the senior management team. "I don't want this getting out to any of the competition and especially to that do-gooding scientist, Jacob Bryant."

Adrian continued, "during my few days in Fiji, I need you to maintain focus on the launch. You know how important this is to the company with the rollout into Asia as the next step. Maintain your focus and if you need any help while I am away, I will check my emails regularly."

With the meeting over, the management team started to gather their bits and pieces together and head back to their desks. Adrian sat back in his chair and became somewhat self-indulgent. *"Things are a lot easier than I thought they would be in dealing with Filipe Matai. A proverbial piece of cake for the*

President of a Anux company. The Fijians won't be able to resist the sizeable carrot I will dangle in front of them. Onward to Fiji and getting the job done. It will be great to shut down that nuisance of an Aussie academic, Jacob Bryant. He won't know what hit him."

CHAPTER 7

Jacob settled back into the passenger seat, as the rain quickly subsided, with the thunderheads rumbling away into the surroundings hills. Laser like rays of sunshine started to filter their way through the clearing clouds.

"Glad the rain is easing," observed a relieved Joeli. "It will make the drive to Suva much easier. It is difficult at the best of times with the crazy Fijian drivers."

"Yes, it certainly was coming down in bucket loads," noted Jacob, a serious look on his face. "I wasn't looking forward to driving in those conditions."

Jacob's head started to move continually from side to side as he took in the surroundings along the roadside and the largely rural landscape. It was all new to him, not experiencing anything like it in Australia, especially next to an international airport. There were fields of growing sugarcane, interspersed with rail tracks, housing wagons laden with cut sugarcane, ready for the journey to the sugar mill.

With the sun starting to peek out through the clouds and the rain gone, it appeared to be a signal for people to emerge from everywhere along the roadside. Indian women in brightly coloured saris, carrying young children on their hips. Fijian and Indian people, waiting at bus stops for the next diesel, smoke spewing, open-sided bus coming up the road. Others were trying to wave down a taxi for a ride back into Nadi Town and some just standing around chatting. Indian men in long pants, shirts with rolled up sleeves to the elbows and wearing thongs. Fijian boys in t-shirts or rugby jerseys, in shorts and typically barefoot. A real mix of people, in a variety of dress and colours. *"What an amazing potpourri of life,"* Jacob thought, taking it all in.

The road was lined with puddles of water from the storm's downpour and the various Fijian and Indian traders were starting to re-open their rickety open, wooden stalls which aligned the main road to Suva. The stalls offered a variety of items including all sorts of local fruit, vegetables, and drinks. Mangoes, coconuts, fresh fish and vegetables, some vegetables he was not familiar with at all.

"That storm will at least cool things down for a bit tonight, but as soon as the sun rises tomorrow morning, the humidity will quickly build again, I am sorry to say," Joeli informed them. "It is going to be about a 2 ½ to 3-hour drive to Suva, so we have plenty of time to get to know each a little better. How about you start Mere and tell Jacob a bit about yourself."

"Sure Tamana," Mere's demeanour becoming notably serious. "The biggest motivation in my life was the tragic death of my Tinana, my Mother. It is why I followed in my Tamana's, footsteps and studied Medicine at his alumni in Auckland. In my mid-teens my Tinana Lute, made a visit to her family's home village in one of Fiji's outer islands. She received a coral cut to her leg while out fishing on the reef with her sister. The wound became rapidly infected and reportedly had taken over her body in only a matter of hours. Being on a remote island with limited medical resources and transport availability, she passed away before any emergency assistance could be provided and she suffered in considerable pain."

Jacob could see tears forming in Mere's eyes. "I am so sorry Mere," Jacob reached behind to tenderly touch her arm.

"My return to Fiji after graduation", Mere said composing herself, "was widely reported in the Fijian media. In an interview for Radio Fiji, I expressed it was my desire to work with my Dad, to find something in Fiji that would help with treating infections and pain. I didn't want what had happened to my Mother, to happen with anyone else."

"Mere's radio interview was heard by Ratu Osea Rokovou, the Chief of the village on Taveuni Island. It motivated him to contact me," Joeli jumped into the conversation. "We went to school together and he contacted me at the Fiji School of Medicine. He explained how villagers had swallowed a draft from the crushed red flowers of the Tagimoucia plant, to provide pain relief, for as long as he could remember."

"Thanks, Dad, for the interruption," Mere glared at her Dad. "We visited Taveuni to meet with Ratu Osea and some of the villagers to learn more about the plant and how it is used. Dad is not as fit as he used to be." Joeli grunted bringing a smile to Mere. "It was up to me, with some guides from the village, to head up to Lake Tagimoucia to see the plant and gather samples. The plant, a vine, inhabits the trees growing alongside the lake. To get to the lake requires a gruelling, steep, four-hour trek, to the top of Taveuni. It is the only place in Fiji where the plant grows, as attempts to grow the plant in other areas have all failed to date."

"Amazing," Jacob was captivated by the tale. "Looks like I will need some hiking gear if I am going to help Mere collect some samples. I did not bring anything suitable with me."

"No problem we can get some gear for you in Suva on Monday," Mere noted. "One other interesting fact is that the plant only flowers during the period October to February, the hottest and most humid time of the year. It is also the cyclone season, so we need to keep an eye on the weather reports before making a decision to go and collect the samples in Taveuni."

"With the samples in hand we returned to the laboratory in Suva," Joeli took over the story. "We prepared some solutions from the crushed flowers and gave the solution to laboratory rats to test their response to pain. We exposed their feet to a hot plate and monitored their responses. This, of course, led to the publication in *Pharmacognosy*, which you subsequently read Jacob and stimulated you to contact us."

"One thing Tamana forgot to mention," Mere interjected. "According Ratu Osea, the drinking of the flower extract reportedly had some strange effects in those swallowing the draft. Some people reported weird dreams and seeing visions. There appeared to hallucinogenic side-effects which we need to look for in the second study with the human volunteers."

"That would certainly create a problem in developing a new medicine based on an extract from the flowers," Jacob advised. "We will need to factor that into the trial with those in the study. They will need careful observation and probably not be able to drive until we check it out, given the potential for a hallucinogenic effect."

"I would concur with that," agreed Joeli. "We will need to be careful with our volunteers. Some of the local medical students have put their hand up to participate in the study."

"It would be fantastic if we can develop a medicine derived from a local source. It could act as a tribute and provide a legacy to your late Tinana. I look forward to getting stuck into the trial work," enthused Jacob.

"You now know what motivated us Jacob. Tell us about yourself," Joeli took a quick glance towards Jacob, before returning his eyes to the road.

"My Dad always wanted me to be a dentist," Jacob turned his head towards Mere in the back seat. "The thought of drilling and extracting teeth from terrified people definitely did not appeal. I had some cousins who were either doctors or nurses, so I thought, why not add a pharmacist to help build the range of healthcare professionals within the Nicholls family." This brought a bit of a chuckle from Mere and Joeli.

"During the four-year pharmacy degree course, I developed a passion for the science of pharmacognosy. As you know it is the study of the medical uses developed from plant sources." The passion came through in Jacob's strong voice. "I was amazed at how many of our modern medicines came from plant sources. Think of the Foxglove plant, from which we derived Digoxin, used to treat various heart conditions. The Chondrodendron in South America, the source of Tubocurarine, which was used in surgical procedures. I knew there must be many more plant-based remedies, that have been used by many cultures for centuries. Your published article really captured my interest, so here I am with you today."

"What about your personal life. Interests, hobbies, any family?" Mere appearing to innocently probe Jacob.

"An easy summary, my work and surfing," Jacob felt wonderfully comfortable with Mere and Joeli. "I have a small one-bedroom apartment overlooking Mona Vale Beach in Sydney and surf most mornings before heading off to work. With my work, I have not had much time for girlfriends and the like, much to my Mum's annoyance. I keep getting not so subtle reminders from her and Dad wanting grandchildren, as they say they are not getting any younger. With a younger sister working in London, I get all the pressure from the folks."

Quickly glancing over at Mere, Joeli noticed the smile on her face following Jacob's answer and grinned to himself. *"I wonder whether Jacob is the catalyst for Mere to take an interest in something beside her work and looking after me, since her Tinana passed away? Jacob's visit is going to be very interesting and hopefully fruitful, in more ways than one."*

The drive to Suva continued, Jacob noting that they appeared to be making good time. This was despite the numerous obstacles one faced in driving in Fiji, even on the supposed national highway. Obstacles encountered included police roadblocks for licence checks and scaling mountainous speed humps to test the suspension on your vehicle to the limit. The number of four-wheel vehicles was very evident. The speed humps were strategically place at the entrance to the various villages that lined the main road, with interesting names like Korovuto and Yako. In addition, the national speed limit was a lowly 80 kmph for cars and even lower for commercial vehicles at only 60 kmph. All this combined with numerous potholes and limited passing opportunities made for a sometimes-nerve-wracking drive. Jacob was starting to make instinctive presses of the brake pedal on the passenger side floor mat, as vehicles continued to approach them on their side of the road. *"I don't think I could ever drive here."*

"Why don't you tell me about the legend of the Tagimoucia," asked Jacob. "Hopefully, I got the pronunciation ok."

"Pretty close," chuckled an amused Mere, "Try this. Tang-ee-mow-thee-a."

"Tang-ee-mow-thee-a."

"Nice try," smiled Mere, as she clapped, while Joeli had a huge grin on his face.

They were continuing to make good time and were now crossing the bridge over the Sigatoka River in Sigatoka Town. This was the part of the journey which followed the scenic, palm tree-lined Coral Coast. "*Now this is how I imagined the paradise of Fiji to be. Look at the waves pounding on the coral reef which hugged the coast like a skirt, around 500 metres from shore. Beautiful horseshoe bays topped with golden sands and surrounded by myriads of coconut trees. Gentle waves were lapping on the shore, with a number of local villagers ambling along the beach in their sulus, enjoying the cool, gentle, afternoon breeze.*" Jacob looking longingly, as the picture postcard continued to unfold before his eyes. The beep of a horn by Joeli and an errant taxi hurtling towards them on their side of the road, brought him quickly back to reality.

"OMG," Jacob cried, his heart pounding, bringing a laugh from Mere.

"Here take a look at this." Mere presenting Jacob with a Fijian banknote. "This is a $50 note, and, on the reverse, you will see there is the floral emblem of Fiji, the red flowered Tagimoucia. I better have that back," smiled Mere holding out her hand.

A grinning Jacob handed the note back to her, "*I really like her sense of humour. It is going to be good to get to know her a lot better over the coming days.*"

Mere took a deep breathe, paused, then began to tell Jacob the legend of the princess and the Tagimoucia, "The legend began long, long ago on the island of Taveuni…

*

"I like it. It sets the scene for our work ahead," Jacob nodded his appreciation at Mere. "However, I don't like the sound of the trek to the lake to see the plant and its flowers. It sounds like a definite requirement, that I'll need to get some suitable gear, to make the trek up to the lake."

They had completed the part of the journey that took them along the scenic Coral Coast and were now at the start of the Serua Hills. The hills are a series of four steep hills, dividing east from west on the main Fiji Island of Viti Levu. This section of the National Highway came complete with hair-pin bends, where one inevitably came across large slowly chugging, exhaust spewing, trucks, or buses. Jacob was starting to the feel the effects of the long day of travel and was quietly nodding off to sleep.

"Dad let him rest. He has had a long day" whispered Mere. "We can wake him once we reach Lami Town on the outskirts of Suva."

"Fine, why don't you lay back as well. I'll be OK," Joeli received no resistance from Mere, who happily dozed off in the back seat.

CHAPTER 8

"Hey Jacob," Mere said, giving him a shake on his shoulder. "We are just approaching the township of Lami on the outskirts of Suva, so not long to go now until we reach home. We will make it just before sunset."

"I must have nodded off," Jacob muttered stating the obvious. "I am glad you let me get a bit of shut-eye, I feel much better." His eyes began to take in the increased activity with people and vehicles on the road into Fiji's capital.

"You will see Suva is surrounded by rugged hills and the growing population is densely crammed in around Suva Harbour," Joeli started a travelogue as he gradually slowed the vehicle, hitting the Saturday evening traffic heading into downtown. "Traffic is always a nightmare around Suva. The windy streets and rugged terrain are not conducive to broad straight boulevards."

"Our place is on Suva Point," Mere interjected. "It has the best breezes coming off the sea and there are some great spots to walk along the waterfront. We can check it out tomorrow."

Joeli started up again. "We have just crossed the Tamavua River and on the left you will see the old Suva Cemetery, the dead centre of Suva," Joeli chuckled, before receiving a wicked glare from Mere.

"Dad, please not that sick joke," Mere smarted. "How embarrassing."

"As we go around this tight bend, on the right you will see the Royal Suva Yacht Club and directly opposite, with the high white walls, Suva Gaol," Joeli quickly pointed here and there. "We are now entering the Walu Bay industrial area."

"Not a very scenic way to enter the capital," Mere mumbled.

"Ah, there on the left is the, Carlton Brewery. I have a cold Fiji Bitter waiting for you at home in the fridge to try," Joeli was hoping for a positive response.

"I think we deserve one or two after that drive," Jacob answered in the affirmative.

"*I am going to like this boy,*" Joeli thought, smiling to himself in anticipation.

Being Saturday night there were people everywhere. They were coming into the city, drawn by the many restaurants, movie theatres and nightclubs, making it a slow crawl through the downtown area. They passed the docks, the market and bus stand before hitting the major commercial street of Victoria Parade and the road to Suva Point. Jacob noted there were only a couple of high-rise buildings in the CBD, with mainly strip shops aligning the street.

"*There is even a Maccas, civilisation has reached Fiji,*" Jacob grinned to himself.

Ten minutes later they were finally pulling into the Koroi residence on Suva Point. It was a Queensland style house, being perched on stilts. This was to allow for the flow of any breeze under the house, to help cool things down with the relentless tropical heat and humidity. Security lights came on as they turned into the driveway.

They were met by two large Dobermans who bounded up to Joeli and Mere. They spotted Jacob as he rolled out of the car and proceeded to bark at him. "It's OK, that's Jacob." Joeli brought them over for a sniff. "He will be with us for a while. Jacob, meet the boys, Bula with the black collar and Vatu with the red collar." Jacob tentatively held out his right hand towards the dogs, who gave the hand the obligatory sniff. It appeared he was ok and would be allowed onto the property.

"I will open up Dad, while you help Jacob with his bags," Mere climbed out of the car and headed up the stairs leading to the front door.

While the luggage was being retrieved, Mere dashed up the steps, opening the front door, followed quickly by the French doors leading onto the balcony which lined the front of the house. She wanted to let some of that Suva Point breeze through the house, to cool things down. As the men entered the house with the bags, Mere had the overhead fan in the living room set to high speed. She then proceeded to retrieve mosquito coils and matches from the kitchen, lighting the coils and placing them under the cane chairs on the balcony, to keep the pesky, biting insects away.

"I am sure the mosquitoes will enjoy the taste of fresh Australian blood," Mere laughed. "Any chance for some drinks Tamana, so we can relax a bit before having something to eat."

"Quality Aussie product here, so I had better take a seat as close to one of those coils as possible. They usually go for me," lamented Jacob, sitting right over the top of the smoking coil.

A laden Joeli quickly returned from the kitchen, "Jacob here, try an icy-cold Fiji Bitter and Mere for you, a glass of your favourite Kiwi Sauvignon Blanc." Joeli was enjoying the role as the waiter. "For me, a wikki-wai. It is what is known as a whisky and water here in Fiji Jacob," Joeli said, keen to sample some of the duty-free Chivas Regal, Jacob had given him.

They watched expectantly as Jacob did not hesitate in taking a large taste of the Fiji Bitter, "That was great, I think I can easily do another," which brought lots of clapping and laughter. "Have I passed the initiation test?" Jacob laughed.

The subject turned to the coming busy week's activities. "As you know, first up Monday morning we will meet with the Minister of Commerce, Filipe Matai. He is keen to learn more about how the pharmaceutical industry operates." Mere began her summary of the week. "We will then head up to the lab at the Fiji School of Medicine campus to show you around and talk about the new study."

"I would like us to review the work done to date in the first study and start planning for the next study with you," Joeli took over the dialogue. "I will also get the department's secretary to arrange flights for you and Mere to Taveuni, along with accommodation. I suggest you head up on the Friday morning. That will give you time to have a bit of a look around Taveuni on the Friday and Saturday. You can then tackle the trek to Lake Tagimoucia on the Sunday morning. There you can collect the research samples to bring back to Suva for the second study on the Monday".

"Sounds like a pretty busy week. I am looking forward to it, especially visiting Taveuni and trekking up to the lake," enthused Jacob.

"Oh, that reminds me Jacob," Mere jumped in, "the current long-range weather forecast is good. However, to be on the safe side we should definitely pick you up a rain jacket and some suitable footwear, so another job for the growing list."

"We better get you something to eat and then you can get off to bed for an early night," Mere said, noticing Jacob attempting to hide a yawn. "There is some chicken and salad in the fridge and some of the local root crop, known as dalo or taro, which is hopefully OK."

"That will be great, I am starting to get hungry, it was only really a snack which was provided on the flight and I certainly felt the effect of that beer on an empty stomach," Jacob said rubbing his belly to stifle a rumble.

"See how you feel in the morning and we can make a plan for the day to show you around Suva," Mere directed Jacob to the dinner table.

After dinner Jacob grabbed his luggage and headed towards the back steps. Mere flicked the switch, turning on a powerful beam of light. The light illuminated the path to the very ample cottage located at the rear of the property. Bula and Vatu, who lived under the house, came out and provided an escort for Jacob and Mere down to the cottage.

The cottage entrance light came on as they approached the screen door and Mere produced a key. She opened the screen door, the main door, before reaching inside to turn on the interior light. It was a comfortable bedsit, with a double bed adorned with a white bedspread. A mosquito net connected to a metal ring in the ceiling draped over the bed. In addition, there was an ensuite with a shower, writing desk, flat screen TV mounted on the wall opposite the bed. Other furnishings included a two-seater couch covered in a light green vinyl with cream cushions and a low, dark-brown, wooden coffee table, stacked with a range of old, well-thumbed magazines. There was also a kitchenette complete with a sink, microwave, and refrigerator.

"This used to be my place before Tinana passed away," reflected Mere. "With Tinana's passing I decided to move back into the house to give Tamana some company and to try and keep an eye on him. Despite his brave face, he has never been the same since her passing. He doesn't look after himself like he used to."

"It looks great Mere; I should be very comfortable in here," Jacob's eyes swept around, taking in his lodgings. "It is going to be much more comfortable than a hotel and I can really stretch out in here."

"You'll find the Wi-Fi network details and password, on the fridge door magnet," said Mere, beginning a hotel like rundown of the room. "In the fridge there is some milk and some fruit if you get hungry during the night. On the coffee table is the TV remote and, on the wall, next to the bed, is the control switch for the overhead fan. In the kitchen there is some spray for any stray mosquitoes and also some coils and matches."

"Thanks, Mere, for your hospitality. You and your Dad, I mean Tamana, have been amazing and so welcoming. I look forward to working with you both and hopefully achieving something worthwhile," Jacob said, holding Mere's gaze.

Mere reached out to hand Jacob the key for the cottage and as their hands met, they looked each other in the eyes, before the both of them turned quickly away from each other. Jacob could feel the warmth in his cheeks as a blush seemed to illuminate his face. With a slight stammer, Mere uttered, "Good night Jacob, see you around eight for breakfast up in the house." Mere closed the main door behind her and with her head down, quickly made her way back to the house, followed by the trusty dogs. She took one quick look over her shoulder back towards the cottage, before rapidly climbing the stairs.

Jacob stood and stared at the closed door, unable to move. Something was happening inside of him, something he had not felt before, with any other woman. *"Dr Mere Koroi is something very special."* Despite being tired, Jacob tossed and turned with his thoughts of Mere. After spraying one errant buzzing mosquito, which was trying to find a way through the mosquito netting, he finally fell asleep. He was looking forward to getting to know Mere and the coming days in Fiji.

*

"*What is her light doing on this early in the morning,*" Joeli wondered, having got up for an early morning toilet break and seeing a faint glow coming from under Mere's bedroom door. He gently tapped then pushed her door open, to see her sitting upright in bed reading. "Can't sleep?"

"Just thinking about the coming days," Mere replied, placing her book on the bedside table. "There is so much to do."

"Try and get some sleep, we have a busy week ahead of us," said Joeli closing the door behind him. "*I wonder if Dr Bryant, features in that thinking?*"

CHAPTER 9

"How did you sleep, Jacob?" queried Mere. "The bed was very comfortable and apart from one annoying mozzie, which I zapped with that handy can of spray, a most restful night," replied Jacob.

"For breakfast there is some pawpaw or papaya to start," Mere being the perfect hostess. "Followed by some scrambled eggs on toast."

"Sounds good to me," Jacob quickly took a seat opposite Joeli, who briefly looked up from reading the rugby news in the Sunday Fiji Times. "England beat Wales 14 to 6," Joeli's eyes returned to the sports section of the newspaper.

"As your tour guide today, let me know what you think of this," suggested Mere. "Before it gets too hot, we can take a walk along the waterfront. That will take us past Government House, residence of the President of Fiji and then next door into Thurston Gardens, where we can stop for something to eat and a drink. I'll make a picnic lunch for us. Bring some bathers and we can head up to Colo-i-Suva waterfall for a swim, to cool down a bit in the afternoon. If you have any energy left, I have made a reservation tonight at Tomasi's Floating Seafood Restaurant, on Suva Harbour for 6.30pm, so it is not too late a night."

"Sounds a great day and I especially look forward to trying some fresh, local seafood at the floating restaurant this evening." Jacob set off to his room to collect a cap and sunscreen for the day's outing. "Be good to get underway before it gets too hot. What about your Tamana?"

"Are you kidding? Him? Walk?" Mere turned to glare at her Tamana. "His eyes will be glued to the television all day, to watch the Six Nations Rugby replays from Europe."

"The replay of Ireland versus Scotland this afternoon," Joeli commented, still firmly engrossed in his newspaper.

The heat was not conducive to a brisk walk along the Suva Point waterfront, located a short drive from the Koroi's residence. Mere parked underneath one of the many, huge Banyan trees which provided a natural umbrella effect, with their branches stretching out over the waterfront footpath towards the harbour. They strolled along, enjoying the gentle breeze coming off Suva Harbour, cooling things a little. However, the heat and humidity began to rapidly rise, in concert with the tropical sun rising to its zenith in the sky.

"Time for something to eat and a drink?" Mere asked raising an eyebrow and turning towards Jacob. "Let's head off to Thurston Gardens and find a shady tree to sit under."

They passed the entrance to Government House, where Jacob paused to take a photo on his smartphone of the on-duty Fijian sentry. The sentry was smartly turned out in a spotless, white sulu and red military top, complete with brass buttons, standing with his rigid back, astride a rifle, in his polished, black sandals. They crossed over the road and entered the gardens, ready to enjoy their picnic lunch.

"No sitting under a coconut tree," Mere said, pointing upwards to the tree laden with coconuts, which were poised ready to submit to gravity and crash earthwards on to an unsuspecting head. "There is a nice shady flame tree."

Jacob spread out the woven Fijian mat and Mere served up some spicy beef and vegetables wrapped Indian style in naan bread.

"Whew, that chilli has some kick," Jacob exclaimed, fanning his mouth with his tongue sticking out and reaching for a sip of some water.

"That was nothing, wait till you try a real local Indian curry," laughed Mere. "We love our curries here."

"Come on. We better finish lunch and get moving, otherwise we will nod off to sleep," Mere starting to stand and gather the bits and pieces together. "Let's get back to the car and we can head on up to Colo-i-Suva for that swim."

"Much quieter downtown on a Sunday in Suva," noted Jacob. "Far fewer people around."

"Yes, the Fijian people are very religious and avid church goers," replied Mere. "Despite family pressures to attend church regularly, Tamana and I have not been ones much for church. Not since Tinana died. Only weddings and funerals get us inside a church these days."

The Colo-i-Suva waterfall and pool was about a 25-minute drive from downtown. They headed up a steep road, Princess Road, Tamavua, which overlooked the city and harbour. Mere turned off down a side street and pulled over to give Jacob a chance to get the lie of the land.

"Wow, what a view," exclaimed Jacob. "Such a beautiful setting."

"There on the right is Lami town, where we first hit the Suva traffic last night," Mere again reverting to tour guide. "There is the cemetery and yacht club and down below us the Tamavua River, with Suva Point to the left. We better keep moving," Mere engaged the clutch and headed back to the main road.

Getting close to the turn off to the waterfall, Jacob noticed the sign for the Fiji School of Medicine. "Is this where we will be heading tomorrow?" Jacob asked, turning to look at Mere.

"Yes, but I won't stop now, better keep moving. We have time for a quick swim and then back home, for maybe a quick rest before getting ready to head out tonight."

They parked the car and headed down the well-worn pathway which led through thick jungle towards the pool. They could hear kids yelling and the splashes as bodies hit the water. The pool area was surrounded by some fragile looking coconut frond thatched shelters. Over the pool a large, knotted Tarzan-like rope dropped from the branch of large tree which drooped over the pond.

Mere took her spot under one the shelters. "Not coming in Mere?" Jacob questioned, moving to grab her arm.

"No way," Mere beating a hasty retreat.

"You're a big scaredy-cat," Jacob teased, then taking off his shirt and shorts headed purposely towards the Tarzan rope.

"*Wow, he looks pretty hot, without his shirt,*" Mere pondered, moving back to take a seat and getting set to watch Jacob in action.

After launching his body out across the water on the rope, Jacob flung his body free and soared through the air, landing in the water with an almighty splash. This caused Mere to shriek as she was hit by the spray.

With a smile on his face noting he had splashed Mere, Jacob dragged himself out of the pool and sat down on his towel which Mere had laid out next to hers. He stretched out and quickly gave in to his body's desire for sleep in the dozy afternoon sun. Mere did not disturb him, content to sit and admire his physique, in the afternoon sunshine. After half an hour she gave him a nudge, which caused him to snap upright.

"Sorry, I must have dozed off," Jacob apologised, stretching his arms out and stifling a yawn.

"Come on, let's get you back home so you can freshen up for tonight," Mere gathered her towel and bag as she stood.

*

Jacob was chatting to Joeli in the loungeroom with the rugby flickering on the television in the background. They were enjoying a beer while waiting for Mere to get ready. Joeli was regularly turning his head towards the screen to get the score in the Ireland versus Scotland game.

"You wait, I will have to chase up Mere for you," Joeli winked knowingly to Jacob. "Mere, hurry up they close at 10pm."

"Very funny, I'll be out in a minute, Tamana," came the tense sounding reply.

Mere stepped in the room and the men's heads turned towards her. Jacob's jaw dropped. She was stunning! Leg hugging tight blue jeans, a white cotton shirt tied at the waist and towering red stilettos. Joeli looked immensely proud and hugged his daughter. Jacob could not remove the smile from his face, as they headed out to the car.

They parked in the Suva City Council carpark and made the dash across the road to the gangplank, which like an umbilical cord, joined the floating restaurant to the waterfront. The vessel was around 100 feet long with a dark-blue hull, parked stern in and riding high in the water. The cabin area above the teak timbered deck was painted white, with dim light seeming to flicker out of the large portholes.

They sized up the swaying gangplank and tentatively stepped out towards the restaurant entrance, firmly gripping the handrails. The journey not made easier for Mere in her stilettos. On the stern was a reception desk where they were met with the universal *Bula*, by the maître d'.

"Table for two, for Koroi," Mere said, taking charge as the maître d' was turning to look at Jacob.

"Certainly madame," the maître d' replied, not missing a beat, and escorting them to their table.

Eyes from the other male diners turned towards Mere, as they made their way to their table. It was a moment not lost on Jacob. They agreed to share the local seafood platter, complimented by a bottle of chilled Kiwi Sauvignon Blanc. It was a perfect evening with Mere and Jacob continuing to warm to each other, their conversation interspersed with lots of smiles and laughter. Reluctantly they agreed it was time to head home to bed. There was a busy week ahead of them.

Despite Mere's insistence, Jacob paid for the meal and they headed for the exit, to be greeted by rain starting to cascade down in tropical strength onto the stern of the boat. The large tropical strength raindrops would soon drench anything they hit.

"Oh poop. I left the umbrella in the car. Tomasi you don't have a brolly I could borrow?" Mere looking forlornly towards the host. "I will drop it back to you during the week."

"No problem for you Mere. Here you are," a friendly sounding Tomasi said, extracting an umbrella from behind the reception desk. "Keep it, someone else had left it behind last night."

With the driving wind accompanying the rain, the boat was starting to rock noticeably as Jacob and Mere stepped cautiously onto the gangplank. Mere quickly removed her shoes, as Jacob slowly opened the umbrella, doing his best to hold it steady and keep them dry, as the wind hit. They scrambled back ashore, the umbrella offering little protection.

Jacob wrapped his arm around Mere, sheltering her, as best he could under the umbrella, as it shook vigorously in his hand. He had a smile on his face as he hugged her tightly to his body, shielding her from the weather, as they made their way to the carpark. Despite the rain, Jacob appeared to be in no hurry to get back to the car. He was enjoying this moment too much, with Mere snuggled close to him. His nostrils were bathed with the sweet smell of frangipani oil emanating from her body.

They made it back to the car with the legs of their jeans drenched. Jacob opened Mere's door, protecting her with the umbrella as she got into the driver's seat. After a good shake of the umbrella, he placed it on the floor behind his front passenger seat and they were homeward bound. The downpour started to ease and had stopped by the time they reached the driveway at home. In the wet conditions, the dogs seemed reluctant to come out of their kennel under the house to greet them.

"That was a great day, capped off by a wonderful dinner, thanks Mere for organising it."

"What was your favourite part of the seafood platter?" quizzed Mere.

"Mm," pondered Jacob, as he placed his right index finger on his chin. "I loved the lightly battered, fried walu fish pieces with of the hint of lime. I will definitely have walu again. I like its meaty texture."

Despite Jacob reaching to open the car door, Mere seemed to linger, but Jacob's head was full of thoughts for the coming week, so he had missed the signal, to stay a little longer in the car and keep chatting to Mere. They entered the house, which was all quiet, with Joeli already in bed, a faint snore coming from his bedroom, his door slightly ajar.

"I suppose I better get off to bed, with what we have ahead of us this week. Thanks again for a fantastic meal and evening, Mere," Jacob slowly headed for the backdoor and to the steps leading down to the cottage.

"I'll get the light for you," Mere's hand moved towards the light switch.

Their hands met at the light switch and their eyes met. Mere had a look of guilt as she quickly removed her hand and started to head towards her bedroom, her mind racing. *"Where is this all going? Can I uphold the oath I made to my Tinana and being alone with him in Taveuni?"* Mere's pulse was racing as she closed her bedroom behind her. She had not had these feelings for a man for an awfully long time.

"What was that all about?" Jacob was pensive as he headed down the path to the cottage. When he reached the door of his cottage, he turned and took a final look back over his shoulder to the top of the stairs. *"Was there some movement behind the curtain?"*

As Jacob turned, Mere flicked the curtain back into place and returned to her bedroom, her heart beating rapidly. *"Oh Jacob Bryant, what are you doing to me?"*

CHAPTER 10

The door of the Minister's Office opened, "Joeli, good to see you again bro'. It's been a while," said the Minister Matai, wrapping his left arm around Joeli's shoulders, while shaking his hand. "Mere, you are getting more beautiful every time I see you. Just like your Tinana." Mere was noticeably embarrassed.

"You must be Jacob. Joeli has told me a lot about you. I'll arrange some tea," Filipe said, herding everyone into his office.

As he entered the large office, Jacob was immediately struck by the panoramic view of Suva Harbour afforded by the large window in Filipe's office. It was on the top floor of the harbourside, Fiji Development Bank Building. To the left was Filipe's large, dark timbered desk, which looked neat and tidy apart from the electrical cables exuding from his computer screen, keyboard, and mouse. On the right were two, three-seater coffee-coloured, textured sofas aligned either side of the huge dark wooden, glass topped, coffee table, engraved with Fijian motifs. Filipe took his seat in his personal matching chair at the head of the table, his back to the window. Joeli sat on one sofa to the right of Filipe, with Mere and Jacob next to each other, to Filipe's left.

"Love the coffee table," Jacob ran his hand over the glass top, which protected the carvings underneath.

"If you can carry it, you can have it," laughed Filipe.

"Filipe and I attended Auckland University together, a very long time ago," laughed Joeli.

"Yes, too long ago," smiled Filipe. "We were in the University's First Team for rugby and we won the New Zealand's National Universities Championship. You can see the team photo on the wall behind my desk. Joeli was the bright one studying medicine."

"You did pretty well yourself, Filipe. First class honours in Commerce if I recollect," added Joeli.

Jacob noticed Filipe's strong build similar to Joeli and imagined Filipe would have been a formidable opponent in his day on the field. He certainly projected a very business-like persona as the Minister for Commerce.

After further reminiscences of the glory days playing rugby, a sip of tea and a bit of chit-chat with Mere as to what she was up to, Joeli gave a small cough with his hand to his mouth, "Filipe thanks for seeing us. I know you are busy, so we better get on with it. Jacob is from the Pharmacy Department at Sydney University. He is on loan to us from the University, to help us with the undertaking of a second study into the pain-relieving properties of the flowers from the Tagimoucia."

"Jacob and I will be heading up to Taveuni on Friday morning," Mere continued. "We are going to collect some flowers for use in the study, which will include the use of human volunteers. We want to see if the results seen in rats can be repeated in humans."

"If the outcomes from the first study in laboratory animals are verified, then there may be something tangible to take to a pharmaceutical company," Jacob interjected. "The ultimate aim would be the development of a commercially viable product, safe for use in humans."

"Very interesting Jacob. How would things progress with a pharmaceutical company, if the study proved positive?" queried an earnest Filipe, leaning towards Jacob.

Jacob warmed to the task, "With verification that the plant extract has pain relieving properties in human volunteers, it would just be the start. A pharmaceutical company with their huge resources, would then need to identify the active ingredient. Further testing would determine the suitable dose form for a potential medicine. It may be effective as an oral tablet or even an injectable product. Most importantly any product would need to be safe to use with little or no side-effects."

"It sounds complex," Filipe looked concerned.

"It is a lengthy process, which is very expensive and high risk, with a low success rate." Jacob paused looking at everyone around the table before continuing. "If there is potential, then there is years of clinical trials. The trials are required to determine safe dosage levels, identify any side-effects and possible toxicity from use of the product."

"Thanks for the background," Filipe seemed pensive. "There is obviously a lot to be considered in discussing the commercialisation aspects of a potential product with a pharmaceutical company Jacob. Your insight may be extremely helpful in the future if things progress."

"I'll be happy to help," Jacob was warming to Filipe. "I also have some good industry contacts, which could prove very useful in the future."

"There are a number of considerations for the Government in considering such an undertaking," Filipe started assuming a ministerial tone. "The Tagimoucia is the national flower emblem of Fiji and is only found in a remote area of Fiji in limited quantities. Attempts to grow the plant in other areas have failed. So, there are a number of cultural and commercial elements to be thought through by the Government, in conjunction with the people of Taveuni. There is the potential for a significant disruption to the people and the environment, if such a development were to take place. In particular, I foresee the need for a formal Environmental Impact Study as a minimum requirement."

"Filipe, you mentioned to me that our meeting today is timely. Why is that?" Joeli asked.

"Well, I have a meeting with a Mr Adrian Nicholls, the President of Anux Pharmaceuticals in Australia this Thursday morning."

"What! That SOB," thundered an enraged Jacob, twisting in his seat and pounding his clenched fist into the palm of his hand. "Sorry Filipe for the outburst. They have wasted no time in coming here. I think I know what he wants." Jacob clenched his teeth and became red-faced with rage.

"Obviously, I cannot say too much, as it is a meeting with a third party,"

Filipe said, noting Jacob's rage. "However, I thought I would mention it to you all this morning, to help me prepare for Thursday's meeting and from what you have shared with me, I understand what he may want to discuss with me."

Filipe went on to describe how Adrian Nicholls' company Anux, was aware of the preliminary work completed and published by Joeli and Mere. He stated it was the type of project his company would be interested in investing in, with it being of mutual benefit to Fiji and his company. As such, he wanted to discuss the commercialisation of products derived from the plant with the Government.

"I have said enough already, so recommend you get on with what you need to do with your studies. You may even like to work with this fellow and his company. I can refer him to you if you like," Filipe suggested, exploring the response he would get from Jacob. The expression on Jacob's face quickly confirmed his thoughts that this was unlikely.

"No way! I do not trust the ethics of Anux and how they are rolling out their new drug," Jacob's voice rose in pitch. "Any development of the Tagimoucia, needs to be handled ethically. We need to work with an organisation, that is prepared to work in line with the International Coalition of Medicines Regulatory Authorities and the World Health Organisation. I do not see Anux doing that. The way they operate, they are only interested in driving sales, to grow their profits and their share price."

"Good to meet you Jacob and I note your passion and I appreciate your insight," Filipe stood, bringing the meeting to an end. "Leave it with me . Keep me informed on your progress with the study, to see if we have something to commercialise, in an ethical manner," he added with a smile.

On their way to the car, Jacob was obviously irritated. "I hope Filipe does not entertain doing anything with Adrian Nicholls and his organisation. Especially after what I said about their *modus operandi*."

With some difficulty and minds clogged with news of the forthcoming meeting of Adrian Nicholls with Filipe Matai, they headed to the laboratory at the Fiji School of Medicine. Joeli and Mere wanted to give Jacob a tour and introduce him to the team, as well as discuss the second study.

"I have known Filipe for many years, and he is a good man. I am sure he will do the right thing for not only the people of Fiji but also the world," reassured Joeli. "The first objective is for us to get on with what we need to do, or there may not even be a medicine to develop."

As a first step Joeli conducted a review of the first study. "As practised by the villagers on Taveuni, we made a solution from the crushed flowers. The solution was fed to rats and their response to the gradual increasing temperature on a hot plate was measured. The rats were able to withstand a significant increase in temperature before starting to become uncomfortable and needing to exit from eating the food placed on the hot plate."

"A good result Joeli," congratulated Jacob. "Definitely vindicates pursuing the second study to verify the results in humans. What about the matter of the hallucinogenic effect as reported from use in the villagers on Taveuni Island?"

"It was not something we observed in the rats," replied Joeli. "There was no evidence of any abnormal behaviour after ingesting the solution."

"As Jacob said when we were coming back from Nadi, we need to be aware of this when we dose our volunteers," added Mere. "Maybe the response is unique to humans."

"I will speak to the people in the laboratory at Sydney University before they start their work on discovering the active ingredient. I will ask them to see if they can identify parts of the molecule that are responsible for pain relief and the unwanted side-effect," Jacob said, busily making notes on his laptop.

"It would be a great opportunity to collaborate with researchers at Sydney University," Mere earnestly replied. "Can we send plant material to Australia for the research?"

"Before coming to Fiji, I checked with Australian Quarantine requirements and we can complete the paperwork to get the necessary permits," replied Jacob. "I will contact Professor Baldwin and the team in Sydney to let them know they are on for the study and to get the paperwork for importation underway at their end."

"Tamana, I need to take Jacob downtown with me before the stores close. He needs to get some gear for our trip to Taveuni," Mere said, standing and picking up the car keys. "He needs a waterproof jacket and some suitable footwear, for trekking up to Lake Tagimoucia.".

"Sure, no problem," Joeli affirmed. "The weather forecast looks ok for the coming week, so I will get Lavenia in the office to make your reservations. I have you heading out Friday morning, with the return Monday morning. I can run you and Jacob out to the airport on Friday morning and also pick you up on Monday."

"Thanks, Dad, see you at home for dinner," Mere took Jacob by the arm.

"Oh, by the way, Mereoni called and was going to whip up something for us for dinner tonight. It will be ready in the fridge and we will just have to heat it up," Joeli said, looking up from the pile of paperwork.

*

"Thank goodness for Mereoni, otherwise we would be permanently on a takeaway diet. She has been amazing since Mum passed away," Mere escorted Jacob to the carpark.

"Who is Mereoni?" asked Jacob.

"Mereoni is what is known locally in Fiji as our house girl, even though she is in her 50's," Mere explained. "Typically, house girls are from rural areas and have limited education. She is really part of the family and been with us for over 20 years. We pay her a wage, look after her and her husband for any medical problems and Dad has paid for her son's education. Her son has done well and is now an ensign in the Fiji Navy. She is enormously proud of what her son has achieved. Mereoni's husband, Malakai, also helps out by keeping on top of the garden for us, as well as feeding the dogs."

After a dinner of his favourite fish, walu in lolo (coconut milk), Jacob was feeling very dozy. A combination of the rich meal and the unrelenting heat and humidity, had him begging for forgiveness at the need to get off to bed. He wanted to be well rested for the week ahead.

"Good night Mere, Joeli. See you in the morning," Jacob pushed back his chair from the dining room table and started to give a big yawn as he stood. He quickly placed his hand over his mouth, drawing smiles from Mere and Joeli.

Joeli smiled to himself as he noticed Mere's eyes look to Jacob's hand as he placed it on her shoulder. He had been around long enough to know things were appearing to develop between Jacob and Mere. "*They would make a very nice couple and it is about time Mere took an interest in someone and stopped making work her only interest in life.*" Joeli understood the drive in his daughter. Since the death of her Tinana, his much-loved wife, she was driven in her research. It had been to the exclusion of everything else. She was always scaring off any would-be suitors.

Joeli was brought back from his reflections by Mere. "Night Dad, I think I will head to bed as well."

"Good night Mere. Hopefully, there are no issues with this Adrian Nicholls fellow," reflected Joeli.

"All we can do is leave matters in the very capable hands of Filipe and expect him to do the right thing," Mere re-assured Joeli. "No use getting stressed about it. It is beyond our control and we have given Filipe plenty to think about in preparing to meet the manager from Anux."

"You are right Mere, we can only do what we can control," added Joeli sagely. "We can't be fixated on Adrian Nicholls. Onward to Taveuni and a very productive few days. I think a nightcap of that Chivas Regal before heading to bed."

"Oh Dad," Mere sighed, shaking her head as she smiled and headed to her bedroom.

CHAPTER 11

After completing arrival formalities, Adrian made his way to the adjacent domestic terminal for the flight to Suva. The domestic terminal was rather primitive, in comparison to the international terminal. It was not air-conditioned and the overhead fans, in the check-in area, did little to prevent the trickle of perspiration beginning to run down his back. "*I should have worn a short-sleeved shirt and certainly do not need my jacket.*"

He was travelling relatively lightly, having checked in his suit bag, carrying sufficient attire for four days on the road. With the flight called, he walked across the tarmac with his light brown leather computer satchel in hand, to board the ATR-42 turbojet flight. The aircraft interior was furnace like, while sitting there on the tarmac and as he took his seat, he immediately got the air blower going at full speed, but it made little impact on the blanket of oven-like heat engulfing the cabin. Relief came quickly soon after take-off, with the air-conditioning thankfully rapidly kicking-in.

The respite was short, as after the 45-minute flight to Suva's Nausori Airport, it was back out into the heat while waiting to collect his checked suit bag, followed by the taxi ride to the hotel. The taxi was not air-conditioned, so Adrian was not in a good mood, being very tired by the time he arrived at the Grand Pacific Hotel in Suva. He was hot and sticky, with the back of his damp shirt clinging to his back like a wet rag.

It certainly was a grand harbourside hotel, the regal Grand Pacific, looking out on to Suva Harbour. It was painted a majestic white, with huge archways and high ceilings capturing any hint of cooling breeze that may waft off the water. Recently renovated from its colonial past, the rooms were spacious and well appointed. There was a huge queen-sized bed, covered in a white doona and backed by a light grey headboard. A white wicker backed chair was positioned under a long, dark brown, timbered desk, which included tea and coffee facilities and a minibar. Adrian immediately fired up the air-conditioning to full speed and lay on his bed, soaking up the cool air. Next, he stripped down and was straight into the shower to remove the layers of dried perspiration. It was the longest shower he had ever taken.

Adrian enjoyed dinner in the cool of the evening, watching the sunset, in the hotel poolside restaurant. The pale-blue water of the huge pool was most inviting, *"I should have brought my swimming trunks."* Over the course of a light meal of grilled chicken and salad, Adrian checked with the concierge as to the location of the Ministry for Commerce's Office. It was located only a few hundred metres down Victoria Parade from the hotel in the Fiji Development Bank Building. Even so, he determined a taxi ride would be more preferable than a walk. It would no doubt not take long to work up a sweat and he wanted to be well-presented in such an important meeting with the Minister for Commerce.

With the air-conditioner continuing to go full blast all night, a travel weary Adrian slept very soundly. He showered again and headed down to the restaurant for a light breakfast of black coffee with tropical fruits and toast. There was no thought of a run or a workout with the heat and humidity. *"It would take a long time to cool down if I were to go for a run around the park over the road from the hotel. I do not want to be red-faced and looking dishevelled for the meeting with the Minister."*

Heading down the stairs from the hotel lobby, he waved to the driver of the first cab in the taxi line-up. Entering the taxi, he gave his destination, "Fiji Development Bank Building, thanks."

"Boss, that is just up the road a few hundred metres and I have been in the line-up for over one hour waiting for a fare. I will then be at the back of the queue. Sure, you don't want to walk it?" The driver pled with Adrian, as he was becoming ensconced in the back seat and looking for the non-existent seatbelt.

"How is twenty bucks for your trouble driver?" Adrian enticed, retrieving his wallet from his hip-pocket.

"Certainly, sir. Would you like me to wait for you until you finish your meeting?" enthusiasm oozed from the driver.

"What is your name driver?"

"Uday Lal boss. Where you from? Why you here?"

"Lots of questions Uday Lal," Adrian said, dismissing Uday's local directness. "Give me your number and I will call you if I have the need to go anywhere else while here in Suva."

Thirty seconds later, Uday leapt out of the driver's seat and came around to the passenger side to open the rear door for Adrian. "Straight in there, boss." A happy Uday directed Adrian towards the entrance.

Adrian entered the building and identified from the wall directory that Minister Matai's office was on the top floor. The elevator was packed with office workers arriving to start their day, which meant a stop on each level on the way to the top 8th floor. The rattling, small overhead fan in the elevator was fighting a losing battle against the heat, so it was a relief to enter the Minister's air-conditioned office.

"Good Morning, I am Adrian Nicholls, President of Anux Pharmaceuticals for Asia Pacific," a confident Adrian announced to the Minister's Personal Assistant. "I have an appointment with the Minister of Commerce, Mr Matai this morning."

"Ah yes, Mr Nicholls. I will let the Minister know you have arrived. Would you like tea or coffee?"

"Tea will be fine, thanks. White no sugar," Adrian took a seat in the reception area, where he picked up a copy of the Fiji Times. He took the opportunity to cool down despite the short journey from the Grand Pacific Hotel to the Minister's office. He sipped his tea and flicked through the newspaper, waiting expectantly for his appointment, confident of doing a deal with the Fiji Government.

Seeing he was getting ink on his fingers from the newspaper, he wiped his hands on his handkerchief and gently replaced the pages on the table next to his hard, wooden seat. He reflected on his arrival in tropical Fiji for the first time. It had proven to be a never-ending cycle of heat, humidity, and perspiration, from the moment the aircraft door opened at the Nadi International Terminal.

As Adrian was escorted into the Minister's office, the Minister stood up from behind his desk, directing him towards the same sofa recently occupied by Jacob.

"Good to meet you in person. Please take a seat," invited Filipe.

"Thank you Minister and likewise good to meet you in person."

Filipe reached to a business cardholder on the coffee table and presented Adrian with his card, Mr F S Matai, Minister for Commerce. Adrian reciprocated with his business card. Filipe was straight onto business and asked Adrian to provide him with some background on Anux Pharmaceuticals. In particular Filipe wanted Adrian to outline in more detail, as to why such a large international pharmaceutical company as Anux, had interest in Fiji's national flower, the Tagimoucia.

"Thanks for the opportunity to meet with you Filipe," Adrian began, settling into his discourse on Anux. It was something he knew by heart. A story he had delivered, many times during the launch of AnuxuDine throughout Europe. "Anux is listed on the NASDAQ, with a market capitalisation currently in excess of Twenty Billion US Dollars. The value of the company is likely to increase substantially, given the immediate success of the company's new blockbuster medicine since its launch in Europe. There is more good news on the horizon, with the forthcoming launch of the product in Australia, only a few days away."

"Given my extensive involvement with the launch in Europe, I was promoted to the position of President of the company's business in Asia Pacific, where I will be personally responsible for the launch in Australia. This will be followed by the rollout into the major Asian markets over the next few years. There will be no stopping Anux, with the planned rapid global expansion for what will become our number one product globally, in the next few years, " Adrian confidently sat back on the sofa and spread out his arms like an eagle, on the back of the sofa.

"That is all well and good Adrian, but how can a small country like Fiji and it's national flower be of interest to such a large and important multi-national organisation like Anux?"

"In our telephone call last week, I mentioned the recent article published in an international scientific journal by the Fijian Doctors, Joeli and Mere Koroi." Adrian paused for effect, before continuing, "Anux sees the potential to develop an anti-pain medication from the Tagimoucia, which would enable the company to maintain leadership in the global analgesic market."

"I do foresee some difficulties, which I will explain later, but please continue," Filipe interrupted briefly.

Adrian reverted into a salesman like mode, "For the rights to be granted to Anux, to commercialise anything developed from the Tagimoucia, Anux would certainly be prepared to pay substantial upfront fees. Most likely in the order of millions of US dollars. There would also be the potential of ongoing royalties to the Government of Fiji on the commercialisation of any plant derivatives. In return, Anux would want exclusivity on commercial development of the plant and complete control over all aspects of the project. We would want no interference or input from any third parties, including the Government. It would be our substantial investment dollars on the line!"

"Given the success of AnuxuDine, it could also mean you had the potential to bury a possible major competitor. The Government would be left with a few million dollars upfront, but see nothing of any royalties," noted a business-like Filipe. "The world could also miss out on an effective new product, should no further testing take place."

"A very astute observation Filipe." Adrian was quick to realise that he had under-estimated Filipe. "I can assure you; we would be working in the best interests of all concerned."

"Adrian, I have limited knowledge of the use of pharmaceuticals; however, I have read about the potential for addiction with opioid pain killers like your product. How does Anux see your current product fitting in with the responsible use of analgesics?"

"Not a problem at all," Adrian attempted to reassure Filipe, but was looking somewhat awkwardly towards the floor. Again, he saw the Minister appearing to be better informed than he expected. "We had no cases of addiction reported to date and the company is providing pain relief to many patients in Europe," conveniently forgetting the feedback from southern Africa provided by Newton Sinclair.

"As intimated earlier, I see there are a number of likely difficulties to overcome," Filipe announced, taking command of the conversation. "I see a problem in attempting to use the national floral emblem of Fiji for commercial gain, albeit for potentially life-saving purposes. Then there is the impact on the island of Taveuni and the villagers on the island. There is likely to be disruption, with the development of infra-structure and associated environmental issues in accessing the plant's habitat."

"It could also see potential employment opportunities in cultivation of the plant," Adrian countered, looking for a positive.

Filipe ignored the interjection and continued. "We are likely to need an Environmental Impact Statement given the fragile and limited habitat of the plant. There will be a requirement for a full feasibility study to be presented to the Fiji Government's Cabinet. It is not only about the money."

"It would appear to be a very lengthy process," Adrian was swallowing hard and looking dismayed, with sweat starting to form on the palms of his hands.

"Adrian, this list is not definitive, and I would believe, once people put their minds to the situation, there will be a lot more questions raised by a lot of vested interests," Filipe at his authoritative best. "It will mean many boxes will need to be ticked. As part of the process, I would suggest you put together a comprehensive proposal. You will need to highlight what is in it for the Fijian people and what Anux requires from the Government in developing such a project."

There was much discussion backwards and forwards in regard to the process and what could be done to speed up the process. None of what was discussed could be seen to rapidly put Anux in a position to control the project and the future commercialisation of anything that may come from the Tagimoucia.

"I understand that the Doctors Koroi, have enlisted the help of an Australian scientist to help with further studies," Filipe said, adding to Adrian's frustration.

Adrian's brain was clicking into gear, "*any positive results from such research being published, before Anux had a commercial contract in place with the Government of Fiji, could potentially have a massive negative impact on Anux, I need to nip this in the bud now.*"

CHAPTER 12

"*It is time for Plan B, I fear.*" Adrian leant forward in his seat towards Filipe. He spoke in almost a whisper, "From our conversation, I can tell you are an astute operator. As the Minister for Commerce, I am sure you understand commercial realities. If the results of a successful human trial were to be published before Anux had a deal in place with the Fiji Government, the ramifications on the company's share price could be significant."

Filipe followed his arms and placed his left hand under his chin. "Please continue Adrian."

"Hypothetically, while we continued to negotiate a deal, what if the availability of the Tagimoucia just disappeared for a little while and the scientists had nothing to work with, say for a year or two?" Adrian posed. "That would give Anux plenty of time to get AnuxuDine well-established in the global market before any development of the Tagimoucia could occur. Work could start in a couple of years' time when the plant became available again. It would not be a permanent situation."

"With what you are suggesting I should have you kicked out of my office! However, I am intrigued to know what you have in mind." Curious, Filipe invited Adrian to continue.

"Filipe, the company would be incredibly grateful for your assistance and no doubt provide a substantial donation to your re-election fund. I understand you have an election coming up early next year, so the timing would be perfect. To keep things tight and only between us, I propose that I personally would fly to the island of Taveuni. There I would attend to matters and not involve any third parties. It would only involve us." Adrian starting to relax.

"Go on, please," Filipe said, appearing eager to learn more.

"What if there was an unfortunate accident and most of the plants on the island were inadvertently sprayed with herbicide. A few plants could survive and ultimately there would be a total recovery, but not for a couple years," Adrian said, waiting expectantly for Filipe's reply.

"Mm, the Doctors Koroi and their fellow scientist from Australia would have nothing to work on. It would preclude them from working on the remaining plants, so not as to endanger those plants which survived a mysterious disease," Filipe sat there nodding with a smile on his face. "It could work, despite being somewhat risky, I like it. Sounds like a win-win," Filipe rubbed his hands together.

"We would continue to work on a commercial proposal over time, giving the plant time to recover, which would allow further testing to eventually be completed. However, it would not impact the rollout of our major new product around the world in the medium term," noted Adrian.

"Make an appointment for tomorrow morning with my PA on the way out. That will give me time to give the matter some more thought and work out the logistics for you," Filipe's mind appeared to churn into gear. "I would also suggest you book to fly up to Taveuni on Saturday morning. You will also need to make provision to transport some equipment to the airport. In addition, I will arrange some support for you. You should not under-estimate the physical demands of undertaking the trek up to the lake in the tropical environment, especially with the need to be carrying equipment with you. At your service in Taveuni, will be one of my most trusted senior officials, Isikeli Cava. He is totally trustworthy and given the demands of the trek, combined with his local knowledge, you will find he will prove to be an asset."

"Filipe, thank you so much for your co-operation. Especially with arranging for Isikeli to accompany me. It has been a pleasure doing business with you. Now what about that donation? As a start, what do you say to two-hundred and fifty thousand US Dollars being transferred into your nominated account overnight?"

With a thumbs up and a big smile, Filipe returned to his desk, indicating he was getting the bank account details. With the details in hand, he retrieved his business card from Adrian and proceeded to write bank account details on the back of the card. Adrian noted the account name as FSM, corresponding with the initials of Filipe's name, Filipe Sitiveni Matai. "I will make a call to the Chief Financial Officer in Sydney as soon as I get back to the hotel. He will ensure the donation is transferred overnight into your nominated account and I will meet you tomorrow morning, to confirm the arrangements."

"I have also written my mobile number on to the back of the card in case you need to get hold of me," added Filipe.

"A pleasure meeting with you Minister and I look forward to progressing our discussions. I will see you in the morning," Adrian stood and extended his right hand towards Filipe. "*I was getting worried there for a while. I can hardly wait to call Newton with the good news.*"

*

Adrian returned to his hotel and immediately called his PA in Sydney. He asked her to re-arrange his itinerary for the flight to Taveuni on the Saturday morning, along with accommodation at the Taveuni Beach Hotel, as recommended by Filipe. In addition, it was arranged for a return flight direct from Taveuni to Nadi on the Monday morning, to connect with the afternoon flight back to Sydney. That would give him Sunday to get the job done. He then spoke to Grant Davis, to arrange for the transfer of the funds to Filipe's nominated account, FSM in Fiji. Grant was asked to transfer the funds from the Charitable Donations Account and to complete the transaction by first thing in the morning . Adrian wanted the funds to be available in the nominated account, in preparation for his follow up meeting with Filipe.

With business out of the way in Suva for the day, it was time to update Newton Sinclair in New York. If he called now, he should get Newton before he left the office for the day. A very smug Adrian placed the call to Newton's mobile.

"Newton Sinclair speaking," Newton answered, noting it was Adrian's number on his screen.

Newton reached into his drawer and put his mobile phone onto speaker mode, while hitting record on his recorder. "Go ahead Adrian, I have been looking forward to the update."

"Hi Newton," Adrian began. "I can report a very successful day in Fiji."

After the polite preamble and a description of the oppressive tropical heat and humidity, Adrian launched into a diatribe of how he twiddled the Fijian Minister for Commerce around his little finger. He then went on to describe how he would take personal responsibility for ensuring any research on the Tagimoucia plant would not be possible for the next couple of years, courtesy of a good dose of herbicide.

"With the Tagimoucia out of the way, at least in the short term, AnuxuDine will be well and truly established globally as a blockbuster product before any research could be undertaken," Adrian sounded incredibly pleased with himself. "With the rapport I have built up with Minister Matai, we will also be in a strong position to secure any future commercial rights as well. All it took was a sizeable donation to the Minister's re-election campaign account," gloated Adrian.

Newton hit the pause button as he began to speak, "Great work Adrian. Keep me posted of how things work out. I am off home now, speak soon."

After disconnecting the call with Adrian, Newton was busy with the record button again. He wanted to ensure that his insurance policy was in place, should things not work out with Adrian in Fiji. "*Adrian as previously directed, you know that I and the Anux organisation cannot condone any inappropriate activity. It goes against everything the Anux organisation stands for. I suggest you arrange to immediately return to Australia and start work on preparing a proposal to secure the commercial rights for the Tagimoucia and stop the processing of any payment to Fiji.*"

The recorder was turned off and safely returned to Newton's top drawer, which was duly locked. "*Adrian's strategy will either work out, or alternatively I have the potential of getting rid of him permanently. At the same time my backside is protected if anything should go wrong.*"

CHAPTER 13

For the rest of the week, Mere, Joeli and Jacob were entrenched in the laboratory preparing for the second study, with the flower samples they would harvest in Taveuni. They were long, busy days in the laboratory and the team was confident the results of the animal study would be re-produced in human volunteers. There was, however, still the uncertainty around the reported hallucinations and they would need to monitor for this potential unwanted side-effect.

From Jacob's international network, they were also building a list of senior executives within potential partner pharmaceutical companies. These were the people and companies Jacob felt comfortable in recommending, in regard to any future commercial and product development discussions. The paperwork was also being put together for Australian quarantine clearance, to forward the bio-samples to the Sydney University laboratories.

Jacob enjoyed getting back home to the Koroi's residence each evening. In particular, he enjoyed relaxing on the veranda with Mere and a cold stubby of Fiji Bitter, after one of Mereoni's substantial meals. "That Mereoni can sure cook," Jacob patted his stomach, which was starting to put pressure on the waistline of his pants. "I look forward to the trek to hopefully get some weight down."

"I am sure that Fiji Bitter has nothing to do with it," Mere teased.

"Yes, Mum," Jacob mocked Mere, resulting in a punch in the arm.

Joeli seemed to be happy to head off to his bedroom after a night cap of his Chivas Regal, leaving Mere and Jacob to talk amongst themselves on the veranda. They would chat away into the evening, seeming extremely comfortable in each other's company and neither of them seeming to want to call it a night.

"Tell me what you have in store for me in Taveuni, Mere."

"How is this for a plan? Mere's eyes were alight with mischief. "After we check in at the hotel tomorrow, I suggest as a first stop, a visit to Waiyevo village. It is where the 180th meridian of longitude passes through the island. Today and yesterday in the same place."

"Any chance for a surf?" Jacob asked, almost pleading.

"Not that I know of. However, we can get a packed lunch from the hotel and head off to Prince Charles Beach," Mere said, hoping the name of the beach would be enough of a drawcard. "The beach was made famous by a visit from Prince Charles, of course. It has beautiful trees that hang over the beach and act as natural beach umbrellas. We should be able to hire some goggles and flippers at the hotel for a bit of snorkelling on the reef."

"Not as good as a surf, but it will be good to hit the beach," agreed Jacob.

"On Saturday I reckon we need to keep moving, to prepare for Sunday's trek, so I recommend we hire a kayak for a bit of fun exploring along the coast," Mere looked as though she was reminiscing on days past. " There is also an amazing natural waterslide, where you can slide down on the smooth stones in your bathers. The kids from the village can show you how to do it."

"Wow should be a fantastic few days," Jacob enthused, looking into Mere's eyes. "That is, apart from the trek up to the lake. I look forward to seeing the plant growing in its natural habitat and collecting those samples, but *ughhh* that trek in all that heat and humidity."

"With the busy days ahead and an early start for the airport in the morning, I suggest we get off to bed," Mere bent over to extinguish the smouldering mosquito coil, protecting Jacob's ankles.

There still seemed to be a reluctance by Jacob to head off to bed, but finally he rose from his chair and stretched his hand to assist Mere rise from her chair. He pulled her towards him and wrapped his arms around her. Looking into her eyes he whispered, "Mere Koroi, you are one special lady." With that their lips met, and Jacob could feel the ache in his loins. He quickly pulled himself away still holding Mere's hands with arms outstretched.

"We had better get to bed," Jacob said, looking over his shoulder as he headed towards the rear steps leading to the back cottage, "I am really looking forward to Taveuni."

Mere moved her hand to her lips, unable to move. She seemed fixed to the spot as she watched Jacob disappear down the path to the cottage. *"What am I to do, Tinana? I am starting to find myself attracted to Jacob Bryant. I am starting to think I cannot live without that person. I am becoming so confused about what to do."*

*

Joeli was up early getting everyone moving. He knocked on Jacob's door, "This is your early morning wake-up call. Breakfast is on the table."

"Go away," Jacob responded good naturedly. " I am up and showered, see you shortly."

Mere was next. "Come on Mere, get moving." The silence was deafening. It took a bit of shake and a lot of coercing by Joeli to finally get her moving.

After coffee and toast, they were on the road just after 5am, to head out to Nausori Airport for the 7am flight to Taveuni on Fiji Link. Jacob chatted away to Joeli about the rugby, while Mere dozed in the back seat. They were travelling fairly lightly, with a small bag each and a carton with plastic bags and garden shears for collecting the study samples. After check-in, they all relaxed in the coffee shop before the flight was called.

All was going well until Jacob saw the plane. His jaw dropped and he stared at the aircraft sitting at the departure gate." Are we going up in that?" Butterflies began to flutter in his stomach. "Good heavens, the rear door forms the steps up into the plane. Is it safe?"

"The Twin Otter is perfectly safe," reassured Joeli. "It is a very reliable member of the airline's fleet."

"It is the smallest plane I have ever flown in," the realisation was dawning on Jacob.

"You will be fine, "reassured Joeli, noting the look of dread on Jacob's face. "They need this type of aircraft for the short runways used on the smaller islands."

"Tamana you are not helping," volunteered Mere.

Joeli shook Jacob's hand and wished him a safe flight before pulling Mere towards him in a big bear hug. He whispered into her ear, "Enjoy yourself with Dr Bryant, you will have him all to yourself."

"Oh Tamana," was followed by a slap on her Tamana's arm, delivered with a big smile.

They turned as they crossed the tarmac and gave Joeli a farewell wave, both yelling out "See you Monday."

Jacob's fears in the boarding process were exacerbated after the unsteady scramble up those rear stairs. Despite stooping over to make his way crab-like down the narrow aisle, he immediately bumped his head on the low ceiling and impaled his left thigh on one of the armrests. " How does your Tamana fit into one of these seats?" Jacob asked, simultaneously rubbing his head and thigh.

With their seatbelts fastened and the safety briefing delivered by the co-pilot, stepping out from the cockpit, the plane's engines spluttered into life. They were soon taxiing to the end of the runway, with the pilot and co-pilot completing the various pre-take off checks. Mere watched Jacob's face with amusement as the co-pilot placed his hand on top of the pilot's hand as they engaged the throttle and with a push the revs of the engine increased, the brakes were released, and they were hurtling down the runway. Instinctively, Jacob reached for and tightly grasped Mere's hand. In response she squeezed his arm and leant into his body. They seemed to take-off within a few metres, the plane rising steeply into the sky.

" We won't get much above seven or eight thousand feet, so you will get a good view of some of the islands in the Koro Sea enroute to Taveuni." Mere retrieved a map from her bag and unfolded it to show Jacob the flight path.

"Sorry couldn't hear you above the engine noise," Jacob smiled as he put his arm around Mere and leaned towards her to speak into her ear.

Mere similarly enjoyed the opportunity to get up close to Jacob, leaning across him to point out the various landmarks on her map. "We will fly over the islands of Ovalau, home of the old capital of Fiji, Levuka. Then over Makogai where there once was a leper colony and finally Koro Island, before heading into Taveuni's Matei Airport."

Jacob was enthralled at what he could see out of his window and was eagerly pointing out highlights to Mere. Coral atolls surrounding the islands. Waves crashing on a reef. Villagers in boats out fishing on the magnificent deep, dark blue sea. He was now oblivious to the intense buzz of the plane's engines, taking in all the scenery below and enjoying Mere's proximity.

Jacob was certainly not objecting being so close to Mere. It was a pleasure being close to her and taking in the energy radiating from her body, with that subtle, tell-tale, frangipani aroma. He was growing very fond of her and was looking forward to his time on Taveuni one on one with Dr Mere Koroi. "*I have never felt this way about any other woman I have met. I hope she is starting to feel the same way about me.*"

CHAPTER 14

"Will we be able to see the lake as we come into land? Jacob asked, breaking the trance like moment.

"Matei Airport is on the north-east corner of Taveuni and we will approach from the south," informed Mere. "On the landing approach we are likely to see beautiful waterfalls cascading into the ocean from the steep cliffs protruding from the highlands. However, it is usually cloudy on top of the island's central highlands, so we may not get to see Lake Tagimoucia. Look there is the island," Mere pointed out the window. "See the cliffs with the waterfalls emptying straight into the sea, like water pouring from a kettle."

"Magnificent," Jacob stared open-mouthed through the window, taking in the scenery.

"Unfortunately, as expected the top of the island is covered in cloud, so we will not get a glimpse of the lake," Mere said, expressing her disappointment.

The pilot came onto the intercom asking the passengers to prepare for landing. Jacob and Mere checked their seatbelts and then Jacob tightly clutched Mere's hand. Mere looked down and smiled, enjoying the feel of the strength in Jacob's grip. They watched out the window as the plane turned, beginning the descent over the sea towards the landing strip.

" You know the landing strip is only 910m long," Mere taunted cheekily, knowing the discomfort it would cause Jacob.

Jacob started to wriggle in his seat as the plane banked, revealing the short landing strip, shrouded by a ring of coconut trees. Mere gave his hand a firm squeeze as they settled in for the landing with those butterflies fluttering overtime as the plane made its final approach.

The wheels hit the ground and the Twin Otter rushed towards the oncoming coconut trees. Jacob's heart raced as the intensity of his grip on Mere's hand increased. The pilot pulled the plane up well short of the trees and Jacob breathed a sigh of relief. "*Made it.*" He was very relieved when the engines were turned off and he was climbing down those rear stairs, already not looking forward to Monday's return flight to Suva.

After collecting their luggage, they were met by a driver from the Taveuni Beach Hotel and were soon underway to check-in. The hotel was located next to Waiyevo village, a 20-minute drive from the airport. It was accessed straight off the main road, via a wide pot-holed concrete driveway which had seen better days. Muddy water still sat in the potholes from the last evening's rain. The hotel was constructed out of massive granite blocks, covered with a vast silver corrugated iron roof.

The car splashed its way through the potholes on the driveway, arriving at the reception area. To the left of the reception was the double storey, accommodation wing, with around 20 rooms on each level. In the centre of the accommodation wing was a staircase leading from the top floor down to the visitor's carpark. Individual car spaces were marked by coconut tree logs sunk into the ground and covered in white, long faded paint.

The driver pulled up under the massive awning covering the wide, breezy, open entrance to the foyer. They collected their luggage from the rear of the station wagon and strode towards the reception desk with overhead fans whirring away, valiantly trying to further help cool the guests.

Despite it being mid-morning and an advertised check-in time of 2pm, they were able to check straight into their rooms. The hotel was much quieter over the summer period. They had adjoining rooms on the upper floor with an interconnecting door. The rooms were located adjacent to the stairwell, leading down to the carpark.

Mere arranged with reception for the hotel driver to take them around the popular spots on Taveuni, starting with a visit to the 180-degree meridian.

The driver waited while they quickly dropped their bags in their rooms, and they were off. The driver obliged by taking photos of them standing astride the marker. One part of them in today and the other part in yesterday.

"A good one to post on Instagram and Facebook, Mere," Jacob said, looking impishly at Mere.

"Don't you dare," scolded Mere. "No social media for me without notice."

They headed back to the hotel, collected their bathers, along with a picnic hamper for the afternoon of swimming and relaxation at Prince Charles Beach. The driver was asked to come back at 4pm to return them to the hotel.

Hand in hand they stepped from the taxi onto the warm golden sands. Mere pointed to a shady tree close to the water's edge. "See a natural beach umbrella, as promised."

"Very beautiful and so quiet. No one else around," Jacob was amazed at the solitude.

They placed their towels on the beach and it had been a long time since their early breakfast, so they started to open their picnic hamper. There were beef and mango chutney sandwiches on white bread, along with some cut-up watermelon and pineapple. Bottles of chilled water were provided in a polystyrene cooler, complete with frozen ice bricks.

As they munched on their sandwiches, they gazed out at the crystal-clear ocean water. The water gradually turned deeper shades of blue, as the depth increased out towards the reef break, several hundred metres from the shoreline. With the waves crashing onto the reef in the distance, Jacob looked up and down the beach, "Do you realise we are the only ones on this beach. A long way from the crowds at a beach back home in Sydney," reflected Jacob.

After allowing his lunch to settle, Jacob asked Mere, "coming for a snorkel?"

"Not for me, you go for it," Mere declined, laying back on her towel, not tired of admiring Jacob as he prepared to go snorkelling.

Jacob was keen to get into the water, so quickly put on the flippers and goggles and plunged in. He was amazed by the warmth of the tropical water, normally he would brace, expecting a tinge of chilliness on entering the water.

"*No need for a wetsuit here.*" His eyes raced taking in the busy marine life, hugging close to the coral outcrops. A huge blue starfish, clams, a few pesky crown of thorns and a myriad a colourful tropical fish darting in and out of the multi-coloured coral. "*I would love to have an aquarium here. You would not need to heat the water.*"

Mere was asleep as Jacob removed his flippers and goggles, heading back to the towels. Mischievously, he shook water onto Mere who woke with a start, "I'll fix you Jacob Bryant."

A honk from the hotel car brought them back to reality. They gathered everything together and headed back to the hotel.

"It's 4.30 now," Jacob noted, stepping from the car. "I wouldn't mind a quick snooze, after this morning's early start. How about I tap on your door at say 6.30 and we head down to the hotel restaurant for a drink and then some dinner?"

"That should give me time for a relaxing bath and to get beautiful."

"You don't need time to get beautiful. You already are."

"Flattery will get you everywhere, Mr Bryant."

"I hope so."

With a gentle punch to Jacob's arm, Mere opened the door to her room and turned towards Jacob with a big smile, "see you soon!" She could feel her pulse was racing and was thinking, "*what is happening to me? Sorry Mum, I will get myself together.*"

Promptly at 6.30 came the tap on the door, which got Mere's heart pounding. Hand in hand they set off for the restaurant, located adjacent to the reception area. It was quiet, apart from a couple snuggling in the booth at the far end. The waitress informed them that they were some honeymooners from Auckland. From the restaurant reception desk, tables of two and four settings of varnished cane furniture aligned a central aisle, leading to the honeymooner's booth. They were seated well away from the honeymooners, on a table dimly lit by a solitary candle, plugged into an old Mateus Rose bottle. The residue of multiple candles slid down the side of the bottle, like a glacier.

They perused the menus which were in place at the table. They were hungry after the day's activities, so Jacob quickly called over the waitress.

"I love the local curries but if I have a curry, we both better have the prawn curry special."

"Why would that be Dr Bryant?"

"You never know, I might like to kiss you good night," Mere laughed and slapped Jacob's hand playfully.

The prawn curry was agreed upon and while waiting for their meals they sipped on their Kiwi Pinot Grigio. They used their index fingers to wipe the beads of condensation forming on the outside of their wine glasses, the moisture trickling down onto the Fijian patterned tablecloth. Chatter turned to the plans for Saturday and ultimately the trek up to the lake on Sunday. For Saturday it was agreed they would take Mere's suggestion of hiring a kayak and exploring along the coastline. They could take a picnic lunch and enjoy some of the remote waterfalls.

They looked up as they heard the sizzle of the prawns on the plates being brought out from the kitchen. Placed in front of them, their nostrils took in the smell of fresh lime and coconut. Their taste buds were anticipating the burst of heat from the red chillies they could see housed in the rich creamy coconut-based sauce.

Jacob dug his fork into his bowl and raised the food up to his nose. With a sniff and a cooling blow, he took his first tentative taste. "Magnificent, a great choice, I think. I love the bite of the chilli and those prawns, how good are they? Beautifully succulent and sweet." They were both fully satisfied after the main and decided not to go for dessert.

Arm in arm they strolled back to Jacob's room. Holding her hand, he reached to unlock the door to his room. As he unlocked the door, he could feel the tension rising in Mere and she suddenly pulled away. *Are those tears on Mere's cheeks?*

"Better get off to bed Jacob," Mere mumbled as she fumbled with her room key, trying to get it into the lock. "We have a busy day tomorrow on the kayaks."

Jacob was confused. He didn't know what had just happened. He sat on his bed in the dimly lit room, trying to understand what had just occurred with

Mere. There was not much sleep that night as he tossed and turned. *"I can't rush her. All in good time. I don't want to do anything to upset her."*

*

Jacob knocked on Mere's door, "Are you coming down for breakfast?"

"Oh, no thanks. I'll see you at reception at 10am to go kayaking," Mere sounded hesitant as she spoke through the door.

No one mentioned the previous night and it was all smiles as they headed off in the hotel transport to hire their kayaks. They hired two single kayaks into which they packed their sandwiches and bottles of water.

They set-off with their guide Pita in the lead kayak and followed along the coastline, protected from the ocean by the reef. They were not in a hurry and gently paddled along, taking in the golden beaches and crystal-clear water. Jacob was shaken from his solitude as a flying fish pounded into the side of his kayak, raising laughter from everyone. The fish wriggled briefly on the deck, before slipping safely back into the water and continue its journey.

On reaching a remote waterfall they pulled their kayaks ashore and called for a lunch break. They relaxed on the beach, enjoying the sound of the cascading water from the waterfall, before reluctantly making the return trip to the hotel.

"Are we on for dinner tonight?" Mere broke the ice, as they waited for their room keys at reception.

"For sure," smiled Jacob, " I will tap on your door at 6.30. Maybe that prawn curry again? It was so good."

CHAPTER 15

Adrian was up early to give himself time for a solid workout in the hotel gym and to provide a lengthy cool down period before his follow up meeting with Filipe. After a light breakfast of tropical fruits and coffee, Adrian slowly made his way from the hotel, down the road to Minister Matai's office. He certainly did not want to get sweaty again before the meeting. Confidently he strode up to Filipe's PA's desk after exiting the elevator on the top floor.

"Good morning Mr Nicholls, the Minister is expecting you. Water, tea?" she offered as she ushered him into the office.

"Water is fine, thanks."

"Ah, Adrian take a seat." Filipe directed Adrian to the sofa opposite the coffee table, where his glass of water was being efficiently placed.

After the PA left the room and closed the door, Adrian could not contain himself, "Have the funds been received into your account?"

"Anux is a very efficient organisation. Thank you very much, I was able to get it confirmed that the donation has been received overnight, which is much appreciated. It will be put to good use," Filipe smiled.

"Can you fill me in on what you have put in place for me," Adrian was business like and obviously keen to get on with matters, his pen paused over his notepad.

Filipe took a deep breath, then launched into the arrangements he had planned. "Your first stop on the way to the airport tomorrow morning, will be to call in at the Suva Hardware and Garden Supplies depot, in Walu Bay. You are to ask for Alipate, the manager. He will have everything boxed and ready for collection. In the carton will be two four litre containers of concentrated herbicide, along with some protective gear. Goggles, facemask, gloves and two backpack hand-sprayer units, for spraying the herbicide. With dilution with water from the lake, there would be more than enough herbicide to do the job, given the plant does not grow too far away from the lakeside."

"Got it," Adrian busily scribing away. "Will they take a credit card for payment?"

"All fixed, you just have to pick it up. While I think of it, I also need your guarantee to spare some plants, to ensure there will be a re-generation of the plant over time," re-iterated Filipe.

"Understood. I will leave enough plants for regrowth. While the plants re-generate, Anux will commence negotiations with you to secure the ongoing commercial rights for the medical use of the plant," confirmed Adrian. "However, we need to ensure, there will be insufficient plant life for the Doctors Koroi and Jacob Bryant, to be able to take any quantities for research in the short term."

"I can also confirm my trusted, senior colleague, Mr Isikeli Cava, will meet you off your flight at Taveuni airport," Filipe continued with the arrangements. "He will store the equipment overnight and then help you on Sunday morning with the climb up to the lake. He will act as your guide with his local knowledge and will help you with carrying the equipment. It will be onerous, given the heat and the demanding four-hour trek up to the lake."

"I must admit I am a little apprehensive about spraying the national floral emblem of Fiji with herbicide in front of a Fiji citizen," Adrian confessed, shifting nervously in his seat.

"Isikeli understands that what is being done is being performed under my instructions and is in the national interest," reassured Filipe. "Isikeli will do as instructed without question. He was formerly with the Fiji Military Forces and understands how to take orders."

"Filipe, thanks for all your help, you have been fantastic. I am sure I can speak on behalf of myself and Anux when saying it has been a pleasure working with you. Anux can no doubt be even more generous in the future." Adrian stood, keen to get on with finalising his arrangements.

As a first step, he would need to pick up a few supplies, given what he understood to be the demands of the trek to the lake in Taveuni. There was going to be a definite need for suitable footwear, sunscreen, insect repellent and definitely a hat. He was going to call Uday the taxi driver and arrange for him to take him around the place, to pick everything up on his check list.

Uday quickly responded to Adrian's call and soon had Adrian stocked with what he needed, at special prices. "*No doubt from stores owned by various relatives*," he chuckled to himself.

Adrian was delivered back to the hotel with his purchases. Uday was confirmed for the pickup from the hotel in the morning, for the airport run, via the hardware store. Uday had a station wagon, so there would not be a problem in loading the cargo for the airport.

Adrian was in a good mood after the meeting with Filipe and having everything in place for the expedition to Taveuni. He celebrated with a spicy beef curry, washed down with a nice bottle of New Zealand Sauvignon Blanc, then it was off to bed for a very contented Adrian Nicholls. He slept soundly, confident all would be well, especially with Isikeli available to assist.

*

Uday was waiting for Adrian in front of the hotel, with his tailgate down, ready for him to complete the hotel checkout and load his now heavier suit-bag into the rear of the station wagon. It was then off to collect the carton of equipment from Alipate at the hardware store. It was rather bulky and weighed around 15kg, given it contained two sprayers, as well as the two containers of herbicide. The consignment was definitely too bulky to manage for one person. "*Thank goodness Isikeli Cava will be waiting for me off the flight and help me to make the climb up to the lake.*"

"Boss, what are you going to be doing in Taveuni with all this?" queried a curious Uday.

"Oh, just helping out a friend," came a curt reply from Adrian. The rest of the drive was in silence as Adrian busily occupied himself on his mobile, working through his accumulated corporate emails.

Pulling up at the Nausori Airport terminal, Uday was quick to assist by getting a baggage trolley. In no time Uday had unloaded for Adrian and wheeled the load up to the check-in counter at Fiji Link. Adrian rewarded Uday with a nice tip, bringing a big smile to his face.

"Boss, any time you are in Suva, you have my number. I will be very happy to be at your service. Next time I will take you home for a curry with the family." A happy Uday saluted Adrian and headed out to his taxi.

Like Jacob, Adrian was not over-joyed to find out that the flight to Taveuni was on a small propeller-driven aircraft. His nervousness was not helped by the entry to his seat, via the fold out rear stairs. With the take-off, his hands gripped the seat arms vice-like, as the plane roared and rattled its way down the runway. There was relief as the plane quickly lifted off the runway. "*The things one does for the company*," he reflected. "*It better be worth it. A big bonus and some company stock options would be a genuinely nice reward.*"

Just as he started to relax, while taking in the scenery out the window, the captain announced for the passengers to get ready for the landing. Looking out the window he could see what he presumed to be the runaway. It was not long and surrounded by coconut trees. "*Surely this could not be it*," he thought as his heart began to pound.

A most relieved Adrian descended the rear steps of the plane and headed towards the baggage collection area. A tall, strongly built Fijian man, mid-thirties, walked towards Adrian with his right hand out-stretched. He was wearing a local bula shirt, patterned with palm trees, jeans, and sturdy workman's steel capped boots "Mr Nicholls?"

"Yes, or should I say bula?" smiled Adrian, extending his right hand. "*He definitely has a military persona and is that a hint of a British accent? Time with the British Army possibly?*"

"Welcome to Taveuni. We have a busy day ahead of us tomorrow," Isikeli said, getting straight to business. "You look in good shape, however, I must warn you, that it is still quite a climb up to the lake, even without the gear we have to cart with us. I understand from Minister Matai, that I am to help you with a project that is in the national interest, which is all I need to know at this stage," which brought a smile from Adrian in acknowledgement.

They loaded Adrian's suitcase and the box of supplies onto the tray of Isikeli's twin cab utility and headed to the Taveuni Beach Hotel. Isikeli dropped off Adrian at the entrance to the hotel for check-in, agreeing to wait for him in the hotel's coffee shop to discuss arrangements for the morning.

Over a coffee, Isikeli confirmed he would store the supplies where he was staying with family friends in a nearby village. "I will be at the hotel at 6.30am tomorrow morning. We need to get underway and as far as possible up the track to the lake before it gets too hot. I will also arrange some food and water for us."

"Thanks for your help, Isikeli. Hopefully, we will get the job done and get back before dark," queried an optimistic Adrian.

"At least the return journey will be downhill and with a lot lighter load," laughed Isikeli. "See you bright and early in the morning."

With Isikeli gone, Adrian chatted to the hotel receptionist and asked what he could do to fill in the afternoon before dinner. The receptionist arranged for a picnic hamper, cold bottles of water and some goggles and flippers, along with transport down to Prince Charles Beach. *"A nice relaxing way to spend an afternoon."*

"Prince Charles Beach, sounds great, let's do it. Oh, do I need to make a reservation for dinner tonight?" Adrian asked as an afterthought.

"No there are only four other guests in the hotel, so it will not be a problem. Dinner is served from 6pm, with last orders before 8.30pm," smiled the receptionist.

With food, drink and snorkelling equipment in hand, Adrian set off for the beach asking to be collected by the hotel driver at 4pm. This would give him time for an afternoon snooze before heading down for dinner. *"This tropical heat and humidity is certainly tiring."*

Adrian enjoyed the afternoon exploring the reef out from the beach with the snorkelling equipment. The tropical water was warm, in some ways too warm to be refreshing. It was like being in a tepid bath. However, he spent what seemed to be hours floating over the colourful coral, watching tiny tropical fish darting in and out of the rock formations. He could see the attraction of an aquarium in his office. "*Maybe something for my office in Sydney? Anux can afford it.*"

*

Refreshed after his powernap, Adrian showered up and headed down to the hotel restaurant for dinner at six-thirty. He walked up to the reception desk and noted the dimly lit restaurant, chuckling at the candles fixed into the necks of the old spherical Mateus Rose bottles. "*How quaint.*" He was escorted to his table adjacent to the solitary booth located at the end of the restaurant.

The booth was occupied by a stunningly attractive Fijian woman and a broad-shouldered, fit-looking European man, picking up what was definitely an Aussie accent. They were engrossed in conversation, interspersed with regular laughter.

The waiter lit the candle on Adrian's table and offered him a menu as he sat down, along with asking him whether he would like a drink. Adrian wanted to try a Fiji Bitter as well as some locally bottled water, the famous Fiji Water, as seen in the movies.

Jacob and Mere looked up and focussed in on Adrian as they heard him place his drink order.

"Definitely another Aussie with that accent," Jacob whispered in Mere's ear. "Wonder what he is doing here by himself?"

The waiter appeared with Jacob and Mere's meals. They had gone for the prawn curry special again, as well as another bottle of the Kiwi Pinot Grigio. A great way to finish off a day of kayaking and preparing for the following day's big trek.

The smell had drifted across to Adrian's table. "Sorry to interrupt, but could you tell me what you have ordered there."

"It's the prawn curry special. We had it last night mate," exuded Jacob. "Very tasty if you like a spicy curry. It was so good we had to have it again."

"Looks good, I think I'll have it as well," Adrian nodded in acknowledgement. "I don't mind a curry."

"What is that bloody Aussie doing with such a beauty?" Adrian wondered, taking a quick peek towards Mere, trying not to stare.

During the course of the meal there was some small exchanges of polite conversation, but no formal introduction or an exchange of names. However, Jacob was sensing that Mere was becoming uncomfortable with the continual stares from the Aussie's table and attempts at small talk.

"Is there anything else Mr Nicholls?" The waiter politely asked, clearing away Adrian's cutlery and crockery.

"No thanks. I have an early start in the morning, heading up to the lake at 6.30, before it gets too hot," informed Jacob, pushing back his chair and standing. "Just charge it to my room, 121."

"That's him. It must be. That is Adrian Nicholls. The Head of Anux in Australia, here on Taveuni." Jacob was suddenly all ears and fidgeting in the booth and whispering to Mere. "It is not a coincidence he is here. Filipe Matai said he was meeting with him to talk about commercialisation of the Tagimoucia, but I did not see that extending to him actually coming to the island. What in the hell is he doing here?"

"He mentioned something about making an early start in the morning," added Mere. "I think we will need to be up early to see what he is going to get up to and especially with him talking about going up to the lake. There must be a local contact to assist him, as surely he does not have any local knowledge."

"OK, I say we get packed and ready to go with all our gear by 6.15am," conspired Jacob. "I will tap on your door and we can head down to take up a position in the carpark. I would like to see what he is up to and with who."

There was no further prospect of Jacob attempting to speak to Mere about what transpired the previous night, with the mood lost. Adrian Nicholls presence had seen to that. Jacob and Mere lay on their backs on top of their respective beds. They looked up at their ceilings, watching their whirring overhead fans and thinking about what the new day would bring on the shores of Lake Tagimoucia.

CHAPTER 16

It was just after 5.30am and the dawn light was starting to creep into Jacob's room. He jumped out of bed and gave Mere's adjoining door a couple of sharp knocks. "Time to get ready Mere."

"Thanks Jacob," Mere called back through the door. "I'm up. Give me a tap on the door when you are ready to head down."

Jacob put on his new hiking boots then arranged his and Mere's backpacks. There were two one litre water bottles and some bananas placed in Mere's backpack. In his, there was the addition of the plastic sample bags and two pairs of pruning shears, plus a bottle of Factor 50 sunscreen.

He had time for a cup of tea and couple of biscuits from his room's facilities and with a quick brush of the teeth, he was ready to go. Mere quickly opened her door after his knock and they were heading down the central staircase in the accommodation wing, to the carpark.

"I suggest we keep out of sight in the bushes on the far side of the carpark," Jacob pointed to a clump of bushes. "Be good if we can glean what Adrian is up to and with whom."

They got into position just as the headlights of a white twin cab utility pulled into the carpark. He pulled up next to the hotel's car, parked adjacent to the hotel's entrance. A tall, fit looking Fijian man jumped out of the vehicle and headed towards the foyer.

"Look, the vehicle has a government registration plate," Mere said, pointing to the rear of the vehicle. "I wonder who our man is meeting?"

"That's very suspicious," Jacob sounded irritated. "Is Filipe somehow involved in all this? How else would he have government connections?"

They heard the Fijian man's "*Bula*" followed by the distinct Aussie accent of Adrian Nicholls, break through the cool morning air, "Good morning Isikeli. You are bright and early as promised. Have we got time for a coffee? Would love one before we get underway."

"No problem," came the quick reply. "Could do with one myself. As promised, I have got us some water and food for the trek ahead, along with the gear for the job, in the tray at the back of the vehicle."

"Perfect." Adrian put his arm on his visitor's shoulder as they headed into the hotel.

Jacob and Mere looked at each other and wondered what job they could be referring to and what was the gear in the back of the vehicle. "I think we need to check out what there is in the vehicle. We need to know what our Mr Nicholls is up to, especially with the arrival of a mystery man, travelling with government registration plates." Jacob's eyes fixated on the vehicle. "What has he arranged in such a short time in Fiji? And now he is about to head up to the lake."

"I agree Jacob, it sounds very suspicious," Mere added. "You better go now as they will be out shortly. I'll wait here with the backpacks."

The rising sun was rapidly illuminating the carpark, so Jacob quickly dashed crab-like across the carpark, keeping below the roof line of the vehicles. He reached the hotel's car where he paused to see if there was any movement from the hotel lobby. Seeing none, he bent down and crept towards the utility, where he cautiously peeled back the cover. There was a backpack containing some plastic bottles of water and some sandwiches, pretty much indicating a day out hiking like themselves.

Next came the big shock, "*Two sprayers, as well as containers of herbicide. Those bastards. You don't have to be a rocket scientist to figure out what they are going to get up to at the lake. Surely they won't destroy the floral emblem of Fiji.*"

Jacob heard voices coming from the entrance and carefully replaced the cover over the vehicle's tray. Keeping low he dashed back to the waiting Mere.

"Mere you won't believe it. They have herbicide in the back of the vehicle with spraying apparatus. I reckon they are on their way up to the lake to destroy our precious plant."

"Surely they would not be so brazen?" Mere's brow wrinkled with concern. "We have no proof of what they are up to and it could all be very innocent. I would like to give them the benefit of the doubt, until we know otherwise."

"Think about it," Jacob grabbed Mere's arms. "Anux knows about your research and he came to Fiji to meet with Filipe Matai. Filipe mentioned Anux wanted to discuss commercialisation of products derived from the Tagimoucia. Maybe the discussions did not go too well, so Adrian has chosen to take some very drastic measures."

"I suppose you could be right," Mere conceded. "Destroying the availability of any specimens, will stop any further research and the possible development of a competitor product to their wonder drug.

"My fear, however, is the unknown man with the government vehicle. Could Filipe Matai have a connection?" posed Jacob. "How else would Adrian Nicholls be able to arrange some local support, including the equipment and transport, in such a short time?"

"I can't believe Filipe is involved," Mere exclaimed, getting somewhat huffy. "He and Tamana went to university together and have been life-long friends. Tamana would never forgive him if he were any way involved."

"That is all well and good, but I reckon we better hit the trail and get up to the lake well before them," Jacob said, gritting his teeth. "We will need to be there ready to take action, should that toxic cargo be destined for illicit purposes."

Keeping low, Mere and Jacob dashed from the hotel carpark, covering the short distance to the start of the trail leading up to the lake. From behind the cover of some dense ferns, they watched Adrian's vehicle pull up and observed the potentially deadly cargo being unloaded.

"Could they really being wanting to destroy the Tagimoucia? What else could they possibly be doing? This is not some coincidence," Jacob pondered. *"Unbelievable and so brazen."*

Mere and Jacob agreed not to challenge Adrian Nicholls here and now. He could easily deny any potential wrong-doing and then be forewarned they were on to him. From here they would make the trek up to the lake side and see what Adrian was up to, with his unidentified companion. They should be able to make much better time than Adrian and his friend, with a lot less to carry.

*

Even though they had started the trek just on sunrise, it did not take long for the temperature and humidity to rise. The climb up the to the lake, around 800m above sea level, was going to be arduous, not aided by the need to make the ascent as quickly as possible. Luckily, there had been no rain over the past couple of days. This would reduce the likelihood they would be slipping and sliding, as they crossed the various rocky creeks that traversed the trail.

The narrow, winding trail was not subject to huge amounts of traffic, so a thick undergrowth of ferns protruded, unchallenged onto the pathway. It was as though they were travelling through a tunnel of foliage. Jacob and Mere continually had their arms raised to fend off the protruding branches, sapping away at their energy. A mass of tall trees provided a dense umbrella-like canopy over the trail, protecting them from the sun as a plus. However, on the downside it trapped in the moisture, raising the humidity, and not allowing the trail to dry out. This made for a number of muddy, slippery patches, concealed by the undergrowth. A musty smell emanated from the rotting vegetation.

They were not long into the journey when Jacob stopped and sat on a large, smooth, rounded boulder on the side of the trail. He placed his backpack on the ground and reached for his bottle of water, also passing one to Mere, along with a banana. The back of his polo shirt was already damp with perspiration.

"How long to go?" Jacob asked, sucking back on his water bottle.

"We have only just started, and you better take it easy on that water, otherwise you will drink it all before we get to the top," chastised Mere. "We also better make sure we keep well ahead of Adrian and his friend."

"Shh, Mere. Look at that beautiful bird, sitting over there on that branch,"

Jacob whispered, crouching down, and pointing just ahead to a tree branch protruding out over the trail.

"I am not a great bird fancier, but I reckon that is an Orange Dove. See the beautiful orange plumage," Mere sounded knowledgeable. "Taveuni is home to many beautiful birds and is a favourite spot for bird watchers."

"Is that voices? Jacob asked, coming back to reality. He stood and peered back down the trail. "We better get moving." The brief moment of tranquillity was lost.

Despite the awareness of the others being on the trail not far behind them, they took regular rest breaks, due to the increasing heat. They maintained low voices, keeping their ears pricked for anyone coming up from behind. During the short breaks they started to formulate a plan of action once they reached lakeside. It was agreed they needed to ensure they not only stopped any potential risk to the floral emblem of Fiji, but also documented evidence of any wrongdoing.

Mere would take up a position, hidden in the undergrowth from where the trail emptied out onto the lake's shoreline. She would have her mobile phone ready in video mode, to record any activity that occurred. If there was action taken to begin spraying, then Jacob would immediately leap into action and challenge the would-be destroyers.

"Even if they attack me, you need to remain hidden," Jacob demanded, seeking Mere's commitment. "People will need to know what happened and I don't want you getting hurt."

"OK, I promise," Mere said, but did not sound fully convincing. "I hope nothing violent happens."

In just under four hours, the exhausted pair, arrived lakeside. They dropped down onto a thick carpet of grass, covering the front shoreline. It was a relief to be at last free, from the clawing, dense jungle foliage. They took the luxury of taking some time to take in their surroundings.

The lake was smaller and not what Jacob expected. "*I thought it would be a great expanse of water, with a yellow sandy beach around the water's edge.*" The lake appeared a dull grey colour, probably due the dense cloud cover, shrouding the lake from the sun. Also unexpected was the thick growth of trees, with the jungle growing right up to the water's edge. There was no sandy beach, thereby making it difficult to walk around the lake.

Standing and moving towards the water, Jacob started to squelch underfoot. The dense grass growing around the lakes edge trapped the frequent rainwater, making it very muddy and slippery underfoot. Something else Jacob did not expect.

"It is not what I envisaged Mere," Jacob said, purveying the area around the lake. "I imagine it will be an exceedingly difficult task to undertake spraying, given the thick undergrowth. Anyway, show me our beautiful flower?"

"If you look amongst the trees growing on the lakeside, you will note there is a vine growing amongst the tree branches," informed Mere, taking Jacob's hand and pointing into the tree line. "There have been attempts to transplant the vine and grow it in other locations in Fiji without success. Look there is one. See the dark red petals that shroud the small white centre of the flowers."

"Ah yes, amazing. I can see why they would be seen as tears, as you described in the legend." Jacob shook his head, clearing the fog and coming back to reality. "We better get ready for our visitors and get into position. We need to be able to observe them as they arrive lakeside and monitor their activity."

As with the princess of the legend, a hide was formed for Mere under a tree housing the flowering vine. It gave her a good view of where the trail emerged from the jungle into the clearing adjacent to the lake. She had an uninterrupted view from here and Jacob could leap into action to prevent any damage being done. They were all set now, it was just a matter of waiting, to confirm their suspicions. In reality, Jacob was hoping his instincts would be proven wrong.

"I pray Filipe has nothing to do with this," stated an emotional Mere. "Tamana will never forgive him."

*

After unloading the vehicle, Isikeli divided the load. They each took a container of the herbicide and the sprayer tank which was strapped to their bodies like a backpack. Isikeli had a heavier load on him, also carrying the two-one litre bottles of water and the food. However, given the load, combined with the increasing heat, humidity, and rugged terrain, it was not long before the trek was having an impact on Adrian. He was starting to feel most uncomfortable.

"I don't think I could have done this by myself. Thank you, Filipe."

"Hell, I forgot the sunscreen and insect repellent," lamented Adrian as he swatted at another buzzing, annoying mosquito. "You reckon over four hours in this heat to get to the top Isikeli?"

"You should be OK. The trail is pretty well covered with the jungle to protect you from the sun and here, take this bit of tree branch. You can use it to deter the mosquitoes from taking a bite," laughed Isikeli. "They love fresh Aussie blood. We will also take short but regular breaks to conserve our energy for the lakeside activity."

It was slow going with the added burden of the equipment to carry up the steep trail. Adrian needed no encouragement to take a break, being blissfully unaware of who was waiting for him up by the lake. They had been going around three and a half hours and Isikeli reckoned they had about another 30 minutes to go to reach the lake. He suggested they take a final rest stop and have something to eat. They would then be able to get straight into the work on arrival at lakeside. It would be best to complete the job as quickly as possible, enabling them to get back to the hotel before it got dark.

"Good idea. I am starting to get peckish and would love another drink of water," Adrian offered no resistance, quickly peeling off his backpack. "I definitely don't want to be on this trail in the dark. I can see a broken leg happening on some of those slippery slopes and rocky creek beds."

After their quick lunch break, they picked up the pace and finally burst into the clearing facing the lake. "We made it, at last," yelled Adrian raising his arms into the air and dropping his pack onto the ground. He removed his sweat-soaked shirt and crossed to the lake's edge. Kneeling down on the muddy shoreline, he splashed himself with the cool, fresh, mountain water. Cupping his hands, he gulped down several handfuls of the crystal-clear, chilled liquid.

"Take it easy, we have plenty to do," Isikeli warned, waving his arms, and beckoning to Adrian. "Let's get organised."

"OK, OK," chuckled Adrian, picking up his shirt and heading back towards Isikeli.

"There is the vine with the tell-tale flowers we need to spray," indicated Isikeli pointing to the trees surrounding the lake. "See the red-blooded flowers, protruding through the branches of the trees.

"It is a shame we have to spray these beautiful flowers," Adrian paused, momentarily reflecting on what he was about to do. "It is only a temporary matter," justifying his actions to Isikeli. "As agreed with Minister Matai we will leave a few vines undisturbed to help their eventual regeneration."

They agreed on a division of labour with Adrian to spray the vines on the west side of the lake and Isikeli to take the east side. They would leave a patch of vines, around 50 metres long on the far north side of the lake unsprayed, to aid the plant's eventual regeneration.

The containers of herbicide were removed from the backpacks and the instructions for dilution of the concentrate reviewed. Each sprayer would hold ten litres of diluted solution, using water from the lake. The hand pump mechanism was extendable, allowing the vines growing in the tree branches to be sprayed, despite the difficult access. It was certainly going to take several hours to get around the lake. There would be no time for a break, if they were to get the job done and be back down the steep trail to the hotel before nightfall.

To the west side of the entry to the lakeside, Mere and Jacob sat quietly in their hiding place. The tension was mounting, and Jacob was coiled like a spring, preparing to leap into action. "As soon as they start to spray, I am going straight for that bastard, Adrian Nicholls and stopping him in his tracks. You get ready to record the action."

"Understood," acknowledged Mere, getting the camera app ready on her smartphone, and checking the battery life.

"Look, they're heading towards the lake to start topping up their spray packs," the tension rising in Jacob's voice. "Ready?"

"Please be careful Jacob," Mere begged, concern showing in her voice. "Don't do anything foolish. There is no phone reception up here to be able to call for help if things go wrong."

Jacob gave Mere a re-assuring smile and a gentle squeeze of her arm. He was waiting for the very first spray of venom to spit out of Adrian's backpack. *"I'm going to stop you causing any damage Adrian Nicholls."*

CHAPTER 17

Adrian and Isikeli filled their sprayer packs with water from the lake. After giving the packs a shake to mix the contents, the men split up. As planned, Isikeli moved towards the east side of the lake and Adrian to the west side, approaching the hidden Jacob and Mere. They observed him putting on his safety equipment of a face mask and goggles, then with a shrug of his shoulders, slipped the sprayer onto his back ready for action. He tried the hand pump mechanism a couple of times to build up the pressure and with a flick of the wrist, a fine milky spray could be seen spurting out of the nozzle. The first victim in Adrian's sights was hanging with its red flowers swaying in a gentle breeze, in a tree adjacent to Mere and Jacob's hide.

With the pump action going, building up pressure, Adrian approached the first vine of red flowers. He twisted the nozzle and began to spray. It was the signal for Jacob to leap into action. "You son of a bitch," yelled Jacob as his body plunged into Adrian's mid-riff sending him sprawling, backwards to the ground, landing with a heavy thud.

Adrian staggered to his feet, facing Jacob who had already sprung to his feet and was standing with fists clenched, ready for action. Mere remained quietly hidden capturing all the action, concerned that Jacob may get hurt if he had to face both Adrian and his Fijian companion.

"What do the bloody hell you think you are up to?" A surprised Adrian snarled, as he peeled off his backpack, mask, and goggles, and prepared to defend himself. "You were that Aussie with that Fijian woman in the hotel restaurant last night."

"Isikeli get over here now" Adrian yelled at the top of his voice. "I need your help."

A startled Isikeli turned towards Adrian. He immediately dropped his backpack and sprinted towards the would-be combatants. "*I need to stop this getting out of hand,*" thought Jacob.

Freed from the burden of his equipment, Adrian did not wait for Isikeli to come to the rescue and rushed towards Jacob. He bent down low and launched himself off his feet, wrapping his arms around Jacob's waist. The momentum carried Jacob backwards, with Adrian falling on top of him, Jacob let out a loud grunt as the wind was forced from his lungs.

Locked in each other's arms, the men jostled and rolled on the muddy shoreline, ending up in the chilly water of the lake. The shock of the cold, mountain water caused them to release their grip on each other. They stood up, in knee deep water with their clothes soaked through. They faced each, glaring with their fists raised in preparation for any further action, with adrenaline pumping through their bodies.

"What the hell was that all about?" exclaimed an extremely agitated Adrian, maintaining eye contact with Jacob. "I have a good mind to give you a damn good thrashing. I hope you can explain yourself."

Still facing each other and poised for action, they edged their way out of the water, to the muddy foreshore. Next to arrive on the scene having removed his spraying equipment was Isikeli, who moved to place himself between the potential warriors. Despite Jacob's instructions, Mere could not contain herself. She moved cautiously out of hiding, still recording the action.

"I am Jacob Bryant, and this is Mere Koroi," Jacob declared, surprised at Mere's emergence from her hiding place. "We saw what you bastards had in the back on your vehicle down at the hotel, this morning," Jacob added in an accusatory tone. "It did not take much thinking to figure out what you pair were up to, in coming up here to the lake."

"So what? You had no right to attack me," Adrian glared angrily towards Jacob.

"When we heard you addressed as Mr Nicholls by the waiter at the hotel last night, we knew you must be Adrian Nicholls from Anux Pharmaceuticals. That combined with those containers of herbicide, could only mean one thing. You are here to destroy the Tagimoucia plant," the tension evident in Jacob's voice. "You wanted to stop our ongoing research, all to feed the greed of the almighty Anux."

"I don't know what you are talking about," came the unconvincing mumbled reply by Adrian, his eyes looking to the ground.

"We have it all recorded," Mere indicating her smartphone. "You are spraying a plant and those drums over there, labelled herbicide. You are in big trouble. Wait till the police get hold of this video."

Adrian made a lunge for Mere's phone. Mere responded, immediately jumping behind Jacob, who thrust his hand out grabbing Adrian's wrist. Adrian chopped at Jacob's arm, causing him to release his grip. They began to eye each other off again, looking as though they were getting ready to resume hostilities.

"I want everyone to settle down," Isikeli finally stepping in between the would-be brawlers. "I am a senior official from the Ministry of Commerce, reporting directly to Mr Matai. Mr Matai has fully briefed me on what is going on and it is my role to keep an eye on Mr Nicholls and his activities."

"Does that include the spraying of herbicide?" Jacob interjected with a sneer. "What has the Minister got to do with this evil plot?"

"I know who you are Dr Bryant and you, Dr Koroi," attempting to appease Jacob. "Mr Matai said there was the possibility I may meet up with you here in Taveuni. I was briefed on what you are up to with your research project. I was hoping to avoid any clash between you and Mr Nicholls but unfortunately we ended up here at the lake at the same time."

"Hoping to avoid a clash," Jacob snarled, dismissive of Isikeli, as he strode towards the drums of herbicide. "You just wanted to assist him to complete this foul deed."

With Mere continuing to record the action, everyone followed Jacob's move towards the containers. Jacob bent over and lifted up one of the containers and examined the label. "Sure enough, it says h-e-r-b-i-c-i-d-e," Jacob spelling out the letters in a rather curt manner, his finger pointing to each letter in turn.

"Now Jacob I would like you to peel back the herbicide label," instructed Isikeli. "What does the removal of the label now reveal?"

Jacob broke out in peals of laughter, as he turned the container towards the group. Adrian had a quizzical look on his face, unsure as to why Jacob was laughing.

"It says Liquid Fertiliser. Nicely done Filipe and Isikeli," beamed Jacob.

"What are you talking about?" stuttered Adrian, his face blushed a bright pink. "I have been tricked, that bastard Filipe," Adrian realising he had been duped. "Wait till I get hands on him and let everyone know he was on the take."

Mere and Jacob looked at each other, wondering what Adrian meant by Filipe being on the take. "Hopefully Filipe can explain to us what is going on," stated Jacob.

Adrian shrugged himself free of Isikeli's grip on his shoulder and ran to the start of the trail. Turning to the group he yelled, "No one makes a fool of Adrian Nicholls and gets away with it. That Filipe is going to hear from me as soon as I get back to the hotel. Everyone will know what he has done." With that enraged outcry, Adrian quickly disappeared into the dense undergrowth at the start of the trail and could be heard thrashing his way through the foliage on his way down the mountain.

Isikeli remained with Mere and Jacob, to fill them in on what had just transpired. He explained how Adrian Nicholls had come up with a plan to destroy the Tagimoucia. This was to prevent any research work being done, for at least a couple of years, until the plant eventually regenerated. That would give time to complete the launch of AnuxuDine around the world, without the hint of any viable alternative product being developed to compete with it in the short term.

"That cunning rat," interjected Jacob. "What was the Minister's role in all the goings on?"

"The Minister came up with the plan to substitute the labels on the fertiliser containers and involve me as a sort of minder." Isikeli launched into an explanation. "The plan was to make Mr Nicholls think he had achieved his aim in spraying the plants with herbicide and then quietly depart Fiji with no actual harm being done. That way the Minister saw Mr Nicholls would not be acting as a loose cannon, operating out of control by himself. Minister Matai did not see that Mr Nicholls would be returning anytime soon to Taveuni to confirm the result of his spraying."

"Very clever, I like it," chipped in an amused Jacob. "We were all fooled."

Isikeli continued," I went down to the garden supply centre in Suva on the Friday afternoon and gave the heads up to the manager to switch the labels on the order. It was then ready for collection by Mr Nicholls on the Saturday morning, on his way to the airport. I headed up here on the Friday evening flight to prepare for his arrival. Mr Matai had arranged for a public works vehicle to be made available for me to transport Mr Nicholls around while he was in Taveuni. I met him on arrival yesterday and took him to the hotel to check-in. It was then arranged for me to pick him up this morning and guide him up here to the lake."

"So, you were able to keep him in ignorant bliss," Jacob really enjoyed Isikeli's explanation of events. "He thought he was actually going to destroy the plants, then happily fly back to Sydney. Hats off to the Minister."

"What did he mean by the comment, he was not going to let Mr Matai get away with what he has done?" queried Mere.

"That I do not know," Isikeli answered, developing a worried look on his face. "That is something between him and Mr Matai, but with you filming him actually spraying, I would be very careful if I was him. He does not want to make any threats to the Minister or there will repercussions for him."

It was agreed that while Mere and Jacob would collect the requisite samples for their second study. Isikeli would tidy up, collecting all the various pieces of equipment, ready for the journey back down the trail. At least it was going to be downhill back to the hotel.

"I will make sure that Mr Nicholls is on the morning flight to Nadi as planned and then join you for the later flight back to Suva." Isikeli confirmed.

"I do not believe we will be seeing any more of Mr Nicholls tonight."

*

An angry, hostile Adrian Nicholls stormed back down the track. He was oblivious to everything around him, ignoring the undergrowth bruising and scratching his body. The sweat poured from him as the afternoon sun beat down. His total focus was on getting back to the hotel and calling that Filipe Matai.

"*Wait till I get hold of him.*" Adrian raged ready to burst. He eventually made it back to the hotel, a hot, sweaty, thirsty mess. Bursting into his room, he went straight to the refrigerator, chugging down two bottles of chilled water. A wiser head was starting to prevail, and Adrian decided to take a shower to cool down, while he gathered his thoughts before calling and confronting Filipe Matai. "*He will be begging for mercy, when I remind him about that bribe, he took. It will soon be all through the media in Fiji. His career will be at an end. I can see the headlines now.*"

Refreshed after his shower and some fish and chips from the room service menu, Adrian prepared for his call to Filipe. He opened his briefcase and retrieved Filipe's business card on which he had written his mobile number. Despite it being Sunday evening, nothing was going to stop him from making this call. He was going to give him a piece of his mind, along with the threat of exposure of the bribe he had taken.

After three rings the phone was answered, "Filipe speaking."

"Filipe, Adrian Nicholls here in Taveuni," announced an enraged Adrian.

"Adrian how did the day go?" asked a hesitant Filipe, sensing the hostility in Adrian's voice.

"Don't give me that, how did the day go, you smart bastard," Adrian hissed, trying with difficulty to remain calm. "I was jumped lakeside by your good friends Dr Koroi and Jacob Bryant, who just happened to be waiting for me. Your associate Isikeli, then revealed how you had arranged for the supposed containers of herbicide, to in actual fact be liquid fertiliser. You think you are so clever, making me look like an idiot."

"There was no way I could risk you being let loose with herbicide and actually destroy the national floral emblem of Fiji." Filipe maintained his decorum, "I suggest you quietly board your flight for Sydney tomorrow and do not ever return to Fiji. You will not be welcome."

"Filipe, no one makes a fool of Adrian Nicholls or the Anux Corporation. I am going to expose you and that donation of two-hundred fifty thousand US Dollars, which was made to your own personal Filipe Sitiveni Matai, FSM account." Adrian assumed a threatening tone, "the accountant in Sydney has all the account details."

"Oh, you mean the sum received from the Anux Donation Account and made to the Fiji School of Medicine, FSM Account?" Filipe remained very calm and considered. "Dr Ranjit Prasad, the Head of School, has already sent a receipt with a letter of thanks to your Sydney office. He was most grateful for the donation. Such a sizeable donation is much appreciated and will be most helpful in the purchase of desperately needed laboratory equipment for the students."

"You smart bastard! You think you are so clever, playing me for a fool" snarled Adrian. "I am going to talk to my boss, Newton Sinclair, in New York and work out a way to fix you up, Filipe. Your political career will be over before you know it."

"I do not take kindly to threats and I would be very careful if I was you Mr Nicholls. My advice to you would be to board your flight back to Sydney tomorrow with a minimum of fuss, otherwise I will see to it that you will be arrested," said an incensed Filipe. "At this point I believe we can avoid any embarrassment to you and your company, by acknowledging Anux's kind donation to the Fiji School of Medicine. On that basis, I do not expect to hear from you again."

After terminating the call with Adrian, Filipe pondered his next steps. Filipe believed the threat of arrest may keep him quiet for the remainder of his time in Fiji. However, Filipe did not trust what Adrian may do once he left Fiji. He decided the best form of defence in shutting down Adrian Nicholls, was attack. A call to Newton Sinclair was the next step.

Just on dark, an exhausted Mere, Jacob and Isikeli made it back to Isikeli's vehicle. They loaded the equipment onto the tray and then Isikeli made the short drive with them, back to the hotel.

"Would you like to join us for dinner Isikeli? I think you have earned a beer or two," offered Jacob.

"Thanks for the offer but I have had it. It has been a long day," Isikeli replied, raising his hands, and politely declining the offer. "I am staying with family in the village and will want to be up early in the morning to make sure Mr Nicholls is on that flight to Nadi. I will then pick you up for the flight to Suva. See you around 8am in the hotel lobby, OK?"

They scanned the hotel lobby area and fortunately there was no sign of Adrian, as they tentatively walked up to the reception desk and requested their room keys. Relieved to get out of their dirty clothes, Mere and Jacob hit the showers. Never had a shower felt so good. Mere had declined Jacob's offer to join her in the shower and scrub her back, costing him a hard punch to his arm.

Freshened up they headed down to the restaurant for the final night in Taveuni. They were not particularly hungry after the events of the day and they both picked over a plate of a medium-steak, salad and chips, accompanied by a small glass of unpalatable, warm red wine. The events of the day with Adrian Nicholls were, of course, the focus of the conversation. They wondered in particular about the threats in regard to Filipe Matai and what that meant. Was this the last that would be heard of Adrian Nicholls and his project of reckless vandalism?

The sanctity maintained of a national icon was a huge relief and the samples were safely in hand, in Jacob's room. The second study would get underway, when they got back to Suva. It would be good to see Joeli at the airport in Suva and fill him in on what had happened and the role of one very clever Filipe Matai.

They did not linger at their dining table after their meal. Side by side they headed up to the stairs to their rooms. Jacob's heart started to race, as Mere stopped outside her room. *"Could this be the moment?"*

"One thing I forget to mention," Mere turned to face Jacob. "Did I tell you that Matai, Filipe's Fijian family name, translates into clever or smart in English."

"You are kidding," Jacob chuckled away. "How appropriate."

With that Mere opened her door, quickly closing it behind her. Jacob was again left in the corridor wondering. "*What is going on inside Mere's head. One moment there are positive vibes, the next second nothing. Will I ever understand her and her continued mixed messages.*"

CHAPTER 18

Following the hostile call from Adrian Nicholls, Filipe wanted to keep a step ahead of Adrian and speak directly to the man he referred to as his boss, Newton Sinclair. With the time difference, Filipe would need to wait to the early hours of Monday morning Fiji time, before attempting to contact him in New York. In the meantime, he would contact the Fiji Consulate-General in New York and get him to use his diplomatic links, to track down a contact number for Newton Sinclair.

Next on the agenda was to contact the editor at The Fiji Times and give him an update on what had transpired on Taveuni. He wanted to make sure that the story made it onto the front page of Monday morning's edition. The editor advised him that he was just in time. Any later and it would have not been possible until the Tuesday edition. A reporter interviewed Filipe and was amazed at what the Minister had described. It was definitely front-page material. The reporter also indicated that given the nature of the story, it would be forwarded to their affiliate news organisations around the world such as The New York Times and The Times in London.

Before heading to bed, Filipe called his PA and asked her to meet him at the office at 6am, as they had some important work to do. With a bit of grumble, mitigated by the promise of an early finish for the day, she agreed to the early start.

*

On arrival at the office Filipe briefed his PA on what was required. It was early afternoon on Sunday in New York, and she was asked to contact the Fiji Consulate General in New York. He was to use his diplomatic contacts to track down Mr Newton Sinclair, a senior manager at Anux Pharmaceuticals. It was to be stressed that this was particularly important and a high priority, even though it is a Sunday.

An hour later the Consulate-General called back. He had been successful in tracking down a mobile number for Newton Sinclair, just as the Monday edition of The Fiji Times was hitting the streets. After a slight hesitation, Filipe fired out the number. After a small delay and several rings, the call was through to the USA.

"*Who could that be on a Sunday afternoon,*" wondered an annoyed Newton noting the call was from an overseas number. He didn't recognise the prefix 679. "*Maybe, it could be one of those international phishing calls.*" However, curiosity got the better of him and in any case, he may be able to have a bit of fun, by leading the caller on. A tentative sounding Newton answered the call, "Hullo."

"Mr Sinclair, my name is Filipe Matai. I am the Minister of Commerce for the Fiji Government and have something of an important nature I need to discuss with you."

Newton's mind began to race. "*Being called by a senior government official from Fiji, could only mean one thing. The call must relate to Adrian Nicholls who was currently in Fiji. I hope there is not going to be a problem.*"

"Minister, how can I be of assistance?" Newton queried, attempting to disguise the quiver and uncertainty in his voice, with his heart pounding in his chest.

"Late last week I met with Mr Adrian Nicholls, the President of Anux Asia Pacific," Filipe stated, getting straight to the point. " Mr Nicholls approached me in regard to securing the commercial rights to any medical usage that may be developed from the national floral emblem of Fiji, the Tagimoucia plant. I indicated to him in reply, that negotiating the commercial rights to such a national icon was going to be a lengthy and complex process, due there being many vested interests. Mr Nicholls was very keen to expedite matters, even so far as proposing to poison the plant with herbicide, to prevent any research work to take place with the plant."

"Minister that is appalling, Anux would not condone such actions," Newton declared, feigning abhorrence.

Ignoring the comment Filipe carried on. "To maintain control of the situation, I co-ordinated with one my trusted employees to accompany Mr Nicholls to the island where the plant grows. The aim was to let Mr Nicholls believe he was destroying the plant with herbicide, which was in fact over-labelled fertiliser."

"*I love it,*" Newton grinned from ear to ear. "*Couldn't have happened to anyone more appropriate.*"

"With the plants duly sprayed, it was expected, Mr Nicholls would happily go away and not be seen again. This was better than leaving him to be an uncontrolled maverick," Filipe continued to explain. "However, there was an unexpected complication, which escalated matters. At the scene, research scientists, Dr Mere Koroi and Dr Jacob Bryant, were collecting samples for their research purposes. Encountering Mr Nicholls spraying the plants with what was believed to be herbicide, they leapt into action. They were not in on the scheme to provide him with fake herbicide."

"Minister, Adrian Nicholls had been in contact with me prior to his meeting with you," Newton said, adopting a business-like tone. " Mr Nicholls raised this crazy idea with me, of using herbicide to kill the plant. I can categorically state that he was instructed by me not to proceed. In fact, I have with me a recording of my explicit instructions to him, to stop any such action. Adrian has acted alone and must face the full consequences of his actions. I can assure you, that Anux will have no option but to terminate his services forthwith. Also, I offer an unreserved apology to you and the people of Fiji on behalf of Anux Pharmaceuticals."

"I understand Mr Nicholls is on his way back to Sydney on a flight departing Fiji in several hours' time, it now being Monday afternoon in Fiji," Filipe informed Newton. "You should also be aware that the story of his activities, has been published on the front page of today's edition of Fiji's national newspaper, The Fiji Times. Mr Nicholls may by now be aware of the publication of the article. It is also quite likely the article will be disseminated around the world by the various newspaper wire services. This may include the likes of The New York Times becoming aware of the situation, so there may be ramifications for your company."

"Minister, I very much appreciate you contacting me personally and advising me of the situation. Again, I must sincerely apologise on behalf of Anux Pharmaceuticals for the action of one rogue employee, which has caused you so much trouble," Newton reverted to a conciliatory mode.

"There is one thing I would ask you to consider," Filipe asked, trying his luck. "I would look most favourably on any assistance Anux could provide to Dr Joeli Koroi's research program. Both Dr Koroi and the Fiji School of Medicine I am sure would be most appreciative of any assistance you could offer."

"Done deal, Minister. I appreciate your understanding in this matter. It is the least we can do in the situation."

"*How could I refuse,*" Newton thought, knowing he had been cornered by Filipe.

"Let's keep in regular contact, in regard to this matter," Filipe said, finishing the call. "Speak soon."

*

"Mr Richards, sorry to call you on a Sunday night but something urgent has come up." A grave sounding Newton started out the call to the corporation's Chief Executive Officer. "I have just been called by a senior government minister from the Fiji Islands."

"The Fiji Islands, what in the hell are we doing in the Fiji Islands?" Mr Richards sounded annoyed. "Get on with it."

"It is an unbelievable tale, sir." Newton began, hesitating. "The President of the business in Asia Pacific, Adrian Nicholls, went to Fiji with a view to destroying their national floral emblem."

"Why would he do such a foolish thing?" asked Mr Richards, growing more irritated and impatient.

"The Fijian plant has shown to have medicinal properties. Adrian was of a view that the plant may have a future impact on the sales of AnuxuDine and therefore ultimately the company," Newton paused before continuing. "He spoke to me of his plan and I dismissed it out of hand. I even have a recording, telling him to stop undertaking such a crazy idea."

"We need to nip this in the bud, quick smart and avoid any public outrage," Mr Richards now focussed on the matter. "I want him terminated and out of the company as soon as possible. Make sure the Human Resources and Legal Departments have a copy of that recording. Also, get the Public Relations agency briefed and ready with a rebuttal."

"I will get on to it straight away, sir." Newton reassured him, "enjoy the rest of the night."

"Are you kidding," a cynical Mr Richards replied. "I am heading for the antacids. I can feel the indigestion coming on."

Newton was next onto the Vice-President of Anux Corporate Human Resources, asking her to contact the HR manager in Australia, Linda Campbell. They were to make arrangements to immediately terminate Adrian's employment and to get him out of the company forthwith. Newton was very keen to get Adrian out of action, so as to be given no opportunity to mention their recent telephone conversations. Even with the recordings, Newton was sure that Adrian would aim to make his life difficult."

"Newton, if you are going to be on the phone all afternoon with work, I am heading for the gym and maybe a bit of shopping afterwards," cried an antsy Lisabeth heading for the door with her gym bag.

"*Looks like an expensive afternoon.*" Newton watched her exit the apartment, "Enjoy yourself darlin'."

After Human Resources, the next priority call was to the account manager at the Public Relations agency. Newton wanted them to get busy with preparing copy to be distributed to all the major media outlets in regard to the actions of a rogue employee. It was important to inform the media that he had been immediately terminated by the company. The timing was perfect given it was Sunday afternoon in New York. He would sign off on all the copy and have it out to the media in readiness for the Monday morning editions.

"*I am extremely glad the Minister from Fiji was able to get hold of me. He never said how he got my number,*" reflected Newton, "*must be very well connected.*"

With all the major items ticked off on his to do list and Lisabeth at the gym, Newton's pulse rate started to return to normal. He turned on the television and it was just about time for kick-off for the Sunday afternoon NFL match. "*A couple of beers and the Giants versus the Cowboys, a great way to celebrate the demise of one Adrian Nicholls. Good riddance.*"

No sooner had he opened a beer and was getting ready to watch the game when his phone rang. "*That's Adrian's number. I need to be careful what I say.*" He moved towards his home office to retrieve his recorder from his briefcase.

"Newton, thank goodness I have got you," Adrian sounded frantic.

*

Isikeli sat in his vehicle opposite the hotel lobby. He observed a very impolite Adrian complete checkout and slam the door as he got into the hotel courtesy vehicle, for transport to the airport. Isikeli followed at a discreet distance and watched from the airport carpark, until Adrian's flight took-off to Nadi. He then returned to the hotel to collect Mere and Jacob for their flight to Suva.

"Adrian is on his way to Nadi," confirmed Isikeli. "I also spoke with Minister Matai last night and filled him in on the day's events. He will monitor his departure from Fiji at his end and also suggested we get a copy of the Fiji Times when we get back to Suva."

"That's good news." Jacob thanked Isikeli. "I am intrigued about the Fiji Times comment. I will get a copy as soon as we get to Suva. Mere and I have had some breakfast and checked out, so we are ready to head home to Suva. There is much to update Mere's Tamana, Dr Koroi."

*

It was mid-morning by the time Adrian's flight arrived at the Nadi Airport Domestic Terminal. He collected his luggage and crossed over to the International Terminal to check in for the flight to Sydney. Flying business class, he was able to access the Fiji Airways departure lounge after completing immigration formalities. He was looking forward to a quiet drink and some time to put his mind to the events of the last 24 hours and his next steps.

He presented his boarding pass at the lounge's reception desk and found a quiet corner, away from the other travellers. From the refrigerator, he selected a chilled Corona Beer and from a large glass jar, scooped up a selection of mixed nuts and placed them into a small ceramic dish. On the way back to his seat he picked up a copy of the local newspaper, The Fiji Times. Taking a long draft of the cold beer, he was starting to feel relaxed, until he read the headline. "Tagimoucia Attacked". His heart started to race, *"What now?"*

Without mentioning him by name, the article went on to describe how a senior manager of a large international pharmaceutical company, Anux Pharmaceuticals, had planned to destroy the habitat of the Tagimoucia. The senior manager had travelled to Taveuni with the intent of spraying the national treasure with herbicide. His aim was to stop research work being undertaken by Drs Joeli and Mere Koroi at the Fiji School of Medicine, into the medical benefits of the plant. A spokesperson for the Government indicated that the Minister for Commerce, Mr Filipe Matai, had been in direct contact with the company. The Vice-President of International Marketing for Anux, Mr Newton Sinclair, said he was appalled by the news. The company would be taking immediate steps with the rogue employee, to rectify the situation, offering an unreserved apology to the people of Fiji.

Adrian stood up and started pacing, while mumbling to himself, bringing him to the attention of the other lounge guests and the receptionist.

"Is everything alright sir? You look upset," queried the concerned lounge hostess.

"Sorry, but I have had some very disturbing news. Is there some place I can make a private call?" asked Adrian with a sense of urgency.

"Yes sir. Follow me. You can use the meeting room," the hostess indicated to Adrian to follow her.

"That would be great," Adrian thankfully replied. "Much appreciated."

CHAPTER 19

Adrian hardly drew breath as he detailed to Newton what had happened in Fiji, "The whole matter has already been splashed onto the front page of Fiji's national newspaper and who knows where else in the world."

"Adrian, the Minister in Fiji has already been in contact with me in regard to the appalling goings on in Fiji," interrupted Newton. "He was able to track me down here at home in New York on a Sunday afternoon, so he must have some serious influence."

"That cunning fox," Adrian ignored Newton and carried on with his diatribe. "He played me for a fool."

"I think you may have done that to yourself." Newton got down to the matters at hand. "There is no way the company can condone what you have done, and steps have already been taken to terminate your employment forthwith."

"You bastard," interjected a belligerent Adrian. "You fully supported my plans and now you hang me out to dry. If I am going down, you are coming with me."

"I don't think so. Just listen to the recording I made of our conversation, which has already been provided to Mr Richards, the CEO of the company and the Vice-President of the Human Resources Department," as Newton hit the play button.

After listening to the doctored recording, Adrian knew he had no leg to stand on. "*I've been outfoxed. There will be no support from Newton or from the company, despite my successes with AnuxuDine in Europe. I'm going down.*"

"I suggest as soon as you get back to Sydney, you head into the office and complete your exit formalities, first thing Monday morning your time," Newton aimed not to get personal and keep matters business-like. "You'll need to return your laptop and any other company equipment. Linda Campbell in the Sydney Office will complete any financial matters with you. We need to minimise any further embarrassment to the company, so we can all get on with life."

"Newton, no matter how long it takes, I am going to get you for this," spat out a vehement Adrian. "You played me very nicely, all for your own ends."

"Have a nice day Adrian and good luck in your new career direction. I do not think we will be seeing you in the pharmaceutical industry any time soon," mocked Newton. "Good-bye."

*

Jacob was relieved after surviving another flight on the Twin Otter aircraft and making it safely back to Suva, albeit having to tentatively clamber down the rear stairs, one more time. He and Mere strode across the tarmac towards the exit, seeing the big smiling Joeli. He was brandishing a copy of what looked like a copy of the newspaper.

"Here look at today's Fiji Times," Joeli enthused, highlighting the banner headlines on the front page.

"Wow, that Adrian Nicholls is in a heap of trouble," Mere noted, quickly scanning the article.

"If you look further down in the article you will note you pair rate a mention," Joeli indicated proudly. " Heroes on the day, saving the national floral emblem from destruction. Unfortunately, I believe that will attract a lot of media attention around you two."

"Well, I'll be," came from a surprised Jacob, with a shake of his head. "Hopefully, we will not be hounded by the local media. That is something I would not enjoy."

"Come on, get your bags, and I'll get you home for some coffee and I am sure Mereoni will have something ready for you to eat," Joeli declared. "There is also some other exciting news. Filipe called me and told me he spoken to a senior manager of Anux Pharmaceuticals' headquarters in New York."

Settling into the drive home, Joeli described how Filipe had been instrumental in securing a sizeable donation from the pharmaceutical giant, to assist with their research project. "The company he believes, wants to make amends for the out of control, unauthorised actions of their rogue employee was the way Filipe described it. I do not know the amount as yet, but it should be worthwhile and most welcome."

"That is fantastic news," chorused Mere and Jacob.

The journey from the airport to their home passed in no time while they all chatted away about what they could do to enhance their research, given the donation from Anux. They were jolted back to reality as they were met by a media frenzy, waiting on the roadway, as they pulled into the home driveway.

Joeli took control and strode towards the waiting pack, as cameras flashed away. In his strong powerful voice he announced, "Dr Mere Koroi and Dr Jacob Bryant will arrange for a press conference at 2pm this afternoon, at the Fiji School of Medicine, main lecture theatre. That is all for now. See you then," Joeli turning his back, striding off to enter the home, as cameras continued to flash.

They remained behind closed doors with curtains drawn, shielding them from any prying cameras. Taking a seat in the lounge room, Mereoni brought out a pot of tea and some freshly baked scones from the kitchen. The warm scones were accompanied by smalls bowls of strawberry jam and cream. Joeli's eyes lit up. Mere playfully slapped his hand as he reached for a spoon to scoop a large dollop of cream onto his scone.

Joeli advised that he had spoken with Filipe and it was agreed that he would lead the session with the media. Joeli would read out a statement that would be approved by the office of the Minister for Commerce. There would be no questions allowed by reporters.

The group sat in the loungeroom while Jacob worked on the statement on his laptop which was sent off to Filipe for review and approval. After several iterations backwards and forwards they were all set for the 2pm media conference at the Fiji School of Medicine.

At the appointed hour, the entourage of Joeli, Mere and Jacob stepped onto the stage at the front of the Fiji School of Medicine main lecture theatre, to be greeted by the flash of numerous cameras. They assumed their seats bringing a hush to the waiting media throng. Suddenly, it was as if the floodgates had opened and a barrage of questions were launched at the group, accompanied by television lights firing up and news cameras whirring.

Joeli stood and roared with his right arm raised, "Quiet, please."

With Joeli's commanding presence, the noise quickly subsided but the hot television lights kept burning. The reporters seated in the front row seats edged forwarded, some with notepads open and pens poised, others with microphones in hand, all ready to fire off their questions.

"I know you all are extremely interested at events that occurred on Taveuni yesterday and reported in today's newspaper. I know you'll have a lot of questions," Joeli capturing everyone's attention. "However, it is early days and based on legal advice, I will only be reading a prepared statement at this stage. Questions may be entertained at a subsequent meeting once more information comes to hand. You will all receive copies of the statement before you leave the building."

With the agreed statement in hand, Joeli began to read it out to the assembled media. It was relatively short and to the point, following the story line already published in the Fiji Times. "*A rogue employee of the large global company, Anux Pharmaceuticals, was allegedly found attempting to destroy the Tagimoucia plant. Dr Koroi and Dr Bryant had travelled to Taveuni to collect samples of the plants' flower, to enable them to continue their important research work. While at Lake Tagimoucia, they caught the person, allegedly in the act of commencing to spray the plants with herbicide. That person is now on their way back to Sydney, Australia. It is stressed, that no harm has come to the national floral emblem of Fiji.*"

Joeli pointed towards the table adjacent to the exit doors, "thank you very much for your attendance. Copies of the statement are available at the door as you leave."

Not unexpectedly the reporters attempted to ask questions. "Who was this person? Was there a fight? Was anyone hurt? Was he arrested?"

Joeli, Mere and Jacob, stood as one and exited via the rear door of the main lecture theatre and returned to their offices. Now as far as they were concerned, the focus was on their research and getting underway with the second study. Farewell to Adrian Nicholls, though they wondered whether they would hear from him, or about him, ever again?

CHAPTER 20

O n the flight back to Sydney, Adrian was restless, as he continued to move about in his seat. He went over and over in his mind, the telephone conversation he had with Newton. He knew somehow Newton had outsmarted him with the recording of their conversations. It would be exceedingly difficult to prove Newton had doctored the recordings, without getting his hands on them.

"I certainly don't have the funds to be able to tackle the Anux legal machine. The system in the USA would bankrupt me if I tried to access the recordings. The legal proceedings could go on for years, without any outcome, apart from me going broke."

After something to eat and a glass or two of red wine, combined with what had already been a long day, Adrian managed to doze off. One of the cabin crew was passing his seat and was about to ask if would like some more wine, when she noticed what appeared to be tears streaming down Adrian's cheeks. She waved to one of her fellow Fiji Airways cabin crew to join her and pointed to the tears. "Look, he is crying in his sleep. Just like the legend of the Tagimoucia." They smiled at each other and quietly left their passenger to his thoughts and dreams.

After dozing for an hour Adrian sat upright in his seat and noticed the salty taste around his lips. The rest had focussed his mind and he was starting to formulate his plans for revenge. Despite it being his actions that had been responsible for his fall from grace, he had rationalised in his mind, that he was going to make sure Newton Sinclair and Anux Pharmaceuticals paid. They had cut him loose without any thought, or support, even though he believed he was acting in the best interest of the company.

His first action was to reach into his overhead locker and retrieve his computer satchel. He booted up the laptop and inserted a USB with a large memory capacity and started to download the contents of his hard drive. In particular he wanted to make sure he had all the information on the negative reports on the use of AnuxuDine in Southern Africa and the associated payments to doctors involved. "*That information could prove very useful to help me plot my revenge, thank you very much Newton.*"

Being in business class Adrian was one of the first to disembark from the Fiji Airways flight. He did not have to wait long for his priority labelled suit bag to appear on the baggage carousel. With nothing to declare at the customs barrier, he was soon headed to the exit.

As the exit door from the customs hall opened, he was hit with the flashes from cameras and a swarm of humanity rushed towards him. There were cries of, "*there he is. Over here.*"

The rage within him surged. "*Those bastards!*" The media pack had obviously been tipped off about the details of his return flight. Camera operators followed his every move. Reporters thrust microphones, labelled with insignia such as 2BG, 3WA and Channel 3 News into his face. "*Why did you do it? Were you arrested in Fiji? What have you got to say for yourself?*"

Shoving his way through the media throng, brushing past their thrusting microphones and bright camera lights, he felt as though everyone in the airport was looking at him. It was with great relief he reached the taxi rank and leapt into the sanctity of a waiting taxi. He quickly tossed his suit bag onto the back seat and slipped into the seat next to it and pulled the door closed. Flashes continued to accompany his ever movement.

"You must be famous," observed the taxi driver, peering into his rear-view mirror and starting to pull away from the curb. "Wait a minute, you're that guy on the front page of today's newspaper. Where are we headed?"

"Attwater Crescent, Neutral Bay," informed Adrian.

"Nice area. Great harbour views I'll bet," the driver said, aiming to strike up an accord with his now famous passenger. "A pretty expensive area I reckon."

"After today I don't think I'll be able to afford it for much longer," replied a candid Adrian. "You don't happen to have a copy of the newspaper?"

"Sure," the driver reached across to the front passenger seat and passed the newspaper back to Adrian. "Front page, mate."

"Where in heaven's name did they get a photo of me?" Adrian stared at the front page. "The company PR agency, I bet."

Adrian spent the rest of the journey reading the article, which was a straight copy of what appeared in the Fiji Times. "*The story must have forwarded around the world on the various news services for it to have been in today's Sydney paper,*" he presumed. He was brought back to reality by the flash of a camera through the taxi's window, as the taxi started to slow in front of his apartment block.

"They must have been tipped off to where I live," Adrian stated the obvious. "Let's get out of here."

The taxi driver accelerated away, weaving the car through the waiting media throng. "Where to next? I don't think you will get any privacy here tonight."

After a moment's thought Adrian fired out, "Edmunds Circle, Mt Willsmore."

"That is a long way down market from Neutral Bay," observed the taxi driver.

"It's my Mum's place," Adrian stated, ignoring the driver's comment. He just wanted to get away from the media and knew he would find sanctuary at her place. He scrolled through his contacts and dialled her number.

"Dorothy Nicholls speaking."

"Mum, its Adrian. I am on the way to your place. I need a place to stay."

"No worries, my boy. You know your room is always here for you," his Mum replied. "Oh, Johnnie Miller is coming for dinner tonight, so there will be plenty for you to eat and he will love catching up with you after such a long time. What was that about you on the TV news tonight?"

"I'll tell you when I get there, Mum, see you soon."

The long journey out to his Mum's place in the outer Western Suburbs, gave Adrian a bit of thinking time and to his relief the taxi driver was perceptive enough to leave him to his thoughts. His Mum had invited Johnnie Miller to come around for dinner, which brought a smile to his face.

Johnnie ran the local gymnasium in Mt Willsmore. He managed to keep a lot of kids on the straight and narrow, despite being in a lower socio-economic area, with high unemployment and many single parent families. Petty crime was rife and there was a ready availability of drugs in the community. Adrian warmed to Johnnie as a surrogate father, with Johnnie taking him under his wing and driving him to succeed. Johnnie saw something in Adrian and encouraged him to apply for the scholarship to the Macquarie Business School, as a vehicle to escape Mt Willsmore. He had not let Johnnie down by graduating with honours and securing the marketing job in Sydney, before heading to London.

"Next turn on the left, thanks driver," Adrian leaned forward from the backseat and pointed out the dimly lit street.

Nothing had changed in the suburb. Most of the streetlights were out of action and the public space in the centre of his Mum's circular street was littered with rubbish and the grass had long died. Cars without licence plates lined the street and typically had panels with non-matching multi-coloured paintwork. "*I am going to get Mum out of here one day. She deserves a better life. Somewhere near the beach would be nice, close to her sister.*"

His Mum's place stood out in the depressing street. She had maintained a little garden in front of the property, behind a waist-high, dark green, picket fence, which was always maintained in good order. She was always vigilant in picking up the cigarettes packs and butts that found their way over her fence. A concrete footpath led up to the dark green door of the two-storey, semi-detached house, in marked contrast to the unkept place next door. Upstairs were two bedrooms with a bathroom. Downstairs there was a lounge-dining area with an adjoining kitchen, through to a laundry and toilet, leading out to a small back garden. His Mum grew a few vegetables, typically tomatoes, beans and potatoes, to save a few dollars.

Johnnie Miller was a great help in assisting her in the absence of Adrian. The word seemed to be around the community that Mrs Nicholls was to be left alone, otherwise they would incur the wrath of Mr Miller and members of his gymnasium.

Adrian handed over his company credit card to the driver to pay the fare and swore when advised by the driver that it had been rejected. "They didn't waste time in shutting me down. Here take my personal card."

Adrian stepped out of the taxi and opened the knee-high picket gate, which he closed behind him with a slight squeak and headed up to the front door. A faint glow highlighted the doorbell which he pressed. The porch light lit up and his Mum opened the front door and then the screen door.

"My boy," she exclaimed, reaching up to wrap her arms around his neck and gave him a big kiss on the cheek. "Come on in, Johnnie is waiting inside."

"Hey, Adrian great to see you," beamed Johnnie. "I have been looking after your Mum for you while you have been galivanting around the world."

"I bet you have," smiled Adrian.

"Adrian, that is enough of that," his Mum slapped his arm. "Drop your bag up in your room and freshen up for dinner."

His room had not changed. It was as he left it those years ago. A single bed under the window which overlooked the back garden. Down one wall a built-in wardrobe, with a full-length mirror on one door. The opposite wall was home to his student desk and posters of past glory days of the Balmain Tigers Rugby Leagues Club. Dropping his suit bag and freshening up he headed downstairs to his inquisitive audience, no doubt wanting answers to what they had seen in the day's newspaper and on the television news.

Conversation was polite over a simple meal of Irish stew, accompanied by freshly baked bread rolls, finished off with apple pie and cream. Nothing could beat his Mum's simple tasty fare. She stood and cleared away the table indicating for the men to retreat to the lounge for a pot of tea. With the tea poured Adrian thought it was time to fill his Mum and Johnnie in on what had recently transpired. He knew they were eager to find out what had happened.

Adrian described how the company had sacked him on the spot. "They didn't give me a chance to speak to any senior managers to discuss the situation." He did not go into any detail about his activities in Fiji, remaining rather vague and not wanting to paint a bad picture of himself to his Mum.

"They didn't deserve you pet. You have better things to do, than work for those ungrateful sods," consoled his Mum.

"I think I will need to move in for a while Mum. Without a job I won't be able to afford to stay in my apartment in Neutral Bay."

"Your room is as you left it and you can stay as long as you like pet," reassured his Mum.

"Thanks Mum," Adrian squeezed her hand in appreciation. "I have got some things I want to work on while I am here, so I will take you up on the offer of that bed. I have money to keep me going for a while, as I got a good bonus from when I was working in London."

He turned his attention to Johnnie who had not changed much, since he was a kid growing up and working out in Johnnie's gym. He was in his mid-sixties, short and wiry with a full head of grey hair. He had become the father figure Adrian was looking for, managing to keep Adrian on the straight and narrow. Johnnie taught Adrian boxing at the gym and encouraged him in his studies. He even slipped him a few extra dollars on the side to help out with various school expenses, which his Mum could not afford being on welfare.

"While you are considering your options, I have something that could be worthwhile and keep you fit at the same time," Johnnie appeared to get excited. "The local technical college put up a poster in the gym inviting applicants, for a new personal trainer course they are starting in a couple of weeks."

"I like the sound of that. It will get me out of Mum's way and help get my fitness level back up," Adrian enthusiastically replied. "I am going into the city tomorrow to hand back my equipment at the office and I will drop in at the technical college as well, to put in an application. Might also drop in at the gym as well for a workout if that is OK?"

"It will be good to see you in the gym again and you may see some of your old school mates," said Johnnie enthusiastically. "The Conti twins are still regulars."

"Those rogues," laughed Adrian. "Are they keeping out of trouble?"

Adrian checked his watch. It was time to head up for the meeting with Linda Campbell and end this chapter in his life. He waved goodbye to Sue the waitress at Giuseppe's Café and strode purposely towards the elevator. He was trying to remain calm and wanted to present a confident persona, albeit he was churning up inside.

"There is no way I am going to give them the satisfaction of knowing I am upset."

The elevator hurtled its way straight to level 42, not helping the churning in his stomach, or the popping in his ears, as it pulled abruptly to a stop. With a ping the doors glided opened and he stepped straight-backed towards Sheila's reception desk and made direct eye contact with her. "Good morning Sheila. I presume Linda Campbell is expecting me. No doubt my staff access card is no longer functional?"

"Yes, Linda asked me to notify her when you arrived. Take a seat and I will let her know you are here Adrian," Sheila maintained her professional composure.

After what felt like an eternity under the watchful of Sheila, Linda emerged from behind the door marked PRIVATE. "This way please Adrian," she instructed without any pleasantries.

"Looks like it is going to be straight down to business. She wants me off the premises as quickly as possible, which is fine by me."

Linda escorted Adrian to her office and pointed to the seat opposite her desk. "Well, I am sorry things had to end this way Adrian." A look of disappointment crossed her face. "You were only with us a few days, but I wish you all the best for the future, whatever that may hold for you."

Adrian reached into his computer satchel, handing over his laptop, mobile phone, along with the now non-functional company credit card and security pass. Linda provided him with a receipt, confirming the return of the items. Linda also provided Adrian with his Australian Tax Office payment summary for his eventual tax return purposes. "One final thing Adrian, I must remind you, that you have a confidentiality agreement in place with the company.

This precludes you from discussing anything about Anux Pharmaceuticals, with anyone. I have been told to reinforce this with you and confirm that the company will come down hard on you for any breaches of confidentiality."

Acknowledging he understood, he asked Linda to give his best wishes to the Australian staff and with a wave to Sheila, headed to the elevator for the last time, forcing himself not to turn around.

"I was the youngest ever President of a Anux Pharmaceuticals business. That was something I can at least be proud of."

CHAPTER 21

"Hey Carlo, come and have a look at this on the TV news," yelled Guido Conti to his twin brother.

"What is it? It better be good," replied Carlo who was busy on his game console.

"It's our old school mate Adrian Nicholls. Looks like he's in a pile of shit," laughed Guido. "Been doin' some dodgy stuff with drug plants in Fiji."

"Drug plants in Fiji?" Carlo's placed his console on the coffee table, his interest suddenly evident, "We better keep an eye on him. You know his Mum still lives out here at Mt Willsmore. May be interesting to hear what he has been up to."

"I'll speak with Mr Miller at the gym, to see if he knows what Adrian's movements are," said Guido. "He is pretty keen on Adrian's Mum from what I hear on the grapevine."

"He was always pretty fit as well. He worked out regularly," noted Carlo.

"Not like us. Too much of Mum's pasta," smiled Guido patting his slight paunch. "About time we got back into it."

*

Carlo and Guido's grandfather Dominic had fled Italy after WWII. He had been a keen supporter of Mussolini during the war and did not see a bright future for his family in post-WWII Italy.

Dominic and Maria Conti had a cousin operating a market garden in a semi-rural town, Mt Willsmore, west of Sydney. The cousin sponsored their migration to Australia and the family was grateful to be out of Italy. They arrived in 1948, to start their new life along with many thousands of other migrants, escaping the aftermath of WWII.

Dominic was a barber and quickly opened a salon in the small township of Mt Willsmore, the only barber for miles around and he quickly built a successful business. He supplemented his income with loans to the many Italian market gardeners operating in the area. It was rumoured no one dared not make their loan repayments, otherwise accidents could occur, such as unexplained fires on properties.

The Vietnam War brought American servicemen on R and R leave from the war into Sydney, accompanied by quantities of cheap illicit drugs. The end of the war created a vacuum in the supply of drugs, a demand Dominic's son Gaetano was keen to meet. Family back in the old country were ready and able to work with Gaetano, who had no passion for the family barbershop and money lending business. There was plenty more easy money to be made in the drug trade.

Suburbia was now encroaching on Mt Willsmore, with many of the market gardeners selling out. They were enticed by lucrative offers from new housing estates and the financial strain of rapidly increasing council rates. In a new industrial estate in the area, Gaetano Conti established the premises of "Conti's – Import and Export."

With the birth of the twin boys, Carlo and Guido, the sign was changed to "Conti Father and Sons – Import and Export." The boys attended Mt Willsmore High School and did not excel academically, as did Adrian. However, they were being groomed to take over the family business, so academic success was not a high priority.

The Conti's dark, red brick warehouse was very understated. The simple, faded signboard on the front of the building, had been there a long time, unchanged, apart from the recent addition of a mobile telephone number. Grey paint was flaking on the giant roller door which only screeched open for deliveries, often late at night when the rest of the estate was dark and quiet. The main entry door to the right of the roller door, was always closed, providing access via a security code panel. It appeared to be a simple wooden door but was backed by a thick sheet of steel which would make it quite difficult for anyone to quickly force an entry, especially the law.

It was a pretty basic warehouse facility with a row of dusty storage racks upon which they stored the contents of the regular containers received from Thailand. The shipments contained boxes of cheap shampoos, conditioners, soaps and handwashes, stocked by the low budget bulk supermarket stores. Mixed in with the consignment, to make detection difficult, were cartons of heroin, disguised as mineral salts. The heroin was smuggled into Thailand by the family connections in Italy and then packed in the container for shipment to Sydney.

An area for an office and an adjacent washroom/ shower had been set aside in the corner of the warehouse affixed to the rear wall. The open-topped office was cheap and simple, comprising a top half of glass and dark timber in the bottom half. There was an open, basic, lightweight timber door revealing two desks piled with papers and a computer on each desk. The office had not been cleaned for some time, with waste bins crammed full of disposable coffee cups. A carpet which had been peeled back revealed an open safe bulging with cash and what appeared to be a trap door, which provided an emergency exit from the rear of the building.

Despite break-ins in other offices in the estate, no one had ever attempted to break into the Conti Brothers warehouse. Rumours abounded of what had happened to people who crossed them, or anyone in their family. Their father no longer appeared to have an active role in the business and seemed content to remain at home with his wife, the grandkids, tending his tomatoes, grapes and making wine.

Papa Gaetano had kept a fairly low profile with the drug trade and made substantial profits without taking huge risks. The twins, however, were looking for more excitement and ways to expand the business and empire.

*

Carlo's mobile phone rang. He looked irritated as he recognised the number on the screen. "It's that dickhead copper, DS Jeffries. He likes all that coded stuff. Calls me Mr Johnson and says it's Mr Roberts calling. Reckons the Federal coppers could be checking us out."

"I'll humour the annoying bastard," Carlo laughed. "Hullo."

"Mr Roberts here. Can I speak with Mr Johnson?"

"Mr Johnson speaking," smirked Carlo.

"I was just following up in regard to some donations I was expecting, which still have not been received."

"You'll get them when I am good ready," snapped Carlo, terminating the call.

"I don't know why we are paying him at all?" queried Guido. "Never seem to get much info from him."

"Bit of an insurance policy. You never know when he might come in handy," noted Carlo. "Who knows when the coppers may decide to raid us to check out one of our shipments."

"Talking of code names, any update on those yachties from the US with the shipment of cocaine," asked Guido.

"Oh, Smith and Jones," smiled Carlo. "As far as I know they are enroute on their yacht *Catalina Express*. They left San Diego a couple of weeks ago for the rendezvous off Mexico to collect the consignment from the Columbians. They will stopover in Fiji to stock up, before heading on to meet with us for the pickup off the coast of Sydney."

CHAPTER 22

In a few days, Jacob's time in Fiji would come to an end and he was starting to think about his return to Sydney University. There was the realisation he was going to have to make some very pretty tough decisions about his future, especially in relation to the feelings he had developed for Mere.

Thanks to the substantial donation from Anux Pharmaceuticals, the research work had progressed very well. It was quite evident that the results they were obtaining in human volunteers were in line with the first study undertaken by Mere and Joeli in the small sample of rats. However, as with anecdotes from the use of the flower extract in villagers on Taveuni, a majority of the human volunteers had experienced bizarre LSD like hallucinations. This was a significant issue to consider and needed to be resolved, before attempting to enter into commercial discussions with a pharmaceutical company.

Fortunately, there was positive feedback emanating from the laboratory at Sydney University. They had been able to identify the separate parts of the molecules found within the Tagimoucia flower responsible for the analgesic effect and the unwanted hallucinogenic side-effect. The focus would become the development of a production process to be able to produce the pain-relieving part of the molecule. With the support of the work from Sydney University, they would have something tangible to present to a possible development partner.

Mere had gone shopping to pick up some groceries which gave Jacob some thinking time. Jacob had fallen in love with Mere, the moment he saw her on his arrival in Fiji. He knew she was the one, however, he was becoming increasingly confused by her lack of response. Some days it appeared she was responding to him and then on other days she would appear aloof and remote, even hostile.

"*I need to speak with her and confront her about her feelings for me. What about my position at Sydney University? What about continuing to work on the Tagimoucia project in Fiji? What about family and friends in Sydney? If I want to stay in Fiji, how would that be even possible with immigration formalities? So many questions.*" Jacob sat perplexed on the edge of his bed in the cottage, head down staring at the floor.

*

Meanwhile, in downtown Suva, Mere was going through similar thoughts in her mind. "*I have grown to love Jacob and want to be with him. Would he even want to stay in Fiji? Could he stay in Fiji? What about his work in Sydney? He has family and friends; would he want to leave them? Could I go to Australia and leave Tamana behind by himself and break the oath I made to my Tinana?*" Mere finally resolved that it was no good wondering and worrying about all these matters, it was time to sit around the table and speak with Jacob. The subject had been avoided for too long.

On arriving at home, Mere gave the groceries to Mereoni to pack away and thoughtfully made her way down to the cottage. She tentatively opened the door and saw Jacob sitting at the coffee table with a notebook, furiously writing away. He turned, looked up and smiled as Mere entered the cottage, then they simultaneously cried, "we need to talk," at which they both laughed.

Jacob took Mere by the hand and led her to the couch, where they sat down. He quickly began to speak, holding up his hand to cut-off Mere's attempt to speak. "Mere I love you and I want to be with you. There are a number of hurdles to over-come including things like employment, immigration, family, friends and my current life in Sydney to name but a few."

"I know Jacob, I feel…," Jacob cut off Mere again.

"My biggest concern is in regard to your feelings for me. I have to get this off my chest." Jacob taking her hand again. "Sometimes I feel you want to be with me, but on other occasions you seem to want to run away. I am getting confused and frustrated. I need to know 100% how you feel about me, before I can think of tackling any of the other difficult questions."

"I am so sorry Jacob," Mere apologised, composing herself before continuing. "I have been trying to fight the feelings I have for you, which is the source of your frustration and confusion. The situation relates to an oath I made to my Tinana at her graveside. It was my pledge to my dead Tinana that I would stay with Tamana and look after him till he dies. My love for you may make that oath I made at her graveside impossible to fulfil and I have feelings of guilt, regret and sorrow, all mixed up inside me."

"Mere I am sure we can work around the pledge you made to your Tinana," soothed Jacob, stroking Mere's hand. "Maybe we can discuss it with your Tamana over dinner?"

"No, I don't want to put him in a difficult position," Mere standing. "I also don't want you to have to compromise your life choices and make me feel guilty." With that she was out the door and back to the house.

Jacob was left stunned and open-mouthed. "*What can I do? I love her.*"

*

Joeli knew something was not right at the dinner table. Mere and Jacob were both noticeably quiet during dinner and only picked at their food. Especially Jacob, who normally devoured everything that Mereoni had cooked. They hardly spoke to each other, just a few mumbles here and there.

"*Something is up. I was dreading this day. It must be Jacob's departure for Sydney on the weekend. Mere is going to be devastated. I wonder what they have in mind for each other, for the future. Surely, this is not the end of things. I really like Jacob. He would make a great son-in-law.*"

"I'm tired Dad. I'm off to bed. See you in the morning," a sad looking Mere took to her bedroom and closed the door behind her.

"Me too, Joeli, I'll hit the sack," Jacob began to head towards the backdoor.

"Everything OK?" Joeli tentatively probed.

"Sure. We are just a bit tired. It has been a busy few weeks finishing up the study, which has caught up with us both," Jacob feigned a yawn.

"*I am not convinced,*" Joeli was concerned for them both. "OK, see you in the morning."

The door to the cottage gave a gentle creak as Mere slowly crept in. Jacob stirred in his bed and rolled over onto his side with a snort, which caused Mere to freeze. She tip-toed across to the coffee table where she placed the envelope, before quietly heading back to the house.

Jacob was woken in the morning with the dogs barking and the clunk of a car door, which appeared to come from the driveway. He sat up in bed and after a big stretch rubbed his eyes. It was then, through the mosquito netting, he noticed a note on the coffee table, addressed to him in bold letters.

"*Dear Jacob, I have explained to you the oath I made to my Tinana, which I aim to keep. To make things easier for you, for your return to Sydney, I have decided to leave Suva today for my Tinana's home village and spend time with the family. With the continued work on the Tagimoucia, we will definitely maintain contact and maybe in time I can see a way forward for us to be together. Mere xxx*"

Jacob was shattered and cried inconsolably. "*My Mere, what have you done?*"

*

It was a sad farewell between Joeli and Jacob as they bade goodbye to each other at Nausori Airport.

"The experience of working with you Jacob has been fantastic and I wish you all the best for the future," Joeli gave Jacob a big bear hug. "I am so sorry about how things worked out with Mere, maybe one day."

"*I cannot mention the oath to him, it would upset him and betray Mere,*" Jacob grabbed Joeli's hand and gave it a firm shake.

"We'll be in touch next month, once the results of the second study are published in *Pharmacognosy,*" reassured Jacob. "I promised you I would engage with some of my contacts in the pharmaceutical industry and introduce them to Filipe. Hopefully, it won't be long before we see each other again and maybe the situation with Mere will change."

With another hug, Jacob turned and after the security check, stepped out onto the tarmac for the flight to Nadi. He turned and gave Joeli a final wave, before once again starting to, tentatively crawl up those dreaded rear stairs on the Twin Otter.

The revs of the twin propeller Twin Otter started to roar on the end of the runway and with brakes released the aircraft surged down the runway. Jacob took one final look out the window and thought he saw a woman in a white sulu with red hibiscus flowers.

"Could it be?"

*

As the Fiji Airways flight started to push back from the departure gate at Nadi International Airport, Jacob tried to hold back his emotions. He reached into his pocket for some tissues and gently dabbed at his eyes, then blew his nose to get some relief from the sniffles starting to irritate his nose. *"Why doesn't she want to be with me? I thought we could have had a life together. Why didn't she give me a chance? Surely her Tinana would not hold her to the oath."* The young blond girl sitting in the centre seat next to Jacob looked up at him and smiled uneasily.

The 737 continued to rumble over the runway apron, on its journey to the entrance to the runway. "Don't be scared Mister. My Dad says these planes are very safe," the little girl said, patting his arm.

"What is your name," Jacob momentarily forgetting about his sadness at leaving Mere behind in Fiji.

"My name is Zoe, and this is my Dad Sam," pointing to her Dad in the window seat. Hardly drawing breath, she pointed to the seat directly behind Jacob. "That is my Mum, Patricia. The plane was full, so we couldn't sit next to each other," Zoe put on her best sad face.

"How about after the plane takes off, I swap with your Mum so you can sit next to her?" Jacob's heart warmed from Zoe's huge smile.

"Would you? Thank you so much." Zoe's face beamed like a beacon of light.

"I have a very good friend in Sydney called Zoe," Jacob whispered quietly to his new friend Zoe. "I will see her first thing tomorrow morning. She is nice, like you."

After take-off, the swap was made with smiles and a thank-you very much all around.

"*Zoe has made my day.*"

*

It was his first surf since he went to Fiji all those many weeks ago. The onshore breeze was building up a good-sized swell and Jacob could feel the wind in his face, as he stood on the beach with his favourite board under his arm. He was lacking a little in confidence after such a long break away from the surf. The joints were a little stiff, so he placed his board down and did a few stretches on the beach to loosen up.

There was a continual stream of "Hey Jacob, where you been?" from his fellow surfers.

"*It's good to be home and at the beach, amongst friends.*"

It did not take Jacob long to get back into the swing of things and he was once again feeling that adrenaline rush as he and his board, as one, flew towards the beach.

"*Oh, I did miss this feeling of exhilaration.*"

Reluctantly he glanced at his waterproof watch and decided to call it a morning. There was just time for a quick coffee at the café before he had to head off for the start of the new academic year. Jacob placed his board at the entrance and boldly stepped inside," Zoe, I'll have a café latte please," his voice booming out and turning heads amongst the regulars.

There was a pause as Zoe slowly turned towards Jacob, "Jacob Bryant, I do declare. You have finally decided to return home," Zoe announced, pouting her lips, and shaking her finger at Jacob.

"I owe you an answer Zoe, to the question you asked me before I headed off to Fiji," Jacob adopted a more serious tone. "The answer is a definite yes, I will be very pleased to accompany you to the wedding next month."

"What makes you think I don't have someone else?" Zoe haughtily replied. Then a big smile came across her face. "OK Jacob, I'd love you to come."

*

After a couple of weeks in her Mum's home village, Mere finally returned home. With her return to the laboratory, she incorporated the data from Sydney University into the study, enabling her and Joeli to get the second study sent off for review by the publishers of *Pharmacognosy*. There would be a peer review and then hopefully publication in the coming weeks.

Mere picked at her food and then bid her Tamana an early good night. An hour later after a Chivas Regal nightcap, Joeli knocked tentatively at Mere's bedroom door but there was no reply. "Mere," he whispered, as he pushed the door gently open to see Mere curled up on her bed, hugging her koala. She looked fast asleep, but there were tears on her cheeks. His princess was "*Crying in Her Sleep*".

CHAPTER 23

Unbeknown to Adrian, the Board of Management of Anux Pharmaceuticals had called an extraordinary meeting in their New York offices, to discuss the situation in regard to the fiasco created by Adrian Nicholls in Fiji. The Board was adamant that they wanted to minimise the impact of any fallout from Adrian's activities in Fiji and the sooner the matter disappeared from front page news in the media, the better.

The Board viewed the footage of Adrian's arrival back in Sydney, the information of his arrival and home address having been leaked to the media. They noted from the television footage he appeared to be unsettled. However, feedback from Linda Campbell, the Human Resources Manager in the Sydney Office, indicated he departed the company with little fuss, seeming resigned to his fate. To avoid any explanation on his part, Newton omitted to make any mention of the threats made by Adrian to him personally.

Given Adrian had gone peacefully, the Board agreed that no further action would be taken with him. It was agreed unanimously, to allow him to get on with his life and the company could then close the chapter on this very unfortunate incident. With the matter quickly dealt with, the small dip in the share price that had accompanied news of the fiasco in Fiji, would quickly be reversed according to most market analysts.

*

The personal trainer course had not been over-subscribed, so Adrian was confirmed as a student on the spot and immediately paid the tuition fee. Pleased with himself, his next stop was to re-join the local Mt Willsmore library. He was keen to use their resources to read the local newspapers and keep up to speed with what was happening in the world of business.

In the Financial Express he came across an article by their Senior Reporter, Karen Nesbitt. It was an interview with Gavin Mills owner of the newly opened, upmarket Sydney CBD located gymnasium, the Gym With A View. It was a top end gym located at Circular Quay in the heart of Sydney, targeting affluent young executives, with its panoramic views of Sydney Harbour. The gym was located on the 40th floor, the top floor of the building located opposite the Anux offices and came with magnificent, uninterrupted views of the Harbour, the Bridge, and the Opera House . Photographs in the article showed it had all the latest equipment, which was being used by some of Australia's biggest pop and television stars. There was a photograph of Karen Nesbitt in action at the gym and she was quite easy on the eye.

The article went on to describe how Gavin was keen to become established on a national scale. He planned a rollout of franchises nationwide, opening similar facilities, with the same theme in Melbourne, Brisbane, Adelaide, and Perth. That got Adrian thinking that there must be an opportunity for him here and the sizeable bonus monies he earned with Anux, to be put to good use. He knew the pharmaceutical industry was definitely a no-go zone, at least for the foreseeable future, but the rapidly growing fitness industry got him thinking. The concept of the Gym With A View was very appealing to him. First things first, however. Complete the personal trainer course, then a trip into the city and a meeting with Mr Gavin Mills. Maybe revenge will need to wait a little longer.

All excited and motivated, Adrian dropped into the gym on the way back to his Mum's. Johnnie had originally established the gym as a centre for boxing, in an old warehouse, in the industrial estate. However, times had changed and the central boxing ring, with punching bags and speed balls on the sides, had all been replaced. The boxing ring had been replaced by a floor area used for group classes, surrounded by weight machines, treadmills and cycling machines. The building was still pretty basic with no air-conditioning, but Johnnie still had a loyal following amongst the locals.

Adrian had his workout kit with him and as he worked in the door with a wave to Johnnie, he thought, "*I must mention Sue's Pilates course to Johnnie, on the way out.*" As he was warming up, Adrian heard his name called out.

"Adrian Nicholls. Long-time no-see."

Adrian turned and initially hesitated, trying to place the faces of the two men before him. Of course, the Conti twins, Carlo, and Guido. They had grown since he last saw them at high school. They were of Southern Italian ancestry, short and stocky but with powerful arms, bulging with muscle, stretching the fabric of their tight-fitting white t-shirts. It was obvious they worked out regularly at Johnnie's gym. The boys were always teased at school about the family being in the Mafia which they accepted good naturedly.

"I do declare the Conti twins, Carlo and Guido. What are you two up to these days?" Adrian wrapping his arms around them.

"Keeping one step ahead of the law," chuckled Carlo, engulfing Adrian in a massive bear hug. "What are you doing back in the old neighbourhood? I never thought we would see you again. Off to London seeking fame the last we heard from Johnnie."

"You probably saw what happened in the newspaper and on television yesterday," Adrian replied. "You might say I am now in between opportunities."

"Yeah, you look like you were really stitched up by the media. Those cameras buzzing around like a swarm of locusts at the airport," noted Carlo. "I would have loved to have given it to a couple of them, especially those shoving microphones in your face."

"What are you fellas up to?" queried Adrian. "From memory you used to work with your Dad. How are the folks?"

"Dad and Mum are fine, though dad is taking it pretty easy these day. For us it is pretty much the same old routine with the family business. Can't get away from it," confirmed Guido with a wink. "Import, export of whatever turns a buck," he added vaguely.

"We only recently got back into the gym," informed Carlo. "Been eating too much of Mamma's pasta."

"What was all that story about in the news and that Fijian drug," asked Guido. "Sounded very interesting."

"It is quite fascinating," started Adrian. "I'll be staying with Mum for a while so maybe we'll catch up for beer and I can tell you all about it." Adrian turned to resume his workout.

"Look forward to it," the twins replied in unison, heading to the change rooms. "Let us know if you need any help."

"Very timely catch up," said Carlo to Guido, as he opened his locker in the changeroom. "In time we may need to know more about this Fijian drug. Could prove to be a worthwhile stopover by Smith and Jones on their way to Sydney."

*

Over the next two months, Adrian completed the full-time Certificate Course IV in Personal Training at the Mt Willsmore Technical Institute. The qualification was recognised throughout gymnasiums in Australia. In between lectures and practical sessions, he continued to keep himself up to date with what was happening in the world of business via the newspapers at the local library. In particular, he continued to read the articles written by the extremely aggressive, senior investigative reporter at the Financial Express, Ms Karen Nesbitt. He checked out her profile online, which indicated she was a member of the Gym With A View. No doubt it was a complimentary membership given to her, following on from the glowing article about the gym.

An idea was starting to form in Adrian's mind. The potential opportunity with the gym, may also provide the solution for his desire to inflict revenge on Anux Pharmaceuticals and Newton Sinclair. Bring on Ms Karen Nesbitt.

As soon as he completed the course, he was straight onto contacting Gavin Mills via email and arranged to head into Sydney to meet up with him. He expressed the meeting to be something that may be of mutual benefit on a national scale, in line with Gavin's expressed expansionist ideas. The very forward approach by Adrian and his impressive CV intrigued Gavin, enough for him to agree to a meeting.

In preparation for the meeting with Gavin Mills, Adrian had busied himself with the development of a comprehensive business plan to open the next franchise in Melbourne. Adrian had been in contact with real estate agents in Melbourne to access information on various costs such as, rentals, electricity, local taxes, and other setup costs. There appeared to be some excellent properties being built that had 360 degree of the City, taking in Port Phillip Bay, out to the Dandenong Ranges in the East and Geelong in the West.

*

Full of his usual confidence, Adrian walked up to the reception desk at the Gym With A View. "Adrian Nicholls for a 2pm appointment with Mr Mills" Adrian declared, smiling at the attractive receptionist.

"Ah, yes. He will be with you shortly" the receptionist advised, slightly blushing, under Adrian's scrutiny. "Just take a seat."

Gavin Mills stepped into the reception area wearing his dark blue, polo shirt, with a logo of the gym emblazoned on the left breast. His polo shirt hung loosely over the top of his cream, pressed Chinos. Adrian noted he was likely to be in his early fifties, around 5 feet 10 inches tall, with a greying, full head of hair. He had a tanned, muscular body which tapered down from his broad shoulders to a trim waist, with not an ounce of fat to be seen. He obviously used the facilities at his gym, including the tanning salon.

"Adrian, welcome to Gym With A View," Gavin extended his right hand. "I understand from your email that you have some interesting plans you want to discuss with me. Let's head to my office."

Adrian followed Gavin through the gym to his office and was impressed with the facilities. It looked as though no expense had been spared, with all the best equipment and that view. What a way to work out.

"Take a seat," Gavin pointed to the seat on the opposite side of his desk. "Before we get down to business, tell me about yourself."

Adrian started with his humble background in the western suburbs and how he had studied hard to win a scholarship to study Commerce at the Macquarie Business School. He went on to describe his success in the pharmaceutical industry, before encountering an exceedingly difficult American boss, while running the business in Australia. He was hoping enough time had passed since he made front page of the newspaper and his past would not feature on Gavin's radar.

"I decided life was too short and resigned from the company," Adrian tried to sound matter of fact. "I have been able to accumulate some cash via good bonuses and was looking for an opportunity to start to build something for myself. I read a recent article on your business in the Financial Express, by Karen Nesbitt which got me thinking. I am a certified personal trainer and have had success working for a global company in international markets. Karen's article indicated you were looking to expand the franchise around the major capital cities in Australia, so I believe I am your man, to help you achieve that aim."

"You have confidence, I give you that and like myself you have done well from humble beginnings. Go on, tell me what you have in mind," Gavin leaned forward in his seat and placed his elbows on the desktop, eyes glued to Adrian.

Adrian launched into his proposal. "The biggest market in Australia is definitely Sydney, though Melbourne is rapidly catching up. My proposal would be to setup a gym in Melbourne's CBD, on the top floor of a building that would provide 360-degree views of the city. This is possible in Melbourne because it is much flatter than Sydney. With a number of major companies headquartered in Melbourne, we would be targeting the same well-paid corporate executives you currently promote the gym to here in Sydney."

"Sounds good in principle, what timelines are you looking at Adrian?" Gavin drew Adrian out further.

"I have given this a lot of thought before coming to see you Gavin," Adrian replied pensively. "My availability is pretty much straight away. It really is a matter of us coming to an agreement. With an agreement in place, I would then head down to Melbourne and get everything moving as quickly as possible. Time is money."

Adrian then went on to describe how he had already been in contact with agents in Melbourne and identified some potential locations. With premises secured, the next step would be to recruit an assistant manager, to access their local knowledge and network. The person would be instrumental in recruiting the rest of the staff and getting publicity underway. Handbills to be distributed to offices and apartments in the vicinity and a full-on social media campaign. We would highlight the VIP members of the gym here in Sydney and offer reciprocal rights for members travelling between Sydney and Melbourne.

"As indicated, I have some funds to put into the venture to secure some of the action," proposed Adrian. "It is not my mindset to want to remain an employee for the rest of my life."

"You are obviously well-qualified and have impressed me Adrian with your thorough planning. There is definite potential for you to make a valuable contribution to the growth of the gyms business. Plenty for me to think about," added Gavin. "From here I suggest you come and work in the Sydney gym as a personal trainer for a period. This will enable us to get to know each other in the first instance and most importantly develop trust with each other. You will also get to understand me, the culture of the organisation and my expectations of working within the gym's organisation."

"I have also developed a business plan with the associated financials, so when you are ready to talk further about Melbourne, I am fully prepared," added Adrian.

"Very impressive Adrian," Gavin stood and guided Adrian towards the door. "If the trial period works out OK, we may well be able to get something going pretty quickly in Melbourne, before someone else tries to copy the concept."

"How about I look at me starting in here next week as a personal trainer?" asked Adrian. "That will give me time to sort out a few personal things, pack up my gear and arrange some accommodation closer to the City, as there will no doubt be some early starts and late evenings with some of the clientele."

*

With the forthcoming return to living nearer to the city, Adrian knew his days in Liverpool living with his Mum were coming to an end. Before he left her again, he wanted to do something nice for her and make her life a little more comfortable.

Adrian sent her away one weekend for a rare treat, to visit her sister near Gosford on the New South Wales Central Coast. While she was away, he managed a complete transformation of her unit, with the help of some local tradesmen, who were regulars at Johnnie's gym. The carpet was replaced, a nice fawn woollen carpet throughout and updating the walls by removing the wallpaper and painting the whole flat in a more modern off-white colour. The flat was now far brighter. New bedroom and lounge suites, along with new built-in wardrobes completed the re-fit. To top things off Adrian bought his Mum a large smart television, fixed to the wall.

"It is going to take me forever to teach her how to operate it."

Adrian told her to close her eyes when he met at the front door. He took her hand and guided her into the lounge and asked her to open her eyes.

She stood open-mouthed, temporarily speechless. "Oh, my son. It is amazing! Look at the place and that television. It will be the pride of the neighbourhood."

"Funny you mention that", Adrian pointed to the new upgraded locks on the door.

"Mum, I have something I need to discuss with you. Take a seat." Adrian indicated the new lounge chair.

"I was dreading this moment, but knew it would eventually have to come," his Mum looked sad and dabbed away the first hint of tears, with the handkerchief clutched in her hand.

"Yes, I am heading off in the morning to live closer to the city. I need to be closer to where I will be working with the gym. The commute from way out here in the West is just too difficult." With the back of his hand Adrian wiped away the tears that were starting to well in his eyes.

"I understand. You know I want the best for you." His Mum patted his knee affectionately.

"Thanks for your support Mum." Adrian stood and lifted his Mum up from her seat and gave her a big hug and a kiss on the cheek.

They had a quiet dinner together and afterwards Johnnie dropped around to say goodbye.

"Don't you worry about your Mum, I'll look after her," reassured Johnnie.

"I know you will Johnnie and I promise I will keep in regular contact with you both," Adrian gave Johnnie a hug. "Once I am settled, I will buy a cheap car, so I can get out every weekend to visit. Might even be able to help you out in the gym."

"I look forward to that," smiled Johnnie.

CHAPTER 24

"What is the matter with Jacob?" asked Professor Baldwin's PA Carol, as she entered the office and closed the door behind her. "He has not been his usual self, since returning from Fiji. I am worried about him. He seems terribly unhappy, despite reports that the work in Fiji went very well."

"Yes. I have noticed it myself," Prof Baldwin replied. "Arrange for him to come in for a chat, thanks Carol. I need to get to the bottom of what is worrying him. Whatever it is, it seems to be starting to impact his work."

Later in the morning, Jacob made his way to Prof Baldwin's office.

"You wanted to see me Prof," Jacob attempted to sound cheerful.

"Take a seat Jacob," Prof pointed to the chair opposite his desk. "I'll get straight to it Jacob. You have not been yourself of late. I sat in the back of one of your recent lectures and it is not the same vibrant Jacob Bryant I know. It has all coincided with your return from Fiji."

Jacob hesitated, "Can I speak with you off the record Prof?"

"You have known me long enough to know I will keep everything in confidence you share with me," Prof replied in a fatherly tone.

"To put it in simple terms," Jacob gave a gentle cough then started his explanation. "During my time in working with Mere Koroi, I fell in love with her. I thought something would come of our relationship. However, she left me confused. There were signs she was reciprocating my feelings, but in the end, she left Suva and was not even there to say goodbye to me. We had been through a lot together, with completing the study and all that business on Taveuni Island with all the media involved."

"Since I have known you, I have never heard you talk about any other woman in your life like that," Prof Baldwin noted. "She must be something special."

"She is special. I tried to forget about her and attended a wedding with the local café owner and long-time friend Zoe," Jacob replied, "but she was just a friend to me, more like a sister. I know it made her sad and she wanted more from me, but my heart was not in a relationship with her."

"Now it all makes sense," Prof nodded knowingly. "Affairs of the heart can be difficult matters. Next week the results of the second study will be published in *Pharmacognosy*, which I am sure will give you reason to maintain contact with her. Things may develop over time. Don't give up on her just yet."

"You are right Prof," Jacob sounded happier. "I will see what may come with Mere after the publication of the study. Joeli on behalf of Mr Matai, the Minister for Commerce in Fiji, has asked me to assist with providing him with contacts in the pharmaceutical industry, to take things to the next step."

"In the meantime, I want you to lift your game," Prof stood to terminate the meeting. "You owe it to your students to give them your best."

With a nod of acknowledgement and a thank you for his support, Jacob stood and left the Prof's office for his next lecture. He owed it to his students to get back to normal.

*

The publication of the results of the second study provided the need for a teleconference between Jacob, Joeli and Mere to discuss next steps. In particular, the success of Sydney University's laboratory in identifying the pain-relieving active ingredient from the flowers' extract added significantly to the commercial viability of the project. Also being able to determine and separate the part of the molecule responsible for causing the hallucinogenic effects was invaluable.

"Bula Joeli," Jacob said.

"Hey bula, Jacob," Joeli answered the call enthusiastically. "I have Mere with me."

"Bula Jacob," Mere greeted Jacob with a tremble in her voice.

During the course of the teleconference, with Mere noticeably not saying very much, the next steps were agreed. Jacob was to distribute copies of the study paper to his preferred contacts within selected pharmaceutical companies. Companies he believed to have high ethical standards, along with the capabilities and importantly adequate resources to undertake the development work.

Jacob would attach a covering letter indicating he would be able to provide assistance with an introduction of the company to the Minister of Commerce in Fiji. This would enable discussions to occur with the Minister in regard to negotiating any commercial rights for any medical uses derived from the Tagimoucia.

"I believe there will be a lot of interest in the published study from a number of companies." Jacob spoke in a business-like manner as he wrapped-up the session. "I will send you a copy of the distribution list and will keep you and Filipe appraised of any developments."

Mere remained silent as Joeli wished Jacob all the best and terminated the call.

*

A few days after Jacob sent out the letters to his distribution list the phone rang in his office. "Jacob Bryant speaking."

"Jacob, this is Mike Starke, Chairman of Mutilin Pharma and I have with me Scott Thomas, our Chief Financial Officer. Are you free to speak?"

"Hi Mike," Jacob recognised the caller. "Good to hear from you."

"We received the copy of the study you co-authored with your work in Fiji," continued Mike. "It hit a sweet spot for us here at Mutilin. As you know our focus is on the development of new non-opioid analgesic agents and we are keen to secure new candidates to investigate."

"You were high on my target list" replied Jacob. "I have been following you since your recent over-subscribed listing on the Australian Stock Exchange."

"The correspondence from you was very timely" enthused Mike. "The active ingredient in the Fijian plant is exactly what we are looking for as a development project. Are you free for lunch today? We have something to discuss, that may be of interest to you."

"Sounds intriguing. Where and When?" Jacob found it hard to restrain himself, not wanting to sound too enthusiastic.

At lunchtime, Jacob was seated in a café, in Newtown, nearby to the Sydney University campus. From his research he knew that Mutilin was a reputable company, going places since their listing, under the leadership of Mike Starke. Mike was well-regarded in the industry as a trustworthy, ethical guy to do business with. It was why Jacob was interested to hear what he had to say, someone he believed he could confidently introduce to Filipe Matai.

Jacob recognised them as soon as they came through the entrance to the café. They were both in their late thirties and casually dressed in slacks and open-necked short-sleeve shirts. Looking relaxed, they greeted Jacob with big smiles and firm handshakes. While they waited for their simple meals of burgers and salads, they exchanged a bit of chitty chat about the rugby and how the Mutilin share price was doing since the company's listing.

"I know you are busy and need to get back, so I better get down to it," Mike adopted a professional tone. "I have had a discussion with the board of directors of Mutilin and I believe we have come up with something which is hopefully a very exciting opportunity for you to consider."

"Sounds intriguing," replied Jacob trying to curb his enthusiasm.

"Mutilin Pharma is going through a massive growth phase. In addition to recruiting a new CEO with international pharmaceutical industry experience to take the business to the next stage, we are searching for someone to fill the position of Director of New Product Development. We would like to offer you the New Product Development position. The job would be based in our Sydney offices and comes with an attractive salary, most likely well-above your University salary. There would also be the opportunity to earn company shares and bonuses, if you and the company meets various performance hurdles."

"Tell me more about the position" Jacob asked, keen to learn more.

"The company needs someone with your expertise in clinical trialling with plant sourced therapeutics" Mike continued. "We want you to oversee our clinical testing programs to enable us to get products to market in a timely and cost-effective manner. I know that is a lot to consider, but we need a fairly quick response. We want to use your skills and contacts in Fiji to help us secure the rights to the Tagimoucia, ahead of any competitor."

"You have given me a lot to think about Mike," Jacob sounded somewhat hesitant. "I have my appointment at the University to consider and I would also like to discuss the matter with the co-authors of the study paper, Drs Mere and Joeli Koroi. They may see there is a conflict of interest, however, my initial thought is that it sounds an amazing opportunity."

"I look forward to hearing from you, but don't take too long. We want to get on with the project as soon as possible and before any competitors emerge." Mike stood. "I'll pick up the check, you head back to work."

After his lecture, Jacob returned to his office and was keen to speak once again with Joeli and Mere, to discuss the news with them. He was keen to get their feedback in regard to the opportunity.

"Bula, Joeli, it's me again. Hope I am not disturbing you," Jacob apologised.

"Bula Jacob, I have Mere with me, go ahead."

Jacob then described how he sent information on the Tagimoucia study to a reputable company in Sydney, Mutilin Pharma. The Chairman of the company met with him today and not only were they extremely interested in the Tagimoucia project but had also offered him a job.

"What sort of job," queried Joeli.

"It would be entitled Director of New Product Development," Jacob boasted, sounding pleased. "Initially, I would have responsibility for discussing the securing of the commercial rights with the Fiji Government for the Tagimoucia. Once the rights are secured, I would then be in charge of developing the clinical program to develop a marketable product. The company is a good company and are cashed up after a recent listing on the stock exchange. They have a reputable Chairman and are currently recruiting an international experienced

CEO to drive the business forward. I believe they will be ethical in their dealings with the Fiji Government and with any eventual marketing of any product developed. If it were not the case, I would not have entertained such an opportunity."

"Do you feel there is any conflict of interest?" quizzed Mere, suddenly becoming vocal.

"I sincerely believe I can operate in a manner that will be fair for all parties concerned," Jacob attempted to placate Mere. "There is no way I could sleep at night knowing that I had done wrong by either you or the people of Fiji."

"Good enough for me," endorsed Joeli. "You have my blessing."

"I am not looking forward to giving the news to Professor Baldwin," Jacob saddened. "He has been so good in mentoring me in my career to date."

*

"Mike, Jacob Bryant speaking."

"Hi Jacob. What news have you got for me?" queried Mike.

"I have spoken with the Korois in Fiji and they are happy for me to go ahead with taking the position with Mutilin," a pleased Jacob stated. "I just need to speak with Prof Baldwin and will confirm with you 100% once I have spoken with him. At a minimum, I will probably need to complete the semester with my lecture program."

"OK, I am sure we can work out something suitable to us and the University to make the transition as easy as possible for all concerned. Let me know how you get on Jacob."

"I am off to see Prof Baldwin now, speak soon," Jacob terminated the call.

Jacob felt the weight of his decision as he made his way to Prof Baldwin's office.

"Prof, I have something important to discuss with you," Jacob announced as he tentatively took a seat.

"How can I help?" asked Prof Baldwin, concern showing on his face.

"It is a difficult one," hesitated Jacob. "I have been offered a senior role in product development with a pharmaceutical company. They were impressed with the work done in Fiji and would like me on their team, to lead development of new products."

"I presume they are offering you a lot more than the University can afford to pay," stated Prof.

"The money is attractive, but I also get the opportunity to hopefully develop something that would be of benefit to humanity," Jacob earnestly replied.

"On that basis, it is difficult for me to stand in your way, especially when you have been given such an exciting opportunity. You will be sorely missed from my department," responded a sad sounding Prof. "What are your timelines?"

"The University has been good to me with all my research and I would not want to sever all ties," Jacob tendered, attempting to be conciliatory. "I would like to discuss with you the ability to continue working the Department's laboratory on an ongoing basis, given what they have achieved to date. In addition, I would want to complete my lectures for the semester and allow you time to recruit a replacement. You have been a great mentor to me, and I would not want to leave you in the lurch."

*

As the newly appointed Director of New Product Development for Mutilin Pharma, Jacob had quickly arranged for a visit to Fiji for himself, Mike Starke, and Scott Thomas. On the agenda were meetings with the Korois at the Fiji School of Medicine and Filipe Matai at the Ministry of Commerce. The meeting with the Korois was held in Joeli's office at the Fiji School of Medicine.

"*Mere was most welcoming. She even gave me a kiss on the cheek and a hug, which I note made Joeli happy, maybe there is still a chance for me.*"

Mere led the discussion, outlining key issues she saw that would need to be addressed in any commercial development with the Government. "You need to think about these matters in preparation for the meeting with Filipe Matai tomorrow," Mere counselled. "The major issue relates to the inability to access adequate quantities of the plants' flowers, given the limited flowering season. However, the work undertaken by Sydney University laboratory has identified the active ingredient. This is where I see Mutilin Pharma adding value, by actually developing a process to manufacture the active ingredient in commercial quantities. With a manufacturing process in place, we will not be reliant on plant sourced material for conducting the clinical testing. That will mean in the longer term, the Tagimoucia would not need to be harvested to produce a commercial product."

Mike entered the discussion. "You are absolutely correct Mere. With the active ingredient having been identified, it will be up to Jacob and his team of skilled biotechnologists, to develop a patented manufacturing process. To assist with the development program, I see we would only need small quantities of the flowers to be collected during the next growing season."

"I believe we have something to discuss with Minister Matai in tomorrow's meeting," Jacob wrapped up. "Are we all on for dinner tonight. How about Tomasi's?" Jacob gave Mere a knowing smile, which was not reciprocated.

At dinner they sat in a wide booth with Mere flanked either side by Mike and Jacob, with Joeli next to Jacob and Scott next to Mike. At the outset, everyone was in a good mood and believed all was set for a successful meeting with Minister Matai in the morning.

As the evening progressed, Jacob could feel the tension building in Mere's body each time their bodies made contact, during the course of the meal. Mere maintained a pleasant facade throughout dinner, but she seemed to be pleased when the night was over and she did not want to linger over coffee or more wine. Mere drove the visitors back to the hotel, Joeli having enjoyed a few drinks during the meal started to doze in the front passenger seat.

"What's up with Mere?" A worried looking Mike asked Jacob. "Maybe you can enlighten me over a nightcap, as to what is going on between you two."

Over a drink in the hotel bar, Jacob opened up to Mike. "I thought we had a thing, when I was here in Fiji working on the second study. This clashed with a commitment she made to her deceased Mother, pledging to look after her Dad and never leave him."

"Wow, that's pretty heavy" exclaimed Mike. "She is an extremely attractive woman. Maybe in time things will work out between you. I better get off to bed, big day tomorrow."

*

"Jacob great to see you again," Filipe welcomed Jacob into his office.

"Minister Matai, this is my boss, Mr Mike Starke, Chairman and Mr Scott Thomas the CFO of Mutilin Pharma," Jacob adopted a formal tone.

"Mike, Scott welcome to Fiji, please call me Filipe. Take a seat."

Mike started out by providing some background on Mutilin Pharma. The company was recently listed on the Australian Stock Exchange and was well-cashed up. There were adequate funds available to undertake the required work with the Tagimoucia. The goal would be to develop a patented process to be able to make commercial quantities of the plant's active ingredient. This would mean the plant would not be endangered given its limited habitat, with only small quantities of the plant's flowers needed for the first phase of the development work.

Jacob continued, "the next step would be to identify suitable dosage forms, in which the product would be stable, for example, as an injection or a tablet. With a suitable dose form there then would be testing in animals to identify suitable safe dosage levels, before undertaking trials in humans. There would then follow formalised trials over a period of time to identify things like side-effects, safe dosage levels and efficacy."

"Sounds quite a lengthy process," noted Filipe.

"Yes, typically it takes some years. With plenty of commercial risk along the way," expanded Jacob. "The other exciting news, following work at Sydney University, is that we have been able to identify the active chemical in the Tagimoucia and separate it out from another chemical which was causing unwanted side-effects."

Mike got down to business. "Minister, I mean Filipe, I have something that I would like to propose to you and the Fijian Government to consider. To secure the commercial rights, Mutilin Pharma would like to provide an immediate upfront payment, of two million US Dollars. In addition, there would be another milestone payment of a further two million US Dollars, once a successful process for making the active ingredient is patented. Finally, the Government would receive an agreed royalty on any eventual commercial sales of any approved product sold around the world."

Jacob leapt in, "as an additional inducement, Mutilin Pharma would be prepared to fund the equipping of a new laboratory at the Fiji School of Medicine. We would bring in some expertise from Mutilin to help train local scientists and work with the Doctors Koroi for an initial period on the project, at a local level."

"Filipe I would also like to affirm to you that Mutilin, is in agreement with all international clinical study protocols and any new marketed products would be used and marketed in a responsible manner," Mike added.

"Sounds a good proposal to me," extolled Filipe. "It appears that it is a good outcome for all concerned. The Tagimoucia habitat and environment would not be impacted. However, Fiji would be recognised around the world as having provided the legacy of an invaluable resource for the development of a potentially new major medicine. There would be the added bonus of substantial ongoing royalties for the Fijian people."

Mike cautioned Filipe's optimism by stating there was no certainty of success. "There was still a lot of water to flow under the bridge and some years of work, before a pack of product appears on a pharmacy or hospital shelf. Nonetheless, the first step in the journey has been taken and it was now over to the lawyers to get a draft contract completed, so it can be reviewed by the Fiji Government."

"Once the contracts are completed, we would plan to commence work as soon as possible on development. *It's all becoming a reality*," beamed a proud Jacob.

"*I can only hope Mere will change her mind about me.*"

CHAPTER 25

"Good morning Sue," greeted Adrian as he entered Giuseppe's café. "Double espresso thanks."

" Adrian Nicholls, I do declare," Sue was thrilled to see him. "I wasn't sure that I was ever going to see you again after your recent brush with fame. To what do I owe the pleasure of your visit?"

"The big news is that I have taken a job as a personal trainer with the Gym With A View, in the building directly opposite," informed Adrian. "A bit of a change from my former life."

"I wish I could afford a membership," reflected Sue. "It would be pretty special being able to work out alongside stars of stage and screen."

"Well at least I will be back for my regular coffee," smiled Adrian. "I will even arrange to give you a tour of the gym."

"That would be great," Sue was obviously keen to take up the invitation. "Where are you staying now?"

"The owner of the gym managed to arrange for some shared accommodation with another trainer," replied Adrian. "Close to the CBD in Newtown and near the train station to make it easy to come in early morning for my clients. I look forward to continuing to enjoy my early morning coffee and croissant, as well as the excellent service at Giuseppe's."

"I look forward to being of service," smiled Sue.

"Oh, by the way, I mentioned to Johnnie Miller the owner of the gym out at Mt Willsmore about being able to offer Pilates to the membership," said

Adrian, immediately attracting Sue's interest. "At first he didn't know what I as talking about, but he reckons it would be worth offering it on a trial basis."

"Thanks Adrian, that's great news." Sue headed off with a swagger in her step and a smile on her face to brew Adrian's coffee.

Over his coffee, before heading up to the gym, Adrian started to put the pieces together as to how Karen Nesbitt was going to help him achieve his plan for revenge on Anux. He was sure she would enjoy looking at the contents of that USB he had kept secure. It would make a huge front-page story in the Financial Express for Ms Nesbitt. Newton may be a more difficult proposition being so far away. Anyway, it was time to start the next chapter in his life and not be too focussed on Newton.

Adrian downed the last of his coffee and headed to the elevator to take him up to the gym. He exited the elevator on the 40th floor and introduced himself to the receptionist.

"Welcome aboard Adrian, Mr Mills is expecting you. I'll go and get him," she announced.

"Adrian, good to see you," greeted Gavin entering the foyer. "I will give you the official tour this morning and introduce you to some of the others in the team."

The gymnasium was relatively new, brilliantly lit with natural light provided by the large floor to ceiling windows. It had all the latest gleaming electronic and weight equipment. A range of classes were offered and included in the expensive monthly membership fee. Classes offered included Pilates, Yoga, Spin Cycle, Zumba, HIIT and Step. A coffee shop and members' lounge appealed to the very wealthy clientele. The facilities were used for business meetings and no doubt a chance to checkout potential dating opportunities in this world of online dating and *swiping right or left*. In addition, there was the offer of personal trainers such as Adrian, who were available to assist the gym's elite clients, with the preparation of individual fitness programs and healthy diet plans.

Posters with photos of the various trainers and what they offered or specialised in were displayed in the members' lounge and on the changing room walls. Adrian was tall, handsome, and fit, with his six-pack, now well and truly in place, courtesy of Johnnie's gym. His services were soon in high demand from the attractive and extremely well paid, female executives. Many an invite for a coffee with his growing clientele were politely turned down, with him trying to maintain a professional distance.

From the gym's database, Adrian made sure he confirmed what Karen Nesbitt looked like. He monitored her regular times in the gym, via her scanned entries through the gym's security access door. The database revealed she was 32 and lived in the expensive suburb of Mosman. He kept an eye out for her and liked what he saw.

Karen was tall, just under six feet, with long blonde hair, which she wore in a ponytail while working out. She was dressed in tight fitting black activewear, enhancing her muscular thighs and the sleeveless tank top revealing her very muscular, tanned arms. She must have been a user of the gym's solarium or a regular at one of Sydney's beaches. The word amongst his fellow male personal trainers, was that Karen regularly rotated her typically male trainers and did not engage in too much small talk about her private life. She only seemed to talk about her work. The impression they got was that she wanted nothing to impede her drive for success in the media world. After a couple of weeks at the gym, Adrian was finally notified by the gym's reception desk, that Karen Nesbitt had booked him for the next Thursday evening, for a trial session.

"*She has taken the bait.*" One step ticked off in completing the complex plan of revenge for Anux that he had formulated.

*

It was 5.30pm when Karen entered the gym, having made the short walk down Pitt Street from her office to the gym. She had time to change and do some stretching to get ready for her 6pm, one-hour session with Adrian. Adrian gave her the once over as she walked towards him from the changing rooms. This was a body that exuded confidence.

Karen pulled her chair right up next to Adrian's, invading his personal space. It was as though it was a test, to see how he would respond. Adrian played it cool, ignoring her closeness and proceeded to work down the questionnaire on his clipboard. What were her fitness goals? Any special dietary requirements? He could smell her subtle perfume and could feel her legs continuing to press against his. He continued to ask his questions and focussed on making his copious notes.

Adrian agreed she was in overall good physical shape. It would be more a matter of working with her in each session, to fine tune her technique and provide variety in her program to keep her challenged. She outlined a hectic lifestyle in the newspaper world of meeting never-ending deadlines. Her regular training sessions helped mitigate the damage caused by too much coffee consumption, company dinners, wine consumption and late nights probing for stories. Adrian suggested it would be beneficial to ease up on the excessive demands of the corporate life, bringing a cheeky smile to her face. They agreed to review progress at the end of each month and look to vary the routine to maintain her interest and extend her fitness goals.

For each of their sessions Karen made sure she was always well-presented and always with a hint of perfume. Her numerous black tight-fitting outfits always seemed to be a size too small, enhancing her physique.

Adrian was enjoying himself, *"She must have cornered the market on black gym gear in Sydney."*

Adrian continued playing a role of being very professional and did not attempt to engage with Karen at a social level, or become too friendly, despite her aggressive approach. He ignored suggestions about a program review over a coffee in the gym café. Over time he began to notice subtle changes in how she presented herself at their weekly session. He noted she had started to back-off on such a strong physical engagement and was moving to a feminine approach. There was more exposure of her adequate breasts and she gradually became more flirtatious, with little touches of the hand, accompanied by smiles and laughter. His nose also began to detect the increasing potency of her perfume.

Adrian was in for the long haul and was playing hard to get. He did not want to appear too eager, in responding to Karen's gradually increasing hints and the newer less aggressive approach. He was sensing the tension beginning to rise within Karen, but he continued to maintain a professional distance. He wanted her to be the one to make the move and be the one full of desire. She was needed as a key element in his planned revenge on Anux. He did not want her to chew him up and spit him out, as she had reputably done with his fellow trainers.

As they started their second month of training sessions, Karen could contain herself no longer and made a move in her very matter of fact style," Adrian, you know how handsome you are. Have dinner with me and let's get to know each other."

Putting on his best professional voice and looking right into her eyes, Adrian responded, "Karen that is very flattering, but it would be very unprofessional of me to engage socially with a client. I am sure you would know it is against the gym's policy."

Touching his arm and with a cheeky smile she added, "blow the gym's policy. We would only be meeting over a meal to discuss my progress and the next steps in my program. What do you say?"

"Well, a chat over a meal could be very productive. It is rather hectic and often noisy here at the gym. What do you suggest Karen?"

After a slight pause Karen proposed, "how about I meet you at Luigi's Ristorante in Darling Harbour, tomorrow night at 8pm. It is a good little Italian place. That should give you time to freshen up after your last client. We could grab a bite and maybe have a glass of wine or two."

"OK, you're on. See you tomorrow night at eight, at Luigi's," agreed Adrian trying not to appear too eager.

Adrian watched an incredibly happy Karen disappear into the changing rooms. The fish had bitten, and his plan continued to evolve. He knew he just had to be patient and have the lovely Karen prepared to do his bidding. Anux here I come.

*

Karen sent Adrian a text message informing him she had booked a table at the restaurant in her name. Being Friday night, Luigi's was busy, noisy, and bustling. It was obviously immensely popular. He approached the maître d's desk with his bag containing his training gear and laptop. Leaning forward he asked for Ms Nesbitt's reservation. It was difficult to make himself heard above the background noise, so he pointed to Karen's name in the reservation book. After relieving him of his bag and laptop, the waiter led him to the table. The waiter seemed to give him a knowing smile.

It was a long narrow café. A bar lined the left-hand wall with stools occupied by people enjoying what looked to be expensive cocktails. Next to the bar was the open kitchen. It was a zone of frenzy, with smoke rising from the grill, accompanied by loud voices, shouting unintelligible instructions as meat was continually flipped on the hot plates. The tables were set in two long rows, separated by a central aisle. Tables with seating for four diners on the left, closest to the bar and kitchen, with tables for two hugging the wall on the right-hand side. Adrian was taken to the far back corner and sat facing the door, to keep an eye out for Karen. He ordered some sparkling water while he waited.

"*I better pace myself with Karen Nesbitt.*"

After about a 5-minute wait, a stunning, Karen Nesbitt walked into the café. She was effortlessly chic. Working from the ground up, Adrian noted she wore small-heeled, open-toed black shoes. There was no need for stockings with her tanned legs. She wore a knee length, tight fitting, mid-grey, speckled dress, over which she wore a cream woollen coat. Her hair was piled up in a bun. His pulse raced. It had been a while.

The gaze of the other diners followed her to the table where Adrian was standing to meet her. After a left and right cheek greeting, he assisted her to remove her coat, revealing her bare, muscular arms. The attentive waiter silently whisked away her coat. She queried, "Been waiting long?"

"Only a couple of minutes," was the nonchalant response. "You look amazing."

" Flattery will get you everywhere, Mr Nicholls," came the cheeky reply.

They ordered a bottle of Chianti and more sparkling water as the waiter left them with menus, advising he would back shortly for their order. As a starter, they agreed to share a plate of olives with sourdough bread for dipping into olive oil and balsamic vinegar. For mains Karen decided on the ham and mushroom fettucine in tomato sauce, with Adrian going for the tuna penne in white wine sauce. They shared a side-order of a green salad, dressed simply with olive oil.

Over the course of the meal, Karen outlined her life growing up in Melbourne where she attended university, completing a course in journalism. She worked her way up through local newspapers, before getting a break with a Sydney suburban newspaper, where she worked in the business section. This ultimately led to the chance to secure a position with the renowned Financial Express, working her way up to senior reporter over the last three years.

Adrian found it hard to concentrate on her story with her perfume wafting across the table and those amazing green eyes, enhanced by those long fluttering lashes. It had been some time since he had been with a woman and he was starting to feel a stirring between his legs. He was brought back to reality when she asked him to tell his story.

"I had better keep my mind on the plan and why I am dining with Karen Nesbitt."

The whole story was not revealed by Adrian. There was no mention of Anux, Australia or Fiji. He described the tough life growing up in a western suburbs housing commission estate with his Mum. " I was lucky enough to have had a mentor in the local youth club," a sombre sounding Adrian explained. " He was a father figure to me and kept me out of trouble. He saw something in me and showed me what I could achieve if I put my mind to it. With his help I gained a scholarship to the Macquarie Business School, graduating with an Honours Degree in Commerce. After graduation I set off to see the world, joining a major multinational pharmaceutical company In London, where I had some success. However, I developed an interest in fitness training leading to the current occupation as a personal trainer."

"Seems a bit of a strange career move to me," Karen noted. "Moving from a management position in the pharmaceutical industry to work as a personal trainer. It seems to be a waste of a degree from such a prestigious college, where do you see yourself in say 5 years' time? Which company did you work for?" probed Karen, rapidly firing out the questions reporter style.

"I certainly don't want to waste the opportunity the degree has created for me," Adrian said, ignoring Karen's question about who he worked for. "My aim is to eventually become the owner of my own franchise within the Gym With A View organisation."

"Sounds like a good plan," then followed another inquisitive question by Karen. "Anyone special in your life?"

"No time for that at the moment," stated Adrian. "Too busy developing my plans for a future with Gavin Mills, hopefully with a Melbourne franchise."

"Let me get this on my expense account and we can head back to my place for a nightcap," Karen waved to the waiter for the bill. "We can talk about my fitness program over a glass of wine," accompanied by a knowing smile.

*

Karen was not shy, reaching for Adrian's hand as they exited the restaurant and hailed a cab to take them to Karen's apartment in Mosman. Adrian placed his arm around Karen, squeezing her gently, feeling the strength in her muscular arm and shoulders. Karen looked into his eyes and smiled, as she pressed his knee firmly.

She fumbled for her key in her handbag to open the door into the foyer. The automatic light came on as they entered the foyer, Adrian noting there were six letterboxes. Either side of the foyer was an apartment door and directly ahead the staircase and no elevator. Arm in arm they ascended to the first landing entering apartment number three on the left, Karen having the key ready in her hand.

"I don't want to damage the new floorboards," Karen slipping off her shoes as soon as the door closed behind them. "Just had the place renovated. Give me your coat," Karen opened a hall cupboard and crammed the coats into the little remaining space amongst a huge range of coats. Her shoes were placed on a shoe rack, home of a number of expensive looking pairs of shoes and boots.

Adrian took off his shoes and seemed to skate towards the faint light coming from the lounge. The sensors fired up the lighting in the lounge as soon as they entered. "Glass of wine? Got a nice Pinot Grigio."

"Sounds good to me," Adrian rapidly took in the plush apartment. It was a bit too modern, with a number of feminine touches, not to Adrian's taste. The apartment was painted throughout in a very subtle grey, to go with the thick-piled fawn woollen carpet. Looking back down the hallway of highly polished light timber, he noticed a series of 12-inch by 12-inch white canvases, splashed with a variety of colours.

"*Must mean something very intellectual. I bet horrendously expensive, but I certainly don't get it.*"

"Do you like the paintings?" Karen following his gaze.

"A bit modern for me," Adrian turned to Karen and watched her opening the wine.

"Take a quick look around," Karen waved her arm towards the bedrooms, located to the left-hand end of the apartment.

The kitchen located in the centre of the living space, had all the mod-cons. Large stainless-steel oven with six-burner stove top, complete with a wok facility. A large, stainless two-door refrigerator, including an icemaker, was well-stocked with plenty of bottles of Karen's favourite white wine, Italian Pinot Grigio. Meals were prepared on the large island bench which housed a huge sink, along with plenty of storage cupboards underneath for the crockery, cutlery, pots, and pans. The island bench also served as a breakfast bar with four chromium legged, wooden topped stools tucked beneath the lip of the bench top. To the right of the kitchen was the dining alcove, featuring a glass topped table and six chairs matching the bench top stools.

There were two bedrooms each with floor to ceiling, built-in robes, which provided a large amount of storage. The smaller bedroom served as Karen's office which she maintained in a very minimalist style. Her very tidy glass desktop sat atop thick adjustable chromium legs. Tucked underneath the desk next to the blue fabric chair, sat a three-drawer cabinet, no doubt home to stationery and files. She used a docking station to connect her laptop to the screen, printer, and cordless keyboard with mouse.

The main bedroom was a little too feminine for Adrian. With various shades of pinks for the bedcover, headboard, and curtains. He started to explore the room, when suddenly he was spun around by Karen. She wrapped her arms around his neck and thrust her hips into his and began a grinding motion, while hungrily beginning to smother him with kisses. He immediately felt a response and was instantaneously rock hard.

As Karen reached for his belt buckle, he suddenly pushed her away at arm's length. His heart was pounding, seeing the puzzled look on her face.

"What's the matter with you," asked Karen, her arms dropping to her side. "Am I not good enough for a former President of Anux Pharmaceuticals."

"You have been doing your homework Ms Nesbitt," noted Adrian as he turned and moved to take a seat on one of the island bench stools. "I think we need to come clean with each other."

"I certainly would not contemplate going to bed with anyone that I had not checked out before hand," stated Karen quite matter of fact, as she dropped on a stool facing towards Adrian. "Somehow you forgot to mention your exploits with Anux in Fiji. I was intrigued to learn what happened to you, as I saw a story in there for me."

"I suppose I was naïve in not expecting a senior reporter from the *Financial Express* not knowing who Adrian Nicholls was. However, I wanted to get to know you a little better, before letting you in on what potentially is of mutual benefit to us."

"I postulate that our relationship to date, may have been a bit of a case of us trying to exploit each other," Karen laughed. "It was not a coincidence that you contacted me, albeit pretending to play hard to get despite my advances and I am keen to know why. My reporter instincts may have given me an ulterior motive in wanting to get you into my bed. Your exploits were splashed all throughout the media and I knew there must be a story somewhere in there for me."

"Sounds like it is time to get all the cards on the table," stated Adrian, as he took a sip of his Pinot Grigio.

"Please go on," Karen looked at Adrian in anticipation.

"What was not reported in the media was that my boss Newton Sinclair had given me the ok to proceed with my actions in Fiji," Adrian commenced. "I believe he also doctored some recordings which infer he told me not to go ahead with the plan. He then hung me out to dry and Anux immediately sacked me on the spot. I was given no chance to defend myself and Newton suffered no ramifications.

"Sounds pretty unfair," noted Karen. "That Newton sounds a crafty fox."

"I have to admit that getting to know you was part of my plan to wreak revenge on Newton and Anux, utilising your reporting skills," stated an earnest Adrian. "I have some information on a USB that describes some indiscretions by Anux in regard to the use of their new analgesic AnuxuDine in Southern Africa. The information was not reported to the authorities."

"That sounds interesting. Definitely front-page material in the Express," Karen's mind raced. "Such a story would definitely enhance my career prospects for entering into television. I have been in discussion with one of the networks in regard to a news program, which I would anchor. A big front-page story might just get me there."

"I think we both got off on the wrong foot trying to be too clever with each other. How about we head off for the weekend?" proposed Adrian. "I'll bring the USB to show you and we can see what you think. We might also be able to have a bit of fun."

"Sounds like a good idea. I like the idea of a bit of fun," enthused Karen. "I know just the place in the Blue Mountains. It is appropriately named the Cloak and Dagger Inn. We can set off straight after lunch next Friday to beat the afternoon traffic. I'll make a reservation for us."

CHAPTER 26

With advice from Filipe Matai's office that a contract was ready for signing, Mike Starke and Jacob returned to Fiji to complete the signing formalities. The short time available in Fiji was likely to be stressful for Jacob on several fronts. Not only was there the matter of finalising the contract but he also wanted to speak frankly with Mere about their future and what he was going to offer Mere. It would be a relief to be heading back to Sydney with a signed contract and knowing what the future would hold with Mere. If there was to be a future, she was definitely worth one last try.

Mere was waving to Jacob and as he and Mike Starke stepped off Jacob's least favourite aircraft the Twin Otter and made their way across the tarmac at Suva's Nausori Airport. An uncertain Jacob gave Mere a hug.

"*Oh, that waft of frangipani fragrance.*"

"Tamana sends his best wishes for the discussion with Filipe," conveyed Mere.

"We are just about there, Mere," Mike added. "I see only a couple of finer points remain to be discussed and hopefully we can sign the agreement while we are here.

On the way to the Grand Pacific Hotel to check-in, Mere provided an update on what she had been working on at the Fiji School of Medicine, since Jacob had departed Fiji. "I have made another trip to Taveuni and met with the village chief Ratu Osea, to arrange for more flower samples. Once the deal is finalised with the Government, Ratu Osea will co-ordinate the collection of samples for us and ship them to us in Suva, to send to you in Sydney, with the permits in place for importation into Australia. With receipt of the samples, Mutilin can then get on with the development of the manufacturing process for the active ingredient."

"Tell us more, please Mere," Mike's full attention was directed to Mere. "I'd like to understand the issues pertaining to the Tagimoucia flowers."

"There are a number of issues in the collection of the flower samples. The flowers have a very short growing season, being over the summer period. The habitat is confined to the lake area at the top of the island and there are a relatively small number of plants that grow and flower in the habitat. Attempts to grow the plant in other regions have failed. We will therefore need to carefully manage what we harvest," detailed Mere. "In addition, Jacob can attest to the difficult trek required to reach the remote lake."

"That's for sure," laughed Jacob. "I am in no rush to test myself again on the trail up to the lake, any time soon. How about after you drop us at the hotel to check-in, you wait for a couple of minutes and take me up to see your Tamana?" proposed Jacob. "I have a couple of bottles of Chivas Regal for him."

"He will love that," smiled Mere. "I will wait in the carpark for you."

"You ok with that Mike?"

"Sure, I have plenty to catch up on," assured Mike. "I will no doubt already have some emails and I will give the contract a final read in preparation for tomorrow's meeting with Filipe."

"Thanks Mike," acknowledged Jacob.

*

The drive up to see Joeli was somewhat uncomfortable. Neither Mere or Jacob appeared to want to discuss what they had experienced on the day of Jacob's departure and his subsequent discovery of Mere's note. Instead, they made polite conversation about Mereoni's cooking and the dogs Bula and Vatu.

The pulled into the carpark at the Fiji School of Medicine and were accompanied by the clank of the two bottles of duty-free Chivas Regal as they made their way into the building. The receptionist told Mere that her Tamana was finishing a meeting with Dr Prasad, Head of School and would be along shortly. They headed off to Mere's office.

Waiting for Joeli, they sat around the small meeting table in the corner of Mere's office sipping tea. The conversation was still polite and very much business focussed, with Jacob still hesitant to address the matter churning him up inside.

"I cannot take this too much longer. I have to speak with her. About us."

Finally, Jacob gave a small cough into hand, "Mere we need to have a serious talk. We cannot go on like this. We have to talk about us. I want a future with us. I love you. You pushed me away, all because of the oath you said you made to your dead Tinana. I cannot believe that if she were alive, she would hold you to the oath, made by you at her graveside. She would only want you to be happy."

"Jacob," Mere struggled, fighting back tears. "I do love you so much and want to be with you, but I did commit to looking after Tamana until he dies. To me, an oath is an oath."

Joeli had been about to enter Mere's office but paused at her office door when he heard them talking. His ears burned when heard Mere mention the oath she had made to his beloved Lute and her Tinana. He could not wait any longer and burst into the room.

"What is this about an oath Mere," Joeli sounding angry. "Looking after me until I die. Why did you make such a commitment without talking to me about it?"

"Tamana, I am sorry I never told you," Mere sobbed faintly, as she turned and reached for a tissue from the box on her desk. "It was something I wanted to do for you, after losing Tinana at such an early age. I wanted to work with you in the laboratory and hopefully discover something as a legacy to the memory of my Tinana. It became the main priority in my life."

"Mere I can assure you that your beloved Tinana would not have wanted you to lock yourself into such a life," Joeli tenderly embraced Mere. He gently pushed her head back and gently wiped the tears from her eyes. "What is more, now that we will have a deal with the commercial rights about to be signed, Filipe Matai has asked me to run for parliament in the forthcoming elections."

"You? A politician? I don't believe it." Mere was astounded and her tears quickly dried as she stared unbelievably at her Tamana.

"That does raise another matter," Jacob could not contain himself any longer. "Mutilin Pharma wants to offer you a position in Sydney as a Research Scientist. "Once the deal is signed, the major focus is going to be on developing the manufacturing process. There is not much to do here in Fiji, apart from arranging continuing supplies of samples of the flowers during the growing season."

"Wow, that is a great surprise," Mere clutched her palms to her chest.

"A very good opportunity for you and your career," Joeli quickly jumped in. "With me considering a move into politics it is perfect timing for you."

"Jacob, I am very flattered and would like to seriously consider the matter," Mere now focussed on Jacob. "However, I would ask you to give me some time, just a week or two. During that time, I would like to visit Tinana's grave in her village and make my peace with her, before being able to consider the offer."

"You mean you are not saying no, you just want some time?" clarified Jacob.

"That is correct," affirmed Mere. "I do love you and the job in Sydney sounds amazing. It will provide the opportunity to create that legacy for Tinana I have dreamed of."

Jacob decided to leave Mere to her thoughts and got Joeli to drop him back at the hotel. Joeli confirmed that he had never heard of the oath and it was something Mere had done, of her own volition.

"Don't worry Jacob. I will speak to her and make her see sense." Joeli was supportive of the opportunity for Mere. "Hope all goes well with Filipe tomorrow." With a wave from his car, he was headed down the hotel driveway and on his way home to enjoy a glass of Chivas Regal.

"He is a good man that Joeli. I hope Mere makes the right choice, so we can be together."

*

"Hey, bula Jacob, Mike. Good to see you both. Take a seat," Filipe said, pointing to the sofas in his office. "Help yourself to tea or water. Our legal counsel will be here shortly, so we can get underway."

"Hopefully, there are not too many outstanding issues with the contract Filipe," Mike quizzed. "Otherwise, I may need to get our legal counsel to dial-in on things as well."

"No, I believe it should be straight forward," Filipe smiled agreeably. "Here is Jioji Qarase our legal counsel. Jioji, meet Mike Starke, Chairman of Mutilin and Jacob Bryant their Head of New Product Development."

They sat down and got straight to the matters at hand. Filipe indicated the major matters of concern related to accessing the Tagimoucia plant and the limited quantities available in its habitat. The Government wanted some sureties around the responsible gathering of the flowers and an assurance that there would be no damage to the natural environment around the lake area and the trail leading up to the lake.

"The Cabinet is happy with the monetary arrangements and wishes your company the greatest of success in developing a product of which the people of Fiji can be proud. It would be a great thing if the floral emblem of Fiji were instrumental in helping relieve a lot of suffering around the world," Filipe was at his political best.

The changes to the wording of the contract were made. They reconvened in Filipe's office in the afternoon for the formal signing of the contract. With handshakes all around it was time to head out to the airport for the return flight to Nadi. There would be an overnight in Nadi before the return to Sydney the following morning.

While waiting to board the domestic flight, Jacob had time for a quick call to Mere. "Mere all went well with the contract discussions and we have a deal."

"That is great news," beamed Mere.

"Mere I know it is important for you to reconcile matters with your Tinana and hopefully you will be able to come to Sydney and work with me." A quiver was evident in Jacob's voice. "Sorry got to go, they have called the flight. I love you."

"Love you too." Mere was not sure if Jacob heard, with the call disconnected.

*

Joeli tapped on Mere's closed door. "It's me, Tamana," he tentatively called, not sure as to what mood Mere would be in, with Jacob's departure.

"Come in Tamana," Mere tried her best to sound cheerful.

Mere was seated upright on her bed, her back braced by a pillow. Moist tissues in her hand indicating she shed some recent tears. Joeli pulled out the chair from Mere's desk and sat down.

"Mere, without Jacob here, I wanted to confirm with you 100% that I fully support you taking the opportunity with Mutilin Pharma in Sydney," Joeli reached out to take Mere's hand. "I can assure I will be ok without you here. I am going to run for parliament, so there will be plenty to keep me busy with the forthcoming elections. Presuming I get elected to parliament, I will be terribly busy with much to learn. It is still confidential, but the Prime Minister is going to retire before the election and Filipe has been asked to take over as PM should we win the election. Filipe has hinted at the possibility of me being appointed as the Minister for Health which will make for an even bigger learning curve and Mereoni will ensure I do not starve."

"That is what I am afraid of," laughed Mere. "I will not be here to tell her to stop feeding you second helpings of dessert."

"I'll be starting a strict diet very soon," Joeli patted his stomach.

"Thanks for your support Tamana," a cheerful Mere replied. "I do love Jacob and do want to be with him and work in Sydney. However, I do need to make the pilgrimage to Tinana's village, tend to her grave and make my peace with her first. I want her to release me from my oath."

"Your Tinana would only want you to be happy," Joeli stood and headed to the door. "See you in the morning."

CHAPTER 27

The Cloak and Dagger Inn was a classic stone country inn built in the early 1900's. It was set right on the edge of the escarpment at the end of Echo Point, Katoomba, about a two-hour drive from the Sydney CBD. The Inn overlooked the famous sandstone rock formation the Three Sisters, with amazing views across the tree laden Jamison Valley. Access was via a long, narrow drive leading from the main road and lined with towering, century old, poplar trees. The rental cars tyres crunched on the white pebbles as it entered the carpark and pulled up in the guests' carpark.

A red brick pathway led up from the carpark to the majestic white painted stone building. Garrets protruded out from under the steep-pitched, charcoal coloured metal roof, with wings running either side of the entry to the reception area. The double entry door had a bottom half of mahogany, which framed the clear glass panels making the top half of the door.

Karen waited in the car to complete some urgent emails and make some calls, while Adrian went inside to start the check-in process. He opened the door which sounded a small bell and stepped inside. He took a moment for his eyes to adjust to the dimly lit interior.

Casting his eyes around he noted the reception desk was straight ahead, with a red carpeted staircase leading to the upstairs garrets. To the left a bar area and to the right a comfortable lounge area, with four huge leather armchairs, two either side of a massive four-seater leather couch placed around a huge rectangular dark timbered coffee table. At the end of the lounge area was a large stone fireplace, the stone blackened from decades of wooden fires. To the left of the fireplace was a double door leading to the dining room. The style of the door was as the entry door from the carpark, a timber bottom half, the top half of clear glass panels. The dining room was currently closed.

A group of men stood at the bar, obviously golfers given their souvenir Blue Mountains Golf Club Caps and gloves protruding from their rear trouser pockets. There was plenty of laughter as they were swapping stories of near misses and balls lost in the notorious ball gobbling lake on the final hole. The golfers turned towards Adrian and nodded, Adrian reciprocating with a nod and a smile.

Having completed a quick check of the hotel layout, Adrian ambled up to the reception desk. The doorbell had done its job in bringing out a youngish, not unattractive receptionist from a rear room, located behind the wall of room keys. "Reservation for Ms Karen Nesbitt, please."

"Certainly, sir," smiled the receptionist, making eye contact with Adrian. "You will be in Room 12. Top of the stairs and second on the left. Please fill in the registration with your details and car registration," she requested turning to retrieve the room key.

"Back in a sec. Ms Nesbitt is in the car and will be in shortly," Adrian noted as he turned and hurried towards the exit. "She will complete everything for you and give you her credit card imprint." Adrian chuckled to himself, after seeing what he believed to be a knowing smile from the receptionist.

"The Cloak and Dagger, may well be the home of the dirty weekend for Sydneyites."

Adrian with their bags in hand, waited while Karen completed the formalities. As they started the climb up the stairs to their room, the receptionist advised them that dinner service was from 6 to 9pm and the bar closed at 11pm.

The century-old stairs and floorboards in the hallway, creaked with each step leading to Room 12, even though they attempted to step lightly on the carpet. Karen opened the door with the large key, which was probably more at home in a dungeon. The dark timbered door squeaked on its huge metal hinges as it opened, followed by the floorboards as they stepped into the room.

"Ms Nesbitt, I think we will have to take it easy when we are in bed tonight, otherwise everyone downstairs will know what we are up to," laughed Adrian, bringing a smile to Karen's lips.

"You are very cheeky, Mr Nicholls. I am looking forward to your so-called fun." Karen playfully gave Adrian a gentle shove with her arms.

For an old-style country inn, the room was reasonably spacious. An ensuite to the left, came with a modern shower and vanity. This contrasted with the dark timber and white-painted stone wall theme which continued in the rest of the room. Single drawer bedside tables, a large four-drawer chest of drawers, upon which sat a small 20-inch colour television, tea/ coffee facilities and the usual information folder. However, their eyes lit up as they took in the major feature of the room, a large queen-sized four-poster bed, including a white lace canopy. The bed was covered with a black and white striped bedcover, along with a pile of random, multi-coloured cushions.

Placing the bags down, Adrian grabbed Karen and fell, laughing with her onto the bed. He started to kiss her, but she gently pushed him as she sat up. "Plenty of time for that tonight. Let's go for a walk. They have great walks around here taking in all the scenery of the mountains. With a walk we will have earned a drink and a good meal. I hear they have a particularly good chef here."

Adrian feigned a pout before laughing and leaping from the bed, "Ok, let's do it."

They followed the sign posted trail leading down from the Inn's carpark towards the lookout for the Three Sisters. The receptionist had provided them with a handy local tear-off map, which highlighted scenic walks of various lengths in the area. They agreed on a 1-hour return walk along the top of the escarpment. The walk would take in the view of the Three Sisters and the start of the stairway leading down into the Jamison Valley. That would be ok for a familiarisation of the area this afternoon, as with evening approaching, they decided to get back to the inn before it got too chilly. Tomorrow was another day and they planned to explore further afield in the morning and head into Katoomba for a spot of lunch.

Hand in hand they strolled down the path towards the lookout. They paused briefly to put on their jackets, with the late afternoon sun not overcoming the cool breeze speeding its way through the valley below.

"You're a local boy," observed Karen. "Can you explain to a girl originally from Melbourne, why are the Blue Mountains blue?"

"Everyone growing up in Sydney knows the answer to that one," chuckled Adrian. "How scientific do you want me to get?"

"Keep it simple, clever dick!" laughed Karen, gently giving Adrian a push.

"Well, it is a reaction between chemicals and sunlight," began Adrian. "The dense eucalyptus forests release huge amounts of oil into the air, which interacts with dust particles, water vapour and sunlight, to create the blue haze."

"Very clever Professor Nicholls," mocked Karen. "So then, what about the legend of the Three Sisters?"

"That is a little more complex, as there are a couple of legends," related Adrian. "The one I liked growing up, was the tale of the three sisters who were in love with the three brothers from another tribe. The tribes did not agree on the union and a battle ensued. To protect the sisters from attack, a witch doctor in the sister's tribe turned them into the sandstone pinnacles we see today. Unfortunately, the witch doctor was killed in the battle and the spell could not be reversed and there they remain."

"Speak of the devil, there they are," pointed Karen. "Look at the view, it is amazing. Maybe we can go the Skyway tomorrow?"

With it continuing to get chilly in the late afternoon sun, the pace was quickened as they crunched their way along the track and in just under the hour, they made their way back to the Inn's bar. Time for a drink before the restaurant opened for dinner. The golfers had departed and their place at the bar was taken by two men, leaning on the bar and sipping on their pints of lager, no doubt waiting for the restaurant to open.

Adrian order a bottle of Spanish Tempranillo and two glasses, which he charged to the room. He and Karen moved to the lounge area and sat near to the fireplace, with the fire having been lit, ready for the evening's guests. Copies of the menu were on the coffee table and they started to look at the choices while sipping on their wine. Gradually other guests entered the lounge and took seats, sipping on an array of drinks, waiting for what was apparently an extremely popular restaurant with locals and visitors. Karen's tip that the chef was good must be right.

A waitress collected their empty bottle of wine and glasses then escorted them to their table in the rapidly filling restaurant. The waitress lit the candle on their table, and they were each handed a copy of the menu. She indicated she would return shortly with some bottled water and take their order. They noted the white, crisply starched tablecloth and glistening silverware, very nice indeed.

Neither Karen nor Jacob went for a starter, just settling for a main course. They could not go past the daily special of freshly caught, local river trout, accompanied by a platter of seasonal vegetables. They would see if they had room for dessert. Adrian selected a bottle of Tasmanian Pinot Noir, which proved to be an excellent choice to accompany the fish.

They did not dwell at the table after the main course. Adrian was keen to reveal to Karen the contents of his USB, so was in no mood for dessert or coffee. The reporter in Karen was also keen to get up to the room to learn about the content of Adrian's mystery USB. They changed into their pyjamas and turned down the bed cover.

They propped themselves up on the large, duck feather pillows and when comfortable, Karen booted up her laptop. Adrian then handed Karen his precious USB, on which was stored the information he had copied from his Anux laptop, before returning it to the Sydney office.

"Here plug this in," Adrian handed Karen the precious item. "Open the file called Anux Top Secret."

Adrian walked Karen through the contents. He highlighted the issues in Southern Africa relating to the unreported side-effects and the rapid development of addiction with the use of AnuxuDine.

"The information on the USB will show you the unethical behaviour of Anux and Newton, in hiding the reports coming out of Southern Africa. With you publishing an exposé on Anux, it should make for a front-page story in the Financial Express and I will get my revenge."

"Mm, I like the thinking," Karen snuggled up to Adrian. "Front page here I come and maybe even that new television program opportunity I have been discussing with the network."

"Sounds as though it could be the win-win outcome I had envisaged," noted Adrian.

As they snuggled closer together Adrian walked Karen through the data on the USB. He highlighted the high incidence of side-effects including rashes, nausea, vomiting, dizziness, physical dependence, and addiction.

"AnuxuDine had been supplied on a humanitarian or compassionate basis, before it had been approved anywhere else in the world," Adrian added. "The supply had not been part of any clinical trial and the reports of the multiple side-effects were buried. This was to ensure that the approval for the launch of the product in Europe was not delayed. The company did not want any hint of any problems with the treatments in Southern Africa to surface."

In his best corporate manner Adrian then described why Anux wanted to bury these reports. "The company was scared that if information came out in regard to side-effects and addiction, then further clinical trials would be demanded by the global regulatory bodies. This would substantially increase costs, as well as delaying the launch in Europe and other markets around the world. In particular there was concern of any impact on the biggest market of the USA. Delays in the USA would lead to a crash in the share price and potentially a loss on the hundreds of millions of dollars invested in developing the product. I should also mention the panic amongst senior management and the likely impact on their bonuses."

"That is some story," responded Karen. "It's definitely front-page material and will give me and the paper a major scoop, once we work it through the legal eagles. Anux are a huge company and we will need to ensure everything we publish is correct to avoid any litigation. "

"With your publication of the contents of the USB, I believe I can then get on with my life having got the revenge I sought for Anux," Adrian tentatively touched Karen's hand. "I have plans with Gym With A View and establishing a gym in Melbourne, once I have finished a trial period working with Gavin Mills in the Sydney gym."

"You certainly will not be letting the grass grow under your feet," noted Karen.

"There is something else I wanted to talk to you about Karen.," Adrian began looking deeply into Karen's eyes. "Is there a future for us somewhere in all this? I reckon we get on pretty well with each other."

"I have been upfront with you about me and my career," Karen forthrightly replied. "I am close to my dream of securing a job in television and will need to commit to Sydney if I am successful. Let's not complicate things with relationship issues and just enjoy our time together for what it is."

Karen smiled and turned off her laptop, placing it on the bedside table and at the same time turning off the room lights. She reached for Adrian, realising he had already slipped off his pyjama pants and from what was between his legs, knew he was ready for action. Karen hoped the floorboards wouldn't squeak too much as they enjoyed this moment of pleasure together, with no obligations.

"*Hopefully I will not regret giving up everything for my career,*" she wondered, as she felt Adrian's fingertips begin to gently stroke her back.

*

After a night spent filling insatiable desires, they were in cheerful moods, relaxing with a late, full breakfast of sausages, bacon, eggs, tomato, and toast with local honey. Waking in the morning there was no further discussion about any long-term relationship, to complicate matters. They were just going to enjoy the weekend together.

After breakfast they took their map and headed off along the escarpment to take the scenic railway down into the Jamison Valley. As they were strapped into their seats Karen was certainly having second thoughts with the 52-degree incline. It gave the impression they were heading straight down the slope and she almost crushed Jacob's hand as they set off down the 300-metre drop.

With hearts pounding they were relieved to step out into the valley floor.

They followed the signpost to the Katoomba Falls, enjoying the abundant wildlife. Koalas resting on the fork of a tree, munching sleepily on leaves. Curious wallabies bounding away into the undergrowth and the prolific birdlife with the non-stop chatter of parrots and galahs. Reaching the falls, they sat hand in hand on a log and just enjoyed the rush of water as it cascaded over the rocky edge and into the pool below. They seemed reluctant to move and break the tranquillity of the moment, but with a squeeze of her hand Adrian stood, "better head on back for lunch."

They hiked into the township where they found a pub. Given the large breakfast they decided not to go into the restaurant area, but rather sat in the bar area settling on a light counter lunch of ham and cheese sandwiches enjoyed with a glass of chilled Chardonnay. Over the course of their lunch, they continued to discuss how and when to implement Adrian's plan for revenge, now including a committed Karen.

"Are you happy to go with aiming to publish the article in next Saturday's edition?" asked Adrian. "It would great to get on with it, now you have the information, from an unnamed source!"

"I will aim for next Saturday, as long as I get the draft to the legal counsel by Wednesday morning. That will give them time to review and comment, giving me time for any rewrite and a sign-off by the editor," Karen ticking off the steps in her mind.

"Cheers to that," Adrian raised his glass of wine and clinked with Karen's.

"*Things are starting to fall into place and Karen has proven to be a surprise. In reality she is a softy under that hard façade. Could there be a life with her. Maybe in time I could change her mind about a commitment? I'll just have to bide my time.*"

CHAPTER 28

Mere tended her Tinana's grave. The outline of the grave was marked on three sides by large, sun-bleached seashells and completed by an engraved headstone. Overlooking the ocean on her home island, the years of weathering had started to take a toll on the engraved lettering on the grey headstone. A lot of the lettering was getting hard to read due to the erosion.

"I must speak to Tamana about getting the headstone re-engraved."

"Lute Koroi. Beloved Watina of Joeli and much-loved Tinana of Mere. Tragically taken from us."

She dug out the weeds surrounding the plot and planted fresh flowers in the soil resting over the grave. A coconut tree provided shade over the grave and after her toil, Mere sat cross-legged on the ground, facing towards the headstone in silent contemplation.

"I miss you my dear Tinana and am torn by the promise I made you to look after Tamana and the love I have for a man who lives far away. Tamana is totally supportive and wants me to go, what do you reckon?"

With that a coconut fell from the tree and landed with a thud on the ground beside her. Mere's heart and mind raced. *"It is a sign from my Tinana. Jacob Bryant, watch out I am coming to Sydney."*

*

After having made the decision to take the position in Sydney, Mere contacted Mike Starke, Chairman at Mutilin Pharma. Mere asked for Mike's indulgence to be able to assist her Tamana during the up-and-coming Fiji elections, while all the paperwork for her Australian working visa was being processed. During the election campaign Mere would complete her employment contract and Australian immigration formalities. She asked Mike to keep it a secret that she had accepted the position, as she wanted to keep her arrival in Sydney a surprise for Jacob. With Mike's OK, it was full speed ahead for the elections.

Not unsurprisingly, an extremely popular Joeli Koroi on the back of the success with the Tagimoucia research, was readily elected to parliament. With the retirement of the previous Prime Minister, Filipe Matai had led the government to victory with a safe majority. Although, he was new to parliament, Joeli was appointed as the Minister for Health. Given his inexperience in politics, Joeli had initially declined Filipe's offer of the ministerial role, however, with Filipe's guarantee of support to aid him in settling into the role, he accepted.

With her visa approved and the election out of the way, it was time for Mere to bid farewell to the land of her birth. There was a series of a never-ending dinners and speeches, all wishing Mere success in her new life and opportunity. Hosts included the Dr Prasad, Head of School at the Fiji School of Medicine, the Prime Minister, Filipe Matai, and her old school friends. Each function contributed to the building up of the conflict which churned within Mere. This was a gigantic step, leaving behind everything and everyone she knew and loved in Fiji, for a life in a city of over four million people, to be with the man she loved.

There were, of course, those seeds of doubt. "*Could I survive in the corporate world? Was I good enough for the job? Will I achieve success with the project and deliver for the people of Fiji? Will Jacob still love me? Will I be homesick?*"

For their final night together, Joeli took Mere to Tomasi's Seafood Restaurant for a farewell dinner. Neither of them felt very hungry but they forced themselves to get through a couple of courses to draw out the night. They had a bowl of thick clam chowder for a starter. For the main, they both had the seared tuna with a side salad. Mere chose a bottle of Pinot Grigio which they sipped, but did not finish, leaving just under a half bottle on the table. It was of a sad affair, rather than a celebration for the close-knit family unit. They were coming to the reality that they would finally be separated, after all the years together as a family and more recently as working colleagues.

They both headed to bed as soon as they got home, neither of them wanting to become teary-eyed and sad. Mere tossed and turned in bed, thinking about what lay ahead for her. Exhausted, she eventually fell asleep with the aid of a book. Joeli woke in the early hours and saw the light coming from under Mere's door. He quietly opened her door and removed the book resting on Mere's chest and was about to turn off bedside lamp when he noticed the dried tears on her cheeks.

"My princess is just like the princess in the legend of the Tagimoucia, crying in her sleep," lamented Joeli. "I will miss her."

Joeli was up early and knocked on Mere's door to get her up and ready for the long drive from Suva to Nadi Airport. Just after breakfast the phone rang.

"Bula Joeli. Its Jacob."

Joeli put his hand of the mouthpiece, mouthing the word *Jacob* to Mere. Mere put her index finger to her lips and shook her head.

"I was wondering if Mere was around," asked a rather forlorn Jacob. "I'd like to speak with her, to see if she had made a decision about taking the job here in Sydney as yet."

"So sorry Jacob. She is not back from the island as yet." Joeli replied, trying to sound convincing under the glare of Mere. "The next boat is due back early next week. I will tell her you called."

"Thanks, Joeli. Send her my best wishes and I look forward to speaking with her soon," Jacob declared with obvious sincerity.

"I am sure she will be speaking with you very soon," smiled Joeli, taking a punch in the arm from Mere.

As she stepped into the car for the drive to Nadi Airport, she turned and saw Mereoni standing on the steps with her husband Malakai. Tears were streaming down their faces. They had known her since she was a little girl. Then she spied Bula and Vatu in the driveway, their tails wagging, uncertain as to what was going on. With all this, the floodgates opened, with Mere leaning forward in her seat and sobbing with her face buried in her hands.

Mere put her arm onto her Tamana's arm, indicating for him to pause their departure. She leapt out of the front seat of the car, wiping the tears from her eyes. She rushed up the stairs to Malakai and Mereoni giving them a final hug. "I promise I will be back regularly to visit. Look after Tamana for me and no second helpings, especially dessert."

With a final pat of Bula and Vatu and a wave to Mereoni and Malakai, they were on their way to Nadi. It was a fairly quiet drive, with just a little bit of polite conversation about what she would do when she got to Sydney. Mainly, they just looked out the window and watched the world go by.

"*I hope Dad will be alright without me.*"

As if reading her mind, Joeli broke the silence, "I will be fine. I have so much to learn about functioning as a Minister in the Government to keep me more than busy. Hopefully, the role will get me a few trips to Australia to visit you and you should be back here periodically for your research work. Sydney is only four flying hours away."

They made good time to Nadi, so after check-in, at the business class counter, a first time for Mere, they had time for a coffee and something to eat in the airport café. Joeli did not say no to some lamb curry and rice, to provide him with some fuel for the solo return journey to Suva.

Joeli had been very strong, trying not to cry, but this was his baby, so when it came time for her to go, the tears flowed. "I did so not want to cry and be strong for you," sobbed Joeli, "but I look forward to seeing you soon. Safe journey. My best regards to Jacob."

Fighting back her tears, yet again, Mere gathered her hand luggage in her left hand and standing on tiptoes, wrapped her right arm around her Tamana's neck. She pulled him towards her, giving him a big kiss on the cheek, "Tamana, I better go. Promise I will call you once I get to Sydney, to let you know I arrived safe and sound." With that Mere entered the security zone and was gone, the automatic doors closing behind them.

"*I can't look back,*" she thought determinedly as she entered the departure zone. "*If I do, I might not be able to go.*"

"Another glass of white wine please and some cashews thanks," Mere lapped up being in business class. Raising and lowering her flat-bed seat. Channel surfing on the in-flight entertainment and enjoying a full meal of the prawn and salad starter, followed by the curried chicken and rice main course. She finished off with dessert of a rich chocolate mousse and the cheeseboard, complimented with a glass of port.

"This is the life for me."

After an exciting four hours and just managing to finish watching a movie, they were on the final approach to Sydney Airport. The flight path took the aircraft over the Northern Suburbs. Mere was seated on the left-hand side which enabled her to get a scenic view of Sydney while landing. She thought she recognised landmarks Jacob had described to her, when talking about Sydney. The Chatswood Shopping precinct, North Sydney Business District and then magnificent views of the Sydney Harbour Bridge and the Opera House. A picture postcard day to arrive in Sydney with beautiful cloudless blue skies.

"The first day of the rest of my life."

With Mere's visa checked and stamped, she did not have to wait long for her priority checked luggage to arrive and was soon exiting the customs arrival hall. Mere was told she would be greeted by a well-dressed man, wearing a grey peaked cap, holding a small electronic signboard with her name in bold letters – Dr Mere Koroi.

"My own driver! Will wonders never cease. I am loving this new corporate life."

"Doctor Mere Koroi?" I am Chris Dimotsos, your driver this afternoon," he introduced himself with a smile. "I will be taking you to your hotel in the City. Follow me to the car please." With that he started to move off, taking her suitcase laden trolley from her hands.

Chris opened the rear door of the Mercedes for Mere and closed it gently behind her. She fastened her seatbelt and squeezed the plush, leather upholstery. With the car loaded they were soon underway to the Intercontinental Hotel in

Sydney's CBD. "Sorry, but I do not have any Australian money and I could surely do with a drink of water after all the wine on the flight. Is it ok if I open the bottle of water tucked into back of the seat in front of me?"

"The water is complimentary Dr Koroi. Help yourself."

"*How dumb am I. Of course, it is complimentary!*"

"Thanks Chris," Mere warmly replied.

The car pulled up in front of the steps leading up to the lobby of the Intercontinental Hotel. Mere was quickly getting used to this door opening routine and waited for Chris to come around from the driver's side to open the door for her. She gave him a big smile and a nod in acknowledgement.

"I will handle your luggage with the bellboy, so you go inside and check-in," Chris tipped his cap to Mere.

Mere confidently stepped up to the counter at the Intercontinental.

"Mere Koroi, checking in." She had gained in confidence with the royal treatment she was enjoying.

"Ah, yes. We have you for two nights, with all expenses covered by Mutilin Pharma," the front desk manager's eyes riveted to the computer screen. "Here is your key card to Suite 1057, on the tenth floor. Your luggage will be up shortly and the elevators are there to the left. Have a nice stay."

Mere stepped out of the elevator, her eyes picking up the sign indicating her room was to the left. She seemed to walk forever, finally arriving at the door to 1057, right at the end of the corridor. She fumbled a little trying to insert the key card but eventually with a click and a flash of green light she pushed open the door.

Her jaw dropped as she took in the view pouring in through the opened, floor to ceiling-curtains. There was the famous Harbour Bridge, which she had just flown over, only an hour ago. She strode over to the window taking it all in. A huge cruise ship was docked harbourside, ferries were rushing all over the water and people everywhere, strolling around the waterfront, enjoying the afternoon sunshine.

"*How magnificent. I know I will enjoy it here with Jacob.*"

A knock at the door forced her to break away from the view. The bell boy had her two suitcases on a trolley. He placed them on the luggage rack located near the room's door. He seemed to linger, asking if everything was ok, or whether she needed him to show her how to use any of the controls.

"No thanks, I can hopefully sort it out."

"Fine," the bellboy curtly added, then turned and exited the room, the heavy door softly locking behind him.

"*You idiot he was probably looking for a tip,*" she laughed and threw herself onto the biggest bed she had ever seen.

Mere went into the bathroom and turned on the light. The shower cubicle was huge, complete with a tray of all sorts of goodies. Shampoo, conditioner, skin cream ,shower gel and even cotton buds. There was also a magnificent bath which included spray jets and bath salts.

"*That bath will definitely get a workout.*"

There was a double wash basin, home to a hairdryer and make-up mirror. Everything sparkled, enhanced by the massive pieces of chrome tapware. Next to the toilet bowl was one of those fancy French things.

"What is it? I know, a bidet. Have to give that a go as well," she giggled, while fondling the controls.

The long day was starting to catch up with her so Mere opted for some in-room dining. A waiter brought in her meal tray, consisting of a chicken burger with fries and a fresh fruit platter to finish.

"Just leave the tray outside the door when you are finished Ma'am."

After finishing her meal, she placed the tray outside her door as instructed and then sat up in bed, propped up by the plump pillows, settling in to watch the massive wall-mounted television. It took some time to figure out the operation of the remote and with so many channels she could not decide on what to watch.

In the end, Mere turned off the television and place the remote on her bedside table.

"*Better get some sleep. Tomorrow is going to be a big day. I can hardly wait to see the look on Jacob's face.*"

＊

Mere was not particularly hungry with all the excitement of heading off to the office and seeing Jacob but forced herself to have some tea and toast with orange marmalade. On the way out of the hotel, the concierge provided Mere with a map on which he marked the building which housed the Mutilin Pharma offices. It was a relatively short distance to walk to the offices from the hotel and would take around 20 minutes. Mere thought it would be good to get the lay of the land and decided to walk to the office, using the map rather than getting a taxi. The Criterion Building was located in Millers Point on the opposite side of Circular Quay to the hotel. After obeying all the *WALK* signs at the intersections, unlike her now fellow residents, she made her way to the entrance of the office block and entered the foyer.

As a building it was older and smaller than those nearby majestic towers that glistened over Circular Quay. Directly opposite the entrance was a staircase, the steps covered in well-worn, red linoleum with corrugated, non-slip metal tips affixed to the lip of each step. A chipped white painted; metallic handrail lined the stairwell. The elevator shaft was located on the right. On the wall directly opposite the elevator shaft was an office directory. Mutilin Pharma was located on the fifth floor.

Mere walked up to the two elevator doors and pressed the "U" button on the central control pad. With a rattle the elevator opened, and she stepped inside the gloomy elevator. The elevator door seemed to take forever to close, but eventually they were underway. With a jolting stop, the door opened, and she stepped out in front of a door marked Mutilin Pharma. An arrow pointed to the intercom, which she pressed.

"Mere Koroi here. I am a new employee starting today. I would like to surprise Jacob Bryant, so please don't tell him I have arrived."

"Come in, Mere. Mr Starke said to expect you this morning."

The door buzzed and she entered the foyer. The offices were in contrast to the entrance to the building. The office had obviously been renovated very recently. Dead ahead the receptionist sat behind a white plastic topped desk, complete with a small desktop switchboard and computer terminal. To the right of the desk there was a door marked STAFF ONLY and on the left a comfortable three-seater sofa covered in a light grey fabric, with chrome legs. There was a side table, either side of the sofa, covered in magazines and newspapers.

Mere stepped towards the reception desk, conscious of her low heels clinking on the light, polished timber floor.

"Welcome Mere, I'm Rebecca, the receptionist," Rebecca stood to welcome Mere. "Just sign in for now and no doubt you will have a company pass issued during the day by human resources."

"Thanks Rebecca. It is good to be here."

"What's this about Jacob Bryant?" Rebecca asked conspiratorially.

Mere just smiled at Rebecca.

The telephone in Jacob's office rang. It was the receptionist telling him that there was someone at reception who wanted to see him but would not give their name. They did say it was important. Curious Jacob got up from his desk and he headed towards reception. He pushed the exit button of the security door and stepped into the office foyer.

He could not believe his eyes, there was his beloved Mere. He rushed towards her, sweeping her off her feet. "Mere, Mere," tears of joy starting to roll down his cheeks, matching those from Mere.

"Oh, sorry Rebecca, this is Mere. She's one of our new employees," Jacob was embarrassed, having forgotten where he was.

"I might have guessed," Rebecca extending a hand in welcome. "Welcome Mere."

"I wish he had welcomed me to the company like that."

CHAPTER 29

Jacob and Mere took advantage of the second night available to Mere at the Intercontinental Hotel, with Mere suggesting Jacob come for dinner after they finished work for the day. Months of anticipation, tension, lust, and desire had been building in both their bodies and they both knew that on this night, their love would finally be consummated. There also needed to be some discussion between them about where Mere would stay in Sydney.

They raced through dinner in the hotel's restaurant, both going for the grilled fish with a side green salad and a shared bowl of fries, with only sparkling water to drink. On getting back to Mere's suite, they ordered a bottle of champagne to be delivered by room service. Mere smiled, noting that Jacob tipped the waiter. Jacob popped the cork and removing their shoes they settled, propped up on pillows at the bed head and clinked their glasses, "Cheers. To the future," they toasted.

"I think I will slip into something a little more comfortable," Mere sprang off the bed and into the bathroom.

She emerged in full length, shimmering, crimson silk pyjamas. Jacob's heart fluttered. He stood, placing down his glass of champagne, his body was raging with desire. He could wait no longer and pulled Mere towards him and their lips met. Mere groaned with desire, as their lips met again and again. They started to explore each other's body with the intensity rising and began to peel off each other's clothing, falling naked onto the bed. Jacob reached for the switch and turned off the light. Their bodies screamed to become united. Jacob had waited a long time for this moment and resisted the urge to immediately drive himself into Mere, despite her urging, almost begging him. He wanted to draw out this special first time together for as long as possible. They continued to hungrily kiss and gently caress each other until they could wait no longer, ready to explode.

Fully spent they collapsed, with Jacob wrapping his arms around Mere, before whispering into her ear, "Mere, I love you."

The night of bliss continued, until their bodies could take no more. They both finally fell into a deep sleep.

In the early hours Jacob woke with the need for some water and a visit to the bathroom. He looked at Mere in the dim light and could see tears on her cheeks. It was though she was crying in her sleep. He gently wiped the tears the away and briefly thought of the Tagimoucia legend before drifting back to sleep.

Over breakfast in their room, snuggly sitting in their fluffy white robes and enjoying the view in the early morning sun, Jacob broached the subject as to where Mere was to stay, now she was in Sydney.

"The logical place for you to stay is with me at my apartment in Mona Vale Beach," Jacob suggested. "It is right on the ocean and will at least be reminiscent of Fiji for you. Each morning with the rising sun, you will be looking back over the sea towards Fiji and can think of your Tamana."

"Sounds good to me," beamed Mere, squeezing Jacob's hand.

"I will arrange for my Mum to pick us up at the office this afternoon and take us home," advised Jacob. "She is desperate to meet you."

Sipping their coffee, Mere excitedly quizzed Jacob about all the landmarks she could see out the window. Jacob looked at his watch, "Come on Mere, we better get moving. We don't want to be late for work and you need to pack and check out," Jacob stood and headed towards the bathroom. "Would you like to join me?" A flying cushion answered the question.

While Jacob was in the bathroom Mere opened her bag and reached for her strip of low dose, contraceptive tablets. In anticipation of joining Jacob, the love of her life in Sydney, Mere knew it was time to commence contraception.

However, in the excitement of packing up and leaving Fiji, she realised she had missed the doses for the last two days. "*I should be ok*," she thought.

*

Jacob's Mum came into the office, to pick up Jacob and Mere, along with Mere's luggage. Mere sat in front, with Jacob in the back seat. Knowing his Mum and the way she went about things, Jacob could sense there was something she desperately wanted to say, as they chugged through the heavy afternoon peak hour traffic. She had given the tell-tale signs of a couple of nervous coughs, followed by a series of quick looks at Jacob, then turning away, with her bottom lip trembling.

Jacob could contain himself no longer. "Come on, out with-it Mum. What have you got on your mind?"

After another little cough, she did not hold back, "Jacob I know you love your apartment by the beach, and I have done my best to help you keep it clean and tidy over the years."

"Mum I know there is a but coming," Jacob leaned forward to squeeze Mere's shoulder.

"Well, smarty pants. Your place is a man-cave." She did not hold back. "You have surfboards everywhere. Basic, ancient furniture. Stuff I gave you when I was going to throw it out, years ago. Mere has come all the way from Fiji to be with you. Your place is definitely not suitable for Mere and if I were you Mere, I would refuse to live there."

Jacob looked suitably embarrassed, "I guess you're right Mum, we can get it all done up over-time."

"Over-time, you are kidding," Mum lectured Jacob. "I have spoken with your Dad and we have set up the spare room for you both. You can stay there with us until your place is fit for habitation."

"Very funny, fit for habitation," Jacob snorted. "What do you mean?"

"We will drop in on the way home, to show Mere," instructed Jacob's Mum.

Mere took a look at the apartment and Jacob could sense that despite the beautiful view of the ocean, she concurred with his Mum's view of the residence. It definitely needed a feminine touch and a complete refit, and those surfboards would have to go to the storage unit in the underground carpark. He knew when he was beaten and it would be to his parent's place, until the works were completed. The new salary package with Mutilin would soon be put to good use in renovating the apartment. A relieved Mum headed off with the happy couple, to the family home in Manly.

It was a nice convenient location for Jacob and Mere to stay with his parents at their Manly home, during the works on the apartment. It was going to take a couple of months to bring Jacob's place into the modern world. A new kitchen with modern appliances. A new bathroom with up-to-date plumbing fittings and painted throughout, with all new furniture. Jacob knew he would not be surfing on weekends for a while. Life would revolve around being dragged through every furniture shop on Sydney's Northern Beaches.

On the positive side of living with his folks, their Manly location was ideal for commuting into the office in the city. Their place was only a 10-minute walk to the ferry terminal at Manly Wharf, from where they would make the daily 35-minute commute by ferry into the city.

With her Fijian heritage, Mere loved being on the water each day. What a way to get to work. A takeaway cappuccino from the coffee shop on the wharf and sit back with the man you love and take in the view. Jacob would spend time pointing out the major points of interest, to familiarise Mere with her new home.

Mere loved it when the ferry started to pitch and roll as it came out from the shelter of Manly Bay and became exposed to the Pacific Ocean swells, surging through the mouth of Sydney Harbour. Spray would cascade from the bow of the ferry as the throbbing diesel engines enabled the ferry to plough its way through the rolling sea, until finally reaching the calmer waters of the inner harbour. She liked an upper deck seat to get a better view of the magnificent Harbour and the surrounds. Jacob's stomach could not handle too much pitching and rolling on the upper deck, so occasionally he would leave her and head on down below, to settle his stomach on those stormy days.

Jacob would point out the highlights of the Sydney city. The entrance to

Middle Harbour, the morning sun glittering off the sands of Balmoral Beach and Taronga Park Zoo on the North Shore. Mere was amazed at the amount of natural bushland that hugged the shoreline, so close to the centre of such a busy city. To the south Jacob identified the busy and exclusive eastern suburbs of Sydney such as Vaucluse and Double Bay. On occasions there was also the excitement of the take-off and landing of the water planes in Rose Bay. She never stopped marvelling at how lucky the Sydneyites were to have such a beautiful harbour, something they seemed to take for granted, in their rush to get to and from work every day. Fixated on mobile phone screens they were oblivious to the magnificent scenery.

*

Once the ferry docked, it was about a casual 20-minute walk from the Circular Quay ferry terminal to the Criterion building and their offices located in Millers Point, right underneath the southern pylon of the Sydney Harbour Bridge. Behind the STAFF ONLY door, it was an open plan style office, apart from the enclosed offices for the senior management located around the fringes with their windows taking in views of the Harbour – Mike Starke Chairman, Scott Thomas Chief Financial Officer and Jacob, Head of New Product Development. There was one vacant office, held in reserve for the soon to be appointed CEO.

It did not take it long for the office gossip column to have it known that Jacob and Mere were an item. As such, Mere and Jacob agreed to have as large a separation from each other as possible during working hours. Mere's desk was located close to the entry from the reception area and Jacob's office was at the far end of the floor space.

Mere's primary function as a Research Scientist was to co-ordinate with the company's laboratory facilities, adjacent to Macquarie University, at Macquarie Park, North of Sydney. Their object was to continue to work on the analysis and purification of the active ingredient from the Tagimoucia. She would then liaise with Jacob's team on the development of the manufacturing process.

Occasionally Mere and Jacob would have coffee together in a nearby coffee shop, but more often it was a case with them being so busy, that their coffee got cold sitting on the desk. However, they made a habit of making time to step out for lunch together and to get out of the office. Today they were going to head down towards a café situated on the promenade leading out to the Opera House. They heard Giuseppe's Café made good coffee and had a good range of food on the menu.

As they were walking along the waterfront a handbill was thrust into Jacob's hand.

"*New gym now open. 50% discount first month. Spectacular harbour views while you work out.*"

"What do you reckon about this gym, Mere?" Jacob asked, as he handed it to her.

"Uh, what?" Mere more interested in the view. "What did you say?"

"A new gym has opened here in the city. Work out with harbour views at Gym With A View."

"Where do we sign up?" Mere's interest evident. "With you not surfing and me eating your Mum's cooking, we need to do something. Let's go and check it out after we have had something to eat."

"Table for two?" asked the attractive blond waitress at Giuseppe's.

"Yes please," replied Jacob, his eyes drawn to her as she led them to their table.

"Ow," cried Jacob as he felt Mere's fist strike his arm. "What was that for?"

"I saw you ogling her backside," smiled Mere.

"I was only window shopping," replied Jacob as he rubbed his arm.

Over their ham and salad sandwiches they discussed it some more detail. "We can work out during the week and I will teach you to surf on the weekend." More of a question than statement from Jacob. Mere seemingly ignored him.

Mere took Jacob's hand as they set off to see the gym after eating their lunch, "Count me in on the gym, but I don't know if you will have time for surfing on the weekend. There will be so much to do around the apartment." This was greeted by a stony silence from Jacob.

*

Adrian was chatting to the receptionist about some client bookings when the elevator door pinged open. His jaw dropped and he could not believe his eyes. Approaching the reception desk, looking at a handbill, was his nightmare from Taveuni, Mere Koroi and Jacob Bryant. Memories of the confrontation by the lake in Fiji flashed into his mind. It was too late to find a place to hide.

Looking up from his handbill, Jacob stopped, gob-smacked, "I can't believe it. It's him."

Mere looked up at Jacob and followed his hand which pointed towards the gym's reception desk. She could not believe her eyes. "The Anux guy from Taveuni. How could I ever forget Adrian Nicholls?"

Adrian stepped out from behind the reception desk and approached Mere and Jacob. "If you give me a chance, I will explain everything," as he guided Mere and a fuming Jacob towards his office. He pointed to seats positioned at a small round table located in the corner of his office and closed the door as they sat down. He certainly did not want Gavin Mills listening in on the potentially hostile conversation.

"This better be good. I was not very happy the last time we met. I never expected to see you ever again," indicated an irritated Jacob.

Adrian paused, "Well, I had not expected to see either of you again. I have started a whole new life and certainly have regrets about decisions I made in my former corporate life."

Jacob's aggression was starting to subside, and he started to relax in his chair. He was very keen to learn about what Adrian Nicholls was doing in Sydney.

Taking a deep breath, Adrian then launched into his story. He described how he believed he had been made the fall guy for what had happened in Fiji and had been cast aside by his then boss and Anux. Life in the pharmaceutical industry had come to end, as no one in the industry would touch him ever again, he was damaged goods, so he needed a new way forward in his life.

Back home staying with his Mum in the western suburbs, he described how he was working out at the local gym to keep up his fitness. A poster promoting a certificate in personal training at the Technical College caught his eye and he was accepted into the course. With the certificate completed Adrian described how he saw the potential of making big money in personal training, with it being such a growth industry.

Seeing interest in those on the other side of the desk, Adrian continued, "My boss here at the gym, Gavin Mills, is very entrepreneurial and is looking to expand the concept around the major cities in Australia. With my qualifications from the Macquarie Business School, I made a proposal to him to establish a franchise in Melbourne. Currently I am on trial with Gavin and if things work out between us, Melbourne here I come, with the opportunity to make a new start in life."

Adrian had omitted to make any mention of his plan to wreak revenge on the company that had ended his career, only a matter of days away with the publication in Saturday's Financial Express.

"That is some tale," an impressed sounding Jacob noted. "You certainly have come a long way from that incident in Fiji and I am sure I can speak on behalf of Mere in wishing you well. We had come up here to sign up to your gym."

There was relief from Adrian with his visitors having calmed down. They appeared to have forgiven him for his past indiscretion and were supportive of his proposed new venture in Melbourne.

"You now know what I have been up to. What have you guys been up to? Something going on with you guys?" a smiling Adrian cheekily asked.

Jacob then launched into his tale of how he and Mere were now employed by a company called Mutilin Pharma, "Our offices are located nearby to here in the Criterion building in Millers Point. The company has come to arrangement with the Fijian Government for the commercial rights to any medicines developed from the Tagimoucia plant. Mere has been appointed as a research scientist working on the sourcing and purification of the extracts from the samples. I am in charge of the development of a manufacturing process for the active ingredient."

"Sounds an amazing opportunity," congratulated Adrian. "I know a guy who was trying to do something similar," he laughed, noting a momentary blushing of Jacob's cheeks. After a slight hesitation he added, "out of interest, what did you mean by purification of the extracts?"

"In the second study in human volunteers we confirmed that the extract from the red flowers of the Tagimoucia, had significant hallucinogenic side-effects. This distracted from the greatly beneficial non-opioid, non-addictive pain-relieving capabilities," Jacob enthusiastically launched into answering the question. "At Mutilin, Mere and I will be working on developing a process to manufacture the active chemical responsible for the analgesic effect, removing the unwanted side-effect of hallucinations."

"Fascinating and all the best for a successful outcome," an earnest looking Adrian replied. "Since our brief encounter in Fiji, I now understand that you have a passion for the responsible use of medicines around the world after appropriate clinical trialling. To help you in that regard, I believe you will see something coming out in the media that you will find interesting and useful. It may repay you for some of the aggravation I caused you and Mere."

"Tell me more, " Jacob moved forward in his chair, his eyes riveted on to Adrian.

"All will be revealed in good time," replied Adrian. "I'll keep you posted."

"Oh, don't forget to fill in your membership applications with reception on the way out. For you both as new members, I will extend the 50% discount for your first three month's membership to six months," said the entrepreneur coming out in Adrian. Mere and Jacob closed the door behind them, leaving Adrian with his thoughts.

Adrian was roused from his thoughts as his phone rang. It was Karen. Hopefully, there was positive news in regard to the publication of the Anux article.

"Good news Adrian. The editor and legal counsel have approved publication of the article," a joyful Karen announced. "I have bought a couple of steaks so reckon you should come around to my place tonight celebrate."

"What time?" a happy Adrian asked, rubbing his hands together with glee.

"See you at eight. That should give you time to freshen up after your last client," proposed Karen.

"Done. Look forward to seeing you then Karen."

CHAPTER 30

Karen greeted Adrian at the door to her apartment with a warm kiss. She looked the homeliest Adrian could ever remember, complete with a floral apron sitting over a simple white blouse, blue jeans, and bare feet. Whatever she wore she always looked attractive and he immediately had his pulse racing, after his experience with her up in the Blue Mountains last weekend. He heard the steaks sizzling in the frying pan as he slipped off his shoes to make himself at home.

Apart from the light above the stove, the apartment's lighting was subdued, enhancing the flickering from the red candle on the dining table. The table was set with bamboo placemats, on which was placed a silver fork and large wooden-handled steak knife. There was a centre piece of small white flowers, a bowl of green salad from which protruded bamboo serving implements. Wholemeal bread rolls sat on the side plates, with no butter.

"Here open the wine." Karen passed Adrian the bottle of red wine and corkscrew.

Adrian looked at the label, "Barossa Valley Shiraz 2010. Looks particularly good."

"It better be at the price," smiled Karen. "Nothing but the best for us to celebrate."

Adrian stood next to Karen at the stove where she was busy attending to the steaks. He opened the wine with a satisfying pop as the cork was extracted from the neck of the bottle and poured the wine, passing Karen a glass.

"Cheers Karen," Adrian said, taking a sip of his wine. He drew Karen towards him, giving her a passionate kiss.

"Wait a minute Romeo. I am trying to cook here," Karen playfully slapped him. "How do you like your steak?"

"Medium is good for me, thanks."

Jacob sat down and then Karen served up the plates of porterhouse steak and green salad, dressed with freshly squeezed lemon juice and a sprinkle of olive oil. They quietly sipped away at their wine when Karen broke the silence, "I have had some positive feedback from the TV 6 network about me joining the network for their new evening business news program, *News Night*. I am sure after the article is published in Saturday's edition and with me starring on the front page, it will be television here we come!"

"That's great news, for you Karen," congratulated Adrian. "I also should hear some news soon from Gavin Mills in regard to my idea to start a franchise of the gym in Melbourne. My trial period will be up soon, and we appear to be getting on pretty well with each other. I'll make time with him next week to discuss the business plan I left with him to review."

Karen did not respond. She finished her wine then stood, blowing out the candle, before taking Adrian's hand and leading him to the bedroom. "Let's forget about life and careers and just enjoy the night together."

After a night of unbridled passion, an exhausted Adrian quietly rose with the glow from the early morning sunshine, peaking through the crack in her curtains. He showered and prepared to head off to the gym for his first client of the day. Feeling conflicted and not wanting to disturb Karen, he left a note on the bedside table.

"The course for the rest of our lives is being set. With you in Sydney and me heading to Melbourne, I just can't see a future for us. I have loved the time we have spent together and all I can say is that I wish you all the best for your future happiness. Yours Adrian xxx"

Karen was woken from a deep sleep with the clunk from the closure of the apartment's door. She felt across the bed and knew Adrian was gone. Turning over she saw the note on her bedside table. A tear rolled down

Karen's cheek as she read Adrian's note.

"Will I regret my decision about pursuing my career above all else? Adrian is the first man I have ever really felt any passion with, or dare I say even love."

*

It was Saturday morning and with no mention of the bedside note, an excited Karen was on the phone to Adrian, "The headlines of the front-page article in the Financial Express reads, *Global Pharmaceutical Giant Cover Up Scandal.*"

"Front-page. Fantastic." Adrian sounded pleased. "I like the headline. That should make a few executives in New York squirm when it makes the news there. They will be worried about their bonuses for sure."

Karen continued, "the article goes into detail on how the paper had been provided with details in regard to the secret goings-on, within the giant global pharmaceutical company Anux. Highlighted was the occurrence of adverse events and the development of addiction with treatments in Southern Africa, with the use of the company's recently launched opioid analgesic AnuxuDine."

"Excellent reporting Ms Nesbitt." Adrian was pleased with what was reported. "No doubt the rest of the global media will be quick to pick up on it and it will be job done on Anux. I would also imagine it will not be so good news for Mr Sinclair."

"Sorry, got to go. My other line is ringing," Karen finished up the call. "I have attracted plenty of global interest in the story and will be interviewed by CNN shortly."

"Congratulations," Adrian added but the call was quickly terminated by Karen.

The weekend media was abuzz with the news. In a television interview, Dr Jacob Bryant, formerly of the Pharmacy Department at Sydney University, re-iterated his views that the Therapeutic Goods Administration (TGA) in Australia had been too hasty in approving the widespread prescribing of AnuxuDine in Australia. He was pleased to note that the TGA, given recent developments concerning Anux Pharmaceuticals in the media, were currently reviewing the approval of the usage of the product in Australia. It was likely further testing would be required before General Practitioners would be able to resume prescribing of the product.

The fallout from the Financial Express article was expected to be immediate and catastrophic for Anux Pharmaceuticals. With the opening of the Monday session of the New York Stock Exchange, market analysts predicted the share price could plummet by as much as 25%, along with international condemnation of their actions by the various regulatory authorities.

Spokespeople from the various leading government agencies around the world, were outspoken, condemning the cover up by Anux of vital patient related information. A review of current approvals of AnuxuDine was being called for. Delays of approvals were expected wherever the product was currently under evaluation. This in particular, affected the review by the USA's, Food and Drug Administration (FDA), the regulatory authority of the world's largest pharmaceutical market.

An Anux spokesperson had come out condemning the actions of a rogue employee who had covered up this vital information and who had already been dismissed. The spokesperson further added that Anux' prime concern was the welfare of all its patients and a full review of the data relating to AnuxuDine would be undertaken immediately by company scientists.

*

Newton's PA was on his intercom, "Mr Sinclair, Mr Richards wants to see you in his office immediately."

Nervously Newton sat outside the CEO's office awaiting the call to be summoned into his office. He tried to remain calm but knew this meeting could not be good with the outcry in the media about Anux. They wanted someone's head and Newton had the feeling it was going to be his.

"You can go in now Mr Sinclair," the PA announced.

"Take a seat Newton," Mr Richards pointed to the seat opposite his massive desk. "I presume you have seen the news."

"Unfortunately, yes sir. It is terrible. I don't know how they could have possibly got that information," noted Newton, hiding the tremble in his hands.

"There are not too many who would have had access to the information, and I am led to believe you were one of them," Mr Richards advised sternly, maintaining eye contact with Newton.

Newton knew he could not admit to having forwarded the information to Adrian Nicholls. It must have been him who was the unnamed source, but that would be hard to prove, without him admitting to being the likely source of the material.

"I have a number of calls with share brokers today as well as the media to try and repair the damage," advised Mr Richards. "You also need to get on with minimising the damage at a sales and marketing level. We cannot afford any impact with the Food and Drug Administration, given the pending launch here in the USA. Maybe it would be prudent if you started looking elsewhere to continue your career."

No sooner had Newton returned to his office and was contemplating a snort of Columbian Heaven to ease his shattered nerves, when his PA announced the Food and Drug Administration on the line.

"Oh no. That was quick. You better put them through," he said to his PA.

"Newton Sinclair speaking."

"Hi Newton. Scott Johnson from the FDA," Scott got straight to the point. "Following the story in today's media we have some serious concerns around the pending approval of AnuxuDine here in the US."

After finishing the call from the FDA, Newton knew his days with Anux were numbered. It was time to take the initiative and think about getting out while he still held a senior position and before his career was in tatters. He kept the drawer containing the Columbian Heaven locked and over a sandwich at his desk, started to look online at advertised senior positions with various pharmaceutical companies. His eye was immediately drawn to a position advertised in Australia.

"Mutilin Pharma based in Sydney, Australia', is looking for a CEO with international experience to oversee the development of their exciting new products and take them to the world. Experience at a senior level with a multinational pharmaceutical company and in particular with analgesic products would be

highly regarded. An appropriate remuneration package and relocation allowance for a successful overseas candidate is negotiable."

*

Newton's online interview with Mike Starke and the Mutilin board of directors went very well. He was able to deflect questions related to the recent media articles about Anux, by indicating a rogue employee had been dismissed over the actions reported. In addition, he received a glowing reference from the Anux CEO, Mr Richards, who was no doubt pleased to assist Newton's departure from the company. Newton's experience in the launch of AnuxuDine in a number of markets, was a big tick. The clincher came when Newton was able espouse his knowledge of the Tagimoucia and the interest shown by Anux in acquiring the rights. The right man in the right place at the right time.

The local candidates interviewed for the position could not match Newton's level of international experience. The board of directors was keen to offer him the position of CEO, subject to a satisfactory face to face interview in Sydney. Newton also stipulated he would like to bring his wife Lisabeth with him to ensure she was 100% happy with making such a big move away from family and friends. He knew he could not take the position if Lisabeth was not happy with what she saw in the way of lifestyle living far away from family and friends in Sydney. However, Newton having been sent some links to potential accommodation options arranged by the Mutilin Human Resources department, knew she would be more than happy with the apartment he had in mind. It would be the envy of all her friends. She would most likely be inundated with requests from visitors to come over from the US.

Once Newton explained the reality of the situation with Anux and what was soon likely to follow in the media if they remained in the USA, he had Lisabeth's full support for a fact-finding trip Down Under. She was keen to check out what life might be like in Sydney, a place she had often dreamed about as a holiday destination. Cuddling a koala was high on the list. Lisabeth was also very keen to see the apartment on Sydney Harbour that Newton seemed so excited about.

The apartment was located right on Sydney's Circular Quay, having spectacular views of Sydney Harbour, including the Sydney Harbour Bridge and the Opera House. The apartment block was located on the eastern end of the Quay, on the 10th floor, with views back towards the CBD and the cruise ship terminal. Underneath the apartment block was a maze of restaurants, cafes and even a cinema. It was a short walk to the ferry terminal, enabling one to travel all around the city, without the need for a car to drive on the wrong side of the road!

It came fully furnished, really the only thing to buy was the bedding and towels. There were two spacious bedrooms complete with king-sized beds, massive built-in robes, and each room with an ensuite. A spacious kitchen came with a stone, island bench top, plus breakfast bar. The kitchen served a ten-place, formal thick timbered dining table. The lounge area with two huge, cream fabric, four-seater couches, looked out onto the wide balcony , occupied by a six-seater teak outdoor furniture set and gas barbeque. A 75-inch television was wall-mounted, the dark screen standing out against the neutral tones of the wall paint.

"Look Beth, there is the Queen Victoria cruise ship, just about to dock," pointed Newton as he headed to the balcony. "Amazing and so huge. I would love us to take a cruise one day."

"It comes as is." The real estate agent sensed a deal was likely, given the smiles on Newton's and Lisabeth's faces.

Lisabeth videoed a walk-through of the apartment and the stunning view from the balcony on her smartphone. ""Wait till the family see this on Facebook and Instagram. When do we move in Newton, honey?"

The meeting in the afternoon with the Mutilin Pharma board of directors went very well for Newton and they were prepared to offer him the position on the spot. The salary was not as high as Newton would have liked, given the comparison with his salary in the US. However, with the magnificent apartment and Lisabeth being very happy, along with an attractive incentive scheme, it was a done deal. There was the added bonus of being able to make a new start on the opposite of the world, away from the business media spotlight in New York.

Looking around the offices with the Chairman after the interview, they were certainly a lot humbler facilities than his office in New York, but what the heck? It was a new start, well away from AnuxuDine and Anux, where his career had reached an abrupt halt. Who knows where success with Mutilin would take him in the future? As a bonus, Mike Starke was a most convivial Chairman, who was very supportive, and the senior management looked very capable from the CV's he was given to peruse.

Newton had a brief meeting with the senior staff in the boardroom, after the announcement of appointment to the stock market. He was particularly impressed with Mere and Jacob and believed from what they described, there was a promising future with Mutilin Pharma. It was an opportunity to take Mutilin Pharma to the world and he was excited about the personal success that would bring.

"Beth, I have accepted the offer. They want us to start as soon as possible," proudly announced. "It is back home to pack up and get our apartment rented out."

"Newton honey, it will give us a brand-new start together," a thrilled Lisabeth replied. "I can hardly wait to get here."

*

Lisabeth knew their relationship had been suffering in New York. Newton's long hours at the office and business travel had seen him become increasingly unhappy. Her escape was to get away from him and spend time with her friends either shopping or working out at the gym. Australia was going to give them a whole new start. Maybe they could even think about starting a family.

The first month in Sydney was one of the best times since the early days of their married life. Newton was walking around the waterfront with Lisabeth after breakfast every morning, before heading off to the office. As a result, he was starting to lose weight and taking a healthier attitude to his diet. As an added bonus Lisabeth had a spring in her step as their love life was much improved.

For Newton he no longer made excuses to need to stay late at the office, attend never ending company functions or always be travelling on business. In addition, the fear of the Australian Customs officials had been enough for Newton to quietly dispose of his remaining supply of Columbian Heaven down into the New York sewer system.

Newton, however, did like the look of the Occidental Hotel over the road from the Mutilin offices. It was a quaint Aussie pub, something he wanted to experience, maybe for a relaxing drink before heading home to dine with Lisabeth.

Lisabeth kept busy by exploring her new city. A ferry ride out to Manly to visit the beach, the Rivercat to Parramatta, a water taxi to Double Bay for shopping in the boutiques and a ferry across to Taronga Park Zoo. She wanted to checkout some of those crazy looking but very cute Aussie animals. They had weird names like kangaroo, wombat, echidna, and numbat. Her favourite, like so many others was the koala, so cute and cuddly, just like a teddy bear.

The Facebook page got a real workout, bringing lots of requests for visits by friends in New York. Her frequent exploring of the city and its surrounds made her ready to be the perfect tour guide for her first lot of visitors, aided by the copious notes she was making.

On his first day in the office Newton picked up a copy of the Financial Express which his PA had set out on his desk along with his morning coffee. He loved the headline.

"Senior US Pharmaceutical Company Executive appointed as CEO of Mutilin Pharma."

"This was the right decision for the family," Newton reflected, as he looked out of his office window at the spectacular Sydney Harbour. *"Lisabeth is happy, I am happy and maybe it is time to start a family."*

CHAPTER 31

"Hey Carlo, come and take a look at this article in the Financial Express," Guido yelled to his brother to come into the office. They were the only two onsite with all the doors locked shut.

"I'm busy unpacking the consignment from Thailand," Carlo called back, preparing to slash open the cartons, supposedly containing bottles of shampoo and conditioner. "We have pickups scheduled for tonight."

"This could be very important," responded Guido.

Carlo threw down his knife and stomped into the office, "what's the big deal?"

"You remember when Adrian was caught up in all that business in Fiji a few months back? Well, a Sydney company has appointed a fella from America to head up the company," informed Guido. "The company has secured the commercial rights to that Fiji drug plant and get this; a major focus will be the purification of the active ingredient to remove the unwanted hallucinogenic properties. I can see some money somewhere in this for us. I like those words, hallucinogenic properties."

"I heard from Johnnie at the gym this morning that Adrian is coming out on the weekend to see his Mum and to give Johnnie a hand with some online promotional stuff for the gym," advised Carlo. "I think we will be due for a bit a workout this weekend and that promised beer with Adrian."

*

Adrian was in a good mood as he was about to meet with Gavin Mills to discuss the future and the possibility of confirming a deal to start a gym franchise in Melbourne. That was until he entered Giuseppe's Café and picked up a copy of the Financial Express while he waited for Sue to bring his coffee. He could not believe his eyes when saw the appointment of Newton Sinclair as CEO of Mutilin Pharma and today was his first day in the office in Sydney.

"What's the matter Adrian?" Sue detected the unhappy look on his face and his wrinkled brow.

"You remember that guy who was my boss in America I told you about, well he has lobbed up here in Sydney," replied an annoyed Adrian. "I don't know how he pulled it off, but it may give me the opportunity to settle the score with him."

"Maybe it's time to move on," added Sue sagely. " He will get what he deserves one day. You have too much to look forward. You cannot continue to be diverted by hatred and must focus positive energy on your future."

"You're right Sue. Thanks for that advice," agreed Adrian. "I am heading into an important meeting with the owner of the gym shortly. We are discussing me establishing a franchise of the gym in Melbourne."

"Oh," was all a despondent Sue could manage in reply, as Adrian drained his coffee and headed out the door.

*

"Come in Adrian. Take a seat," Gavin Mills pointed to the seat on the opposite side of his desk. "I know you are keen to discuss the commencement of the franchise in Melbourne."

"Most definitely," Adrian enthusiastically replied. "I believe during my trial period that we have got on very well together and developed a high level of trust. Have you studied the business plan? Do you have any questions?"

"Adrian, you have done a great job in the gym and you have an excellent rapport with your clients, resulting in many new members being recruited. I believe we can work very well together in building the Gym With A View franchise nationwide," commented Gavin. "You have obviously thought about the Melbourne franchise for some time, which I can see from all the effort put into your business plan. The background work on costs and potential profit has pretty much clinched the deal for me. Do you have any reservations about proceeding?"

"I am all set to go. We just need to put a franchise agreement in place," noted Adrian.

"With the capital you have available to invest, I propose a 25% equity in the business for you," proposed Gavin. "Over time you could reinvest your share of the profit to build up your equity. What do you think of that?"

"I have studied the standard franchise agreement and it all looks fair to me," replied a smiling Adrian. "Hopefully, it is the start of a very lucrative partnership. Let's shake on it."

Gavin and Adrian then discussed next steps in more detail. Adrian would start the process of registering the business name in the State of Victoria. He would also re-establish contact with the real estate agent in Melbourne he had identified. It would be good to work on securing the lease of the ideal premises, complete with the desired 360-degree view of Melbourne and surrounds.

Using an online App, he would place an advertisement to recruit the assistant manager, who could eventually take-over the operation, if Adrian continued to drive expansion of the franchise around the country. Local knowledge would be important in recruiting the rest of the staff and getting publicity underway. Adrian planned for handbills to be distributed to offices and apartments in the vicinity of the gym, as well as a full-on social media campaign. Gym With A View direct from Sydney with its elite clientele would be sure to attract interest. There was the added benefit of membership, for members to enjoy reciprocal rights while visiting Sydney on business or leisure and maybe bump into some of those stars mentioned on the website.

Adrian was keen to hit the ground running. So once the franchise agreement was finalised with the lawyers, the next stop was to the bank, to open an account for the Melbourne gym.

It would be a difficult visit with his Mum this coming weekend. She would no doubt be happy for him and his success in starting the business in

Melbourne, however, she would be sad to be losing him again, so soon after his return to Sydney from London.

At least it would take a few months to set everything up, so she still would have time with him in Sydney for a little while yet, as he commuted backwards and forwards to Melbourne. Confirming the lease on the premises, arranging for the shipment of the equipment, recruitment of staff, setting the gym up and beginning the promotion of the business, would all take time.

*

It was late afternoon, and a happy Mum smothered her son in kisses when she opened the door. "Come on in. I'll put the kettle on for a cuppa. Then you better tell me all about these plans for heading off to Melbourne I am hearing about."

Adrian put his bag in his room and took a seat on the new sofa. His Mum brought out scones with cream and strawberry jam, along with the pot of tea. "Mum, those scones look great, but they are not good for my waistline."

"Your waistline. What are you talking about. You can work it off while you are helping Johnnie at the gym over the weekend. He is looking forward to having you around. I have arranged for us to have dinner with him tonight at the local pub. They do a good meal in their restaurant," she started to pour the tea.

"It will be good to spend some time with Johnnie again," said Adrian. "You seem to be seeing a lot of him these days?"

"He is great company," replied his Mum. "I love having him around to watch my new television and we get out and about a bit."

"Is it becoming serious with Johnnie?" probed Adrian with a smile on his face.

"You may remember his Mary died last year with the cancer," informed his Mum. "Since you came home to Australia and met up with him, he has invited me along to bingo in the church hall on Tuesday nights and we head out occasionally for a meal at the Sports Club."

"Well, I'll be Mum," laughed Adrian. "A bit of life in the old dogs.""

"You behave yourself Adrian Nicholls," Mum looked embarrassed. "He'll be here shortly to pick us up, so you better finish up your tea."

A few minutes later the doorbell rang. It was Johnnie ready to take them out. He was unusually all spruced up for a meal at the local pub. Polished black shoes, pressed grey slacks and a white shirt with navy blue tie.

"You look very dressed up for a night at the pub Johnnie," observed Adrian. "The pub must have gone up market, since I was last there."

"Nothin' too good for your Mum," laughed Johnnie.

Adrian entered the pub holding his Mum's arm. Johnnie led the way into the dining room and confirmed their reservation to the hostess. Being a Saturday evening the restaurant was busy with the smell and smoke of barbequing cuts of meats filling the room. The carpet was a black and red floral design, probably hiding years of spilled drinks and meals. The well-worn dark timbered tables and chairs were setup in settings of four and eight. The far side of the restaurant housed an alcove from which rang the incessant sounds pinging out from the banks of poker machines. Players sat on stools in front of the screens, their eyes fixated, while sipping on their drinks, oblivious to their surroundings. A proud Mum took her seat at their table, next to her son Adrian. As she sat down, Adrian noted his Mum giving Johnnie's hand a squeeze and smiled to himself.

"*It was about time Mum found a bit of happiness with a man in her life.*"

They dined on a simple dinner of roast lamb, thick gravy and seasonal vegetables. The men enjoyed a pint of lager and Mum a glass of house white wine. They could not refuse the dessert of hot apple pie and clotted cream. After tummies were full and the tea poured, Adrian shared his plans with them for Australia.

"Thanks to Johnnie and getting me to do the personal trainer's course, I got the trial position with the Gym With A View in the city," Adrian relaxed and detailed his plans. "I got on well with the owner, Gavin Mills. He was keen to expand the business around the country and I suggested opening up in Melbourne as a next step."

"I can thank Johnnie for losing you again," Adrian's Mum glared at a sheepish looking Johnnie.

"Mum, you found Johnnie as a swap for me I can see," teased Adrian, watching his Mum blush. "Is there a bit more developing between you two? You are even a little taller than he is, the perfect couple."

"Enough with your goings on," Mum got huffy. "Anyway, you better finish off telling us about your plans."

Adrian went on to describe how his proposal for opening in Melbourne was accepted by Gavin and they had agreed on a franchise agreement. "It is a great opportunity and who knows, I may be opening up some other franchises in the other capital cities."

"When do you head down to Melbourne?" asked Johnnie.

"Things have progressed really well, but I will be flying to and from Melbourne for a few months yet, as it will take some time to get set up," informed Adrian. "I will have the opportunity to spend a few more weekends with you both."

"That is good, as there is something important, I have to tell you," Johnnie became formal. "Your Mum and I are going to get married and want your blessing."

"That is fantastic news. I could not be happier for you both. I wish you all the best," beamed Adrian, standing to hug his Mum and shake Johnnie's hand.

"You have done really well," stated a proud Johnnie. "I promise you I will look after your Mum. Also, I want you at the ceremony to give your Mum away."

"An absolute pleasure appreciate the opportunity, thanks Johnnie," Adrian signalled the waiter for the check. "Better head home as we have a busy day at the gym and the Conti brothers want to catch up with me for a beer."

*

"Hey Guido, hey Carlo. Good to see you guys again," Adrian greeted the twins as they entered Johnnie's gym. "Are you still on for that drink? We can head off to the pub once you finish your workout."

"Good one," replied Carlo. "We will grab a quick shower in the changeroom and then we can head off."

When they reached the pub, Guido ordered the beers, and they took a seat in a quiet corner. There was a bit of small talk about the rugby league and the lack of success of the Tigers, before Carlo asked Adrian how things were going with the gym. Adrian indicated things were going well and mentioned the plans of establishing a gym in Melbourne.

"Wow, sounds impressive," chorused the boys.

"What are you guys up to these days?" asked Adrian.

"A bit this and a bit of that," replied Carlo. "Just had a big shipment of shampoo and conditioner for the supermarkets from Thailand. Seems to sell pretty well as it's nice and cheap."

'One thing we wanted ask you about is Mutilin Pharma," Guido was not able to contain himself. "We play a little bit on the stock market with some spare cash and have recently seen articles on them in the Financial Express. They have recruited some big shot CEO from New York so they must be doing ok. Thought you might be able to give us a heads up."

"I know the bastard concerned," fired in Adrian. "He used to be my boss and did the dirty on me which got me fired in the end. He is a bit of sleaze from what I heard on the office grapevine in the US. It was even rumoured he liked to snort a bit coke, but it was never confirmed."

"We'll have to stitch him up for you," laughed Carlo.

Adrian was not sure if he was joking given the brothers reputation in the community.

"What is all this business about this Fijian plant?" Guido became business-like, as he leaned forward.

"It appears the plant has excellent properties to provide pain relief, putting it in simple terms," informed Adrian. "Problem is that there is a part of the plant that causes these hallucinogenic side-effects like LSD."

"Sounds very interesting," chorused the brothers. "Tell us more."

"Well, the scientists they have recruited at Mutilin are very capable," continued Adrian. "They will be bringing in samples of the plant from Fiji into the laboratories into Sydney. In the labs here, they will undertake the development work to create the chemical that does not have the side-effect and can be used to make a commercial product."

"Into Sydney you say," noted Carlo. "Fascinating, so you reckon they could be worth considering as a stock for our portfolio."

"I would say so in time," reckoned Adrian. "However, it will be a few years for the stock to boom, so you'll have to be patient. Of course, there are no guarantees with pharmaceuticals."

"We will have to monitor this purification process and see how they progress," noted Guido.

"I suppose I better get to the gym," Adrian reluctantly stood up. "Better finish this social media stuff for Johnnie as I am heading back into the city tonight."

"Great catching up Adrian," smiled the brothers as they exchanged handshakes. "We'll keep an eye on Mutilin. Thanks for the information."

With that Adrian was up and out the door and back to Johnnie's gym.

"Hallucinogenic," mused Carlo." I say it would be incredibly good if we can get our hands on that plant material when it comes to Sydney."

"Let's see what we can learn about Mr Newton Sinclair," reflected Guido. "Maybe a night with Miss Trixie could do the trick, to get him onside. She has been especially useful in the past to loosen lips."

With a laugh they downed the remains of their beer and headed to their car and back to the warehouse. There was some planning to be done to get their hands on this new drug but back to the warehouse but firstly there were shipments to be collected this evening.

CHAPTER 32

Melbourne commercial space was eye-wateringly expensive, especially anywhere in the CBD. However, Adrian knew if the Gym With A View business model was to succeed in Melbourne, he needed a well-equipped, professional facility in the right location, to attract those high fee-paying clients. The property shown to him by the agent did not disappoint. The full-length windows facing Port Phillip Bay provided the stunning 360-degree panoramic views Adrian wanted. He had no hesitation in agreeing to lease the entire floor-space, on the 50th floor of the building in Collins Street. It was close to Southern Cross station, a major commuter hub and a source of a large pool of potential gym members.

"Gavin, Adrian calling. Sorry to call you early morning, but I wanted to let you know I have secured the lease on the building. You can now ship the equipment once the paperwork is finalised and the deposit paid."

"That was quick," Gavin noted. "We will start packing the consignment and get it ready to go from the warehouse here in Sydney as soon as we get your go ahead. You should have everything within a couple of days of you giving the word. In addition to the gym equipment, we will include some branded merchandise including drink bottles, t-shirts, tracksuits, towels, sweat bands."

"Great news. I am itching to get started," Adrian enthusiastically replied. "I will get on with developing the promotional campaign and recruiting the staff. We want to get income being generated as soon as possible given the rent we are paying."

"Keep me posted," Gavin signed off.

*

Adrian wasted no time in preparing to get the gym operational, with the appointment of an assistant manager, Aaron Kennedy. Aaron was keen and liked the potential of working with an organisation that was in expansion mode. Aaron like Adrian was early 30's, just over six-feet tall, blonde-haired, well-built, with broad shoulders tapering to a narrow waist. He was well-tanned and extremely fit. He had completed courses in nutrition and management. His qualifications, combined with a good network in the local fitness scene in Melbourne, made him an ideal appointee.

With Aaron's assistance they recruited a number of personal trainers prepared to operate out of the gym. They would pay a proportion of what they earned from each client, as a contribution towards the use of the gym. There was an additional sessional fee if their client was not a gym member.

Next came the establishment of the various social media platforms and the barrage of publicity surrounding the opening of the new prestigious gym. Attractive young, fit guys and gals distributed handbills to commuters in the CBD, or as they stepped off the trams and trains arriving in the city. The gym was promoted as offering a unique experience with panoramic 360-degree views while you worked out. This brought the gym to the attention of some local radio programs which secured Adrian valuable airtime. On air he was able to name drop some of the VIP's who were members of the gym's Sydney facility. Gym With A View would also offer a reciprocal arrangement for Melbourne gym members, with the facility in Sydney, generating a lot of buzz from interested callers into the radio programs.

The modern gym included changerooms complete with showering facilities, lockers, a range of health foods, gym gear, the latest equipment from Europe and a group of personal trainers to assist with the development of training programs. Specialists offered sessions with a variety of options including Yoga, Pilates, Step, Spin-cycle and the like. It was going to be expensive to join the gym, so they decided on a trial period, offering 50% discount for the first month, to get people through the door. They believed once people started with this unique gym and its amazing views, they would be impressed and the turnover rate would subsequently be relatively low, as was the case in Sydney.

"*Fingers crossed.*"

Adrian was impressed with what he and Aaron had achieved in such a short time since the arrival of the shipment from Sydney. They put in long hours and were all set to launch in two weeks. From the elevator a gym member would immediately be able to access the gym by scanning their membership card at two turnstiles located to the left of the reception desk. A receptionist handled membership enquiries and all the merchandise related transactions – health food, clothing, and the like.

Once through the turnstiles it was a hard left and down a corridor to the changerooms and lockers. To the right were the two large rooms operating the various specialist sessions. One quiet room for Yoga and Pilates. The second outfitted with bikes for spin classes and room for other activities such as Zumba, all enjoyed with Bay views. Opening out from the entry turnstiles was the main gym floor split between an area devoted to electronic equipment such as treadmills and rowing machine and an area for free weights for the body builders. Floor to ceiling windows ensured as many as possible would enjoy the Bay and surrounding city while working out.

"Gavin thought I would give you a virtual tour," Adrian having initiated a Skype call to walk him through the premises.

"It is even better than I imagined. Wow, that view. I look forward to a visit at some stage. Maybe for an official opening function," extolled Gavin. "I am very happy with the setup, congratulations and all the best."

"I'll back in the office in Sydney tomorrow morning Gavin," advised Adrian. "I still have plenty of loose ends to tie up in Sydney, including my Mum's wedding this weekend, before taking up full time residence in Melbourne. Meanwhile, my Assistant Manager, Aaron Kennedy is doing a great job. He has great connections amongst the major local football teams. Getting some of the top players using the gym would provide great promotional opportunities and interest."

Despite the potential he saw in a relationship with Karen, Adrian knew her desire for success in the media in Sydney, combined with his move to Melbourne, was not a recipe for a successful relationship. However, he realised there was a special lady he wanted to ask to accompany him to his Mum's wedding.

*

Adrian entered Giuseppe's Café and received a big smile from Sue as he entered and took his usual seat near the entrance, which gave him a good view of the street.

"Sue have you got a second," Adrian asked indicating the spare seat at his table.

"Sure," Sue took a quick look around the café, noting everyone had been served.

"What would you say to accompanying me to my Mum's wedding this Saturday afternoon?" Adrian coyly asked, as he fiddled with the sachets of sugar on the table.

"I would love to. I thought you would never ask me out on a date," Sue leapt up and gave him a hug and a kiss on the cheek. "I'll have to get a new dress and new shoes and…."

"We can make arrangements for me to pick you up for the wedding during the week," Adrian interrupted Sue who headed off to get his coffee.

A beaming Sue with a swagger in her step placed Adrian's coffee on his table and smiled when he gently squeezed her hand. With Sue starting to serve other customers, Adrian picked up his coffee and was about to take a sip, when his jaw dropped. Passing by the café was none other than Newton Sinclair, dressed in business attire, carrying a computer satchel and accompanied by a very attractive blond-haired woman in activewear. Adrian left his coffee on the table and with a wave to Sue and holding his hand up to indicate he would call; he was off in pursuit of Newton.

Adrian followed from a discreet distance, observing as the couple stopped occasionally to admire the view. Adrian followed Newton to an office block, where Adrian saw Newton kiss the woman, who he presumed was Newton's wife and he then entered the building. The wife looked as though she was ready to head off on a run, or a walk around Sydney's harbourfront. In addition to her activewear of 7/8 length black tights and a white, tight fitting t-shirt with a Quicksilver motif, she wore shiny silver runners with white ankle socks, complete a with pair of pom-poms over-hanging the rear of the runners. She was topped off by a white sun visor with NY in gold letters on the peak.

"Very nice indeed. What does she see in Newton?"

With Newton heading into the office, Adrian saw his chance and strolled casually up to Lisabeth. "Good morning Miss. You look set for a busy morning of exercise."

"Do I know you sir?" queried Lisabeth in her distinctive New York accent. "I don't usually talk to strangers."

"Love your accent," noted Adrian warming to his mission. "You must be a tourist so you would not be interested in a gym membership," as he handed over to her a Gym With A View handbill.

"My husband and I have just relocated to Sydney from the US," informed Lisabeth. "Matter of fact, I would be very interested in checking the gym out with you."

"I can see you like to keep fit," smiled Adrian. "My company Gym With A View, sits on the top floor of that building, overlooking the harbour," informed Adrian, as he pointed it out. "You can come by and check it out when you are ready. You will see the view of Sydney Harbour in the gym is amazing. There is no better way to work out in this city. We offer a 50% discount for the first trial month, with no ongoing obligation. My name is Adrian. The handbill has all the details of the gym. Ask for me at reception and I will personally look after you."

"My name is Lisabeth, I am living in that apartment block adjacent to the gym's building, so will definitely drop in to check it out," Lisabeth turned with a spring in her step, heading off towards the Opera House in a brisk walk.

"Very impressive location for their apartment," thought Adrian, as he admired the rear view of Lisabeth. *"They must be paying him a good salary."*

*

The next morning Adrian was on the phone to Aaron in Melbourne, discussing matters relating to the opening, when the elevator door pinged open and there stood Lisabeth Sinclair. She stepped up to the reception desk, all set for action in tight, skin hugging 7/8 leopard print leggings and matching zipped up tracksuit top. Gucci sunglasses were pushed back above her forehead. A gym bag was in her hand, so she was ready to sign up and prepared for an immediate workout.

"Good morning my name is Lisabeth Sinclair," she stated. "I met Adrian yesterday and he promised to look after me personally in regard to a tour and signing me up for a membership."

"He is busy at the moment on a call, but shouldn't be long," replied the receptionist. "How about you take a seat in his office and I will let him know you are waiting for him. Follow me."

Lisabeth sat down and while waiting for Adrian saw a gym brochure on his desk, which she stood to retrieve. Her hand paused above the brochure when her eyes caught the words NEWTON SINCLAIR, on an unopened manila folder on Adrian's desk. "*What was this all about? How would this guy have a file on Newton? He may have some explaining to do.*"

Curiosity got the better of her, so she picked up the file she and sat down. On opening the file, she was immediately hit by a newspaper article. It described the actions of Adrian Nicholls in Fiji and him being dismissed by his manager at Anux Pharmaceuticals, Newton Sinclair. "*It could not have been a coincidence that Adrian spoke to me. Wait till he gets here. What is this all about?*"

Adrian's face dropped as he entered the office and saw Lisabeth with the open file on her lap and scanning the newspaper clipping.

"Do you mind telling me what this is all about?" asked a hostile Lisabeth, throwing the folder back onto the desk. "I would have to believe our meeting was not a coincidence. Your explanation better be good."

"I'll start at the beginning," Adrian took a seat. "As the article indicates Newton was my boss and I had his OK to undertake the action in Fiji. I believe he did something rather devious with a recording which exonerated him and made me the fall guy."

"I think I know the device you're referring to," Lisabeth settled back in her seat. "A favourite toy of his."

"Anux terminated me on the spot without giving me any chance to defend myself," Adrian continued. "My mind was full of plans for revenge on both Anux and your husband."

"In the circumstances I can understand that, but how and why did you bump into me? It could not have been a coincidence," probed Lisabeth. "You mentioned the word revenge. What did you mean by that?"

"I have to admit that with the loss of my career in the pharmaceutical industry and Newton's part in that, I wanted the same outcome for him," Adrian earnestly replied. "However, I have got on with my life and moved away from any plans I had for revenge with Newton. I have taken a whole new career path and have been successful with this gym business. In fact, I am shortly relocating to Melbourne to start a new franchise for the company."

"What about you approaching me yesterday?" Lisabeth pushed for more certainty in regard to Adrian's motives.

"I was having coffee in the café down below when I saw you and Newton walk past," continued Adrian. "I could not believe my eyes when I saw Newton. I knew from the newspaper that he had accepted a job in Sydney. I followed you to that office block and with you in your activewear, couldn't miss the opportunity to approach you and give you a handbill."

"OK." Lisabeth relaxed.

"I am more than happy to catch up with Newton," Adrian passed his business card to Lisabeth. "I mean him no harm. I want to get on with this new chapter in my life."

Reassured, Lisabeth stood, "I better get on with completing the paperwork and getting underway with my workout. I will let Newton know I met with you. It will be interesting in what he has to say. You should also know we had our personal difficulties, and this has been a good move for us. Newton has changed, certainly for the better, since we have been here in Sydney."

*

Newton finished work and being a warm evening thought it would be a good idea if he stopped in at the Occidental Hotel, for a pint or two of lager. He was enjoying the unique Aussie pub experience, a couple of nights per week. He didn't want to completely undo all the effort he was putting in with Lisabeth to get fit. The hotel was located directly over the road from the Mutilin Pharma office block and had seen better days. It had been spared the developers wrecking ball due to its heritage listing, with its unique early 1900's architecture and original fittings.

From the street view, to the right-hand end of the building was a small dining room offering simple pub food. Burgers, fries, meat pies and fish n' chips. The décor was basic. Small round, dark-timbered tables with matching wooden chairs, with the centre of the table furnished by a metal basket in which was housed salt, pepper, sauces, cutlery and paper serviettes. The walls were lined with dark timber, with dark green carpet. The low level of light emanating from the few operating bulbs in the dusty chandelier, did nothing to enhance the dark ambience.

The lounge at the left-hand end was similarly out-fitted apart from the dark wooden furniture being replaced by low lounge chairs and coffee tables, covered in coasters which looked as though they were stuck to the tabletops. A narrow corridor over which rose the stairs leading to the now defunct upstairs accommodation, housed the toilets and a door leading into the lounge.

Behind the massive, central, dark-timbered bar was a huge ornate mirror, featuring native Australian floral designs – kangaroo paws, wattle and gum blossoms. Sitting on top of a huge refrigeration unit sat rows of bottles of wine and spirits. Protruding from the top of the bar were beer taps dripping with condensation.

It was amongst all this that Newton liked to sit in the quiet alcove under the staircase. He perched on his bar stool and relaxed with his beer watching the world go by. In particular he enjoyed listening to the Aussie accent and slang, much of which he was still trying to understand. There were the office workers grabbing a drink before joining the throng of commuters down at Circular Quay, lining up to catch a ferry home. The old regular retirees who seemed to sit sipping the same beer for hours. Their eyes glued to the horse racing, broadcast by the television screens housed on the wall above the entrance. In his American way he tipped the bar staff, so he was always promptly served as soon as he raised his hand for another drink.

It was time to head home to Lisabeth who had his favourite fried chicken on the menu at home tonight. It was not good for the waistline, but he loved it occasionally. He waved goodbye to the bar staff and a couple of the regulars and headed out the door, for the casual stroll to his apartment on the other side of the Quay.

"Darlin' I'm home," announced Newton as entered the apartment. "I can smell that fried chicken. I can hardly wait."

Lisabeth waited for them to sit down to dinner before breaking the news about her meeting with Adrian. Newton had a big grin on his face as picked up a leg of chicken and tore off a mouth full of chicken from the bone.

"You wouldn't believe who I met today," teased Lisabeth. "An old friend of yours."

"An old friend, here in Sydney?" Newton placed the bone on his plate. "Who was it?'

"Adrian Nicholls was his name," Lisabeth smiled.

"What that scumbag," Newton's face became bright red with rage. "Where in the hell did you see him?"

"Settle down. He explained his history with you, and he has got on with life," informed Lisabeth. "He is a partner in a gymnasium, which I have joined today."

"Joined? How could you?" Newton raised his voice. "I don't trust him one bit."

"He would like to catch up with you. He wants bygones to be bygones," placated Lisabeth.

"I'll have to think about," Newton became pensive. "Well that certainly ruined my mood tonight."

*

"Mr Conti, Bruno calling."

"What's up Bruno," responded Guido.

"The American fella has just left the hotel and is heading to his apartment," informed Bruno. "He seems to make a regular habit of stopping off for a couple of beers, usually on Monday and Friday nights each week after work."

"That is very helpful, Bruno," thanked Guido.

"Hey Carlo, that was Bruno," Guido yelled. Carlo was in the office at the back of the warehouse, counting cash, before putting it into the open safe. "It looks like we may be able to arrange for Miss Trixie Desire to meet up with our Mr Sinclair. I am sure she will be very helpful in enabling us to find out when the that next shipment of flowers is coming in from Fiji."

CHAPTER 33

Adrian knocked on the door at Sue's place. She was still living with her parents to save money. Sue opened the door, and he was left speechless, his mouth opened, and he just stared. This was not the same woman who served him coffee, wearing black tennis shoes and blue jeans covered in a checked apron. There was no white t-shirt, hair tied back in a ponytail, or a pencil stuck behind her ear. Before him stood a complete transformation.

Sue presented in a cream dress with a black cross across the chest. The shoulders were bare over which draped her long, glistening blonde hair. The dress fell to just below the knees with a central split up to a mid-thigh length. Her stockinged legs fitted into open-toed black, high-heeled shoes, tied around the ankles. She held a black wrap in her right hand and a black patent leather purse in her left.

"Miss Sue McKenzie, you are absolutely beautiful," gleamed Adrian. "Will you be so kind as to accompany me to the wedding?"

"It will be a pleasure Mr Nicholls," replied Sue with a slight curtesy. "You better say hello to the folks. They are desperate to meet you."

With the uncomfortable formalities out of the way in meeting Sue's folks, they were off to Mt Willsmore, Anglican Church. There was a small crowd assembled outside the church chatting to the reverend in his long flowing robes with Bible in hand. There was a nervous Johnnie awaiting the arrival of the bride to be, dressed in his best navy-blue suit, white shirt, a navy-blue tie, and a white rose pinned to his left lapel. Also in attendance was Johnnie's sister, her husband, and grown-up children with their families. There were a few of his and Mum's friends from bingo, to bolster the numbers.

The presence of the glamorous Sue drew plenty of stares from the crowd. She certainly stood out in Mt Willsmore on a Saturday afternoon. Adrian introduced her to Johnnie who made her feel welcome and introduced her to the other guests.

"Everybody inside and take your seats, the bride is not too far away," announced Adrian.

"I will head off now to join Mum for the ride to the church," Adrian advised Sue. "You head inside with Johnnie and I will see you with Mum shortly."

As Adrian pulled into front of his Mum's place, he noticed the limo was waiting and saw a nervous Mum pacing up and down on the footpath leading to the front door. She waved to Adrian as he pulled up.

"I was getting worried love. Thought you were going to be late," said his nervous Mum, who continued to fidget with her bouquet of petite white roses.

"Mum you are beautiful," Adrian noted her knee-length, floral design, champagne dress with matching jacket and shoes. "Shall we go?"

A proud Adrian escorted his Mum down the aisle, giving her away to Johnnie before taking his seat next to Sue. She grabbed his hand and gave it a squeeze and did not let go. Much to the annoyance of the reverend, the happy couple were sprayed with confetti as they exited the church, despite the *No Confetti* sign. He would have a clean up to perform, to get ready for the Sunday morning service.

The bride and groom, along with the guests retired to the private function room at the local pub to celebrate the wedding. In his speech, Adrian thanked his Mum for the sacrifices she made for him while he grew up which brought tears to the crowd. He also thanked Johnnie for being his mentor and surrogate Dad. "I would never have achieved what I did without your support.

*

Later that evening Sue and Adrian pulled up in front of Sue's place and Adrian turned off the engine, "I hope you had a good day," asked Adrian.

"It was wonderful. Your Mum is a special person and she looked incredibly happy with Johnnie. They made a lovely couple," noted Sue as she leant towards Adrian and gently kissed him on the lips.

He responded with increased intensity, placing his hands-on Sue's cheeks to wipe some tears away. "You are a special lady Sue McKenzie," he said as he looked into her eyes.

"Took you long enough to notice," she replied.

"Yes, you are right about that. One thing I have to remind you about is my forthcoming move to Melbourne, before we start taking things too far."

"I like the shopping in Melbourne," noted Sue. "Let's see how things develop, before you have to permanently move down there."

"How about I pick you up for lunch tomorrow?" asked an expectant Adrian. "I'll book somewhere down near the beach and pick you up around noon."

"See you then," Sue gave him a lingering sensuous kiss. "I am looking forward to it."

Next morning on the way to pick up Sue, Adrian stopped at the local 7-Eleven store to fill up the car and get himself a coffee and newspaper. He relaxed in the car opening up his newspaper and after seeing not much in the headlines turned to the business section. His eyes were drawn to the lead article; *Mutilin Pharma Announces the Arrival of the Tagimoucia Samples from Fiji.* The article described how the samples would arrive in Sydney on Monday from Fiji and would be available to commence the testing work in the laboratory, after customs clearance by the end of the week.

"Hopefully, they are successful," Adrian muttered to himself. "Even with Newton in charge."

*

It was 6pm on Monday evening and Newton entered the bar at the Occidental Hotel . He would have a couple of beers before heading home to Lisabeth. She had mentioned heading down to China Town for dinner. Seated in his regular corner at the bar, there was a rather glamorous woman who certainly stood out amongst the usual male crowd, who frequented the front bar at the Occidental.

She was dressed in a short, black cocktail dress, which did not leave much to the imagination. Her large breasts looked as though they would pop out of the top of the dress at any moment. There was a flick of her head as she cleared the shoulder-length, jet black hair away from her face and long false eye lashes. She crossed her legs over as he approached the bar, drawing his eyes automatically to them.

"Well, hello," she greeted. "My name is Trixie."

"Newton," he replied with a grin. "I haven't seen you here before."

"Love the accent. American no doubt," she observed. "Which part?"

"New York City. Can I buy you a drink Miss Trixie?" Newton asked, being friendly.

"*This could be a bit of fun before heading home for dinner,*" he mused.

"That would be nice, but how about we go into the lounge at the rear and make ourselves a little more comfortable while we chat," Trixie started to stand.

"Sure, what are you drinking?" Newton retrieved his wallet. "I'll bring it through."

"The house white wine would be fine," Trixie headed towards the entrance door to the lounge bar.

Drinks in hand Newton entered the dimly lit, empty lounge and noted Trixie had taken a seat near the rear fire exit. The dark wooden tables and old lounge chairs had certainly seen better days but were comfortable enough.

"Oh, before you sit down, you couldn't get me some peanuts to nibble on?" asked Trixie. "Feelin' a bit peckish."

"No problem, but I haven't got too long here. I will need to get home after this drink," Newton turned to head back to the bar.

Trixie quickly reached for the phone in her bag, "Bruno, the fish is dangling at the bait. Get the van backed up in the alleyway and be ready to go as soon as I open the door. Don't forget the *closed for cleaning* sign at the door leading in from the main street. We don't want anyone coming in unexpected."

From her bag she extracted a small plastic ampoule containing a clear solution, which she opened and tipped the contents into Newton's beer and gave it a quick stir with her right index finger. Newton returned with the peanuts, emptied in a glass bowl, and sat down picking up his beer. "Cheers," he clinked his glass with Trixie's.

Bruno had placed the cleaning sign in front of the door leading in from the street entrance to the lounge. Once Newton had entered the lounge with the peanuts, he place another sign in front of the door leading in from the bar area. He then quickly headed out the front door of the bar and around the side of the building, to his van waiting in the alleyway at the rear. As soon as the rear fire exit opened, he would be in to collect his cargo and Trixie.

After a large mouthful of beer by Newton, the date-rape drug did not take long to have its effect. Newton's head slumped forward, and Trixie sprang to her feet, pushing on the central bar to spring open the fire exit. Bruno was waiting and with his huge, muscular body picked up Newton like a feather. Newton was tossed onto the mattress on the floor at the rear of the van and Trixie jumped into the passenger seat. The rear door was closed, and they were gone in seconds.

*

The Conti brothers maintained a central, unmarked warehouse in the back streets of Sydney's red-light district Kings Cross, not far from the CBD. The van pulled up in front of the silver roller door, covered in graffiti and Trixie pulled out her phone, "Delivery for Mr Johnson."

The door screeched its way to the top and when Bruno had the van inside, the door creaked closed with a shudder as it hit the ground. The rear door of the van was opened, and Bruno soon had his cargo on his shoulder and on the way to a room set up at the rear of the rather empty, uninviting building. There were a few empty storage racks, some spare tyres and a large work bench fitted with a range of hand and electrical tools.

Opening the door Newton was unceremoniously dumped onto a queen-sized, brass bed, his unconscious body giving a slight grunt. With the layout of the room, it appeared as though it may have been used on regular occasions. A video camera was setup just inside the door with photographers' lights pointing towards the bed, which was set perpendicular to the wall. To the right of the bed was a lounge chair over which Newton's clothing was being placed as Trixie stripped him naked and then began to remove her clothing.

At the head of the bed, Newton was being propped up by a pile of different coloured cushions, ensuring his face was revealed to the camera. His naked body now spread-eagled on the white bedspread exposing his genitalia. Trixie then began her work, engorging Newton's penis in her mouth, then straddling his face with her thrusting hips. Newton appeared to be responding to Trixie's actions in his drug induced state.

"I think that is a wrap guys," announced Carlo. "Let's see. From his business card we have his email address where we can forward the footage of him and Miss Trixie, fulfilling their sexual desires. Clear out the cash in his wallet to make it look like a robbery and then call Vince's taxi to come and get him, to drop him off at his apartment. We need to ensure he gets home safely, ready for tomorrow's email."

The taxi pulled up in front of the warehouse and the roller door opened with a toot of the taxi's horn. "Here Vince, take the cash and leave him with the concierge at his apartment block. Here is the address," Guido handed the driver the note.

It was only a short drive from Kings Cross down to Circular Quay and the taxi pulled up at the entrance to the apartment block, with Newton beginning to groan and come to, his head pounding. The concierge came out of the building and was told by the taxi driver that he found the passenger wandering around Kings Cross and it looked as though he may have been robbed, as he has been groaning and feeling his head.

"He was able to give me his address, so I brought him straight here," advised Vince.

"That was good of you. Here is $20 for your trouble and I will get it back from him later," responded the concierge, as he assisted Vince to get Newton out of the taxi and into the foyer.

With Newton's arm draped around his shoulder, the concierge assisted Newton inside to the safety of the building and finally into the elevator to be taken up to his apartment.

By now Lisabeth was beside herself with worry. It was now nearly 11pm and Newton had been expected home around 7pm for dinner. He had not called and did not answer his phone.

There was a knock at the door. "Is that you Newton?" called Lisabeth, as she rushed to answer.

Opening the door, she was shocked to see Newton supported by the concierge. Lisabeth quickly grabbed the other arm and assisted in taking Newton to the sofa, carefully placing on his back.

"What happened?" an urgent look crossed Lisabeth's face.

"A taxi driver brought him here, indicating he thought Mr Sinclair had been mugged up at Kings Cross," informed the concierge, gradually getting his breath back. "I slipped him $20 for his trouble. He appears to look OK. I did not see any cuts or bruises."

"What in the hell was he doing at Kings Cross?" asked a perplexed Lisabeth. "He normally has a drink after work at the hotel near his office."

"Sorry, I don't know," replied the concierge. "If there is nothing else, I better get back to the desk."

"Thanks for your help," acknowledged Lisabeth. "I'll drop in the $20 in the morning."

With the concierge gone, Lisabeth moved over to the couch as Newton was starting to sit up. He braced himself with one arm on the back of the couch before crashing back into the cushions. "What happened?" he groaned, his eyes starting to flicker as he was coming back to reality.

"It would appear my darling, you were mugged in Kings Cross and luckily brought home by a saint of a taxi driver," Lisabeth slipping onto the couch and placing Newton's head in her lap. "Do we need to call the cops?"

"There's not much I can tell them," as Newton began to regain his faculties. "Last I remember is sitting down to have a drink with this woman at the bar and the rest is a blank. I suspect my drink was spiked."

"A drink with a woman," Lisabeth started to become annoyed. "Serves you right. You are lucky to have got home alive. You might have to put it all down to experience."

"I will certainly keep an eye out for that bitch," said Newton with anger in his voice.

*

After a morning walk along the waterfront with Lisabeth, followed by a healthy breakfast of freshly squeezed orange juice, muesli with cut up banana and a black coffee it was off to the office for Newton. He still had a slight headache but was looking forward to the day ahead, especially with the arrival of the Tagimoucia flowers into the warehouse and getting ready for the testing to begin.

He had another coffee at his desk while scanning the Financial Express and particular liked reading any articles written by Karen Nesbitt. He liked her style and would miss her offerings with the move into television on Network 6 that had been announced. There was a knock on his office, and it was his PA with an envelope for him.

"This was left at reception for you, Mr Sinclair."

Newton took his letter opener and opened the envelope, careful not to damage the contents. Inside was an A4 sized colour photograph of him in a very compromising situation with a woman. "*She was the one from last night at the hotel.*" He picked up the note which fell from the envelope.

"*Dear Mr Sinclair, I hope you enjoy the enclosed photograph. You will also like the videoclip coming through shortly in your email.*"

Newton was speechless, his mouth dropped open. "*I have no recollection of this. Somehow I must have been drugged by that woman.*"

The note went on to provide a threat of releasing the photograph and the videoclip to his wife, as well as to the Chairman of the company. It did, however, provide a simple remedy for Newton to avoid a public shaming and to get his hands on the original. The simple solution lie in Newton providing the location for the storage of the Tagimoucia shipment.

Newton slumped back in his chair and then turned on his computer. He noted an email which came through in the early hours of the morning without any subject. He initially hesitated then opened the attachment. Tears started to form in his eyes as he saw himself in a series of disgusting positions with that woman, memories of her starting to flash back into his mind from the previous evening. The email finished with a final paragraph; *"We want the information texted to the number of the burner phone available for one call only by noon today, otherwise we will release the material. Have a nice day, as you say in America."*

Newton paced up and down in his office. *"What am I to do? I cannot let Lisabeth see me like that, or the media get hold of the footage. It's only a few plants and no one will get hurt."*

CHAPTER 34

Newton was sitting at the kitchen bench when Lisabeth called from the lounge where she was watching the morning news on the television, "Newton quick. Come and watch this. It is about Mutilin Pharma."

"I am here out front of the Mutilin Pharma warehouse in North Ryde. The warehouse manager has indicated the warehouse was broken into last night and the only thing stolen was the recently arrived shipment of the red Tagimoucia flowers from Fiji."

Newton downed his coffee, "I'd better get to the office. No doubt the media will be calling the office this morning." With that he was out the door.

On the approach to the office Newton noted the television camera crew parked in front of the office building. He entered the building and headed up to the office where a reporter and camera crew were confronting the receptionist.

"Here is our CEO, Mr Sinclair," she announced to the reporter with the microphone.

Newton took charge with the television camera lights firing up as he spoke, "I have just seen the report on the news this morning and have come straight to the office. If you could wait just a moment until I come up to speed with what happened, I will be back shortly with a full update."

The management team were called together in the boardroom where Jacob was able to provide an update, "I have spoken to the warehouse manager and he has confirmed the break in last night, resulting in the theft of the consignment from Fiji. The police have been called in and the CCTV footage has been provided to them."

"I presume this relates to the recent reports of the hallucinogenic effects of the plant extract," interrupted Newton. "We need to advise the police in that regard, as we are probably looking at some drug gang related activity."

"Yes, I think you would be right," agreed Mere. "To help us get back on track, I will put in a call to the Fiji School of Medicine to arrange for a second shipment, so we can get started on our work. It will take two or three weeks to get here by the time we get the permits and collect the samples from Taveuni."

Newton headed back down to the awaiting news crew and related details to them about the break-in and confirming the theft of the Tagimoucia shipment. He warned the public to keep an eye out for the distinctive red flowers which could prove dangerous in the wrong hands given the potential for abuse by drug takers."

"Are you OK?" asked Jacob as Newton came back into the office from the meeting with the media.

"Just a bit shattered by the news," Newton replied. "Hopefully Mere can get replacement stock in as soon as possible so we can get underway with the project. Maybe we can get together with her this afternoon to discuss it?"

"I know it's not a good time with what happened overnight, but could we make the meeting early afternoon?" Jacob looking anxious. "Mere and I are heading out for dinner tonight to celebrate the completion of the renovations in our apartment and we can move back in this coming weekend. Mum and Dad are great, but we can hardly wait to move into our place. Over dinner tonight I am going to propose to Mere. I have the ring safely in my pocket. It is a big secret; she doesn't know."

"That's fantastic news, getting engaged. Congratulations," Newton shaking Jacob's hand. "We can meet straight after lunch, so you can get away early. Promise I will mention it to no one."

Jacob and Mere headed back to the office after the lunch their break and were preparing to meet with Newton. Mere was looking forward to going out for dinner that night, despite the events of the day. Celebrating the completion of the renovations and the pending move into their own place, Jacob had been most insistent that they dine somewhere special and had booked an expensive restaurant at the Sydney Opera House.

Mere was just about to leave her desk and head to the meeting room when the phone on her desk rang. It was Rebecca the receptionist. "Sorry, Rebecca. I am just about to go into this afternoon's meeting with Newton and Jacob, can you take a message?"

"You'll need to take this call. The caller said he is Fiji's Prime Minister," announced Rebeca.

"Oh, you better put him straight through," instructed Mere, wondering why Filipe would be calling her.

"Mere, Filipe here. I will get straight to it. Your Tamana has had a heart attack this morning and collapsed at his desk. He has been admitted to Suva's Colonial War Memorial Hospital."

For a moment Mere could not speak as she started to hyper-ventilate. She took a deep breath and calmed herself, "Is he OK?"

"The doctors tell me it was a significant event, and it will take some time and rehabilitation for him to fully recover," informed Filipe.

"I'll arrange to get to Fiji on the next flight out of Sydney," said Mere fighting back tears. "Thanks for letting me know."

"I am sorry I had to speak with you in such difficult circumstances," soothed Filipe. "When you get home, I want you to make time to come and see me, once you've had time with your Tamana."

"Mere, Newton is waiting for you to get started," called Jacob as he approached her desk.

He stopped, seeing the tears streaming from her face, "what's happened?"

"Tamana has had a heart attack. I need to get back home on the first available flight," sobbed Mere.

"Of course. I will let Newton know. You need to make your arrangements," Jacob moved to embrace Mere. "Let me know what you need me to do. I will run you out to the airport as soon as you have booked your flight."

"You go on into the meeting and I will get things organised. Thanks, Jacob, for your support and sorry to ruin your plans for dinner tonight. I will need to get back to your Mum's place and pack ready to go."

"I'll ask Newton to cancel the meeting and get you out of here," Jacob headed off to Newton's office. He was about to knock on the door before entering, just as Newton took a call. He paused, deciding to see if Newton was going to be quick on the call.

"Mr Sinclair, a Mr Johnson on the line," announced Rebecca. "He says it is very important about last night's theft."

"Mr Johnson, how can I help?" a cautious Newton asked.

"How did you like those photos? They would look nice in a frame next to your bed," laughed the supposed Mr Johnson. "I think information on one more shipment, might just do the trick before we destroy the originals."

"You bastard, you will not get any more information from me about shipments. Goodbye." Newton slammed the phone down.

Jacob knocked and entered Newton's office, "everything OK?"

"No, its fine," Newton curtly replied.

"I need to cancel the meeting this afternoon. Mere's Dad in Fiji has just had a heart attack," informed Jacob. "I need to get her home, packed and on the first available flight to Fiji."

"Sure, that's fine," Newton looked relieved. "I've got a lot on my mind."

As Jacob left the office Newton's phone pinged as a new message arrived. Opening the message sent him into a rage and he started pounding his fist onto his desk. What to do? This cannot go on. It was another photo from the night, with the caption – "*Friendly reminder. I'll be in contact in regard to a future shipment. Your contact number for the new burner phone is 0319 555 321. Regards Mr Johnson.*"

Jacob turned as he heard Newton slam his door and head quickly towards the elevators. He seemed in an awful hurry. "*What was that all about?*"

Newton crossed the road purposefully and into the Occidental Hotel. He stepped to the barman, "Sean, is Mr Drysdale in his office? I have a favour to ask him."

"He's in. Top of the stairs, second door on the left," Sean was happy to be of help, as a regular recipient of Newton's tipping at the bar.

Newton bounded up the stairs and tapped on the door marked OFFICE.

"Come in," called out Tom Drysdale.

"Newton, good to see you," greeted Tom. "Nasty business about your company on the television news. What can I do for you?"

"I had strange incident the other night in the lounge area, where I think I had my drink spiked," detailed Newton. "I ended up being put in a taxi and was dropped off at my apartment with all the money in my wallet gone, but the not the credit cards. It was very strange. You wouldn't happen to have CCTV footage from Monday evening?"

"I should have, but we only cover the main bar area with CCTV," indicated Tom.

"That will be good enough," Newton became excited. "There was a woman sitting in my usual spot and she was a bit of fun and invited me into the lounge to have a drink with her. I thought it would a bit of a laugh. Little did I know."

"Here we go," Tom reached to a rack of discs on top of his filing cabinet. "Hope that helps with what you are looking for."

"Thanks Tom, I owe you one," Newton picked up the disc and headed for the door feeling very smug with himself.

With a big grin on his face, he headed back to his office. Entering the office, he locked the door and inserted the disc into his player. He scanned through the disc until he reached 6pm. There she was sitting in his corner, in her skimpy black dress. "How could I have fallen for it. A boy from New York after all ," Newton berated himself. He made a copy onto his laptop along with a covering note. Next, he placed the original disc in an envelope along with the details of what had transpired, culminating in the theft of the Fijian shipment from the warehouse. It would be placed in the drawer of his home office for safe keeping.

He reached for his phone and typed a text message for Mr Johnson. "*Mr Johnson, I have procured the security disc from the Occidental Hotel on Monday, in which your accomplice is featured in her tiny black cocktail dress. If there is more in the way of threats or contact from you, the disc will be going to the police.*

I am sure your friend will be known to them and lead them to you and your activities. Yours NS"

One of the many burner phones buzzed on Carlo's desk out at the Mt Willsmore warehouse. "Hey Guido, it is our Friend at Mutilin already. He was quick."

"Holy shit," Carlo exclaimed as he stood and stepped across to Guido's desk. "We underestimated our man. Take a look at this. He has been able to get footage of himself at the Occidental with Trixie on Monday night. He has threatened to take the disc to the police if we don't back off."

"Let me see that," Guido took the phone from his brother. "Under pressure from the cops she may give us up, so we better start making alternative arrangements for getting our hands on more *Red T*. When is the yacht from Mexico, carrying the *ICE*, due into Fiji?"

"Last feedback I got was that they are expected to arrive in Nadi any day now. You better make contact with our local man Tevita," noted Carlo. "They were stopping in Fiji to re-provision, for the last leg into Sydney. Their stop in Fiji could prove timely and very useful. It looks as though a visit to that place Taveuni, would make a nice stopover for them. Better get Tevita on the line straightaway."

*

After a lengthy flight delay out of Sydney and the drive from Nadi to Suva, it was an exhausted Mere who finally made it to her Tamana's bedside in the hospital. He seemed to have tubes everywhere, connected to various machines and was indeed not at all well. Casting her professional eye over the situation, she was relieved to see he had at least stabilised and was receiving excellent care. Mereoni and Malakai had been up to visit as well as Filipe and his Prime Ministerial entourage.

As she tenderly stroked her Tamana's hand, Mere advised him of the request she had from Filipe to meet with her and wanted to know if he knew what it was about. "Sorry," Joeli replied in his very weak, croaky voice. "Mentioned nothing to me. Let me know how you get on."

The appointment was made to meet with the Prime Minister the next day. She was full of curiosity as to what it could be about and dressed up in formal Fijian attire, being a full-length cream coloured chamba sulu. She sat patiently awaiting the call to enter his now much grander office, in Suva's Government Buildings.

Time seemed to pass slowly while waiting and Mere was becoming restless and began to shake her right leg. This brought her to the attention of Filipe's PA who raised her eyes from the paperwork on her desk, which caused Mere to stop the nervous fidgeting. Finally, the PA's intercom buzzed. "The Prime Minister will see you now."

Filipe emerged from behind an immense mahogany desk piled with papers and folders to greet Mere. He took her by the arm and directed her to the huge raintree coffee table, carved in the shape of a turtle and sat her down on the plush dark green leather sofa. Filipe started with the pleasantries enquiring about her Tamana and life in Sydney, Mere found it hard to concentrate, her mind wondering what the meeting was about.

"Let me get down to why I called you in Mere," Filipe adopted a formal tone and noted Mere's demeanour. "Your Tamana will not be able to come back to parliament for a very long time, if at all and there is much work that needs to be done. What I want to propose to you, is that you come back to Fiji to serve your country and undertake your Tamana's work, by taking his seat in parliament."

"How would that be possible?" A concerned look developed on Mere's face.

"Joeli would resign from parliament on health grounds and you would stand in the by-election for his seat. As his daughter and with your profile in the community, your election would be a virtual certainty," noted Filipe.

"That is quite a surprise and given me a lot to think about," the shock evident on Mere's face. "I have started to build a career and a relationship with a man I love in Sydney."

"I know it is hard, but your country needs you and I have a particular project in mind for you to manage, that was raised by your Tamana. Given your medical background and the urgency of the situation," Filipe passed Mere a document marked HIGHLY CONFIDENTIAL. "Your man in Sydney may well be invaluable in assisting you."

Dear Prime Minister
HIGHLY CONFIDENTIAL
Since being appointed as Minister for Health, I have been made aware, by the Chief of Police, that there are significant issues with the use of illicit drugs in Fiji. The use of the drugs is destroying our youth here in Fiji. I fear there are also implications for the people of Australia and New Zealand, with Fiji being used as a central hub for drug distribution, across the Pacific, reportedly by yachts in transit across the Pacific Ocean, from North and South America.

In addition, the publication of the article about the hallucinogenic effects of the Tagimoucia in Australia, may only exacerbate the situation and draw further interest in Fiji from overseas drug cartels.

I seek your immediate support in providing the resources to tackle these rapidly emerging problems, before it is too late.
Yours
Dr Joeli Koroi
Minister for Health

"Prime Minister, you have given me much to think about. I would like to think about it over the weekend and get back to you on Monday. I need to talk to Tamana about his letter to you and there is also consideration of the work I have only just started to undertake in Sydney. Most importantly I need to speak to the man I love," Mere stood to close the meeting and get back to her Tamana.

CHAPTER 35

The yacht *Catalina Express*, a 40-foot ketch, had cleared customs in Nadi and was anchored in the Denarau Marina. Its illicit cargo of *ICE* safely hidden in a false bottom, housed under the toilet. Tevita walked up to the yacht, "My name is Tevita, Mr Smith and Jones I presume," Tevita continued, "Mr Johnson from Sydney sends his regards and looks forward to a spot of fishing with you off the coast of Sydney in the coming days."

"Tevita come aboard," invited the blonde-haired Mr Jones in the board shorts and sky-blue Hawaiian shirt with white coconut tree motifs. "What news do you bring from Mr Johnson?"

"We need to take a trip to the island of Taveuni this afternoon, along with a little of your precious cargo," advised Tevita. "Some local boys have packed up something that Mr Johnson is keen to get his hands on. Some of your cargo the Taveuni boys will happily accept as a swap . I will accompany one of you. Just bring an overnight bag and we'll return to Nadi on the first flight tomorrow morning with the cargo."

"Mr Smith, you look after the yacht and I'll head off with Tevita and pick up the cargo," Mr Jones decided.

With that, Mr Smith retrieved some of the hidden sachets containing translucent crystals and passed them to Mr Jones. Tevita and Mr Jones then headed off to the Nadi Domestic Terminal for the afternoon flight to Taveuni.

They were met at the airport in Taveuni by a couple of young Fijian youths in an old four-wheel drive that had seen better days. There was more rust evident than the paintwork and new tyres would not have gone astray. Apart from the obligatory *bula* welcome, little was said, and they were driven straight to the hotel.

In the driveway at the hotel, two cardboard cartons in the rear of the vehicle were removed and handed to Tevita. In return, Mr Jones passed an envelope containing the sachets to the youths, who were quickly back in the vehicle and gone, huge smiles on their faces.

Tevita and Mr Jones did not speak during the evening, both eating in their rooms, only getting together at checkout time to head back to the airport for the return flight to Nadi, along with the cartons. Tevita dropped Mr Jones back at the Marina and with a wave was gone.

The next morning the *Catalina Express*, fully provisioned and having cleared customs, was ready to get under sail to Sydney. Guido's phone rang, "Mr Johnson , it's Mr Jones here. We managed to land a big fish on the boat and look forward to some fishing with you in about a week's time."

*

Mere dropped her phone onto her bed and sat staring at the wall. She could not believe what Filipe had just told her. Two youths in Taveuni were dead and six others injured, when their old four-wheel was wrapped around tree. They were reported to be high on *ICE* provided to them by an American and a Fijian man. The *ICE* was given to them in return for stripping all of the Tagimoucia vines of this season's growth of flowers. Traces of the red flowers were found in the back of the vehicle. There was no sign of the men who made off with the boxes of flowers.

After pausing for a moment to think, Mere had made up her mind and it was time to speak to Jacob. She dialled his mobile phone which was quickly answered, "Jacob, its Mere. I have just had some terrible news about the Tagimoucia flowers."

"Slow down," Jacob sensed the tension in Mere's voice. "Firstly, how is your Tamana?"

"Tamana is definitely on the improve thankfully," Mere started to relax a little. "However, you won't believe it but the entire growth of flowers has been stripped from the vines up by the lake. It would appear that some youths were given *ICE* in return for harvesting the flowers. It was given to them by a couple of men, including one American. My guess is that the flowers are destined for Australia and most importantly, there is not one flower available for any testing in the Mutilin labs on Taveuni."

"That is shocking news," replied a crestfallen Jacob. "We can only hope there is still enough left in the School of Medicine to give us something to work on until next year."

"The other news I am afraid you will not like," Mere sounded close to tears. "Filipe has asked me to remain in Fiji and take over Tamana's seat in parliament. He also wants my help with a major project to battle the scourge of drugs starting to impact the youth of Fiji. Then there is also the matter of Tamana's health. I cannot leave him by himself with no family around him, so with all this happening I am going to have to remain in Fiji. I hope you can forgive me."

"There is nothing to forgive," Jacob's brain raced. "I can understand where you are coming from and with my love for you, I am happy to support you in whatever you do. Somehow we will make things work between us."

"Thank you my darling," Mere sounded happier given Jacob's support. "You don't know what that means to me. I will be calling upon you regularly for your help. Hopefully, we will see a lot of each other, with you visiting the labs in Fiji for Mutilin, to work on the remaining flowers we have at the Medical School. It is also likely I will get to Australia, to meet with Australian health officials. Can you update Newton on my situation and that I will need to resign from the company?"

"I'll let Newton know and will aim to get over to Suva as soon as possible to visit the laboratory and see your Tamana," informed Jacob. He ended the call fiddling with the box on his desk containing the engagement ring. "*Will I ever be able to place this on Mere's finger."*

∗

Newton was at his desk and picked up a copy of the newspaper. His eyes became fixated on the headlines - *"Red T Hits the Streets."* He was appalled and ashamed of what he read in the article about the deaths of young people having taken the extract. "It is all my fault," he yelled pounding his right fist into the top of his desk. The article described how according to his friends; a young man had soared off the top of an apartment block believing he could fly. He was found with bits of dried red flowers around his mouth. Another young man was found in his car, wrapped around a tree, also with bits of a red flower around his mouth. According to the media, Red T had quickly become all the rage and was in high demand at music festivals and nightclubs, this new phenomenon fetching extremely high prices in the streets.

Newton hesitated, then decided he must go to the police and tell them what happened. He didn't want any more deaths on his conscience. Online he checked out the number for the headquarters of the Sydney, Criminal Investigation Division and was put through to a Detective Sergeant Jeffries. "My name is Newton Sinclair. I am CEO of Mutilin Pharma, the company who was robbed some days ago of that shipment from Fiji. What was stolen has turned into what is known as Red T in the illicit drug market. I have information that might help you identify the culprits. I can't live with the information any longer even though it may involve me."

"Can you email the information to me and then come in to meet me this evening?" queried DS Jeffries. "I just have to make a court appearance this afternoon and will be free after 6pm."

"That will be fine, as I have a couple of meetings myself this afternoon. Let me have your email address."

After speaking with Detective Jeffries, Newton called Lisabeth, "Darlin' have you seen today's newspaper article about those deaths from the people having used Red T?" asked Newton.

"Yes, it sounds terrible," there was concern in her voice.

"Regrettably, those deaths were a result of the samples stolen from our warehouse." Newton was obviously dismayed. "I have information I need to share with the police about the theft and have made an appointment to meet with a Detective Jeffries this evening after I finish work. These deaths cannot go on. I may be late so don't wait for me for dinner."

"Are you OK?" Lisabeth asked, but Newton had already ended the call.

*

"Carlo, good news the shipment of flowers is underway, and it will take them about a week to get here from Fiji," muttered Guido conspiratorially. "I think a spot of offshore fishing will be in order one evening. You never know what you might catch."

"The Red T is selling like hot cakes at $50 a sachet and with more Red T enroute, the safe will soon be bulging with cash," laughed Carlo. "With what they have onboard the yacht, plus the *ICE,* we must be looking at millions. I think I will take that Ferrari for a test drive after all."

"Now we have the consignment on the way, I think it is time we think about taking out our friend, Mr Sinclair," stated Guido. "I don't want him getting some sort of conscience after the article that appeared in today's newspaper."

"What article was that?" quizzed Carlo, as Guido handed the morning edition to him. "Wow, I reckon that may drive demand. Everybody will want Red T."

Guido's phone rang. "Mr Johnson, this is Mr Roberts. A friend of yours is coming to see me this evening at home and wants to tell me about some special flowers and where you can get them from. He sent me some interesting footage of a very dear friend of ours, as well. I will be most disappointed if he can't make it."

"Carlo, get Bruno on the line we have a job for him."

*

It was getting dark as Newton turned off his computer and began to prepare himself for heading off to the meeting with Detective Jeffries. While he thought he may be in some trouble for revealing the information about the consignment from Fiji, it was done under the threat of blackmail. He was now coming forward to not only help identify the crooks, but mostly importantly prevent any more tragic deaths, irrespective of the impact on himself.

As Newton stepped out of the building into the quiet, dimly lit street, he saw an elderly looking man in overalls, fall into the open side of a white delivery van. The man was groaning and clutching at his chest, Newton instinctively dashed forward to assist. Bruno sprung from the rear of the van crashing a metal rod into the back of Newton's head. He collapsed falling into the open door of the van. The door was quickly slammed shut and in seconds the van was gone.

*

It was after 10pm and Lisabeth had still not heard from Newton. She started to become agitated and paced up and down. Calls to his phone went straight to voicemail. In desperation she checked the online directory for police headquarters and called asking for Detective Jeffries.

"I'm sorry Detective Sergeant Jeffries has finished for the day," noted the Desk Sergeant. "Can I be of assistance?"

"My husband, Mr Newton Sinclair was going into your offices to meet with Detective Jeffries earlier this evening and has still not come home," advised a concerned Lisabeth. "I have tried his mobile and only get his voicemail. He has just disappeared, and I am very worried."

The Desk Sergeant flicked through the logbook, "I have checked our entry log and there is no entry for a Mr Newton Sinclair having come into the building." I am sure he will be OK, but just in case, can you text through a recent photograph of him and I will get it out to the city patrols."

"Thank you for your help officer, appreciate it," Lisabeth was somewhat appeased that some action was underway to find Newton.

With nothing more that she could do Lisabeth tried to get some sleep, but she tossed and turned, seemingly seeing each hour of the night tick by on the bedside clock. She had finally drifted off to sleep just before sunrise due to exhaustion but was awakened by the buzzing from the building's intercom. It was the concierge sounding rather distressed, "Mrs Sinclair, I have a Detective Sergeant Jeffries in the foyer, along with a uniformed policewoman wanting to speak to you urgently."

A shaking Lisabeth met them at the door. Jeffries smelt of cigarette smoke and it looked as though his black suit had seen better days, with a sheen on the crease of the well-worn trousers. A coffee stain stood out on his red tie. Lisabeth ushered them in and invited them to take a seat on the sofa, "Have you found him? Is he OK?"

"Mrs Sinclair, I regret to say we have found Mr Sinclair's body at the base of the cliff at South Head. A note was found in his coat which indicates he committed suicide," advised a most solemn Detective Jeffries. "I can't leave it with you, but here is a photo on my phone of the note in which he expresses his love for you, *his Dear Lizabeth* and asks for your forgiveness. He further states he could not live with himself being responsible for those recent deaths. Can you tell me anything about what he meant by that? I am concerned, because he did not show up to meet with me last evening as arranged. That is why I made sure I was able to meet with you this morning."

Lisabeth began to sob uncontrollably, the policewoman moving quickly to console her, wrapping a comforting arm around her shoulders. It took some time for Lisabeth to compose herself before replying to Detective Jeffries, "all I know is that he was going to meet with you, as he wanted to tell you something about the theft from the company's warehouse."

Jeffries left Lisabeth with the policewoman who was making her a cup of coffee. He retrieved a second phone from inside his jacket and dialled. The call was quickly answered at the other end. "Mr Johnson, Mr Roberts here. I can confirm our friend did not show up last night to meet with me. I think he hurt himself. and his other half knows nothing. Other bits and pieces he forwarded to me have disappeared. Bye."

*

"Carlo, Mr Roberts called," Guido beaming. "It appears things have gone to plan; our friend has met an unfortunate self-inflicted end, according to preliminary reports."

"I think a nice spot of fishing in a few days, will be a nice way to celebrate," laughed Carlo. "We better get the boat fuelled and ready to go to meet Smith and Jones."

CHAPTER 36

As the sun was setting, the Conti brothers fired up their open-topped 20-foot speed boat, powered by a 200hp outboard engine, from the mooring at Brooklyn, located on the Hawkesbury River, North of Sydney. It could outrun anything that the police force could put on the water in the way of a pursuit. The weather had been good with the gentle, offshore westerlies keeping the ocean relatively calm. It would be a perfect night for a spot of fishing.

Using their GPS, they headed out of the mouth of the Hawkesbury River into the Pacific Ocean. It was far too deep to be able to anchor, so they drifted in the gentle rolling ocean as darkness descended. They sat quietly sipping on bottles of beer, springing into action when they saw the flash of three white lights, followed by three red lights. The mighty engine was fired up and with its throaty roar, powered towards the flashing lights.

"Mr Jones, Mr Smith," Carlo yelled into the night after he cut the engine.

"Mr Johnson," came the reply followed by a splash and a bobbing beacon flashing in the water. "Happy fishing."

Guido hooked the object with a gaff and with Carlo's help hauled it alongside and over into the boat. He turned off the flickering light which sat on top of a large plastic buoy. With his torch alight, Guido opened the hatch door, revealing red flowers packed in plastic bags, Red T. There was condensate on the plastic bags indicating they had been chilled onboard the yacht to maintain freshness. At the base of the buoy were large plastic bags of *ICE*, all the way from Mexico.

Mr Jones and Mr Smith did not stop and continued into the night, sailing towards Sydney Harbour to complete customs clearance procedures the following morning. The Conti brothers fired up the beast and sped back to Brooklyn, where Bruno awaited with the van, ready to load their precious cargo and return to the Mt Willsmore warehouse.

*

Apart from Adrian at the gym, Jacob at the office and Mere who was now in Fiji, Lisabeth was pretty much all alone with no friends or family in Sydney. However, with the help of the American Consulate who liaised with the police, matters were in hand to repatriate Newton's body back the US, once the autopsy was completed and clearance given by the police. She would accompany the casket and return home to her apartment in New York.

Jacob had been a great help in sorting out matters with the office and referring Lisabeth to a tax accountant to help wrap up a financial matters before heading back to the US. Her next task was to start packing up the apartment, ready for the carriers to come in for the repatriation of their personal effects. She went to the spare bedroom which served as Newton's home office. Lisabeth placed an empty, open carton on the floor next to the desk and pulled out the chair from under the desk. She sat down, pulling open the drawer, ready to scan the contents and decide what to keep or throw out.

Sitting on top of the contents of the drawer was a sealed envelope marked "Lisabeth Only". She pushed a pen into the flap of the envelope tearing it open, tipping the contents on to the desktop. Tears started to flow from her eyes as she saw the lewd photographs of Newton in a series of compromising position. He looked sort of spaced out, not with it. There was no life in his eyes.

Gathering herself she started to read the accompanying note. Newton explained how he believed his drink had been spiked at the hotel by the woman in the photographs and she had him taken to some isolated place where he was photographed and set up to be blackmailed. He further detailed how he had retrieved the disc of the CCTV footage of the woman from the night concerned, from the manager of the hotel. It was noted that copies of the information and disc had been forwarded to a Detective Sergeant Jeffries.

Then the penny dropped. Something had been niggling at the back of her mind. It was the copy Jeffries had shown her of the suicide note. In the note her name had been spelt wrongly, using a Z rather than an S in Lisabeth. Newton did not write that note and Detective Jeffries seemed very keen to wrap things up and move on.

She got on the phone and called Adrian at the gym.

"Hi Lisabeth. How are you coping? Do you need any help?" queried Adrian. "You were lucky to get me. I just got back from Melbourne, where we are close to opening the new gym. I was just going to have a shower here at the gym and then head out for dinner with Sue."

"I can use your help. I have something important I need to run by you," stated Lisabeth. "Jacob is going to meet me at the gym shortly for a coffee, to help me tidy up a few things and maybe you could join us?"

"No problem I'll see you shortly," Adrian wondered what was so important.

They all sat around the table in Adrian's office and Lisabeth presented the contents of the envelope she discovered in Newton's home office. She highlighted the meeting that had been arranged with the Detective Jeffries and how he had visited her to advise of Newton's supposed suicide. "He showed me a copy of the suicide note he reckons was written by Newton, with my name spelt wrongly, for heaven's sake." Lisabeth shook her head then continued, "Jeffries seemed to pump me for information to see if I knew anything else and then promptly left. It smells to me that he is a dirty cop. The information Newton had shared with Detective Jeffries has cost him his life."

"There is a whole lot of crazy stuff going on in Fiji as well," interjected Jacob. "Mere had to return to Fiji to see her Dad who has had a heart attack. She informed me that all the Tagimoucia flowers had been stripped from the vines in Fiji and disappeared, leaving mayhem behind with doses of *ICE* released into the community."

"Terrible news about Mere's Dad," they chorused.

"He is in good hands," replied Jacob.

Getting to the topic at hand Adrian summarised matters. "We have a situation with Newton mysteriously dead after trying to tell the police about the Sydney robbery of the Tagimoucia flowers. We then have all the current growth of the flowers stolen from the habitat on Taveuni. I have a gut feeling I know who may be involved with all this."

"What do you know Adrian?" asked an intense Jacob.

"There is the Conti family whose twin sons I went to school with," began Adrian. "They were always rumoured to be involved with illicit activities, but they never did wrong by me. I worked out with them, at my now stepfather's gym in Mt Willsmore. They have a warehouse out close to the gym, which would make the perfect place for distributing what has become known as Red T in the media. I would not be surprised if they were not up to their necks in all of this. They were pumping me for information on the Tagimoucia and Mutilin Pharma. They reckon they were going to invest in the company."

"We can't go to that Jeffries," snarled Lisabeth. "Any other ideas how to proceed? I want revenge for my Newton."

"One of the members here at the gym is a bright young Detective, Adam Charles," Adrian paused before continuing. "I propose I call him and get him in here straight away and give him the story and what you discovered in Newton's desk." There were nods all round and Adrian retrieved Adam's membership information from the gym's database.

Adrian had stimulated Adam's interest and he arrived within the half hour at the gym. Adam was young, enthusiastic and had rapidly risen through the detective ranks. However, he would need to proceed cautiously when accusing a fellow officer of corrupt behaviour. He was over six feet tall with trimmed, jet black hair. He obviously worked out with his large upper torso. He was conservatively dressed in a light grey suit with black pointy shoes, black belt, and black tie. Adrian pulled another chair into his office and they repeated their individual pieces of the puzzle to Adam.

"From what you have described, Jeffries is up to his neck in something bad and we cannot trust him," noted Adam. "I reckon I need to go over his head to Detective Inspector Sutton. I will speak with him first thing tomorrow morning when he is back on duty and show him everything you have here.

Jeffries won't be on roster until the afternoon shift this week, so hopefully we can take action before he is aware of any activity against the Conti's."

"Thanks, Adam, for all your support with this," acknowledged Adrian. "I speak for all of us when I say we don't want Newton's death to be in vain."

"I'll keep you informed," promised Adam. He took the package of information from Lisabeth and the others, to prepare for his meeting with Detective Inspector Sutton the following morning.

*

After meeting with Adam and reviewing the information, Inspector Sutton agreed time was of the essence and approved a raid on the Conti's warehouse. A call was made to the SWAT team to get them ready. All that was required was receipt of the signed search warrant from the Magistrate. Adam paced up and down hoping they would get underway before Jeffries arrived. He agreed with Inspector Sutton that the raid on the Conti's was a priority and once that was over, they would investigate Detective Jeffries.

The search warrant was in hand, just as Jeffries arrived to start his afternoon shift. "What's going on?" he asked as he sipped on a coffee. "SWAT team here. Armoured vehicle out the front. Pretty heavy duty."

"Got a raid on this afternoon to catch a couple of bad guys," replied Adam nonchalantly.

"Anything I was working on," probed Jeffries, his alarm bells ringing, given Adam's body language.

"Not one of your cases that I know of," Adam vaguely replied. "Sorry got to get going."

Jeffries waited for the office to clear and the vehicles to head off, before he returned to his office. After they had been underway for 15 minutes or so, Jeffries called one of the guys he knew in the raiding party, Mike Collins, on his mobile.

"Mike, Jeffo here. What's going on with this raid? Seems all very hush, hush," Jeffries fished for answers.

"We are hitting some warehouse in Mt Willsmore. Something to do with all that Fijian flower stuff," replied Mike. "Gotta go."

"Who was that Mike," quizzed Adam. "I thought I said no calls."

"It's OK, it was just Jeffo feeling left out on the raid," laughed Mike.

"OMG, we think he is a dirty informing cop," barked Adam. "Step on it" Adam announced across the radio network. "It looks like they will now know we are coming, so we better be prepared for a hostile reception."

"I didn't know, I'm so sorry," apologised Mike.

After speaking with Mike, Jeffries quickly scoured Adam's desk. He sifted through the information lying on the desktop. There were notes relating to Red T and the Conti Brothers, as well as suspicions about Newton Sinclair's death. He pulled out his personal mobile and dialled the Conti's, using the agreed coded language, "Mr Johnson, Mr Roberts here. I am letting you know that some friends of mine will be coming to visit you very, very soon. I would suggest we both take that well-earned holiday far away and do not see each other for an awfully long time." With that Jeffries was gone out the door of the police station with a grim look on his face. He did not look back as he headed to his car.

The police vehicles arrived at the warehouse where everything appeared to be quiet with all the doors closed. The commander of the SWAT retrieved a bullhorn from the armoured vehicle and roared, "this is the police! Open up straight away otherwise we start smashing your doors in."

There was no response, and all remained still. They tried the telephone number on the signboard but no reply. The commander gave the signal, and the crew pounded a sledgehammer into the wooden side door. The hammer was flung to the ground with the SWAT member ringing his hands. It had slammed into the steel backing panel, now exposed from behind the splintered external wood façade of the door.

"We won't be able to budge that in a hurry. We'll have to bulldoze it open with the armoured car," roared the commander.

After several attempts the door was finally loosened on its hinges and they were inside. The SWAT team had to turn on their head lamps on entering the dimly lit interior. Above the bench on the right, they found the light switches and lit up the warehouse. All was quiet but there was obviously recent activity with small plastic sachets filled with red flower material covering the bench top. The team cautiously approached the rear office with guns raised to shoulder height, fingers poised on their triggers.

The office door was pushed open revealing a carpet pulled back and draped over one of the desks, exposing an empty safe with a couple of $20 notes, a few loose bullets, and an adjacent, open trapdoor. The SWAT team proceeded cautiously down the escape hatch with guns poised. A dark tunnel lead out into a dense bush area at the rear of the warehouse. Fresh tyre marks revealed a vehicle had very recently been in the neighbourhood.

"Shit!" was all an exasperated Adam could manage. "That bastard Jeffries. Wait till I get my hands on him. He is going away for a long time."

*

"That was Jeffries. Looks as though all that money we have been paying him has finally proved worthwhile," stated Guido with tension in his voice.

"What did he have to say for himself?" asked Carlo sensing something was not right.

"Not good news I am afraid. The cops are on to us and they are on their way here and we need to move fast," replied Guido. "I'll call Bruno to come and get us. They'll be here shortly so we have no time to destroy the ICE and Red T sitting out there in the warehouse. We better get away otherwise we might be sitting in prison for a long time."

Carlo grabbed a couple of satchels and started loading cash from the safe, just as the roar came from the street. *This is the police*! There was no time to waste, so with the cash loaded, guns and false passports in hand, they opened the trapdoor. The building seemed to shake as the blow from the sledgehammer crashed into the security door.

Carlo and Guido opened the external trapdoor hidden by bushes and raced towards the waiting van. They threw in the satchels of cash and hurled themselves through the open van door and slammed it shut. Bruno immediately put the van into gear and headed down the track and towards the entrance of the M7 freeway.

CHAPTER 37

"Papa, this is Carlo."

"What's up son?" asked Papa Conti.

"The cops are on to us and we need to get away for a while," replied Carlo.

"I told you boys to keep a low profile," fumed their Papa. "You and your big plans which have got the cops interested."

"Sorry, got to go Papa. Tell Mamma we will be fine, and we will contact you as soon as we can," Carlo terminated the call, not wanting to engage any longer with his very unhappy Papa.

"What are we going to do?" asked Guido.

"I am going to call our friends Smith and Jones," conspired Carlo. "I reckon a nice cruise to the Fiji Islands would be an ideal way to spend our time. From there with our cash and new passports, we could look at heading to Italy and stay with the relatives till the heat dies down. The guys are due to sail back to the States tomorrow, so I'll call them now."

Guido tapped Bruno on the shoulder, "Bruno, head towards the Macquarie Shopping Centre so we can pick up some supplies. We need to pick up some clothes and bits and pieces, then on to the boathouse at Brooklyn. We should be safe from the cops there."

"Mr Smith? Mr Johnson here," said Carlo with a laugh. "We are in spot of bother and will need a ride with you and have plenty here to make it worth your while. I note from our call earlier today that you are heading home tomorrow."

"Always happy to be of assistance," replied Mr Smith. "We are anchored at

Neutral Bay and yes we will set sail tomorrow morning, after completing our Customs clearance formalities. Suggest you come onboard tonight so we can have you well hidden away before the Customs inspection.

"Bruno you'll need to fuel up the boat for a run tonight, down to the Harbour," requested Carlo.

*

An exasperated Detective Charles slumped into a chair in the warehouse. "We better get out an all-points bulletin to track down those bastards," he commanded. "As a first step you better get around and check out their parents place. Not that I expect their Dad to say anything as to their whereabouts."

Detective Charles started to look through the papers strewn on the desktops. He picked up a piece of paper upon which were written the words Catalina Express along with the word "tomorrow".

He called over one of his colleagues and asked, "what do you make of this?"

"Catalina is in the US, so some American link, maybe?"

"I reckon with the quantities of ICE and Red T here in the warehouse, I would believe it was most likely smuggled into Australia by boat," declared Adam Charles. "I'll give my mate in Australian Border Force a call to see if he can help."

"Good idea," said his fellow officer.

Adam picked up his phone, located the number in his contacts and hit the speed dial.

"Steve, long time no speak," said Adam. "I need a favour."

"Why else would you be calling," laughed Steve. "Only time I ever hear from you is when you want a favour. You still owe me a beer from last time."

"Can you check on a boat or yacht called Catalina Express?" asked Adam. "Yes, I know I still owe you a beer and here is another one to add to the slate."

"Just a second, I'll take a look," replied Steve tapping at his computer. "Here it is, a yacht which cleared customs here in Sydney. Arrived a week ago from the States via Fiji. The crew has booked a Customs clearance inspection for tomorrow morning and they will then set sail with the US as their final destination, again via Fiji."

" A long way to come for a week," observed Adam. "Something definitely not right there."

Adam then filled in Steve on the raid at the premises in Mt Willsmore, with the two suspects having fled. He described how he found the note which mentioned the Catalina Express and believed they may be making their escape on the yacht.

"We need to get a plan of attack together with your team Steve," said Adam. "I'll head on into your offices now and we can get something together to surprise them in the morning. We need to be careful; they're armed."

"While you are getting here, I will arrange for the yacht to be put under surveillance," said Steve.

*

On the way back into the city for the meeting with Steve at the Australian Border Force offices Adam gave Adrian a call to give him an update.

"Adrian, Detective Adam Charles calling."

"Did you catch the Conti's," asked Adrian.

"It is not good news I'm afraid Adrian," replied Adam. "Believe it or not they had a secret escape tunnel so got away, but the good news is that we think we know where they are and expect to make an arrest in the morning."

"Great. I have the others here with me so will give them an update," said Adrian.

Adrian had Lisabeth, Sue and Jacob still in his office at the gym waiting for news of the raid. They were devastated to learn from Detective Charles that the Conti's had evaded capture but buoyed by the prospect of their capture in the morning. Even though they were not very hungry given their personal situations, Lisabeth and Jacob agreed to join Adrian and Sue for dinner, better than being alone in the circumstances.

*

Over dinner Jacob filled everyone in on the situation with Mere and her return to Fiji. "She has decided to stay in Fiji and support her Dad, as well as taking over his seat in parliament, at the request of the Prime Minister."

"How do you feel about that?" asked Adrian. "What about your future together?"

Jacob reached into his pocket and drew out the engagement ring, "I was about to propose to her when she got the call about her Dad."

Lisabeth and Sue looked admiringly at the ring. Sue lifted her head and stared towards Adrian. A point not lost on Adrian, who shuffled uncomfortably in his chair and gave a gentle cough.

"I have spoken to Mike Starke, the Chairman of Mutilin Pharma and he has agreed to allow to work out of Fiji for a period", advised Jacob. "I will aim to set up the labs at the Fiji School of Medicine to the appropriate standard, to enable them to perform the necessary work on the remaining samples of the Tagimoucia flowers. After the setup I can then move to and from Fiji on a regular basis. It is not ideal but at least I can see Mere."

"What about permits to work?" quizzed Adrian.

"All set. I spoke with the Prime Minister and explained the situation and given what Mere has sacrificed, he totally supported the plan," replied Jacob. "I expect the work permit any day and plan to head off to Fiji on Sunday week on the 11am flight, ready to start on the Monday. I am going to surprise Mere."

"I am expecting everything to be finalised with Newton's body during this week and as such, have booked to fly out to the States Sunday week as well. Let me see," Lisabeth reached into her bag. "My flight to the States is at noon."

"Well as everyone else is in a flying mood, how about Sue and I join you Jacob on the flight to Fiji," smiled Adrian as Sue's jaw dropped open, leaving her speechless. "I have had a pretty busy period setting up in Melbourne and a short break would do me good, before getting stuck into the opening of the gym in Melbourne."

Sue snuggled up to Adrian and gave him a huge kiss on the cheek. Everyone laughed and Adrian thought champagne was in order. Jacob said he would book a limousine to take them all out to the airport together, so they could have a final farewell before flying out.

*

The Conti's waited until it was dark before loading the boat for Bruno to take them to board the *Catalina Express*. The yacht was moored at Neutral Bay, close to the Sydney Harbour Bridge, ready for the morning's customs clearance inspection. They loaded their duffle bags filled with the purchased clothing and toiletries, along with the satchels of cash.

The powerful motor of the speedboat enabled the Conti's to make good time down the coast from the Hawkesbury River and into Sydney Harbour. However, with speed restrictions in the harbour it seemed to take forever to reach Neutral Bay and they didn't what to draw any attention from the Water Police by speeding down the harbour.

As they approached the yacht Carlo called to let Smith and Jones know they were on approach. The men were waiting on the stern and threw a line to Bruno who fastened the speed boat alongside. Carlo and Guido tossed their bags to their hosts and with Guido onboard, Carlo spoke with Bruno.

"Thanks for everything Bruno," Carlo turned and hugged him. "There is one loose end I would like you to clean up and that is Detective Jeffries. I suggest you pay him a visit in the early hours and see to it that he sleeps with the fish. He knows too much about us."

"As soon as I get the boat back to the marina, I will see to it," Bruno replied and with that helped Carlo board the yacht.

"Once we get to Fiji, we will keep you informed of our plans so you can let the folks know. I am sure the cops will be monitoring their movements," the brothers waved as they gently pushed the speedboat away from the yacht.

"Great to see you guys in the flesh," smiled Smith and Jones. "It was a bit of pit stop in the dark last time. Here take a cold beer and then we better start getting ready for the customs inspection in the morning."

The plan was to hide the brothers in the forward cabin. There were two single beds forming a V-shape towards the bow of the yacht. Under each mattress was a wooden base which is where Carlo and Guido would be hidden. It would be tight, but it would only be for short period until they were cleared and set sail. The forward cabin was separated from the main cabin by the galley to port, the bathroom facilities to starboard and a wooden louvered bi-fold door.

After a couple more beers Smith and Jones tidied up the main cabin, wanting to ensure that there was no evidence of multiple passengers onboard. They would be up before sunrise to stow the brothers away in their hiding places, ready for the inspection.

Meanwhile on the nearby foreshore, a voice crackled over the radio, "I can confirm the parcels have arrived. Let's get ready for action in the morning. Will advise of any change of status overnight."

*

Bruno made good time back to the marina. He drove the boat inside the boatshed and closed the electronic door with a press of the remote control. In the office he peeled back a couple of floorboards to retrieve a gun wrapped in an oily rag. He checked the mechanism before loading in the clip containing the 9mm bullets. He screwed a noise suppressor into the barrel and headed to the van, all set to meet with Detective Jeffries.

It was now the early hours of the morning when Bruno parked in front of Jeffries' house in the quiet Northern Sydney suburb of Westmead. The front light was on and the front door open, with light streaming from the interior. The boot of the car was open with a large suitcase inside. The front light was turned off and Bruno saw Jeffries emerge, closing the front door quietly behind him. Bruno quietly exited the van and strolled over the road towards Jeffries.

Jeffries headed towards the car with a suitcase in his left-hand. Suddenly he noticed movement from the roadway. He knew it was not a good thing when he saw Bruno heading his way. "Hi Bruno, what brings you out this way and so early in the morning. Can't sleep?"

"The boys just wanted me to check on you and make sure you were ok," replied Bruno as he gently slipped his hand into coat pocket.

The movement was not lost on Jeffries who took Bruno by surprise by appearing to stumble on the footpath leading to the car. Jeffries released the suitcase and reached for the gun in his right ankle holster and fired off two quick rounds which struck Bruno in the chest. Bruno dropped to the ground clutching his chest, a surprised look on his face, with blood starting to ooze from between his fingers.

"Take that you bastard," cried Jeffries. "Is this how the Conti's try to repay me. I hope they rot in hell."

With a neighbour's light coming on, Jeffries dragged Bruno's body into his garage and closed the door. With the car loaded, he was off to a safe place in the country, an hour's drive North of Sydney. It was where he stored a false passport and cash he had accumulated from his regular payoffs, for such an eventuality in his life. A cop on the take, he knew, could not last forever. Now as George Hutchison, he would be flying out of Sydney to start a new life in New Zealand.

*

The Conti's were safely hidden away just before sunrise and Smith and Jones set about readying the yacht for the customs clearance process. Just after 9am, with a toot from the boat's horn, the Australian Border Force boat pulled alongside the *Catalina Express*.

The Border Force officers appeared to take a cursory look through the yacht and in loud voices declared all was ok and the *Catalina Express* was cleared to set sail. The officers guided Smith and Jones to the stern of the yacht where Detective Adam Charles pulled out his warrant card with his left hand and then placed his right index finger to his lips.

In a whispered voice Detective Charles said, "We know the Conti's are onboard and suspect they are armed. I suggest you co-operate and let us know where they are hiding, otherwise you will be going away for a long time. We don't want anyone to get hurt."

Smith whispered, "they are under the mattresses in the forward cabin and they are armed."

"Thank you for your assistance and co-operation which is duly noted.

Now join my fellow officers onboard the boat," Adam pointed to the waiting fellow members of the New South Wales police, with their handcuffs ready for deployment.

Adam and three other detectives took up positions in the yacht's main cabin with guns drawn, as the Border Force boat moved away from the yacht. With two police officers bracing either side of the door leading to the forward cabin, Adam let out a muffled cry, "all clear guys."

The detectives could hear the Conti's make their way out of their hiding spots and the groans as they stretched their bodies after being released from the confined space.

"Fooled those bastards," laughed Carlo as he and Guido stepped into the main cabin looking for Smith and Jones.

The smiles faded from their faces when they heard the click of the guns coming from behind them and the words, "you are under arrest. Hands on your head."

The Australian Border Force vessel quickly returned, and the very unhappy Conti brothers were reunited with Smith and Jones.

CHAPTER 38

The arrest of the Conti Brothers was the lead story on all the television networks, and it was a relieved Adrian who called Lisabeth. "I know it is not going to bring Newton back to you, but at least those responsible have been arrested. That is, all except that Detective Jeffries who has disappeared. They found a dead body at his residence, identified as one of the Conti Brothers goons."

"Our life had been going so well here in Australia," lamented Lisabeth. "I hope they get justice. I am certainly prepared to fly back from the US if required as a witness in any court case."

"Jacob has arranged the limousine pick-up for all of us to get to the airport next Sunday," confirmed Adrian. "It will be a sad farewell, but I am sure we will keep in contact.

"Thanks Adrian. I better get back to my packing as the removalists will be here shortly, not that there is much to send back. I have given most of Newton's things away to charity and there are only some of things I have bought since arriving," said Lisabeth. "Speak soon."

*

The limousine picked up Jacob from his apartment at Mona Vale, then headed on into the City to collect Lisabeth from her hotel and finally Sue and Adrian from Adrian's apartment enroute to the airport.

Jacob had arranged a chilled bottle of champagne for the limousine, which helped the mood and got the conversation going for the drive to the airport. After speaking with Detective Charles during the week, Lisabeth confirmed that it was likely she would be back in Sydney for the trial of the Conti Brothers. She would be required to identify the documents she discovered in Newton's desk and the matter of the misspelled note.

Adrian confirmed that he and Sue had booked a resort at Denarau for five nights before heading back to Sydney and then onto Melbourne to get the gym up and running. Sue would join Adrian in Melbourne at the completion of her Pilates course and would run Pilates sessions in the gym.

While Sue was momentarily distracted, rummaging in her handbag to ensure she had her passport, Adrian signalled to Jacob and Lisabeth a circling around his ring finger and pointing to Sue. This draw smiles and claps. Adrian was going to propose to Sue while in Fiji.

"What's going on?" asked Sue looking at the smiling faces.

"Nothing," they all chorused with smug looks on their faces.

They unloaded the luggage onto trolleys at Sydney Airport with the assistance of the driver. Lisabeth headed off to United Airlines for the flight to Los Angeles and the others to the Fiji Airways counter for the flight to Nadi. They agreed to meet up at the *Wings Across the Sky Café*, located just past all the duty-free stores.

Given the extra clearance time required for the flights to the US, Lisabeth was the last to arrive. The others had already started with a coffee and sandwich.

"What can I get you Lisabeth," asked Jacob.

"No, I'll get it. I have some Aussie money I need to get rid of," replied Lisabeth.

Lisabeth picked up a tray and joined the line up to order a coffee and something to eat. Her tray nudged the tray of the gentlemen in front of her. "Sorry," she automatically said.

The gentleman turned and was about to reply when the smile on his bearded face disappeared. There was an instant of mutual recognition. He avoided further eye contact by quickly turning away and he left his empty tray and moved quickly out of the line.

Lisabeth replaced her tray at the head of the queue and rushed back to the table. "I think I saw that Detective Jeffries. He had a beard, and I am certain he recognised me, as he up and left the line as soon as he saw my face."

"Are you sure," probed Adrian.

"As sure as I can be," replied an agitated Lisabeth. "That's him in the black hoodie heading towards Gate 52."

"I have got Adam Charles' number in my mobile. I'll call him straight away," said Adrian as he picked his mobile out of his carry-on bag.

"I'll follow him," said Jacob as Adrian placed the call.

"Detective Adam Charles speaking."

"Adam, Adrian Nicholls. I have some important info for you."

"Fire away," replied Adam.

"I am here at Sydney Airport with Jacob, Sue and Lisabeth," commenced Adrian. "Lisabeth was in the line to get something to eat when she bumped into someone, she believes is our Detective Jeffries. He seemed shocked to see her and immediately left the line. Jacob has followed him."

Jacob arrived back at the table and reported what he had seen to Adam. "He is sitting at departure gate 52 for the flight to Auckland which is boarding in 30 minutes. The black hoodie he was wearing has been removed and placed in his carry-on bag. He has put on sunglasses and a black baseball cap and is holding up a newspaper to hide his face."

"That's great info Jacob. I will call my mate at Australian Border Force to make sure he does not get away," responded Adam and then immediately called Steve. "Steve, we need your crew to apprehend a fugitive. It is likely we have discovered the whereabouts of that Detective Jeffries who was tied up in the Conti Brothers case."

"Tell me what you have, and I'll alert the guys at the Airport," informed Steve.

They remained calmly at their table at the coffee shop and after a wait of around 20 minutes they saw a team of four Border Force offices enter Gate 52. Moments later they emerged with a man struggling in handcuffs.

As the entourage passed the group in the coffee shop, the struggling man turned to the table and yelled, "bastards."

With hugs and kisses, with some tears, the group finally had to break up and head to their respective departure gates. There were promises made to keep in touch and add each other to their Facebook friends list.

*

After clearing customs at Nadi Airport it was time for a final farewell. Jacob wished Adrian and Sue all the best for the future, with a knowing wink towards Adrian.

"What was that wink all about," quizzed Sue.

Adrian just smiled and shrugged his shoulders as he reached to shake Jacob's hand. "After our first meeting in Fiji, who would have thought we would have ended up as friends."

"Yes indeed," smiled Jacob. "All the best to you both."

"Please pass our best wishes to Mere," said Adrian and with that Jacob was headed to the domestic terminal for the flight to Suva on his worst nightmare, the Twin Otter. His least favourite aircraft in the world. "One more time," he muttered to himself as he cautiously crawled up the stairs and tried not to bang his head or knock his knee while taking his seat.

*

From Suva's Nausori Airport Jacob took a taxi direct to the Koroi family home. He stepped on to the driveway with suitcase in hand and headed towards the stairs leading up to the front door. Bula and Vatu rushed forward.

"Hi boys," called Jacob, hoping they would remember him. He was relieved as he received licks and wagging tails. They happily escorted him up the driveway.

Jacob climbed the stairs and knocked gently. A surprised Mereoni opened the door and tears of joy immediately started to flow. "Oh, Mr Jacob. So good to see you."

"Don't tell Mere I am here. I want to surprise her."

"Take a seat in the lounge and I will go and get her," said Mereoni. "She is out in the back garden with Malakai.

"Mere. You have a visitor," yelled Mereoni from the top of the rear staircase.

"Who is it?" asked Mere.

"He didn't say who he was, but said it was important," replied Mereoni.

"Tell him I'm coming."

Mere straightened her clothes and headed for the lounge. As soon as she saw Jacob, she could not contain herself and leapt into his waiting arms. She smothered him with kisses. "I am so pleased to see you. I have some exciting news."

"Sorry, me first," said Jacob taking Mere's hand. "We better take a seat." He filled Mere in on what had happened in Sydney since she returned to Fiji and then proudly produced his Fijian work permit. "I spoke with Filipe and have arranged a permit that will enable me to set up the lab at the Fiji School of Medicine to take a lead role in Mutilin Pharma's development of the Tagimoucia project."

"That's great news, it means we can see a lot of each other," Mere grinned. "Now my turn."

"Just wait a moment longer as I have one more very important matter." Jacob stood then knelt on one knee as he extracted the ring case from his pocket. He opened the case and held it up for Mere to see. "Dr Mere Koroi, will you marry me?"

A smiling Mereoni tip-toed down the rear stairs to give Malakai the happy news.

"Of course, you big romantic." Then longingly kissed Jacob. "It is a very timely proposal as my news was to tell you that you are going to be a Tamana."

"Me a Tamana. Wait till I tell my Mum. She will be over the moon. She never thought she would see the day."

—

THE END

ACKNOWLEDGEMENTS

As a recently retired company executive, I was looking for a creative project to keep me busy and away from watching too much daytime television. It has been a long journey over many months, involving a number of re-writes to complete this, my first novel.

A big thanks goes to all those family and friends who have helped me along the journey. Their positivity and inputs has kept me motivated through periods of writers-block, critiques, and doubts about ever finishing the book. My wife Bev has been especially understanding given the time involved in writing, with me locked in my home office for hours on end, tapping away on the keyboard.

A special thanks goes to Roderic Grigson, author of *Sacred Tears* and two other novels. Rod encouraged me to attend his excellent beginners and advanced writing classes, which became the catalyst for my story. I can highly recommend the writing classes which gave me the basic tools and enthusiasm, to make the attempt at writing *Cry In Your Sleep*. Rod's ongoing mentorship, and encouragement has kept me going through multiple re-writes and during periods, when completing the completion of the manuscript seemed impossible. I can remember Rod's early advice that, "I would need broad shoulders to handle the criticism that comes the way of a would-be writer." Never a truer word said, especially after presenting my very first draft for his review. Rod's experience has also proved invaluable with him taking on the publication of the book.

In my early re-writes I received invaluable input from Sharon Brown, Director of the Melbourne Village Arts Festival, Derbyshire, UK. Sharon's feedback was most helpful in the development of the main characters and she has a great eye for detail. Thanks to Sharon for the many hours she has devoted to reviewing my drafts. For those visiting the UK, I can highly recommend a visit to the Arts Festival, usually held in the second weekend of September each year.

Rod also introduced me to my editor, Melissa Sayers. Melissa has a quiet, softly spoken manner. However, she proved to be firm in her suggestions which contributed to the improvement in my writing style. Without Melissa's experience and comments, *Cry In Your Sleep*, would have been a far lesser novel.

Also, a special thanks to Mark Thomas of Coverness.com in the UK for this book's design, as well as the development of my author website *(hewettwrites.com)*.

Having survived what came with writing this my first novel, hopefully those same family and friends, may be prepared to saddle-up for a second novel. Maybe another visit to Fiji to see what happens to Mere and Jacob.

Bruce Hewett

ABOUT THE AUTHOR

After graduating as a pharmacist in Perth, Western Australia, Bruce set off to see the world but fell in love with his first stop in the Fiji Islands. During the next 10 years in Fiji, he managed a community pharmacy in Suva, established his own community pharmacy in the township of Lami and represented Fiji in the 1984 Los Angeles Olympic Games in yachting.

Bruce married a local Fiji gal Beverley and following the birth of their first child, the family made the difficult decision to leave behind family and friends in Fiji, to commence a new life in Sydney, Australia. In Sydney, Bruce joined the pharmaceutical industry where he spent the next 35 years in a variety of senior management roles in Australia, New Zealand, and the UK, as well as, establishing his own successful consulting business.

Now living in Melbourne, Australia, Bruce spends his time as a non-executive director of two companies. He also enjoys keeping fit, voluntary work with a charity and spending time with his two children, Vanessa and Sean and their families.

Cry In Your Sleep is Bruce's first novel.

To discover more about Bruce and his writing, please visit:

hewettwrites.com

Printed in Great Britain
by Amazon

58630437R00177